John Adams Vinton

The Symmes Memorial

A biographical sketch of Rev. Zechariah Symmes, minister of Charlestown,

1634-1671, with a genealogy and brief memoirs of some of his descendants. And

an autobiography

`

John Adams Vinton

The Symmes Memorial
A biographical sketch of Rev. Zechariah Symmes, minister of Charlestown, 1634-1671, with a genealogy and brief memoirs of some of his descendants. And an autobiography

ISBN/EAN: 9783337113834

Printed in Europe, USA, Canada, Australia, Japan

Cover: Foto ©Raphael Reischuk / pixelio.de

More available books at **www.hansebooks.com**

John A. Winslow

A

BIOGRAPHICAL SKETCH

OF

REV. ZECHARIAH SYMMES,

MINISTER OF CHARLESTOWN, 1634-1671,

WITH A

GENEALOGY AND BRIEF MEMOIRS OF SOME OF HIS DESCENDANTS.

ALSO

Embracing Notices of many of the Name, both in Europe and America, not connected with his Family.

AND AN AUTOBIOGRAPHY.

BY

JOHN ADAMS VINTON,

AUTHOR OF THE "VINTON MEMORIAL," OF THE "GILES MEMORIAL," AND OF THE "UPTON MEMORIAL";
MEMBER FOR LIFE OF THE NEW ENGLAND HISTORIC, GENEALOGICAL SOCIETY; CORRESPONDING
MEMBER OF THE MAINE HISTORICAL SOCIETY, OF THE BUFFALO HISTORICAL
SOCIETY, AND OF THE STATE HISTORICAL SOCIETY OF WISCONSIN.

Fortes creantur fortibus et bonis,
Doctrina sed vim promovet insitam.—HOR.
The glory of children are their fathers.—SOLOMON.

BOSTON:
PRINTED FOR THE AUTHOR BY DAVID CLAPP & SON.
1873.

AUTOBIOGRAPHY OF THE COMPILER.

As there are indications, scarcely to be mistaken, that my life on earth is drawing to a close, I deem it proper, for the satisfaction of those who may come after me, to make some statements concerning the manner in which my life has been passed.

I was born in Winter Street, Boston, Feb. 5, 1801; just five weeks after the commencement of the nineteenth century. I was the eldest son of Josiah and Betsey (Giles) Vinton, who were married in Boston, April 7, 1800. I was named JOHN ADAMS, from the strong attachment entertained by my father for his kinsman, the second President of the United States; my father's mother, Anne Adams, being a daughter of Boylston Adams, a first cousin of the President, whose term of office was then just expiring.

On the side of both father and mother, I trace my ancestry to no less than thirty-five men of different names, in the first generation of New England people. On the side of my father I am descended from the Huguenots of France, exiled 300 years ago.

Though feeble in body, I was always disposed to mental effort, the more perhaps on that very account. I was able to read at a very early age, and when five years old could read a psalm in the Bible without serious difficulty. When seven years of age, I had read the New Testament through. I could also make rude letters and figures on a slate. I began to write on paper the summer after I was seven years old.

My advantages for education were always very limited. I never attended a public school in Boston, of any kind. This was not then permitted to children under seven years of age. In Boston I went to women's schools, supported by private subscription. After the removal of the family to Braintree, in March, 1808, I attended a woman's school in summer, and a man's school in winter; each of them, perhaps, three months in length. The teachers in those days were poorly qualified; and I learned but little, except by myself in private. My knowledge of arithmetic I obtained by turning round in my seat and witnessing the operations of the older boys, some of them young men, in the seat behind me. I soon became able to assist them, and show them how to solve a question in arithmetic. My grammar and arithmetic were acquired, chiefly, without any help from the

1

master. In August, 1811, my father took me into his store to assist him. I still attended school part of the day in winter; but several months before I was thirteen my school-days ceased entirely. Since November, 1813, I have never attended school.

I was extremely fond of reading, especially in books of history. My father took no newspaper during several years; but when I could get hold of one, it afforded a perfect treat. He had some valuable books, which I devoured with the keenest appetite. Before I was thirteen, I had read through Josephus, 6 vols.; Prideaux's Connections, 4 vols.; Marshall's Life of Washington, 5 vols.; Rollin's Ancient History, 6 vols., and Pinkerton's Geography, 2 vols.; most of them large octavos. He had also an atlas of 60 maps. These books were to me treasures of untold value.

My fondness for books, however, did not please my father. He thought I must get my living, as he had, in a store. He never seemed to think that my desire for an education could be turned to any good account. He always frowned upon it. He often told me, with great emphasis, that if I spent so much time over books, I should STARVE! He persistently discouraged, even till after I entered college, my desire for an education. The feeling went through the family. My brothers and sisters seemed to look upon me as an inferior sort of being, because I wanted to *know something*, to be a man of education and refined *culture*, a man of *thoughts* and *ideas;* instead of giving all my attention to the acquisition of *wealth*. I well remember, as though it were a thing of yesterday, how, from my father's dry-goods store on Washington Street, the part at that time called Cornhill, I watched the boys of the Latin School, then situated on School Street, Boston, as they were returning from school, swinging the satchels containing their books; and how sad I felt that the opportunities they were enjoying could not be mine. My thirst for an education was always subordinate to an earnest desire to be useful; to help others, if I could, to be good and to be happy.

The Spirit of God strove with me from my childhood. My father, being a church member, was wont, of a Sunday afternoon, after meeting, to take his children into a room by themselves, and hear them recite the answers in the Assembly's Shorter Catechism; closing the service with prayer. This was about all the religious education I received. There was no explanation of the catechism; no attempt to make us understand it. Even in my childhood, I wondered that the exercise was so mechanical and formal. Still the exercise was not lost. The impression was good, and remains to this day. Oh! if my parents had talked kindly and tenderly to me of the love of Christ, and my duty to love and obey him, how different had been my early life! There were no Sabbath schools in those days: I never attended one till, in 1817. I attended as a teacher. Ministers seldom or never preached to the young.

When I was between eight and nine years of age, a small book, intended for children, came to my hands, entitled a Memoir of Dinah Doudney, of Portsea, England, written by Rev. John Griffin, a minister of that place. I think this was the first book, except the spelling-book and Testament, that I ever read, and it impressed my mind very strongly. It was an account of a little girl, about my own age, who was a remarkable example of early piety. That a child of my own age could be devotedly pious, and could die and go to heaven — the impression never wholly left me. The book, I think, was, many years after, issued as a tract by the American Tract Society.

I do not remember any special concern for my salvation after this, till October, 1811, when I was in my eleventh year. The solemn, earnest preaching of Rev. Daniel A. Clark, then just settled as our minister, in East Braintree, and the death of a young girl in the neighborhood, gave rise to many solemn reflections, and drove me to secret prayer and earnest cries for mercy. These impressions of divine truth were never wholly lost. I find in my diary, which I began to keep in my eleventh year, a great deal that indicates a strong desire to be a true christian, and even a belief, two or three years later, that I was one. At the age of fourteen, I deliberately and solemnly entered into a written covenant with God, to be His only, and forever. I never wholly lost the impressions of that hour; though I wandered away from God, lost the spirit of prayer, and at times had fearful experience of a heart in rebellion against my Maker. I can conceive of nothing more truly indicative of a renewed state of mind than some things which I wrote the winter I was fourteen, particularly a prayer which I have lately found among my papers. But months and years elapsed ere I obtained a confirmed hope. I remember, and find it so written, that in the autumn after I was fourteen, I had earnest desires to be a minister of the gospel. But none of my friends, and nobody else, encouraged this desire. The desire, however, remained; it had existed, in some degree, ever since I was ten years old.* Now, at the age of fourteen, I made it a matter of fervent prayer for the divine guidance. My feelings continued to be very tender, and my impressions from divine truth were at times overpowering. I prayed much and earnestly. Yet I said nothing to any of my friends; for I knew it would do no good.

I read the works of Jonathan Edwards, of Joseph Bellamy, and other writers of that stamp. The views therein set forth, and the preaching I heard from Park Street pulpit, after our return to Boston, in November, 1813, impressed me very deeply. The effect was to make me feel myself unutterably sinful, loathsome and vile; lost and undone forever. I knew that God was merciful, but only to the truly penitent. How could I become truly penitent? I labored under the great mistake that I must become so by my own endeavors; and I felt that I could as soon make a world, as to change my own heart and make myself truly good: that I could as easily chase away the darkness of primeval chaos, as to produce one sincere emotion of true love to God. Oh! if I could have known that such a work was not expected at my hands; that all I had to do was to surrender myself absolutely and forever into the hands of God, give up my will to his, devote my all to him, and to trust wholly in Christ for this great salvation! what a relief it would have been!

At length, after years of struggle and of unspeakable distress, I came to see all this. I came to see, as in the noon-day sun, that my efforts to make my heart better would never amount to anything; and that Christ was ready to take me just as I was, in all my sin and guilt, and to make me his own, immediately and forever. Now, fifty-four years afterwards, the tears burst from my eyes as I remember what a change then took place in me. It was like the clearing of the sky after a storm: it was the noonday brightness after stark midnight: it was the sensible flowing in of the divine life upon the soul: it was a RESURRECTION FROM THE DEAD! Nobody

---

* Mr. Clark, our minister at Braintree, speaking to my father, and referring to me, once said—"That boy will get an education, if he has to wait till you and your wife are both dead."

can have any idea of it but from experience. I enjoyed a heaven upon earth. At times, I was perfectly overcome. Everything around me was changed. More than all, God, who had formerly been contemplated with alarm and terror, if not with aversion, now appeared unspeakably glorious and excellent. Never, from that day to the present, have I doubted the reality of the change.

I am at this time tenderly and deeply impressed with God's wonderful goodness, in bringing me so early and so distinctly to know HIM as my FATHER, REDEEMER, and SANCTIFIER. I well remember exercises of mind, when only sixteen years of age, which could only have been felt by a renewed soul. During four or five years I suffered extreme distress, in view of being in an unconverted state, and, as such, exposed to the wrath of God through interminable ages. God was to me an object of unspeakable terror, as a holy, just, and righteous Being, the inflexible Enemy and Punisher of sin. I knew he was not vindictive; but that HOLY LAW of his he must maintain. I could not flee out of his hands; I could not render myself acceptable to him; I could not even produce in my heart the repentance and faith which the gospel requires; what could I do?

I now see that I gave way, unduly, to a certain morbid tendency of mind, a disposition to look too much on the dark side. This has always afflicted me. I was looking into my heart for comfort, and no comfort could possibly arise thence. Oh! if I had fully realized that Christ came to save the lost; that I might apply to him just as I was, bad as I was, wretched and undone as I felt myself to be; and that it was safe and proper to cast myself simply and wholly on HIM, an all-sufficient SAVIOUR, giving myself wholly to Him, relying on His boundless grace, His unspeakable love, His infinite power; it had been well with me! Foolish creature that I was, to think I must make some preparation for believing in Christ! when, according to scripture, and to every christian's experience, believing in Christ, trusting wholly in Him, is the very first step in the way to Heaven!

Oh! what relief I felt when I came at length to realize Christ's infinite ability and willingness to save! when I felt that I had nothing to do, in the affair of my salvation, but to cast all my burden, all my care, my whole soul, on Christ! I felt just as the Pilgrim felt when he came in sight of the cross. The tears now start freshly from my eyes, at the bare recollection of what I felt more than fifty years ago, and for a long time after.

I was one of twelve young persons who made a public profession of religion in Park Street Church, Boston, June 1, 1820, being then a little over nineteen.

When I became of age, February, 1822, I was released from my long and irksome service in my father's store, which had continued, with some intermissions, from August, 1811. For this long service of ten years or more, I received nothing but my board and clothing; and my clothing was for the most part, I think, made up from my father's old clothes. After trying, four or five months, without success, to get into business in Boston, I went to Philadelphia, at the invitation of my two uncles there, my father's brothers, and assisted in their wholesale dry-goods store until the spring of 1823. All this while, my mind was exercised on the subject of a preparation for the gospel ministry. At length my mind became fully settled, and I made known to my uncles and my father my fixed purpose, if life were spared, to become a minister. My father said plainly that he could not assist me. My uncles warmly approved my design. They said they had ever thought that I ought to receive a liberal education, and had even intended to send me to college at their own expense; but were prevented by reverses in business. As it was, they agreed to bear a certain part of the expense.

I returned to Boston in May, and found the Providence of God had prepared the way before me. It was decided that I should go to Exeter, N. H., and apply for admission on the Phillips Fund. I walked nearly all the way thither, forty-eight miles, under a burning sun, at the summer solstice, carrying my bundle of clothing and books, and arriving there faint and weary. A good lady, Mrs. Halliburton, took me to board at a little more than half price.* After a few weeks, I was made a charity scholar on the Phillips Fund, receiving one dollar a week from it, which paid nearly two-thirds of my board.

At Exeter, to make up felt deficiencies, I studied very hard, even till twelve or one o'clock at night, and got along well, even to the wonder of the other students, who, nevertheless, sometimes could not suppress feelings of malignant envy. In fourteen months I was found prepared to enter any college in the land. I entered Dartmouth College, Sept. 22, 1821.

I was punctual in all the exercises of college, never absent, and never late, but for just cause. I made good progress in my studies, and soon gained the confidence of the Faculty, and of my fellow-students. I taught school every winter, which helped to defray my expenses. In the summer, I was engaged in Sabbath schools in the vicinity of Hanover.

There was a great revival of religion in college and in the village, during the spring term of 1826. I enjoyed the season greatly, and did what I could to promote the work. And here I may remark, that from the time when I began to indulge a settled hope of my own salvation, I was disposed to speak to others, as I had opportunity, especially to those about my own age, respecting their need of salvation. An eminent clergyman of our denomination, who has occupied important spheres of usefulness, both as a pastor and as an officer of one of our great national societies, to whom the christian church is indebted for some of our sweetest, noblest hymns of praise — hymns that are used wherever American christians meet for worship and pious conference — said to me, at a casual meeting, some years ago — "I remember, Brother V., how you used to walk, and talk with me about my soul!"

While a member of college, I employed my winter vacations in teaching school, and my spring and fall vacations in pedestrian tours. I visited Northampton, Hartford and the towns along Connecticut River to its mouth nearly, New Haven, Providence, Middlebury, Burlington, Lakes Champlain and George, Cape Ann, Portland, the White Mountains and many other places, going on foot nearly all the way, the foot travel amounting to more than one thousand miles. In these journeys I was careful to take religious tracts with me and distribute them by the way, and to converse on the concerns of the soul as I had opportunity, often with entire strangers. I found my health greatly benefited by this course.

I was chosen a member of the Phi Beta Kappa Society in June, 1827, at the first election made from my class. The whole number then elected was nine. Four were elected afterwards. I graduated, August 20, 1828, having the fifth appointment, the Greek Oration, in a class of forty members. Six of those who ranked after me, subsequently became

---

* She gave me four weeks' board out of ten.

professors in American colleges. I might have held a similar position, had not my inclination led me another way. I had the degree of A.M. from Dartmouth College.

But it is time to state what my expenses were at Exeter and at college, and whence my supplies were derived. I kept an accurate account all the while; and it is now before me.

Expenses at Exeter, while fitting for college, from June 23, 1823, to Aug. 20, 1824, nearly all of which was for board, say 52 weeks — leaving out vacations — at about $1.50 per week, $102.11.

Rec⁴. of my father,	$ 4.30
Rec⁴. of the Charity Fund of Phillips Exeter Academy, one dollar a week, during the time I was thus aided,	43.00
Rec⁴. of my uncles, T. & A. Vinton, Philadelphia,	40.00
Rec⁴. of Richard Chamberlain, Boston,	20.00
Rec⁴. of George J. Homer, Boston,	5.00
Rec⁴. of John Kent, Boston, a young friend,	5.00
Rec⁴. of William T. Boutwell, my room-mate,	.50
Rec⁴. of Mrs. Ladd, for cutting wood,	1.50
Total receipts for fourteen months,	$119.30

My total expenses during those fourteen months, including vacations, travelling, and incidentals of all sorts, were exactly $121.92, which amounted to one hundred dollars for a year, nearly.

At college, the sum total of my expenses was $693.63

viz.: Freshman year,	$153.76
Sophomore year,	192.04
Junior year,	165.00
Senior year,	182.83
	$693.63

At Exeter I had nothing to pay for tuition, being a charity scholar. At college, being a charity scholar, one-half of the amount of my term bills, or seventy (70) dollars in all, was remitted. My board at Hanover, in the entire four years, cost me $175; room rent, $27.80; travelling, $77.47; clothing, $152.50. I gave in charity, $20.

My receipts, while in college, were as follows:

From my father, in the whole,	$150.00
For my own labors, of which were $156.87 for teaching school four winters,	180.00
From Mr. Richard Chamberlain, Boston,	80.00
From Mr. George J. Homer, Boston,	120.00
From my uncles, T. & A. Vinton, Philadelphia,	116.64
From George Vinton, my brother,	22.00
From my mother, besides bedding and some clothing,	2.61
From Mrs. Carter, Peacham, Vt.,	5.00
From a society in college,	4.60
Total receipts in four years,	$680.85

My expenses in Andover Theological Seminary, three years, were $628.26. Tuition is free at Andover Seminary to all the students.

Received from my father,			$170.00
"	"	my brother George,	25.00
"	"	my mother, $3.00; sister Eliza, $3.00,	6.00
"	"	George J. Homer, Boston,	25.00
"	"	Daniel Safford, Boston,	20.00
"	"	American Education Society,	80.00
"	"	Ropes Fund, Andover,	20.00

Avails of personal labor, of which I received for clerk
hire, $38.64; preaching, $15.00; writing for the press, } 165.00
$24.00; agency for N. H. Bible Soc. 5 weeks, $30.00,)

Total, $511.00

The amount received from the Ropes Fund I afterwards repaid, as also the greater part of what I received from the American Education Society; I also repaid $114, received from Seminary Fund, with interest, in 1839, eight years after. The Ropes Fund was established by Mr. William Ropes, an eminent christian merchant of Boston. Mr. George Joy Homer was one of the partners in the well-known firm of Homes & Homer, hardware merchants, Union Street, Boston.

I entered the Theological Seminary at Andover, Oct. 31, 1828. Every thing there concurred to promote my intellectual progress, and spirituality of mind. The light shone brightly upon my path, and I found myself as it were in the very suburbs of heaven.

The subject of Foreign Missions had for many years occupied my mind. I read and conversed much on the subject. Dr. Woods, the professor of theology, and others, warmly approved of my inclination to be a foreign missionary. He advised me to cherish the desire I felt. After due deliberation and much prayer, I made a formal tender of my services to the American Board of Commissioners for Foreign Missions. I was willing to go wherever they might wish to send me. The offer was kindly received; but after some delay, Dr. Anderson, the secretary, told me frankly, in February, 1831, that my own slender health, and that of my intended wife, presented an insuperable bar to its acceptance.* The matter had been by me fully laid before Dr. Woods, who was a member of the Prudential Committee, and supposed to be acquainted with the missionary work in all its bearings. I had told him about Miss Haskell's health, and every thing else I could think of, bearing on the case; I had talked the matter over and over, with him, several times; and he had uniformly and strongly approved of my going as a missionary. The matter had also been

---

* My tender of myself to the Foreign Missionary Society was declined in the following letter:

"*Missionary Rooms, Boston, Feb.* 17, 1831.

"MY DEAR SIR: I stated your case to the Prudential Committee as you described it to me, particularly in relation to your intended partner's health; and it appeared to them so very doubtful whether duty required you to go on a mission, that they were not prepared to vote you an appointment at present. This is the reason why none is sent you. They have long made it a rule not to give an appointment, unless the case is a clear one. You will not consider this, however, as a *refusal* of your services. The committee mean to say nothing more than this:—that, as circumstances now appear, they do not feel warranted to decide in favor of your becoming a missionary to the heathen. May the Lord enlighten your path, and render you eminently useful wherever may be your field of labor.

"I am, my dear Sir, very truly yours,
"R. ANDERSON."

"Mr. John A. Vinton, Theol. Sem., Andover."

laid before my class in the seminary, and their opinion requested; and thirty-nine out of forty, by express vote, said it was my duty to go. The students in the other classes took the same view. Mr. Evarts, also, the former secretary, who knew me well, both being members of the same church in Boston, told me in an interview at Andover, in August, 1830, that it was probable the Prudential Committee would wish to send me out as a missionary, and he bade me get my testimonials ready. Bridgman, afterwards missionary to China; Schauffler, now and for many years missionary at Constantinople; Emerson, missionary to the Hawaiian Islands; Munson and Lyman, the martyr-missionaries of Sumatra — all these were intimate friends of mine, all being members of the Society of "Brethren," and all, of course, consecrated personally to go out as missionaries, if God should open the way; we all talked over the matter together, and all approved of my going. I was therefore surprised at the letter of Dr. Anderson, and not only surprised, but disappointed. After the lapse of more than forty years, it is my decided belief that I ought to have been a foreign missionary. I now regret nothing so much as that I was not a missionary. I should have been a translator, and my work done chiefly within doors. The fatigues and exposures of a missionary life in the Turkish Empire, would, I apprehend, have been no more oppressive or injurious to our health than those which I and my wife actually endured in America. She lived but six years after marriage, here, in New England. Very likely she would have lived as long in Turkey. For myself I must say I have never been satisfied with the life I have since passed in the United States. I should have been far happier and more useful abroad. It has always afforded me comfort that I did, after much deliberation, fully make up my mind to go; I am sure it was from love to Christ and his cause; and I trust that, as in the case of David, God accepted the will for the deed.

The writer begs permission to say, that from those days to the present, he has been able to conceive of no human employment so worthy, so noble, so congruous to all our true relations to God and to eternity, so much in harmony with the example of Christ and the genius of his gospel, as that of making known to the benighted, perishing heathen the infinite riches of a Saviour's love.

I completed the full theological course of study at Andover, Sept. 28, 1831, and immediately entered on the work of the ministry at Bloomfield, Me., now called Skowhegan, on the Kennebec river. Here and in the neighboring towns my labors were incessant, arduous and exhausting, though to myself unspeakably joyous. The glad anticipations of many years now began to be realized. Through the divine blessing, my labors, though I had help from others, resulted in a precious revival of religion, just about doubling the church. The church was saved from extinction; but, as often happens, the consequences to me were personally disastrous. Worldly people were displeased with me; and the church, to please the worldly people, and to secure a continuance of their favor, after giving me a unanimous call to be their minister, retracted the vote.

I was ordained pastor of the church at New Sharon, Me., May 16, 1832. I was married at Hanover, N. H., June 6, 1832, to Orinda Haskell, who was born in Strafford, Vt., Jan. 14, 1805, daughter of Thomas L. and Orinda (Carpenter) Haskell, successively of Strafford and of Hanover.

I need not detail my subsequent labors in Maine, where I spent, in all, seven years; nor in Vermont, where I passed four or five years; nor in Massachusetts, where I spent about four years. I found the work very

laborious and exhausting. Part of the time, I was almost constantly in the
saddle.   I labored under the great disadvantage of weak lungs, and a
slender physical frame. From these causes, I could not hold competition
with men of Herculean stature, of Milonian strength, and of a Stentorian
voice. It would have been far better for me to have labored in Western
Asia. My labors were very inadequately recompensed. Only in one or
two instances, did I receive even the small salary that was promised, never
exceeding five hundred dollars a year, and very often less than four hundred.   Part of the time, my family barely escaped absolute want.   In
many instances, my services were given away, or nearly so.

At length, when I had been in the ministry twenty years, my health, and
that of my wife, utterly broke down: we could stand it no longer. What
little strength we had, wholly failed. We could no longer endure such
hardships and such treatment. These hardships and this treatment had
cost me the life of one beloved wife, and of three sweet infants; the
confirmed ill health of another wife, and my own permanent disability.

My former wife died Aug. 4, 1838, during my ministry at Chatham,
Mass. I was married to my present wife, Laurinda, daughter of Deacon
Reuben and Sarah (Vinton) Richardson, at Stoneham, Feb. 24, 1840.

I have no hesitation in saying that no dereliction of duty, as a minister,
was ever laid to my charge. Weak lungs, imperfect health, and advancing
years, and nothing else, compelled me to quit the pulpit.

Since leaving the ministry, in 1852, much of my time has been occupied
in writing for the press. This employment commenced, indeed, when I
was but little more than seventeen years of age. I have a list of one
hundred and thirty-four articles written by me between 1817 and 1872,
which have appeared in eight or ten influential periodical publications, such
as the old Boston Recorder, the New England Puritan, Congregationalist,
Christian Watchman, Christian Mirror, Vermont Chronicle, Spirit of the
Pilgrims, Boston Traveller, Congregational Journal, Congregational Quarterly, Genealogical Register, &c. Most of them were religious in character,
though many were historical and literary. Some were articles of considerable length, as, "Japan," 18 pages, 8vo.; "Reminiscences of the Early
History of Park Street Church, Boston," in 8 numbers; "Memoir of Rev.
Jonathan Parsons," 22 pages; "Memoir of Rev. Parsons Cooke," 26 pages;
"History of the Antinomian Controversy of 1637," about 80 pages; and
some others.   For a time, my articles prepared for the Boston Recorder
were printed as editorial. Seven bound volumes, compiled by me, have
issued from the press, viz.: The Vinton Memorial, Giles Memorial, Upton
Memorial — which is still in press, nearly finished — Sketches of the Vinton
and other Families, The Sampson Family, The Female Review, and The
Bill Family. Some of these contain from 500 to 600 pages, octavo. In
these volumes may be found memoirs, more or less full, of between thirty
and forty Families descended from early settlers of New England. They
have cost me much time and labor, and have afforded little pecuniary profit.

To as many as fifteen extensive and valuable historical works, written by
others, and extending through thirty or more octavo volumes, I have
prepared analytical indexes. The works are: Bancroft's History of the
United States, 9 vols.; Plutarch's Morals, 5 vols.; Parkman's Conspiracy
of Pontiac, 2 vols.; The Jesuits in North America; The Discovery of the
Great West; Wood's New England Prospect; The Hutchinson Papers;
Mourt's Relation; Church's Indian War; News from Virginia; Lechford's
Plain Dealing, and I know not how many more. I have also prepared a

2

Supplement to Dr. Anderson's History of the Mission to the Sandwich Islands; a Supplement to his History of the Missions to the Decayed Oriental Churches; a Supplement to his History of the Missions in Ceylon and Southern India; each containing about thirty octavo pages. I have assisted other authors in their works. The Triennial Catalogue of the Theological Seminary at Andover for 1870, is partly my work. Indeed, something of the sort has been constantly in hand for the last twenty years.

After leaving the pulpit, I resided in South Boston about eighteen years, or till July, 1870. I then removed to Winchester, a pleasant town eight miles northwest of Boston, where I now reside. I have suffered much, and still suffer, from ill health, and the present indications are that I have but a little longer to live. Notwithstanding the gloomy forebodings of some of my friends, fifty or sixty years ago, that if I indulged my literary inclinations, I should come to utter want, I am happy to say, through the Divine Goodness, that period has not yet arrived, nor does it at present seem near.

In what I have said of the discouragements offered to me by my father, I wish not to be understood as in the least impeaching his integrity. He was a man of great uprightness and unspotted purity of character, a good christian, a useful man; a friend to all worthy enterprises. But his means, unfortunately, were at that time quite limited, and he honestly supposed that he could afford me little or no aid in obtaining an education. He did not even feel able to hire help in his store. Hence he kept me with him during those ten gloomy years of my life, from the age of eleven till twenty-one. My father's intentions were good, but he erred in judgment. Success is seldom or never attendant on the efforts of any one who enters on a business which he utterly dislikes.

This sketch of my life has been committed to writing for two reasons:

I. To honor and commemorate the wonderful goodness of God, my heavenly Father, towards me; first, in recovering me from that abyss of sin and ruin, in which all men are sunk by nature, and from which they cannot, by any efforts of their own, deliver themselves. He, through the grace of the gospel, has done this for me; and for it I will praise His glorious name forever and ever. And secondly, by wonderfully opening the way before me into the ministry of the gospel, and giving me some souls as seals of my ministry, and crowns of my everlasting joy.

II. For the encouragement of young men, who, like myself, may be longing for an education, but find themselves beset with difficulties apparently insurmountable. Their hindrances cannot be greater than were mine for many years. But let them hope! hope in God, and hope in themselves. Let them examine their motives; let them see to it that they are aiming to be useful in the world; let them lay aside all thoughts of becoming great and honorable; let them commit their case to God in prayer, and He will, by some methods now unthought of, open the way before them.

Ever since God was pleased to speak peace to my soul, now fifty-four years ago, I have been able to feel His sustaining arm, and to see his finger pointing out before me the way I should go. I have been as sure of it, as of my own existence. I do not refer to any miraculous interposition, to any thing like special revelation, or divine impulse; to nothing but what every true christian has, or at least may have, if faithful to his Lord.

I had nearly forgotten to mention that the dagnerreotype likeness, from which the frontispiece was copied, was taken in July, 1857, sixteen years ago, and therefore does not accurately represent me as I am now.

INTRODUCTION.

THIS work owes its existence to a desire entertained by the compiler, to collect, treasure up, and preserve, all that can now be known of one of the worthiest of the founders of New England — whom he is happy to recognize as his own ancestor — and of his descendants to the present day. To render the work as full and complete as possible, no effort has been spared. The materials have been drawn from a great variety of sources, and nothing has been admitted which is not believed to be authentic. The author, now in failing health, and as he trusts he may be allowed to say, "on the bright side of seventy," dedicates these pages to those of the Symmes Family who now follow in the steps of that man of God who is here commemorated.

The writer is not solicitous to enter on a labored defence of the propriety and value of a work such as is here attempted. If some persons — existing only in the present, regardless of every thing which does not minister to the wants of the passing hour, and as careless about the past as they are about the future — can look with a stolid indifference on such inquiries as are here answered, there are many others who would not willingly let the honored names of worthy ancestors perish in oblivion.

It is most certain that those who are thus willing to forget the past, will not themselves perform anything worthy of remembrance. Such persons betray, too plainly, a lack of sound moral sentiment, a stupid indifference to high and noble ends, which will not suffer them to deserve well of future generations.

A distinguished American clergyman has remarked: "There are riches of moral power in such an ancestry as ours." One of our most eminent divines said in a letter (the writer being in his eighty-first year) : "I am ashamed, my dear Sir, that the business of gene-alogy has, in times past, engaged so little of my attention ; and that now, when I see so much of its real value, a great deal truly interesting to me has irrecoverably gone." Multitudes have had occasion for a similar acknowledgment !

Washington, in the midst of his duties as President of the United States, in 1792, found time to collect and write out the genealogy of his family ; and Benjamin Franklin, when in England, undertook a journey for the express purpose of ascertaining his lineage and connections.

It cannot be doubted by any reflecting mind, that New England is largely indebted to her traditions of the past for her culture and refinement, her high intellectual and moral character, and even for her commercial and manufacturing prosperity. Equally true is it that as you go south and south-west, the civilization, the moral principle, the intellectual energy, and even the power of commercial achievement, diminish in exact proportion to the reverence entertained by the people for their ancestors.

The considerations now presented have, if we mistake not, a special application to the case now in hand. It is not difficult to discover, among the descendants of Rev. ZECHARIAH SYMMES, a train of most happy influences operating all the way. With com-paratively few exceptions, his posterity have sustained a high moral character. None of them, so far as we know, have taken to vicious courses, and none have come to want. Many have been distin-guished for virtue and piety. A number have been worthy and useful ministers of the gospel. Others have borne office in civil life. One of the number was a Justice of the Superior Court of New Jer-sey, Lieutenant-Governor of that State, and one of the founders of the State of Ohio. His daughter became the wife of a President of the United States. Several distinguished themselves in the late War for the Union. So far as the writer is informed, all the living are useful and happy.

While we fully admit that truly religious persons become such "not of blood, nor of the will of man," but by the free grace of God, we firmly believe that the influence of personal character and exam-ple, subtle and unseen though it be, is for the most part decisive from generation to generation, and that children, as a general fact, walk in the footsteps of their parents.

I take pleasure in expressing my obligations for aid rendered in the compilation of this work, to Mr. Edward Symmes, of Westford, Mass.; to Rev. Francis Marion Symmes, of Crawfordsville, Ind.; to Miss Harriet Symmes, of Charlestown; and to Miss Mary Wright Symmes, now of Winchester, Mass., my near neighbor. The materials which they had been collecting during many years, and which were truly valuable, were freely placed at my disposal, and were essential to the proper execution of my design. For the Appendix, I am largely indebted to Mr. Isaac J. Greenwood, of New York city, and Mr. George C. Mahon, of Framingham, Mass.

I have also availed myself of information contained in the following publications: Johnson's Wonder-Working Providence, Mather's Magnalia, Winthrop's New England, edited by James Savage, Hutchinson's Massachusetts, Felt's Ecclesiastical History of New England, Allen's Biographical Dictionary, the several volumes of the Register of the New-England Historic, Genealogical Society, the American Quarterly Register, Brooks's History of Medford, Perry's History of Bradford, the Records of Middlesex and Suffolk Counties, and the Records of many towns; besides deriving much aid from private correspondence.

I should do injustice to my own feelings, did I not express my high sense of obligation to the worthy printers, Messrs. David Clapp & Son, Boston, for the tasteful and accurate manner in which the mechanical execution of the work has been performed.

The origin of the name is lost in obscurity. There is no end to conjecture; but we have no information relative to the history of the family farther back than about 1390. Two generations later, the whole realm of England was convulsed by the Wars of the Roses; and it is said that a portion of the Symmes family then took refuge in Scotland. This corresponds with what we know to be the fact, viz., that in later times, and now, there has been, and is, a branch of the family in Scotland. There is also at the present time a branch of the family in Ireland.

The family has been long seated in Northamptonshire, in England. There are also branches in the counties of Devon and Somerset. Jeremiah Symes, a younger son of the Northamptonshire family, was rewarded by Charles II. for some services, with a grant of lands in Middleton, in the county of Wexford, in Ireland. The name soon spread into the adjoining county of Wicklow. From him descended several clergymen and other men of note, among whom was a Michael Symes, lieutenant-colonel of the 76th regiment, ambassador to the court of Ava, who was killed at Corunna, 1809.

The name has been variously spelled, as fancy or caprice dictated: as *Sym, Syme, Syms*, in Scotland; *Symes, Syms, Sims, Symmes*, in England and Ireland. Several coats of arms are known, indicating respectability, if nothing more. In the city of New York, as will appear in Appendix II., the name is spelled in seven different ways.

This work is the result of, at least, eight months' severe labor, performed under the pressure of constant and immedicable illness, often when the writer was scarcely able to be about house, or even to stand, and when he was unable to see company or to converse. He could think and write, but he could do nothing else. He could not even go to the post-office, though less than half a mile distant, nor has he been able once to attend church during the eight months past. Gladly would he have been excused from the labor attendant on this work, and only a solemn sense of duty prevented. The labor has been exceedingly arduous: none but those accustomed to such employment can have any tolerable idea of what it is.

Winchester, Massachusetts, July 31, 1873.

EXPLANATIONS.

THE plan of this volume is simple. A consecutive numbering runs through the whole, beginning with Rev. ZECHARIAH SYMMES, of Charlestown, the original emigrant, who came to this country in 1634. This numbering is found on the left hand of the page, before the name of each individual in the series of his recorded descendants. Thus, on page 33, are found eight children of William and Ruth Symmes, numbered from 53 to 60, inclusive.

This mark +, immediately preceding a consecutive number, denotes that a distinct and additional notice of the person to whom that number belongs is reserved for a separate and subsequent paragraph. The place where this promise is fulfilled may be found by looking for the same consecutive number in heavy type, like this, **80**, in the middle of a line, and occupying a line by itself. Thus, Thomas Symmes, whose consecutive number, found on page 40, is 80, is afterwards found on page 46, as the head of a family.

Only one consecutive number belongs to an individual. By means of this, and in the use of a copious *index* at the end of the volume, he is immediately found, and his ancestry and posterity are easily traced.

If there be occasion to mention an individual elsewhere, his place in the series is indicated by his consecutive number in brackets, thus : [102].

A small figure after a name, and just above the line, thus, William Symmes,² denotes the generation to which the individual belongs, and serves in part to distinguish him from others of the same name.

When a woman's name occurs in this fashion, ELEANOR (THOMPSON) MOODY, the name in parenthesis was her original or maiden name, and the name following was the name acquired by a former marriage.

The name of the head or parent of each separate family is found at the beginning of the notice of such family, printed in capitals. It is found to be a great convenience to insert, immediately after the parent's name, the names of his or her American progenitors, thus : TIMOTHY SYMMES⁴ (*Timothy,³ William,² Zechariah¹*).

The families are ranged in the order of seniority, as they occur in the second generation. Thus, the posterity of Zechariah,² second son of Rev. Zechariah Symmes,¹ follow, in each generation, the posterity of William,² the eldest son.

When a town is named without any specification of State, Massachusetts is to be understood, unless the place be universally known, as Portland or Cincinnati.

H. C. 1733, means that the person graduated at Harvard College in that year.

Previous to the year 1752, two methods of reckoning time existed in Great Britain and her colonies. According to one of these methods, the year began on the 25th of March—this being supposed to be the time of the conception of our Saviour. By this reckoning, February was the twelfth month; this was the *civil*, *legal*, or *ecclesiastical* year. According to the other method, the year began, as among the Romans after the time of Julius Caesar, on the first of January; this was the *historical* year, closing with December. In old records these two methods were frequently combined, thus: Feb. 9, 1723-4, which means that the year was 1723 of the *civil*, but 1724 of the *historical* year. When in dates between January 1 and March 25, only one reckoning occurs in an old record, a year is for the most part to be added, to make it conform to our present usage. In the following pages, this practice of " double dating " will occasionally be found. To change Old Style into New, add ten days to dates between 1600 and 1700; or add eleven days to dates between 1700 and Sept. 3, 1752, at which date the New Style was inaugurated by act of Parliament—the 3d of September being counted as the 14th, and the year made to begin with January.

To find the name of an individual recorded in this volume. Suppose it to be Timothy Symmes, the father of Hon. John Cleves Symmes. Thirteen persons of that name are recorded in this book. *This* Timothy was born in 1711. Find the name Timothy among the Christian names of the Symmes Family in Index I., preceded by 1711, the year of his birth, and following the name is the consecutive number, which you will find in its proper place in the body of the work.

THE SYMMES MEMORIAL.

First Generation.

1.

Rev. ZECHARIAH SYMMES[1] was the ancestor of most of those who bear the name in America, so far as is known. He was born in England of most respectable and worthy parents, who had been steadfast in the faith of the gospel, even in the worst of times.

His grandfather, WILLIAM SYMMES, was a truly religious man, and a firm protestant, in the reign of the bloody Queen Mary, from 1553 to 1558. His wife was like-minded. Their son,

Rev. WILLIAM SYMMES, was ordained to the ministry of the gospel in that famous year 1588. He exercised his office faithfully, at a time when it exposed him to great suffering. Queen Elizabeth was afraid of carrying the Reformation too far. She had set up a standard of her own in things ecclesiastical, retaining many of the old Popish rites, and she determined that all her subjects should conform to it. She inherited the stern, unrelenting spirit of her father, and was fond of the old ceremonies in which she had been educated. The year after her accession, the parliament made her the supreme head of the Church of England, and conferred on her the right of regulating all its affairs. Her authority was thus made to supersede the authority of the Lord Jesus Christ; and the power thus conferred she was not slow to exert. She was in effect the Pope of England.

She claimed, and pretended to exercise, supreme authority in matters of faith, to determine what every man between the four seas should believe, in what manner he should worship God, and what should be the terms of his acceptance with his Maker. To enforce these high claims a court was erected, called the Court of High Commission, which was little else than the Spanish Inquisition in disguise. If any persons did not conform precisely to the orders and decrees of this tribunal, the court were authorized to punish them by fine or imprisonment, at their discretion. This power was exercised with the most unrelenting severity. Many of the best people in England, both ministers and laymen, were fined far beyond

1

their ability, and to their utter ruin; others were shut up in prison without a trial, and kept there for months and even for years, none of their friends, not even their wives, being allowed to speak to them except in the presence of the jailor, and twenty or more excellent ministers perished in jail. Many hundreds of faithful ministers, whose only offence was that they chose to obey God rather than man, were turned out of their parishes, and their families left to starve. Some, of whom the world was not worthy, were executed as felons.*

Such things rendered the condition of upright, conscientious men in England intolerable. To escape the sufferings which awaited them there, great numbers went over to Holland, and thousands at length sought refuge beyond the stormy Atlantic. It was such a state of affairs which, in the reign of the weak and bigoted Charles Stuart, compelled Zechariah Symmes and his family to emigrate to America.

Amid all these dangers our Symmes ancestors stood firm. Cotton Mather relates that Rev. William Symmes charged his sons Zechariah and William never to defile themselves with any idolatry† or superstition, but to derive their religion from God's holy word, and to worship God as he himself has directed, and not after the devices and traditions of men. He says, in a passage preserved by Cotton Mather: "I went to Sandwich in Kent to preach, the first or second year after I was ordained a minister, in 1587 or 1588, and preached in St. Mary's, where Mr. Rawson, an ancient godly preacher, was minister, who knew my parents well, and me too at school." How long he remained at Sandwich we do not know.

He had at least two sons, Zechariah and William. It is uncertain whether William came to America.‡ There is no evidence that he did come, as we have found his name in no early record, save his brother's will. He was living in 1664, as we learn from the document just mentioned. From that document we infer that he possessed some property, some of which had been used for the relief of the suffering brother and his family.

Rev. Zechariah Symmes, son of Rev. William, and grandson of Mr. William Symmes, already mentioned, was born at Canterbury, in England, April 5, 1599. He gave evidence of piety at an early age. He was educated at Emanuel College, in the University of Cambridge, where he was graduated in 1620. The next year he was chosen lecturer at St. Anthony, or Antholine's, in the city of London. Being frequently harassed by prosecutions in the Bish-

---

* Henry Barrow, a lawyer, John Greenwood and John Penry, clergymen, to gratify the spite of an angry prelate, were executed without any legal authority, and by the mere sentence of the High Commission, in 1593, after being kept three years in prison.
† The worship of the Church of Rome, some of which still lingers in the Church of England, is essentially idolatrous.
‡ Could he have been the father of Miss Sarah Simes, who died in Cambridge, near Boston, June 11, 1653?

op's courts * for his nonconformity, he removed to Dunstable † in 1625, where, as rector, he continued for eight years his labors in the gospel. Still annoyed by prosecutions of this nature, he at length determined to remove to America.

He arrived in Boston, with his wife and seven children, in the ship Griffin, September 18, 1634. This ship brought over about two hundred emigrants, among whom were William and Anne Hutchinson and Rev. John Lothrop. Mr. Lothrop, after preaching in Scituate three or four years, settled in Barnstable in 1639. This emigration, and others that took place in the six years following, were greatly promoted by an apprehension now entertained by godly people in England, that there "was a special providence of God in raising this plantation, which generally stirred their hearts to come over."‡ Mr. Lothrop, for instance, was accompanied in his voyage by about thirty of his former charge in London.

Mr. Symmes, and his wife Sarah — of whom more in the sequel — were admitted to the church in Charlestown, December 6, 1634. On the 22d of the same month, on a fast-day appointed for the occasion, he was elected and ordained their teacher.

There is no reason to doubt that Mr. Symmes was set apart to the ministry of the gospel by the church in Charlestown themselves, on the very day of his election. He had received Episcopal ordination in England; but our fathers, on their arrival in this country, threw off entirely the yoke of bishops, which had set so uneasily on their necks. The churches of New England, in the early times, claimed and exercised the power of ordaining their own officers — pastors and teachers, as well as deacons and ruling elders. Rev. John Wilson, the first minister in Boston, was set apart to his office, Aug. 27, 1630, by imposition of the hands of the church. "This was done," says Gov. Winthrop, "only as a sign of *election* and *confirmation*, not of any intent that Mr. Wilson should renounce his ministry received in England." Rev. John Cotton was chosen teacher of the church in Boston, Oct. 10, 1633, and on the same day, immediately after, the pastor, Mr. Wilson, and two ruling elders, laid their hands on him, in behalf of the church, solemnly designating him to his holy office. Rev. Thomas Carter, the first minister of Woburn, was ordained by the laying on of hands of two private members of the church, one of whom probably was Edward Johnson, the author of the "Wonder-Working Providence." The transaction, which took place Dec. 2, 1642, is minutely related both in the town records and by Johnson in the Wonder-Working Providence.

---

* The execrable William Laud was then bishop of London, a fit instrument of arbitrary power. He was archbishop of Canterbury from 1633 to 1644. He was beheaded on Tower Hill for his agency in subverting the liberties of England, Jan. 10, 1644-5.

† In Bedfordshire, thirty-four miles N. W. from London.

‡ This statement was made by Mr. John Humphrey, who with his wife Susan, a sister of the Earl of Lincoln, arrived in Boston, July, 1634. The lady Arabella, wife of Isaac Johnson, who came with Winthrop in 1630, was daughter of that nobleman.

Nine ministers were present, one of whom was Mr. Symmes, the nearest minister, yet none of them took part in the ordination. Mr. Carter himself preached and prayed. Other instances of this sort might be mentioned, all of which show that such was the prevailing, as it was the primitive practice.*

The First Church, Boston, was originally formed in Charlestown, July 30, 1630.† But it being found difficult to cross the river, especially in winter, the church was removed to Boston, where a majority of its members resided, and a new church, consisting of sixteen men and their wives, and three unmarried men living on the north side of the river, organized in Charlestown, Nov. 2, 1632. Of this new church, Rev. Thomas James, who arrived in Boston with Rev. Stephen Batchelor and Rev. Thomas Welde, June 5, 1632, was chosen the first pastor. It being customary for each church to enjoy the labors of two ministers, Mr. Symmes, in December, 1634, was ordained as colleague with Mr. James, taking on him the work of *teacher*, while Mr. James confined himself to *pastoral* labors. Difficulties soon arose between the two ministers, a majority of the people adhering to Mr. Symmes, which occasioned the calling of an ecclesiastical council. This council, on the 11th of March, 1636, advised Mr. James to ask a dismission, which was accordingly done. He went to Providence in 1637, and thence to New Haven, where he engaged in teaching. In October, 1642, he accompanied Rev. Messrs. Knowles of Watertown and Tompson of Braintree, in their unsuccessful mission to Virginia, returning with them in June of the following year. Not long after this, he returned to England; was resettled at Needham in Suffolk; was deprived of his parish for nonconformity, and died about 1678, aged 86. In all his trials he approved himself as a faithful servant of Christ, and appears to have been a truly good man.‡

---

* It was held, and such is the theory at the present time, that by the appointment of Christ himself, all church power, under Christ, resides in the church itself; i. e., in the body of church members. Every church, therefore, has the right of choosing its own officers; a right which no man can take from it. But the power of *election* implies and includes the power of *ordination*. For, as the Cambridge Platform says, "Ordination is nothing else but the solemn putting a man into his place and office in the church, whereunto he had right before by election. Ordination is to follow election. Ordination doth not constitute an officer, nor give him the essentials of his office. . . . . In churches where there are elders, imposition of hands in ordination is to be performed by those elders. . . . . For if the people may elect officers, which is the greater, they may much more impose hands in ordination, which is less."

To this practice the churches of New England seem to have adhered for many years. The earliest instance of departure which has been observed, was at the ordination of Rev. Moses Fiske, of Braintree (now Quincy), Sept. 21, 1672, when Rev. Mr. Oxenbridge of Boston *and the deacons joined in the laying on of hands.* This is Mr. Fiske's own account.

At length, near the close of that century, ministers began to claim the power of imposition of hands in ordination as their exclusive right, and the churches by courtesy yielded it to them. Still, to the present day it is held that ministers, in ordination, act only in behalf of the church as their agents, by their appointment, and not by any right in the ministry itself.

† For some time they met for worship under the shadow of a great oak, "where," says one, "I heard Mr. Wilson and Mr. Phillips [afterwards of Watertown] preach many a good sermon." This tree was alive and flourishing nearly a century after.

‡ Felt's Eccl. Hist. of New England.

The Rev. John Harvard, who, with Anna his wife, came over in 1637, was with her admitted a member of the Charlestown church, Nov. 6, in that year. He graduated at Emanuel College, Cambridge, in 1631, and took his second degree there in 1635. He must have been, therefore, at this time, a young man. He has usually been reckoned one of the ministers of Charlestown, and a colleague with Mr. Symmes.* But though a resident in Charlestown, and a member of that church, it is next to certain, says Rev. Samuel Sewall, that he never was called to office in that church. The only notice to be found of him in the church records is of his admission as a member, at the date already mentioned.† He died of consumption, Sept. 14, 1638; and this fact appears, not from the church records, but from Danforth's Almanack for 1649, printed at Cambridge. But his generous bequest to the college, which has so long borne his name, has insured to him a perpetual remembrance. The legacy amounted to £779 17 2 — a large sum for those days, and one half of all his property. Johnson speaks of him as an earnest christian and as an impressive preacher.‡

Rev. Thomas Allen was admitted a member of the church in Charlestown, Dec. 22, 1639, O. S., answering to Jan. 1, 1640, N. S., and soon after, if not at the same time, became the colleague of Mr. Symmes. He was the *teacher*, whereas Mr. Symmes, from the time of the dismission of Mr. James, 1636, was the *pastor*. Mr. Allen was born in Norwich, Eng., 1608; graduated at Caius College, Cambridge, 1627; was minister of St. Edmund's Church in his native city, but was deprived for nonconformity, 1636, and came with his wife Anne to New England in 1638. It is supposed that she soon died, and that he married the widow of John Harvard.§ In 1651 Mr. Allen visited England, spent the rest of his life there, and published several books. In 1659, he was again minister in Norwich. He was again ejected, as were two thousand other faithful ministers, in 1662, but still preached to his people, as opportunity offered, till his death in that city, Sept. 21, 1673, aged 65.‖ He was called "a holy man of God and faithful servant of Christ."

Mr. Symmes had one other colleague, in the person of Rev. Thomas Shepard, born in London, England, April 5, 1635, eldest son of

---

* Eliot, in his biography, calls him "pastor of the church in Charlestown." In a list of its ministers, drawn up in modern times, and inserted in the second volume of the church records, Mr. Harvard is numbered among them. But all this appears to be founded in mistake.

† See American Quarterly Register, vol. xi. p. 49.

‡ As early as May, 1636, measures had been put in train for a college in Massachusetts. Salem was at first proposed; but in November, 1637, the legislature resolved on the erection of a college in Cambridge, then a part of Newton, for the support of which it was agreed to give four hundred pounds, whereof two hundred pounds to be paid the first year, and two hundred pounds when the work was finished.—*Felt's Eccl. Hist. N. E.*, vol. i. pp. 251, 263, 326.

§ The General Court, June 6, 1639, granted to Rev. Thomas Allen five hundred acres of land, "in regard to Mr. Harvard's gift."—*Felt's Eccl. Hist. N. E.*, vol. i. p. 377.

‖ Am. Quar. Reg. vol xi., pp. 46, 49; vol. xiii p. 44.

the eminent Thomas Shepard, of our Cambridge; grad. H. C. 1653; was ordained *teacher* of the church in Charlestown, April 13, 1659. The imposition of hands was by Mr. Symmes, Rev. John Wilson of Boston, and Rev. Richard Mather of Dorchester, *at the express desire of the church*, and acting in their behalf.[*] He died suddenly, of small-pox, caught while visiting one of his flock, Dec. 22, 1677. President Oakes, in a Latin oration, pronounced at the Commencement after his death, extolled him "as holding the first rank among the ministers of his day."

Mr. Symmes was admitted freeman of the colony, May 6, 1635.

Not long after his settlement in Charlestown he became involved in the celebrated controversy with Mrs. Ann Hutchinson[†] and the Antinomians. As already observed, he was a fellow-passenger, 1634, with Mrs. Hutchinson in the voyage from England. Mrs. Hutchinson had startled him and other passengers by some eccen-tricities and speculations of her own in matters of religion, and especially by "revelations" which she professed to have received. According to her statement, revelations from heaven were with her matters of frequent occurrence. After her arrival, Mr. Symmes felt it his duty to inform the Boston church of what he had heard her say during the passage. This caused some delay in her admission to that church, which, however, took place early in November.

---

[*] Ibid. vol. xii. p. 244.

[†] She was the daughter of Rev. Francis Marbury, of Lincolnshire, and was baptized at Alford, July 20, 1591. At the age of twenty she was married to William Hutchinson, a prosperous merchant of that place. At the time of the controversy spoken of in the text, she was forty-five years of age, and had several children already come to maturity. She was an exceedingly capable and resolute woman. After her banishment from Massachu-setts, she and her husband went to Rhode Island, where he died in 1642. She then went to reside under the Dutch jurisdiction at Pelham Neck, near New Rochelle, N. Y., where she was killed by the Indians, with most of her family, in September of the following year. Some of her children and grandchildren arose to wealth and distinction in Massachusetts. Thomas Hutchinson, her great-great-grandson, was governor of that province, 1771-74.

The following is the testimony given by Mr. Symmes on the trial of Mrs. Hutchinson before the court at Newtown (now Cambridge) in 1637. We find it in Hutchinson's History of Massachusetts, published in 1767.

"For my own part, being called to speak in this case, to discharge the relation wherein I stand to the Commonwealth, and that wherein I stand to God, I shall speak briefly.

"For my acquaintance with this person, I had none in our native country, only I had occasion to be in her company once or twice before I came, where I did perceive that she did slight the ministers of the word of God. But I came along with her in the ship, and it so fell out that we were in the great cabin together, and therein did agree with the labours of Mr. Lathrop and myself, only there was a secret opposition to things delivered. The main thing that was then in hand was about evidencing of a good estate, and among the rest about that place in John concerning the love of the brethren. That which I took notice of was the corruptness and narrowness of her opinions; which I doubt not I may call them so; but she said, when she came to Boston there would be something seen. . . . .

"And being come, and she desiring to be admitted a member, I was desired to be there, and then Mr. Cotton did give me full satisfaction in the things in question.

"And for things which have been here spoken, as far as I can remember, they are the truth; and when I asked her what she thought of me, she said, Alas! you know my mind long ago. Yet I do not think myself disparaged by her testimony; and I would not trou-ble the court, only this one thing I shall put in, that Mr. Dudley and Mr. Haines were not wanting in the cause, after I had given notice of her."

Thomas Dudley came to New England with Winthrop in 1630; was deputy governor of Massachusetts, 1630-1633; governor, 1634 and 1640; died July 31, 1653. John Haynes came with John Cotton in 1633; was governor, 1635; governor of Connecticut many years; died March 1, 1654.

Soon after her arrival, she began to hold meetings once or twice a week, at first for women only, afterwards meetings at which men as well as women were present. Sixty or eighty or even one hundred women attended these meetings, some of them from the principal families of the town. On these occasions she urged her peculiar opinions with great earnestness, and with no small measure of success. Among them were such sentiments as these: — That the outward life is not a sure test of character; that the evidence of our acceptance with God, need not, any part of it, be exhibited to the view of others; that the evidence of a man's piety is and must be shut up in one's own breast, and cannot be increased by any outward manifestation. She insisted very strongly on an inward witness of the Spirit, amounting to an immediate revelation from God, that the person is in a state of favor and acceptance with him. Of course, if I have a promise coming immediately and specially from God that I shall be saved, what need of further evidence?

The ministers of the colony, who held that the evidence of a man's piety must, partly at least, be furnished by a holy life, and must therefore be patent, thus far, to the eyes of others; that a man must be a good man outwardly in order to be a true Christian — she denounced, in no measured terms, as holding to a "covenant of works," and therefore as preaching no gospel at all. As she made herself very prominent in this affair, she was of course opposed by the ministers whom she thus misrepresented, and by none more decidedly than by Mr. Symmes.

The promulgation of Mrs. Hutchinson's views, in the manner and style which she chose to adopt, soon raised a prodigious ferment. The whole colony was shaken to its centre. Her teachings were regarded by the most judicious and sober-minded persons as not only dangerous to the souls of men, but as tending to revolution in the state. If, as she claimed, revelations from God were to be expected, and were actually enjoyed by her, not only in the affair of our salvation, but in reference to the more important concerns of life, these revelations having equal authority with the Scriptures, who could tell how far they might extend, what direction they might take, or what line of conduct they might prescribe for her followers? Suppose Mrs. Hutchinson to have a revelation requiring her followers to take the sword; what then?

Serious apprehension existed, therefore, that the whole fabric, civil and religious, for the erection of which our fathers had left their native land and incurred all the toils and perils of the wilderness, might be overthrown. The followers of this able and daring woman appeared likely to carry the controversy, thus awakened, to the most dangerous extremes. It became necessary, therefore, to resort to extreme measures. The General Court, impressed with the belief that the peace of the civil community and of the churches demanded a decisive course, found Mrs. Hutchinson and a large number of her adherents guilty of sedition, and proceeded to disarm, disfranchise and banish from the colony seventy-five of the more prominent men, and banished Mrs. Hutchinson herself.   If this measure was a stretch of power, it at least saved the country from ruin.   Mr. Symmes took part in these proceedings.

Mr. Symmes appears to have been held in esteem by his cotemporaries, and when we remember who they were, this is no small praise.   In regard to literary attainment, he appears to have been respectable.   He had for those times a good library, containing the works of the able divines of his day.   But so far as we can now discover, he was more distinguished for practical talent and general usefulness than for intellectual eminence.   He must have been a man of no small ability to retain a firm hold of such a parish for so many years.   He wrote his sermons, and left a large number in manuscript, most of them bound up in volumes.   "He knew his Bible well," says Cotton Mather, "and he was a preacher of what he knew, and a sufferer for what he preached."

Of his wife, Edward Johnson, in the Wonder-Working Providence, writes as follows: "Among all the godly women that came through the perilous seas to war their warfare, the wife of this zealous teacher, Mrs. Sarah Symmes, shall not be omitted.   This virtuous woman, endued by Christ with grace fit for a wilderness condition, her courage exceeding her stature, with much cheerfulness did undergo all the difficulties of those times of straits, her God through faith in Christ supplying all wants, with great industry nurturing up her young children in the fear of the Lord; their number being ten,* both sons and daughters; a certain sign of the Lord's intent to people this vast wilderness.   God grant they may be as valiant in fight against sin, Satan, and all the enemies of Christ's kingdom, following the example of their father and grandfather, who have both suffered for the same; in remembrance of whom these following lines are penned:

> " Come Zachary, thou must re-edify
>   Christ's churches in this desert-land of his,
>   With Moses' zeal, stamped unto dust, defy
>   All crooked ways that Christ's true worship miss.
>   With Spirit's sword and armour girt about,
>   Thou layedst on proud prelate's crown to crack,
>   And wilt not suffer wolves thy flock to rout,
>   Though close they creep, with sheep-skins on their back.
>   Thy father's spirit doubled is upon
>   Thee, Symmes! then war: thy father fighting died.
>   In prayer then prove thou a like champion!
>   Hold out till death, and Christ will crown provide."

If these lines have little poetic merit, they aptly express the spirit and life of the Charlestown pastor.

---

* We have the names of twelve, of whom ten were then living.

Woburn was settled from Charlestown in 1641. The first settlers had been members of Mr. Symmes's church and congregation.
The first sermon ever preached in Woburn was by Mr. Symmes, Nov.
21, 1641, from the text, Jer. 4: 3: "Thus saith the Lord, break up
your fallow ground, and sow not among thorns." Very appropriate,
certainly, to the occasion. Mr. Symmes was present at the formation
of the church, Aug. 24, 1642. On that occasion he "continued in
prayer and preaching about the space of four or five houres."* He
was also present at the ordination of Mr. Thomas Carter, the first
minister, December 2, following.

He preached the Election Sermon in 1648.

In July, 1656, the Quakers first came to Boston. The sect then
bearing that name were not the peaceable, order-loving citizens now
known to us under that designation. They were people who, pro-
fessing to have revelations and impulses directly from heaven, made
it their special business to disquiet all who differed from them, to
the utmost of their power. In England George Fox and others
travelled through the land, declaiming against the ministers and
churches, interrupting public worship, and refusing any respect to
the civil magistrate. Some of them, even females, went into meetings for public worship stark naked. Many opened their shops on
the Lord's day, in defiance of the laws. Others went about the
streets of London denouncing the judgments of God against the
government.†

The advent of these people to New England was dreaded as
among the worst of evils. But in 1656, two Quaker women came
from Barbadoes to Boston, as they expressly stated, to propagate
their contempt of the ministry and of the civil power. A month
later, several other Quakers arrived with similar intent. They continued to come. They would not have been molested, if they had
been quiet and peaceable. But they were not peaceable. On Martha's Vineyard they tried to induce the Indians not to hear Mr.
Mayhew, and not to read the scriptures.‡ In other places their
conduct was in the highest degree riotous, turbulent and provoking.
They were continually disturbing congregations assembled for public worship. Margaret Brewster went into a meeting-house with her
face smeared over with black paint. Deborah Wilson went through
the streets of Salem naked, as a sign to the people. Lydia Ward-
well went into a meeting-house in Newbury, as naked as she was
born. The Quakers in those days were not so much a religious
sect as a band of miscreants. Bishop Burnet, whose opinion is worthy of respect, says they were dangerous to the peace of the community.

---

* Johnson's Wonder-Working Providence; Sewall's Hist. of Woburn.
† Neal's Hist. of the Puritans, vol. iv. pp. 175, 176.
‡ Felt's Eccl. Hist. of N. E., vol. ii. p. 162.

2

The General Court of Massachusetts passed an act against the Quakers, imposing heavy fines, sentencing offenders to prison and banishing them from the colony. Some of them, after being sent away, returned a second or a third time, notwithstanding that the penalty of death was denounced upon them in case of their return.*

The government were very reluctant to proceed to extremities. But exercising the right which every householder has to clear his house of disorderly persons, and finding that these wretches, after being sent away, would still return, and, as some of them avowed, for the express purpose of defying and trampling upon the laws of the land, the executive authority made use of the last resort; they hanged four of these Quakers.† But they were not hanged for being Quakers; they were not thus dealt with, nor were they fined, imprisoned or banished, for opinion's sake, but for riot and sedition, for endeavoring the overthrow of the civil authority, and for disturbing the public peace.

While some of these Quakers were in prison, Mr. Symmes visited them for religious conversation suited to their need. For this and similar efforts he was grievously reviled by the Quakers.

The latter part of the life of Mr. Symmes was embittered by the conduct of some of the members of his church, who were among the founders of the First Baptist Church in Boston. This church was originally gathered in Charlestown, about the year 1665. Thomas Gould, a member of Mr. Symmes's church, had a child born to him in 1655, which he withheld from baptism. For this, and for absenting himself from the worship and ordinances of that church, in disregard of covenant vows, he was repeatedly admonished, and at length, with some others, excommunicated. They were also prosecuted in the civil courts. The Baptist historians blame Mr. Symmes for the part he took in these proceedings. But he, in common with his brethren, honestly regarded Mr. Gould and his associates as disturbers of the public peace. They remembered the disturbances and murders caused by the Anabaptists in Germany the century previous. They feared the influence of the principles now held by the Baptists in common with those incendiaries. Mr. Symmes and those who acted with him, are not to be blamed for not possessing the light we now enjoy. Moreover, the Congregationalists of that day supposed that as they had, at the cost of much labor, expense and suffering, procured on these shores an asylum for themselves and their brethren of like faith, it was a grievous wrong for persons of a different faith, and maintaining other forms of worship, to intrude among them, when there was room enough elsewhere. They considered themselves as acting in self-defence. These considerations should shield them from the charge of persecution. The charge is utterly groundless.‡

---

* Ibid, vol. ii. 211, et seq.; Palfrey, ii. 461, &c.
† Felt's Eccl. Hist. N. E., ii. pp. 208, 211 et seq. 251; Palfrey, ii. 464 et seq.
‡ Felt's Eccl. Hist. N. E., ii. 138, 151, 341, 362, 371, 513; Palfrey, iii. 89, 90.

In 1648, and about that time, the salary of Mr. Symmes was ninety pounds sterling. Only one other minister in the colony, the eloquent and eminent John Cotton, of Boston, had as much. Thomas Weld of Roxbury, John Knowles of Watertown, and Ezekiel Rogers of Rowley, had eighty pounds each. Others had from seventy pounds each down to twenty pounds. Thomas Allen, the colleague of Mr. Symmes, had sixty pounds. These salaries and public taxes generally, were paid, for the most part, not in cash, but in the produce of the farm.*

The church of Charlestown was gathered Nov. 2, 1632, and the records, still in existence, and in good preservation, begin at that time. From that date till 1677, it appears that five hundred and twenty persons were admitted to full communion in this church, of whom two hundred were males. Of this period of forty-five years, thirty-seven years belonged to the ministry of Mr. Symmes. It is probable, therefore, that during his ministry, more than four hundred persons were added to his church.

A synod, assembled in Boston in 1662, introduced into the New England churches what has long been known as the "half-way covenant," whereby persons baptized in infancy, on coming to maturity and owning the covenant made by their parents at their baptism, were entitled to have their children baptized, without themselves coming to the communion. This new practice was strenuously resisted by many, while others, among whom was Mr. Symmes, were its zealous advocates. The practice was immediately introduced into his church. In this affair, as in others, he acted in concurrence with such men as Richard, Eleazar and Increase Mather, Thomas Shepard, John Wilson, John Allin, Samuel Whiting, Thomas Cobbett, John Higginson and John Ward.†

The town of Charlestown gave Mr. Symmes a tract of three hundred acres of land, extending from the north end of Mystic Pond to the borders of Woburn. In his will he calls it "my farm near Woburn." It continued for a long time within the limits of Charlestown, but is now included within the town of Winchester. A more particular description is reserved for the notice of his eldest son William, who owned it after the father's death. Part of it, fifty or sixty acres, remains in the possession and occupancy of his descendants to this day.

The town of Charlestown also granted to Mr. Symmes three hundred acres in the "Land of Nod," the history of which is as follows:

The town of Woburn was separated from Charlestown in 1642, but the divisional line between the two towns was not established till

---

* Feit's Eccl. Hist. N. E., ii. 3; Palfrey, ii. 57; Sewall's Hist. of Woburn, p. 50. Silver was scarce; the most that had been brought over, was sent back to England for supplies.
† The compiler hopes that in this instance, as in others, he will be understood simply as acting the part of the faithful historian, in stating the facts as they were. He does not undertake any justification of the practice.

eight years after. There had been some misunderstanding about the line, which was at length quieted by an arrangement entered into July 29, 1650, by a committee mutually chosen. By this arrangement Charlestown relinquished to Woburn five hundred acres of land, beginning at the east corner of Edward Convers's farm, which was in Woburn, and running north to Charlestown Head Line; in exchange for which Woburn ceded to Charlestown three thousand acres lying further north.

Edward Convers lived near where the Orthodox church in Winchester now stands. His farm, of course, was in the neighborhood of his house, including what was long known as Convers's Mill, on the Mystic River, in the present village of Winchester, and now in the occupation of Joel Whitney, or very near it. Mr. Symmes's farm lay immediately west of the farm of Convers. The arrangement now entered into gave to Woburn the farms and lots on "Richardson's Row," now Washington Street, in Winchester, respecting a part of which there had been some dispute. But Woburn relinquished to Charlestown three thousand acres of land, of which the rights of property were to be vested in Charlestown, though considered to be within the bounds of Woburn. When Woburn was incorporated, October, 1642, it was four miles square, and the three thousand acres lay at its northern extremity, within the limits of the present town of Wilmington. It was long known as the "Land of Nod," and is so called by many at the present day.* This name was probably suggested by its forlorn condition, so far from church ordinances, which seemed to justify a comparison with that distant region to which Cain banished himself when he went from the presence of the Lord—Gen. 4 : 16. This tract of land lay for many years in a neglected, uncultivated state. It was divided by Charlestown, in 1643, among twelve of her prominent citizens, of whom Mr. Symmes was one. The share given to him was three hundred acres; none had more than this, some had less. But the lots were not surveyed nor staked out till 1718, and were considered of so little value, that several of the gentlemen resigned their grants to the town again.† In 1671, Mr. Symmes's three hundred acres were valued at only five pounds.

Mr. Symmes continued to be pastor of the church in Charlestown till his death, which took place Feb. 4, 1670-1,‡ at the age of 71 years and ten months. His wife Sarah survived him, dying in 1676. Mather says his epitaph§ represents him as having lived with his wife forty-nine years and seven months, and as having had by her

* A mill in that vicinity is still called "Nod's Mill."
† Sewall's Hist. Woburn, pp. 8, 23, 29, 540, 541.
‡ A different date is given in the N. E. Geneal. Reg., vol. xiii. 207, viz., Feb. 24, 1671. But Mather, in his Magnalia, says Mr. Symmes died Feb. 4, 1670, which of course is old style. Ten days must be added to make it conform to the new style, and the true date, according to our present mode of reckoning, is Feb. 14, 1671. This also corresponds with the date as given in Hobart's Journal and in Judge Sewall's interleaved almanac. (See Geneal. Reg., vii. 206.) Moreover, the inventory is dated Feb. 15, 1670-1.
§ It is to be regretted that this epitaph now exists only in the Magnalia.

five sons and eight daughters. According to this statement he must have been married to her as early as July, 1621, the year after he graduated at college. He resided in London from 1621 to 1625, and his two eldest children seem to have been born there. We have the names of twelve children, none of whom were born previous to 1625.

He was honorably interred at the expense of the town. His grave was "covered and set comelie" by a stone-work laid in lime, together with a tomb-stone, procured by the selectmen of the town and the deacons of the church, in pursuance of a vote of the town. The epitaph, which has been wholly effaced by the ravages of time, contained the following lines:

> " A prophet lies beneath this stone :
> His words shall live, though he be gone."

His will is dated Jan. 20, 1664–5; it was proved March 31, 1671, and is recorded Midd. Prob. 3, 234. I have carefully examined the original document, written with his own hand, which I shall here quote exact and entire.

The twentieth day of January 1664, I Zechariah Symmes of Charlestown, New England, being at present, through God's free mercy, in some competent measure of health, yet daily wayting for my change, have revised the last former draught of my will, but revoking it, do establish this following as my last will and testament, and do hereby appoint my dear and faithful wife Mrs. Sarah Symmes sole executrix thereof.

First, I commit and commend what I am and have into the hands of my most loving Father and Gracious God in Christ Jesus: my soul immediately upon my death to be received into those heavenly mansions which my blessed Saviour hath prepared for me ; my body to be for a time, in a comely, but not over costly manner, interred, in assured faith and hope that my Saviour will in his time raise up my vile body and make it like his glorious body, and, uniting it to my soul, will continue them forever with himself in perfect blessedness and glore.

For my temporal estate wherewith the Lord hath blessed me, it is already in good parte disposed of by reason of the mariage of my eldest sonne William, and of six of my daughters, viz., Sarah, Marye, Elizabeth, Huldah, Rebeckah, Deborah. To each of these seven I have already given such a portion, as our own necessities would permitt, and that without any partialitie farther than a legacy given to my daughter Brock, and daughter Savage did equity require ; therefore my earnest desire and will is that none of them grudge at any of the other, or trouble their mother in the least wise any further demand, or motion about what is already disposed of.

For Ruth,* my wife hath already set by for her such a portion as with a very small enlargement (which I leave to my widow's discretion) may equal her portion with her sisters.

For my two sonnes Zechariah and Timothy,† to the former upon his

---

* Ruth was the seventh daughter, not then married. Deborah, younger than she, had been married a few weeks previous.

† No other sons are mentioned in the will than these three, William, Zechariah and Timothy.

going to Rehoboth I gave some books, with some household stuff, and to make up his first dividend, I assign unto him all my library, except what is after mentioned, and provided that soone after my death he oblige himself in a bonde of eighty pounds, together with his heirs and assigns, to pay unto his brother Timothie fourty pounds sterling in money, or merchantable goods at money price, within one year after my decease, or in case his brother Timothy dye before the year expired, then to pay it to my other children surviving, in equal portions, reserving a double portion to my eldest sonne William.

Other legacies doe some of my dear friends deserve, and therefore may probably expect, but considering my dear widos probable necesseties, and that farr most of our first estate came by her, I trust they will take it well though I do dispose of the remainder of my estate in the manner following.

First, my debts being discharged (which are none that I know of but what my wife is privye unto) and one legacy of five pounds to my dear brother Mr. William Symmes, to which I know my wife will be as willing as myself, it being but a small remembrance of his very great love and costs to us and ours, I then give and bequeath to my faithful and dearly beloved wife, the whole use and benefit of all my temporal estate, consisting in lands, houses, cattell, moneye, plate, with all other goods and moveables which the Lord hath given, to her own proper use, to have, hold and enjoy during the whole time of her widowhood. In case she shall see good to marry, which I suppose she will never do without good advice, then I take it for granted that it will be with one that may bring some comfortable outward estate with him, and therefore in case she shall marry I give a third part of my whole estate to be equally divided among my children then living, only a double part to my eldest sonne, and at her death the other two thirds to be alike divided, only I give her liberty and power at her decease to dispose of fifty pounds sterling to any of her children or any other of her relatives or friends as she shall see mete. Further, out of my books and papers, I give her that large English Bible w[ch] was her mothers, also such books as I have of Doc Sibs or Doc Prestons,[*] also a book of Baynes letters,[†] and about comfortable walking with God. Also all my notes of my sermons, one book in octavo upon 16th Mat. 24 and 17 cap of John, 2 small books of my latter sermons, one in decimo sexto, the other hath yet but a few sermons. Also I give to my eldest sonne Fulke[‡] on Rhem. Test. with 4 books in quarto of Mr. Bolton's works,[§] as also a fourth part of such manuscripts either mine owne or my father's sermons, as are in papers or sticht, but not bound up. All my written books besides I give to Zech: with the rest of the manuscripts, yet so as upon their requests not to deny the lend-

---

* Dr. Richard Sibbes, a celebrated Puritan preacher, and the author of some highly approved works, the most noted of which was " The Bruised Reed," to which Baxter says he owed his conversion. He died in 1635, aged 59. Dr. John Preston was another distinguished Puritan divine, master of Emmanel College, Cambridge, and might have been bishop of Gloucester, but he refused. He was a remarkably eloquent preacher, and died July, 1628.

† Paul Baynes was a preacher of great learning and exemplary piety, and the author of several valuable works. He suffered much for his nonconformity, and was reduced to great poverty and want for religion's sake.

‡ Dr. William Fulke, an eminent and learned Puritan divine, born 1510, died 1589. He exposed the mistakes in the translation, and the false glosses put upon the sacred text, in what was called the Rhemish Testament; which was an English version from the Latin Vulgate of the New Testament, made in the (Romish) English College at Rheims, France, in 1582.

§ Robert Bolton, born 1572, died 1631, was a very learned Puritan minister, a most awakening and able preacher, a very devout and holy man. He could speak Greek with almost as great facility as his mother tongue.

ing of them for a small time to any of their brethren or sisters to peruse for their owne private use onely, for I never intended nor prepared anything of mine to be put in print.

Item. At my wives death I give my farm neere Woburne and land at Nottimos* to my eldest sonne, provided that he bynde it over to pay unto the rest of my children a hundred pounds in equall portions in two years time: 50 pounds per annum.

Item. I give to all my sonnes in law, at the death of my wife, to each of them thirty shillings for a ring, or any other meanes of remembering my love to them; and to each of my grandchildren, by nature or by law, thirteen shillings four pence for a spoone."

Witnesses. Francis Norton, Joshua Teed [Tidd].

There is a codicil dated Dec. 19, 1667, making no essential change.

INVENTORY of Estate of Mr. Zechariah Simmes, deceased, made Feb. 15, 1670–1. [Exactly copied, as was the will, from the Probate Records.]

Dwelling house and outhouses, wth orchard & yard	£200.	0. 0
Two acres of land by Thomas Carters	30.	0. 0
Ten acres of meadow by Mr. Palgraves	50.	0. 0
Two Cow Commons	10.	0. 0
A farm bordering upon Wooburne with 6 acres of land at Monotamie [W. Cambridge, now Arlington]	160.	0. 0
Fourty seven acres of Woodland	5.	0. 0
Three hundred acres in ye Land of Nodd	5.	0. 0
	460.	0. 0

In Cattell	£7. 0. 0		
In Waring apparell	20. 0. 0		
His Library	85. 10. 3		
In Plate and Mony	20. 0. 6	132. 10. 9	

Household Goods.

Pewter, £10. 0. 0 ; Brass, £5. 10. 0			
Iron ware, £7. 15. 0		67. 11. 6	
Beding & bedsteds,	£24. 15. 0		
Lynnen	£19. 11. 6		

Coverlets, Blankets, Searge, Flannell, Flax, Yarn, Carpets, &c.	£7. 19. 0		
Eleaven Cushions	1. 6. 0		
One clock	2. 10. 0		
In trunks, chests, Tables, Chaires, Stooles & Desks	8. 2. 0		
In Lumber	1. 0. 9	20. 17. 9	

£681. 0. 0

Signed by Thomas Linde, William Stitson, Lawrence Hammond, and Joshua Tidd, appraisers.

Midd. Probate Records, 3: 237.

* Menotomy in West Cambridge.

The following is, with some slight omissions, the will of Mrs. Sarah Symmes, as found on record in the Suffolk Registry, vol. vi. fol. 145. It was proved Dec. 28, 1676.

WILL OF SARAH SIMMS, relict of Zechariah Simms, late of Charlestown.

I do freely give and resign my soul into the hands of my blessed Creato' and Redeemer, desiring for the merit of Christ alone to be accepted, and desire with thankfulness to acknowledge his grace for that measure of assurance thereof which bee hath vouchsafed unto mee. And for that temporall Estate which I have which is onely fifty pound, which my husband in his last will and Testament gave me liberty to dispose of as I saw good, I do dispose and give as followeth

I do give unto my son Zachary Simms fifteen pounds.

I do give to my grandchild Margaret Prout ten pounds.

I give to my son Timothy Simms seven pounds.

I give unto my grandchild Margaret Davis five pounds.

I give to my grandchild Hannah Davis five pounds.

The remaining eight pounds I give to my son William Simms, to my son John Broke and to his wife, to my son Zachary Simms and to his wife, to my son Timothy Simms and to his wife, to my son Thomas Savage and to his wife, to my son Timothy Prout and to his wife, to my son Humphrey Booth, to my son Edward Willies and his wife, to each an equal part for to buy each of them a Ring, which I desire them to accept as a token of my love, I not having farther to give unto them.

Thomas Savage and Edward Willis were Executors.

Mr. Symmes had by his wife Sarah, according to Cotton Mather, thirteen children, five sons and eight daughters. We find but ten mentioned in the foregoing will; the same number assigned to him by Johnson — this being the number living in 1652, the date of the "Wonder-Working Providence." Eight were born in England, of whom seven accompanied him to this country. Five were born afterwards.

Born in London, Eng.

2. A son,[2] born about 1623. This must be supposed, to make out the number assigned to him by Mather. Died early.

+3. SARAH,[2] b. about 1625; m. first, Rev. Samuel Haugh; m. second, Rev. John Brock, both of Reading.

Born in Dunstable, Eng.

+4. WILLIAM,[2] bapt. Jan. 10, 1626-7; m. first, Sarah (?) ——; m. second, Mary ——.

+5. MARY,[2] bapt. April 16, 1628; m. Thomas Savage.

+6. ELIZABETH,[2] bapt. Jan. 1, 1629–30; m. Hezekiah Usher.

+7. HULDAH,[2] bapt. March 18, 1630–1; m. William Davis.

8. HANNAH,[2] bapt. Aug. 22, 1632; unm.; d. early.

9. REBECCA,[2] bapt. Feb. 12, 1633–4; m. Humphrey Booth.

Born in Charlestown, New England.

10. RUTH,[2] b. Oct. 18, 1635; m. Edward Willis, June 15, 1668.

+11. ZECHARIAH,[2] b. Jan. 9, 1637–8; m. first, Susannah Graves; m. second, Mehitable Dalton.

12. TIMOTHY,[2] b. May 7, 1640 ; d. Sept. 25, 1641.
13. DEBORAH,[2] b. Aug. 28, 1642 ; m. Timothy Prout, Dec. 13, 1664—
   his second wife ; his first wife's name was Margaret.
+14. TIMOTHY,[2] b. 1643 ; m. first, Mary Nichols ; m. second, Elizabeth
   Norton.

The baptisms of the children born in Dunstable appear in Mr.
Savage's " Gleanings."

Second Generation.

3.

SARAH SYMMES,[2] daughter of Rev. Zechariah and Sarah
Symmes — the eldest of their children except a son who died in
infancy — was born in England about 1625 ; accompanied her father
to America in 1634 ; admitted to the church in Charlestown, April
17, 1642 ; m. first, Rev. SAMUEL HAUGH,[*] in 1650. He was born
in England, son of Atherton Haugh, who came in 1633 from Boston
in Old England, where he had been mayor, and settled in Boston,
New England. He came in the ship Griffin, of three hundred tons,
with Messrs. Hooker, Stone and Cotton, the last of whom was probably his pastor in England. He was an adherent of Mrs. Hutchinson in 1637, and representative from Boston with Vane and Cod-
dington. Samuel, the son, was a member of the first class in Harvard College, though for some reason he did not graduate. He came
to Reading, or what is now Wakefield, in 1648, and was ordained
pastor of the church there, March 26, 1650. He was the second
minister of the place, succeeding the Rev. Henry Green. He died
at the house of his brother-in-law, Hezekiah Usher, in Boston, March
30, 1662. He left three daughters, and a son *Samuel*.

She married second, Rev. JOHN BROCK, of Reading, now Wakefield, Nov. 14, 1662. He was born in Stradbrook, in Suffolk,
Eng., 1620 ; came to this country in 1637 ; grad. at Harvard College, 1646 ; began to preach, 1648, first at Rowley till 1650, then to
the fishermen at the Isle of Shoals, where he labored twelve years.
He was ordained at Reading [Wakefield] Nov. 13, 1662, as successor to Mr. Haugh, and on the day following married his widow. He
was eminently a devout and holy man, and was supposed to exercise
what is called a " particular faith " in prayer, or an assurance that
the very thing prayed for will be granted. He died June 18, 1688,
aged 68.

---

* Pronounced *Hoff*.

3

4.

Capt. WILLIAM SYMMES,[2] the eldest son of Rev. Zechariah[1] and Sarah Symmes who came to maturity; born in Dunstable, Bedfordshire, Eng.; bapt. Jan. 10, 1626–7; came to New England with his parents at eight years of age; and was twice married. The name of his first wife is not known. As she had a daughter *Sarah*, this may have been her name.* The second wife was Mary ——.

Not much is known respecting him. He resided in Charlestown, in that part which lay north of Mystic Pond, and which is now included in Winchester; was chosen tything-man there in 1679.

The Indians gave a deed of the land afterwards known as Chelmsford, April 3, 1660. Of this deed William Symes was a subscribing witness. The others were Samuel Green and James Convers. [See Allen's History of Chelmsford, page 163.]

Sept. 21, 1674. In behalf of the proprietors of the Land of Node, William Sims and Edward Wilson, both of Charlestown, received from the town of Woburn a quit-claim of that tract, being 3000 acres.†

He appears to have adhered to the royal government during the melancholy time from 1684 to 1689. The charter of Massachusetts, under which the colony had prospered for fifty-four years, was vacated in October, 1684, and the people now lay at the mercy of the king. In December, 1686, Sir Edmund Andros arrived in Boston as royal governor of all New England. His government was oppressive in the highest degree. He pronounced the titles under which the inhabitants held their land utterly worthless. Their land, he said, belonged to the king of England. If they would retain possession, they must take out new titles from him or his agents. In March, 1688, he and his council passed an act which struck at the root of that system of town government, which is the safeguard of our civil liberties. This act forbade that more than one town meeting should be held in a year, on any pretence whatever; and this only for the election of town officers; and this meeting must be called, not by the selectmen, but by certain justices of the peace within the county.

The town of Woburn met in March, as usual, and chose five worthy men for selectmen. But within a fortnight the election was declared null and void, and the inhabitants were directed to meet for a new choice, by a warrant issued by Jonathan Wade of Medford,

---

* We find on file in the Probate Office at East Cambridge, the will of " Sarah Simes, of Cambridge, Mass. Bay in New England," dated April 4, 1653. She makes bequests to her brother John Stedman, her dear pastor Mr. [Jonathan] Mitchell, Elder [Richard] Champney, Elder [Edmund] Frost, her brother William French, Deacon [Gregory] Stone, Deacon [John] Bridge. All of these were highly respectable Cambridge men, members of the church, and all were freemen of the colony as early as 1640. There is nothing further to indicate the condition of the testatrix; but we cannot avoid the conclusion that she was the first wife of Capt. William Symmes. By the inventory it appears that she died June 11, 1653. Amount of inventory, £44 11 9, all personal estate.
† Sewall's Hist. of Woburn, p. 540.

John Brown of Reading, and William Symmes of Charlestown, three justices of the peace for the County of Middlesex. These justices had been appointed by the arbitrary royal Governor, and were expected to be subservient to his will.*

After his father's death, and probably before, he resided on the farm given to his father by the town of Charlestown, and which by will the father gave to him to be his after his mother's death, on condition that he pay to his brothers and sisters one hundred pounds in equal portions within two years. This condition was never performed, as we learn from a document, dated 1692–3, which will now be quoted. It was signed by his brother, Zechariah Symmes, of Bradford, and the other children then living. After speaking of themselves as the children of the Rev. Zechariah Symmes, late of Charlestown, deceased, and of his having made a will devising his property, they say that "Mr. William Symmes, eldest son of the aforesaid Zechariah, having died in an untimely, aggravated and sudden manner,† and his affairs having been left in a complicated and unsettled state," they have taken it upon them to look into and settle his affairs, or something to that amount.

The document proceeds as follows: "That whereas our brother William, deceased, being our father's eldest son, at our honored mother's death, concerning whom the will runs thus: 'Item. At my wife's death, I give my farm near Woburn and land at Menotomy to my eldest son provided that he bind it over to pay unto the rest of my children a hundred pounds in equal portions in two years time;' which condition as yet has not been performed: therefore we the subscribers of this instrument do resign up all our inheritance and claim to and interest in the aforementioned farm upon these provisos, viz. 1. That the debts due from the farm be first responded. 2. That his relict, as administratrix, and his heirs as they come of age, do subscribe with their hands and seals to this instrument of accommodation and concord. But if they refuse, this instrument is of no force to secure the farm to them."

Signed by

ZECHARIAH SYMMES and others.

INVENTORY of the Estate of Capt. William Symmes, Esq. [sic] of Charlestown, who deceased Sept. 22, 1691.

Housing and lands			£624. 0. 0
Money and Plate	£22.	5.	6
Horned beasts, sheep, horses & swine	28.	5.	0
English & Indian Corn	5.	4.	0
Goods in the Hall	18.	1.	0
Goods in the chambers, garret, kitchen & cellar	58.	3.	0
Table linen & other linen	7.	15.	8

* Palfrey, Hist. of New England, vol. iii. p. 550; Sewall's Hist. of Woburn, p. 129.
† He died, as per Inventory, Sept. 22, 1691. We know not the manner of his death.

Books, £6. 11. 0 ; Wearing apparel, £10. 0. 0　　16. 11. 0
Arms and ammunition　　　　　　　　　　　　 4. 0. 0
Cart, plow, chains & other utensils of husbandry　 4. 10. 0
Sundries　　　　　　　　　　　　　　　　　　 3. 7. 0
　　　　　　　　　　　　　　　　　　　　　　 ────────
　　　　　　　　　　　　　　　　　　　　　　　168. 2. 2

　　　　　　　　　　　　　　　　Total　　£792. 2. 2

　Desperate debts, £38. Rates, &c. £34. 8. 3. Funeral charges, £11. 0. 0
Appraisers—
　　James Convers, Sen.　Matthew Johnson, Sen.　James Convers, 2d.*
　　This Inventory was exhibited in court, Jan. 3, 1693–4.

　As an index to the housekeeping of those days, even in good families, we introduce the following, exactly copied from the original.

　"John Warner of Lawfull age doth testefy y^t he lived with $Capt^n$ Wm Syms late of Charlestoune a many years, in perticuler he lived there at y^t time when y^e Reverend Mr Moses flisk, courted and Marryed his daughter Mrs. Sarah Syms, and s^d Mr. flisk rec^d and had Caryed to Brantre a Considerable quantity of Goods y^t were Mr. Symses. Imp†† two tables one forme six Joynstools and two or three chests y^t went not away Empty. Six chairs of John Larkin at $Charlest^n$ also 90 weight of fethers, and a new ticking for those fethers that cost three shilling a yard, also a considerable sum of money laid out at y^e vpholsters, for his Master's daughter $afores^d$, and $Consid^{be}$ sum for Ditto at a Braziors shop, and she had som plate viz one silver Beaker‡ and two silver cups and 3 silver spoons, & brass, one brass kittle from hom y^t would hold about three pailfuls, and one or two Iron pots, and fiue pounds cap^{tn} Syms paid towards Mr. flisks purches at Brantre, also a pair of hand Irons & a Spitt or two, and a tramills§ made by Hen: Balcomb at $Charlst^n$, likewise she had som pevter out of the hous, and four pounds more he gaue her at Mr. $Rich^d$ Barnads.
　"Likewise when my Master was a widower, his s^d daughter caryed away at twice, two considerable quantetyes of Linen, sheets and napkins and such like, which was by my Masters order.
　"my Master spake of giueing his s^d daughter fifty pound vpon Marriage, y^e which I doubt not but he $perform^d$ with great advantage. how many cows and sheep I do not remember.
　"also my Master lent M^r flisk a Larg Concordance y^t sum did Judg was well worth forty shillings.
　"also M^r flisk borrowed a small birding piece of my Master very Injenious work, my Master was offered twenty S. for it, these he promised to returne again."

　This paper has no date, but must have been used in settlement of Capt. Symmes's estate.

---

　* James Convers, Senior, was son of Dea. Edward Convers, one of the founders of Woburn, and father of Maj. James Convers, the third appraiser and the gallant defender of Storer's garrison in Wells, in June, 1692.
　† Imprimis, first in order.
　‡ A cup of peculiar construction, ending in a *beak* or *point*.
　§ A trammel, a sort of pot-hook that might be varied in length, to hang kettles over the fire.

Capt. Symmes received that title from being an officer in the train bands. He was a lieutenant in 1687. At the time of his death, Sept. 22, 1691, he was in his 65th year.

There is a long interval between the birth of his daughter Sarah in 1652, and the birth of his next child Mary, which was in 1676. We know of no other child than Sarah by the first marriage. The conviction forces itself upon us that his first wife died in 1653, in Cambridge, while living apart from him, and that he lived in a widowed state till about 1675. Probably his second wife was considerably younger than himself. She had by him six children, and outlived him nearly thirty years.

Unfortunately, no record of Capt. Symmes's family has been preserved.* We derive our information from other but authentic sources, especially the court records and the will of Mrs. Mary Torrey, who had been the second wife of Capt. Symmes.

Capt. Symmes left no will. His widow Mary was appointed administratrix, and gave bonds in the sum of £1200, with Matthew Johnson, Sen., and John Carter,† both of Woburn, as sureties, to exhibit an inventory of the goods and chattels of the deceased in court on or before Jan. 3, 1693–4. This inventory has been already quoted.

Commissioners were appointed to attend to the settlement of the estate of Capt. Symmes. They reported that William, the eldest son, should have his share in upland.

Mary, the old house, &c.

Timothy, part of the new house, &c.

Elizabeth and Zechariah, to have shares.

Nathaniel, the old mill, &c.

Mr. Fiske, a portion of the swamp.

Mr. Fiske's wife Sarah, a portion.

Here we have the names of all the living children of Capt. Symmes, none of whom, except Mrs. Fiske, were then of age.

This document was signed by the commissioners, Josiah Parker and others, March 10, 1693–4.

This settlement of the estate was consented to by the widow of Capt. Symmes, and by Rev. Moses Fiske, husband of his eldest daughter Sarah. But no division or appraisement was made at that time.

Mrs. Mary Symmes, the widow of Capt. Symmes, was married to Rev. Samuel Torrey, of Weymouth, July 30, 1695. He was born in England, 1632; was brought by his father to this country in 1640; was educated at Harvard College, but left that institution the year he was to have graduated; labored fifty years in the minis-

---

* There are many deficiencies in our early town records. There was no law then requiring the registration of families. One reason for the deficiency in this case may have been the fact that Capt. Symmes lived seven or eight miles from the town clerk.

† Matthew Johnson was the son of Capt. Edward Johnson, the author of the "Wonder-Working Providence." He was often employed in town business. John Carter was a son of Capt. John Carter, one of the founders of Woburn.—*Sewall's Hist. of Woburn.*

try, three years in Hull and forty-seven in Weymouth; and died April 21, 1707, aged 75. He was probably much older than his wife Mary; and his children, at least two of them, seem to have married hers. Cotemporary writers represent him as possessing commanding mental abilities, richly ornamented with science, and as truly a great and good man. He was three times chosen by the legislature to preach the Election Sermon, in 1674, 1683, and 1693; and all three of the sermons were printed. He was chosen president of Harvard College, 1684, but declined the honor.*

No division of Capt. Symmes's estate was made till July 31, 1705. At that date a survey of the farm was executed, and a plot of it made by Capt. Joseph Burnap, of Reading, a noted surveyor. This plot may now be found among the papers on file in the probate office at East Cambridge. I have given it a careful examination, and an exact copy is now before me. The farm is to my eyes quite a familiar object. Indeed it came up within a few rods of the spot where I now write. It extended from the north end of Mystic Pond to the confines of Woburn. It had Mystic Pond on the south-west; the Gardiner farm, originally granted to Increase Nowell, of Charlestown, afterwards owned by Samuel Gardiner, and recently by Hon. Edward Everett, on the west; on the north it extended to what was from 1753 till 1850, the boundary line between Medford and Woburn. It lay on both sides of the Aberjona (by some called Mystic) River.† It had on its west border the road which is now known as Church Street. Most of it, nearly all, lay west of what is now Main Street, in Winchester. The farm, originally granted to Dea. Edward Convers, and long occupied by his descendants, lay on the north-west. The main body of the farm, on which the houses stood, was found, on the survey, to contain 279 acres and 64 poles; the meadow, called Bare Meadow, which appears to have been in the south part of what is now Stoneham, 11 acres and 126 poles; and the salt marsh‡ at Menotomy, 9 acres and 15 poles: the whole making out the 300 acres granted by Charlestown to Rev. Zechariah Symmes. There was also a parcel of Swamp on Alewive Brook, at a little distance south-east, containing 7 acres, 41 poles.

East of the river were 111 acres 53 poles; west of the river were 126 acres 99 poles. All this lay in a compact body; besides which were several smaller detached parcels.§ The "old house, barn and die hous," were near the north end of the farm, near the river, and on its west side. A "new house" appears on the east side of the river, near the centre of the farm. It was a few rods east of where

<hr/>

* Am. Quar. Reg., viii. 57.
† It was often called Symmes's River.
‡ Farmers in those days, and ever since, have thought it desirable to have a piece of salt marsh. This piece lay two or three miles south of the farm, on Mystic River, where the tide ebbs and flows.
§ One piece, of twenty acres, lay near Spot Pond, at a distance of about two miles east, valued at £9 10 0.

John Bacon and his sister Ann Bacon now live. That part of the farm which lay on the river was low, and often overflowed. Indeed, several acres are now permanently flowed for the supply of the Charlestown waterworks.

The farm is of course very greatly altered since that time. Most of it has gone out of the family. Forty acres, however, remain in the present possession and occupancy of Marshall Symmes. Smaller portions are owned by Theodore Symmes, Hosea Dunbar, whose wife was a daughter of Edmund Symmes, and other heirs.

One third of the farm, or 98 acres and 75 poles, were at this time, July, 1705, set off to Mrs. Mary Torrey, the relict of the deceased Capt. Symmes. This was the south and south-west part, near Mystic Pond. It contained the new house, barn, mill, mill-pond, and an orchard. It was appraised at £148 10 0. The remainder, 186 acres and 149 poles, could not be divided without spoiling the whole, and was therefore assigned to William Symmes, clothier, of Charlestown, eldest son of the deceased, March 7, 1705-6, on his giving bond, in the sum of £566 5 0, with Josiah Convers, of Woburn, maltster, as surety, to pay the other heirs, the children of the deceased, their several shares of the estate. William Symmes lived on the farm, and was now 28 years of age. The final settlement was made April 4, 1709.

Mrs. Torrey also had, as a part of her dower, one third of Bare Meadow, 3 acres 147 poles, valued at £7 0 0; one-third of the salt marsh at Menotomy, 3 acres 5 poles, valued at £24 0 0; and one-third of a wood-lot near Bare Meadow, 13 acres 54 poles, valued at £5 15 — the aggregate value of her third part of the farm being estimated at £189 8 4.

The whole farm at this time lay in Charlestown. In 1753 it was annexed to Medford. Since 1850 it has been included in the town of Winchester.

William Symmes, the clothier, afterwards bought his mother's third, and thus came into possession of the whole.

Mrs. Mary Torrey, in her will dated June 26, 1720, bequeaths various articles of household furniture to her eldest son, William Symmes, of Charlestown; to her son Timothy Symmes, of Scituate; to her daughter Mary Torrey, to whom she gives all her wearing apparel; to her daughter Elizabeth Torrey, a ticking bed and feathers, lying in the best chamber. Her son Nathaniel Symmes she makes her executor and residuary legatee.

From all which we gather that the children of Capt. William Symmes were — by first wife:

+15. SARAH,[3] b. 1652; m. Rev. Moses Fiske, of Braintree.

By second wife MARY, afterwards Mrs. Torrey:

16. MARY,[3] b. 1676; m. —— Torrey.
+17. WILLIAM,[3] b. 1678; m. Ruth Convers.

+18. TIMOTHY,[3] b. 1683; m. Elizabeth (Collamore) Rose.
  19. ELIZABETH,[3] m. —— Torrey.
+20. ZECHARIAH.[3]
+21. NATHANIEL.[3]

One of the above daughters was the wife of Joseph Torrey. This is certain, because Mrs. Torrey in her will says her oldest brass kettle was then lent to her son-in-law. Joseph Torrey. He was probably the husband of Mary; but which it was we do not know. Joseph and the other Torrey were probably sons of Rev. Samuel.

5.

MARY SYMMES,[2] sister of the preceding, and second daughter of Rev. Zechariah Symmes,[1] of Charlestown; born in Dunstable, in the county of Bedford, England, and baptized there, April 16, 1628; was brought by her father to this country in 1634, when a little more than six years old; admitted to the church in Charlestown, July 9, 1648.

She married THOMAS SAVAGE, of Boston, Sept. 15, 1652.* She was his second wife, and much younger than her husband. His first wife, to whom he was married about 1637, was Faith Hutchinson, born at Alford, in Lincolnshire, England, and baptized there, Aug. 14, 1617 — the daughter of William and the famous Anne (Marbury) Hutchinson; came with her parents to this country in the Griffin, with the Symmes family. She died in Boston, Feb. 20, 1651-2. By this his first wife Mr. Savage had *Habijah*, b. 1638; *Thomas*, 1640; *Hannah*, 1643; *Ephraim*, 1645; *Mary*, 1647; *Dionysia*, 1649; *Perez*, 1652.

Mr. Savage — admitted freeman, May 25, 1636 — was a successful merchant and eminent citizen of Boston, though for a time unhappily implicated in the Hutchinson controversy. He rose to wealth and high respectability; was deputy from Boston to the General Court, 1654–1676; was Speaker of the House of Deputies in 1660; Assistant, 1680–1; and rose through all the military grades from sergeant to be commander-in-chief of the Massachusetts forces in the early part of Philip's war. He died suddenly, but greatly respected, Feb. 15, 1681-2.

The will of Maj. Thomas Savage was dated June 28, 1675, the very day he commenced his march against the Indian chieftain Philip; proved Feb. 23, 1681-2; recorded Suff. Prob. vi. 370. He gives to wife Mary Savage the use of his new house at Hog Island, with the new garden and orchard, forty acres of marsh, five cows, two oxen, eight swine and seventy sheep, divers articles of house-keeping

---

* She and her sister Elizabeth were married by Increase Nowell, Esq., of Charlestown. It was customary then for justices and other magistrates to solemnize marriages—marriage being held to be a civil ordinance. I discover no foundation for the statement in Brooks's History of Medford, p. 512, that Mary Symmes married a second husband, Anthony Stoddard.

goods, sheets, beds, &c., also a negro maid. To his daughter Hannah Gillam, £180, and £50 to each of her three children. To his son Thomas Savage, £150, and £50 to each of his three children. To his daughter Mary Thacher, £150, and £50 to each of her four children. To his grandson Thomas Savage, son of testator's son Habiah Savage, deceased, £150, and £50 to each of his two daughters. To Habiah's widow Hannah, £50. To the testator's son Ephraim Savage, £150, and £50 to each of his three children. To the testator's daughter Higginson, all his land in Salem Town, or £200, whichever she may choose. To her daughter Mary Higginson, £50. To the testator's daughter *Dinnie* (Dionysia), £100. To his son Ebenezer, £300. To his son Benjamin, £300. To his son Perez, £300. Total, £2830, besides the house, farm, &c.

The children of THOMAS and MARY (SYMMES) SAVAGE were:

+22. SARAH (Savage), b. June 25, 1653; m. Hon. John Higginson.
   23. ZECHARIAH (Savage), b. Dec. 26, 1654; died Aug. 23, 1656.
       Probably also:
   24. EBENEZER (Savage).
   25. BENJAMIN (Savage).

6.

ELIZABETH SYMMES,[2] sister of the preceding; bapt. at Dunstable, England, Jan. 1, 1629–30; came with her parents to America in 1634; admitted to the church in Charlestown, Sept. 23, 1652; married HEZEKIAH USHER, Nov. 2, 1652. She was his second wife. His first wife was Frances ——, who died April 25, 1652. By her he had *Hezekiah*, 1639; *Elizabeth*; *John*, b. April 27, 1648; *Hannah* and *Peter*. His son John was a printer and bookseller in Boston; was a Mandamus Councillor, 1686–1689, under Dudley and Andros, and Lieut.-Governor of New Hampshire. He lived in Boston, 1689, but afterwards moved to Medford, where he died Sept. 25, 1726.

Hezekiah Usher was a prominent merchant of Boston; a man of decidedly religious character; one of the original members of the Old South Church, 1669, and ready to good works. He assisted in the redemption of Mrs. Rowlandson, wife of Rev. Joseph Rowlandson, from Indian captivity, in 1676. He died soon after. We know of but one child of Hezekiah and Elizabeth (Symmes) Usher, viz.:

   26. ZECHARIAH (Usher), b. Dec. 26, 1654.

7.

HULDAH SYMMES,[2] sister of the preceding; bapt. at Dunstable, England, March 18, 1630–1; was brought by her parents to America in 1634; admitted to the church in Charlestown, Nov. 27, 1652; married WILLIAM DAVIS.

4

He was an apothecary in Boston in 1647; freeman, May, 1645; a prosperous merchant. 1655; chosen selectman, 1655, 1656; one of the original members of the Old South Church, 1669; and was often employed in public business.

His first wife was Margaret, daughter of William Pynchon, of Springfield.*

Thomas Davis, an innholder of Boston, a son of William and Huldah (Symmes) Davis, married Hannah, daughter of Gov. John Leverett.†

11.

Rev. ZECHARIAH SYMMES,[2] second son of Rev. Zechariah Symmes,[1] of Charlestown, was born in Charlestown, Mass., Jan. 9, 1637–8; baptized three days after. He had two wives.

He married, first, Susannah Graves, Nov. 18, 1669 (8, O. S.). She was born July 8, 1643, daughter of Thomas Graves, of Charlestown, a prominent citizen of that place.‡ She died July 23, 1681, and he married, second, Mehitable (Palmer) Dalton, Nov. 26, 1683. She was the daughter of Henry Palmer — one of the founders of Haverhill, and a distinguished citizen there — and widow of Hon. Samuel Dalton, of Hampton, N. H.

He was admitted to his father's church in Charlestown, Aug. 22, 1658, and grad. H. C. 1657. He is the first named of his class in the catalogue, which indicates that he was the first scholar in rank. He became one of the fellows of the college. The Latin inscription on his tombstone says that he was distinguished for learning and piety. He went to Rehoboth (now Pawtucket, R. I.) to preach as early as 1661 — probably a year or two before. In September, 1661, the church and town voted that he should receive £40 a year, "besides his diet at Mr. Newman's." This was Rev. Samuel Newman, who was pastor of the church there, and compiler of a valuable concordance; a very learned and excellent man. He died July 5, 1663, aged 63. He revised the concordance by the light of pine knots.

Mr. Symmes was admitted an inhabitant of Rehoboth, April 13,

---

* Felt's Eccl. Hist. of New England, vol. ii. 65.
† Geneal. Reg., iv. 134.
‡ Thomas Graves was born in Ratcliffe, near London, in England, June 6, 1605. He was a seafaring man, and master of several ships, as the Whale, the Elizabeth Bonadventure, the James, the Trial, that made voyages from Old to New England. He came every year, from 1629 to 1635, inclusive. He at length settled in Charlestown, or between that place and Woburn, and married Catharine Coytmore, dau. of Thomas and Catharine Coytmore, of Charlestown. He and his wife Catharine were admitted to the church in that place, Oct. 7, 1639. Some of his descendants are still living in Charlestown. He was one of those who undertook the settlement of Woburn, but became discouraged and returned to a seafaring life. For his good conduct in capturing, though in a merchant ship, a Dutch privateer in the English Channel, he was put in command of a ship of war and made a rear admiral by Cromwell. He died in Charlestown, July 31, 1653.—Sewall's Hist. of Woburn, pp. 69, 70; Frothingham's Hist. of Charlestown, pp. 139, 140.

1666. About this time, or a little earlier, Rev. John Miles, who had been pastor of a Baptist church in Swansea, Wales, came to the place — or rather that part of it which is now Swanzey — and preached, and the people became divided in religious sentiment. A Baptist church was formed there in 1667. Mr. Symmes left Rehoboth that year and came to Bradford, a new town on the Merrimack, previously known as Rowley Village — incorporated as a town in 1675. There he became permanently established in 1668, and was the first minister of the town, though not ordained till Dec. 27, 1682. The people built a house for him in 1668, which was standing in 1838. There was no church in the place, regularly organized, till the date just mentioned. His salary was fifty pounds a year, besides which the people gave him forty acres of land, and chose a committee from year to year to provide for having his work done. The whole period of his ministry in Bradford was forty years. He died there, March 22, 1707–8, aged 70 years.[*]

He was much beloved by his people, and respected in all the region around.

His children were all by his first wife, and all born in Bradford, except Catharine, who was born in Charlestown. The family record is copied here:

27. SUSANNA,[3] b. Oct. 11, 1670; m. first, John Chickering, of Charlestown; second, Benjamin Stevens, Oct. 18, 1715.
28. SARAH,[3] b. May 20, 1672; m. Joshua Scottow, May 25, 1697.
+29. ZECHARIAH,[3] b. March 13, 1674; m. Dorcas Brackenbury.
30. CATHARINE,[3] b. March 29, 1676.
+31. THOMAS,[3] b. Feb. 1, 1677–8; m. first, Elizabeth Blowers; second, Hannah Pike; third, Eleanor (Thompson) Moody.
32. WILLIAM,[3] b. Jan. 7, 1679–80; m. Eliza Langdon, Boston, June 13, 1706.
33. REBECCA,[3] b. July 20, 1681; m. Ebenezer Osgood,[4] of Andover, Dec. 20, 1710. He was born in Andover, March 16, 1685, son of John[3] b. 1654, son of John[2] b. 1631 in Old England, who came with his father John[1] Osgood, and settled in Andover, 1644, or 5. The children of Ebenezer and Rebecca (Symmes) Osgood were—*Ebenezer, Rebecca, Susanna, Ruth.*

14.

TIMOTHY SYMMES,[2] youngest son of Rev. Zechariah Symmes,[1] of Charlestown; probably born there in 1643; married, first, MARY NICHOLS, Dec. 10, 1668. She probably died soon after the birth of her only child. He married, second, ELIZABETH NORTON, Sept. 21, 1671.

---

* Felt's Eccl. Hist. of New England, ii. 317, 387; Am. Quart. Reg., x. 245; Budington's Hist. of First Church in Charlestown, p. 210.

He resided in Charlestown; and died of smallpox, July 4, 1678. His widow probably married Capt. Ephraim Savage, son of Maj. Thomas Savage, May 12, 1688.

His children were—by first wife:

34. TIMOTHY,[3] b. Sept. 6, 1669; died in infancy.

By second wife:

35. TIMOTHY,[3] b. November 18, 1672.
36. ELIZABETH,[3] b. July 24, 1674; m. James Herrick, Jan. 19, 1708–9.
37. SARAH,[3] b. Aug. 6, 1676.*

Third Generation.

15.

SARAH SYMMES[3] (*William,[2] Zechariah[1]*), daughter of Capt. William Symmes,[2] of Charlestown; born 1652;† married Nov. 7, 1672, Rev. MOSES FISKE, pastor of the church in Braintree, then including the present town of Quincy.‡

Moses Fiske was born in Wenham, 1643; grad. H. C. 1662, in the class with the renowned Solomon Stoddard, of Northampton; was ordained at Braintree, now Quincy, Sept. 11, 1672, being the third minister of that place; and was pastor there thirty-six years, till his death, Aug. 20, 1708, aged 66.§

He appears to have enjoyed and retained the affections of his flock. The following testimony to his worth is given in the Diary of John Marshall, who sat under his ministry and knew him well:

" This excellent person was ordained pastor of the church in Braintree, in September, 1672, in which sacred employment he continued till his dying day, a diligent, faithful laborer in the harvest of Jesus Christ; studious in the Holy Scriptures, having an extraordinary gift in prayer above many

---

* Geneal. Reg., xiii. 136.
† Marshall's Diary.
‡ He was the youngest son of Rev. John Fiske, of Wenham and Chelmsford. The father was born 1601, in the parish of St. James, Suffolk, Eng., and was educated, it is believed, at Emanuel College, Cambridge. He not only preached, but practised medicine, upon a thorough examination, in England; came to this country in 1637, bringing with him a large property; was admitted freeman, Nov. 2, in that year; resided in Salem about three years, engaged in teaching and occasionally preaching. About 1640, he commenced preaching in Wenham, the settlement of which began in 1639, and continued there till 1655; when he removed, with a majority of his church, to Chelmsford, then a new town; being in each case the earliest minister. He continued pastor at Chelmsford till his death, Jan. 14, 1676–7. He was highly esteemed, both as a divine and as a physician. In the course of his ministry, he expounded almost the whole of the Bible to his people; and went twice through the Assembly's Catechism. Suffering from the gout and the stone, he was carried in his latter years in a chair to and from the pulpit, and preached in a sitting posture. He was an eminently laborious and godly man.
§ At the time of Mr. Fiske's death, the number of polls in Braintree was 195; oxen 219, cows 738, horses 199, sheep 1575, swine 78.

good men ; and in preaching equal to the most, inferior to few ; zealously diligent for God and the good of men ; one who thought no labor, cost or suffering too dear a price for the good of his people. His public preaching was attended with convincing light and clearness, and powerful, affectionate application ; and his private oversight was performed with humility and unwearied diligence. He lived till he was near sixty-five years of age, beloved and honored of the most that knew him. On the 18th of July, being the Lord's day, he preached all day in public, but was not well. The distemper continued and proved a malignant fever. Small hope of his recovery being entertained, his church assembled together and earnestly besought the Great Shepherd of the sheep, that they might not be deprived of him. But Heaven had otherwise determined, for on Tuesday, August 10 [equivalent to Aug. 21, N. S.], he died about one in the afternoon, and was with suitable solemnity and great lamentation interred in Braintree, in his own tomb, the 12th day."*

The town of Braintree voted, June 18, 1672, to give Mr. Fiske, by a town tax, the sum of sixty pounds in money as a yearly salary, with the use of a house to be kept in good repair by the town, and six acres of land to be fenced by them. In 1674 his salary for that year was increased to eighty pounds. During his ministry one hundred and forty-seven members were added to the church. The baptisms were seven hundred and seventy-nine.

Mrs. Sarah (Symmes) Fiske, his first wife, died Dec. 2, 1692, having borne him fourteen children. His second wife, to whom he was married Jan. 7, 1700–1, was Ann (Shepard) Quincy, born 1663, daughter of Rev. Thomas Shepard, who has been already mentioned (pp. 5, 6) as a colleague of Rev. Zechariah Symmes, of Charlestown. She was the widow of Daniel Quincy, born 1681, son of the second Edmund Quincy, of Braintree. She died July 24, 1708, aged 45, less than three weeks before his own decease.

The following were the fourteen children of Rev. MOSES FISKE, by his first wife, SARAH SYMMES :

38. MARY (Fiske), b. Aug. 25, 1673 ; m. Rev. Joseph Baxter, minister of Medfield, and a native of Braintree. She died March 29, 1711.
39. SARAH (Fiske), b. Sept. 22, 1674 ; m. Rev. Thomas Ruggles.
40. MARTHA (Fiske), b. Nov. 25, 1675 ; d. Nov. 28, 1675.
41. ANNE (Fiske), b. Aug. 17, 1677 ; d. June 9, 1678.
42. ANNE (Fiske), b. Oct. 29, 1678 ; m. Rev. Joseph Marsh, June 30, 1709. He grad. H. C. 1705 ; succeeded her father in the ministry in Braintree ; d. March 8, 1725–6, aged 44. A very able man.
43. ELIZABETH (Fiske), b. Oct. 9, 1679 ; m. —— Porter.

* By some unaccountable mistake, the valuable Diary, from which this interesting extract has been taken, and which extends from 1697 to 1711, has been attributed to Daniel Fairfield and quoted as his. The real author was John Marshall, then of Braintree, formerly of Boston, an ancestor of the compiler of the present volume. Daniel Fairfield, who married the mother of John Marshall, was of Boston, and died there Dec. 22, 1709, aged 77. He *could not* therefore be the author of the Diary. For a full account of John Marshall, and the affecting elegy which he wrote and printed, after the death of his excellent and beloved wife, see the compiler's GILES MEMORIAL, Boston, 1861, pp. 349, 550.

44. JOHN (Fiske), b. May 29, 1681 ; d. Aug. 5, 1681.
45. MOSES (Fiske), b. July 19, 1682.
46. JOHN (Fiske), b. Nov. 26, 1684 ; admitted to church, Aug. 26, 1705 ; grad. H. C. 1702 ; was a preacher, 1710.
47. WILLIAM (Fiske), b. Aug. 2, 1686.
48. SAMUEL (Fiske), b. Feb. 19, 1687 ; d. March 4, 1687.
49. SAMUEL (Fiske), b. April 6, 1689.   (See the note below.*)
50. RUTH (Fiske), b. March 24, 1692 ; d. June 6, 1692.
51. EDWARD (Fiske), b. Oct. 20, 1692 ; d. Oct. 25, 1692.

This record is copied from the Town Register of Braintree; but an evident mistake occurs in the date of Ruth's birth.†

17.

WILLIAM SYMMES³ (*William,² Zechariah¹*), eldest son of Capt. William² and Mary Symmes, of Charlestown; born 1678; married RUTH CONVERS,⁴ Dec. 7, 1704. She was born in Woburn, May 28, 1686, and was the eldest daughter of Capt. Josiah³ and Ruth (Marshall) Convers, of that place.‡ Though living in two separate towns, the two families were near neighbors.

---

* Rev. Samuel Fiske was born in Quincy, then part of Braintree, April 6, 1689. He graduated at H. C. 1708; taught school till 1710; was chosen minister of Hingham, Feb. 11, 1716-17, as successor to Rev. John Norton, but did not accept the call. He was ordained pastor of the First Church in Salem, Oct. 8, 1718, as successor to Rev. Geo. Curwin. In 1734, a violent disruption of that body took place and an embittered controversy arose, which continued many years. A majority of the church—it was a bare majority—with Mr. Fiske, their pastor, left their old house of worship, and founded another church, which yet, till 1762, claimed to be the First Church. In 1762, they took the name of the Third Church. Since 1775, it has been known as the Tabernacle Church. The charges made against Mr. Fiske in 1734, do not seem to be entitled to serious consideration. They did not affect his moral character. He died in Salem, April 7, 1770, aged 81.
One of his sons was General John Fiske, born in Salem, April 10, 1744. He "early engaged in the business of the sea;" was successful in business; and was a gentleman of much distinction. He was a major-general in the militia, and died of apoplexy, Sept. 28, 1797, aged 53. He had three wives: 1st, Lydia Phippen, married June 12, 1766 ; died Oct. 13, 1782. 2d, Martha (Lee) Hibbert, a widow, daughter of Col. John Lee, of Manchester; married Feb. 11, 1783; died Nov. 30, 1785. 3d, Sarah (Wendell) Gerry, June 18, 1786. She died Feb. 12, 1894, aged 58. She was widow of John Gerry, of Marblehead, and daughter of Major John and Elizabeth (Quincy) Wendell, of Boston. Elizabeth Quincy, her mother, was daughter of Hon. Edmund Quincy, who was brother of Daniel Q., already mentioned, and son of Col. Edmund Quincy, and grandson of Edmund Quincy, who came from England 1633, and was progenitor of the Quincy family in America.—*Am. Quar. Reg. ; Geneal. Reg.* vii. 252; xii., 111 ; *Giles Memorial,* p. 19.
† For most of what has here been said of Mr. Fiske and his family, I am indebted to the Centennial Discourse of Rev. William P. Lunt, delivered Sept. 29, 1839.
‡ EDWARD CONVERS¹ came from England in the fleet with Winthrop, 1630, and settled in Charlestown. In 1631, a grant was made to him of the first ferry between Boston and Charlestown. He was admitted freeman, May 18, 1631; was selectman of Charlestown from 1635 to 1640; and was a member of the First Church there from the beginning. His name stands first of the seven men appointed by that church for the settlement of Woburn, and for gathering a church there. From the incorporation of that town, he was one of its most esteemed, active, and useful citizens. He and John Monsal were the first deacons of Woburn church. He was chosen as one of the selectmen every year from 1644 till his decease. He died Aug. 10, 1663, aged 73. His residence was very near where the Orthodox Church in Winchester now stands, and also near the mill once called by his name, now occupied by Joel Whitney. Several of his posterity dwelt in that vicinity many years. By his wife Sarah, who accompanied him from England, he had three sons, JOSIAH, JAMES and SAMUEL, and a daughter MARY.
JOSIAH CONVERS,² his eldest son, accompanied him from England, and to Woburn, in 1641. He married, March 26, 1651, Esther Champney, daughter of Richard Champney, of

Mr. Symmes was a clothier by trade, as we learn from some old papers. He had the whole of his father's large landed property. Some of it came by inheritance, and some by purchase from the other heirs. Until 1754 it was regarded as being in Charlestown; but in that year it was annexed to Medford, and is now in Winchester.

The town of Medford had long been straitened for room. Several attempts had been made for an enlargement of its territory. At length a petition, dated Dec. 13, 1753, was signed by a committee of the town, appointed for the purpose, asking that a certain tract in Charlestown, lying south of Medford, and another tract in Charlestown, lying north of Medford, might be annexed to Medford. The petition says: "The northerly tract is bounded on the south by the north line of Medford and the southerly bounds of Mr. Symmes's farm, west by the line that divides Mr. Symmes's from Mr. Gardiner's farm, north by the line of Woburn and Stoneham, east by Malden line." The reasons assigned were, the contracted limits of Medford, containing only about two thousand acres, surrounded almost wholly by Charlestown, and the fact that the inhabitants of the northerly tract [the Symmes family, &c.] were but two miles from the Medford meeting-house, where they attended meeting without paying for the privilege; while they were obliged to go seven miles to attend town meetings, trainings, &c., in Charlestown.

This petition was presented to the General Court, and granted April 17, 1754. After that date, Mr. Symmes's farm was in Medford till 1850, when it became part of the new town of Winchester.*

Tradition reports that the land included in the Symmes farm was formerly the abode of a portion of the tribe of Indians called by the euphonious name of Aberginians. It is said that it contained twenty-seven wigwams. The story is likely to be true; for here were Mystic Pond and the Aberjona River,† both very convenient for fishing. Nanepashemit, the sachem of the larger tribe called the Pawtuckets, whose sway extended to the Merrimack River, and who was killed, 1619, in an attack upon his tribe by the Tarratines from the Penobscot River, lived in the near vicinity, somewhere on Mystic or Aberjona River. It was his son, Sagamore John, of Mystic [Medford], who, before his death at Medford, Dec. 5, 1633, wished to go to the God of the Christian people. The widow of Nanepashemit, in 1639, sold to the town of Charlestown all the land on the west of Mystic Pond, bounded north by Increase Nowell's lot (the Gardiner farm), west by Cambridge Common, south by the land of Mr. Cooke. This

Cambridge, a ruling elder in the church there. He like his father was a deacon in the church in Woburn, 1674-1690.

JOSIAH CONVERS,‡ son of the preceding, born March 15, 1660, married Oct. 8, 1685, Ruth Marshall. They were the parents of Ruth Convers‡ in the text. He was much employed in town business, and was familiarly known as "Captain Josiah." He died July 15, 1717, aged 58.—*Sewall's Hist. of Woburn.*

* Brooks's History of Medford, pp. 107-109.
† Here known as "Symmes's River."

seems to have included the Symmes farm; for after her death, it was
claimed, March 25, 1662, by William Symmes, son of Rev. Zechariah.
Or rather the claim was for land at the upper end of the Pond,
which the squaw-sachem had reserved for her use and the use of the
Indians, to plant and hunt upon, "and the weare above the Pond for
the Indians to use in fishing." during her life. This "weare" must
have been in the Symmes farm.* It is where the Aberjona River
enters the Pond, and we are sure that this river at that place, and
for some distance north, divided the Symmes farm from the lot of
Increase Nowell.

Mr. Symmes built a clothing mill on the Aberjona River, near
where the railroad bridge now crosses that stream. It was a little
north of the spot where, not long ago, Mr. Robert Bacon's dam stood.
A little island in the small pond, near the railroad bridge, shows
where the waste-way was. His house was on the left bank, or eastern side of the river, nearly opposite the house of Mr. John Bacon,
son of Robert Bacon. He afterwards built a large house on the spot
where John Bacon's house now stands. This was on the west side
of the river; it was occupied by his sons Timothy and John after
him. His grandson John Symmes was born there. The first house
built on the farm, where Capt. William Symmes probably once lived,
was further north, on the west side of the river, and very near the
old line between Charlestown and Woburn.

William Symmes, of Charlestown, gentleman, was surety, March
24, 1726, with John Richardson, of Medford, for Elizabeth Richardson, widow of Capt. James Richardson, late of Woburn.

His papers, still in existence, show him to have been a man of
business and of influence. His farm had been reduced to eighty
acres at the time of his death. This was caused by his having conveyed portions of it to his sons during his life-time, the deeds not
having effect till after his death.

He died May 24, 1764, aged 86. His wife Ruth died March 16,
1758. The gravestones of both are standing in the old cemetery in
Woburn.

His will is dated Nov. 27, 1761; proved April 16, 1766; recorded Midd. Prob. Records, xxix. 192. He calls himself William
Symmes, of Medford, yeoman. He leaves legacies to his sons Zechariah, Josiah, Timothy, John and William, and his daughter Mary
Munroe. To his sons Zechariah, Josiah, Timothy and John, he gives
his dwelling-house, barn, the mill, and about eighty acres of land;
the land to be equally divided among these four sons. The portion
of each is particularly described, and cannot conveniently be noted
here. To his son William he gives the whole expense he, the father,
had incurred for his education at school and at college, and £13 6 8
besides — equivalent to forty dollars.

Inventory of his estate — Real, £490 3 4; Personal, £33 16 1.

---

* Brooks's History of Medford, p. 72 et seq.

The children of WILLIAM³ and RUTH SYMMES were:

53.   WILLIAM,⁴ b. Oct. 10, 1705 ; died young.
+54. ZECHARIAH,⁴ b. Sept. 1, 1707 ; m. Judith Eames.
+55. JOSIAH,⁴ b. April 7, 1710 ; never married.
+56. TIMOTHY,⁴ b. 171– ; m. Elizabeth Bodge.
57.   MARY,⁴ m. —— Munroe.
+58. JOHN,⁴ b. about 1720 ; m. Abigail Dix.
59.   ELIZABETH,⁴ b. May 7, 1722 ; died young.
+60. WILLIAM,⁴ b. Nov. 1729 ; m. first, Anna Gee ; m. second, Susanna
        Powell.

18.

TIMOTHY SYMMES³ (*William,² Zechariah¹*), brother of the preceding, and second son of Capt. William Symmes,² of Charlestown; born about 1683; married ELIZABETH (COLLAMORE) ROSE, July 31, 1710, widow of Jeremiah Rose and daughter of Capt. Anthony Collamore, of Scituate.

Weymouth, which was the home of his mother, and his home for many years, is but a few miles from Scituate. We are not surprised, therefore, at finding him there in 1707, nor at the fact that he spent the remainder of his life there.

I have before me a letter from him to his brother William, dated Scituate, June 28, 1707. He sympathizes with him in the loss they had lately sustained (the death of their step-father, Rev. Samuel Torrey, of Weymouth, who died April 21, 1707), and proceeds: "My heart's desire and prayer to God is, that he would make us sensible of our sins against him, which provoke him to .... remove him who was so eminently serviceable for Christ and his kingdom. We all have great cause to say, ' Against Thee, Thee only have we sinned,' &c. Let us fly to Christ for mercy and pardon. He has promised that he will hearken to our cries and pardon our iniquities, though great." He then reverts to his temporal affairs; speaks of working at a trade, and of his master as exceedingly kind, and loth to part with him, but as not wishing to hinder him in any plans he may make for his own advantage. "For reasonable terms," he says, "I shall depart." He then proposes that his brother meet him on the ensuing Wednesday, to talk over his plans for the future. He thinks of going to Woburn to settle in three or four weeks. At the close he says : " Give my duty unto uncle and aunt, and my kind salutations to the lady of my best affections, Miss R. B."

The uncle and aunt probably were his mother's brother and sister. The " Miss R. B." he did not marry, as it seems.

He at length settled on a farm near the centre of South Scituate, Mass., on the Boston road, where his grandson, John Cleves Symmes, visited him in 1762. He died in 1765, aged 82.

5

His children were, so far as is known:

  61. HANNAH,[4] b. May 12, 1712.

+62. TIMOTHY,[4] b. May 27, 1714; m. first, Mary Cleves; m. second,
      Eunice Cogswell.

  63. ANTHONY,[4] b. Sept. 22, 1716.

20.

ZECHARIAH SYMMES[3] (*William,*[2] *Zechariah*[1]), brother of the
preceding, and third son of Capt. William Symmes,[2] of Charlestown;
born 168–. Unmarried.

About all we know of him is derived from a letter written by him
to his brother William Symmes[3] and wife, dated Jan. 21, 1706,
which is old style, and is equivalent to Feb. 1, 1707, N. S. From
this letter it appears that about three weeks previously he had sailed
from Boston in a vessel commanded by Capt. Mears, with a cargo
of farm produce, such as onions, cranberries, &c., suited to a West
India market. The vessel could not have been of large size, since
he mentions as officers only Capt. Mears and the mate, a brother of
the captain. Some days after sailing, a conspiracy was discovered
to take possession of the vessel, after first taking the lives of Capt.
Mears, his brother, and young Symmes. There were, he says, three
blood-thirsty men who had this design, two of them Frenchmen, and
the third a runaway, a deserter from the navy. The design having
been discovered, Capt. Mears, his brother, and young Symmes, armed
themselves, took possession of all the ammunition, drove the con-
spirators below, and kept them prisoners under the hatches eight or
nine days, until they came under the guns of a fort in Jamaica, when
they delivered them to a British man-of-war, receiving better men in
their room. He ascribes his deliverance to the mercy of God. The
letter breathes the language of ardent affection for his brothers and
sisters, and for his "honoured parents," who at this time were Mr.
and Mrs. Torrey of Weymouth. He says nothing about a wife, and
it is probable he had none.

His home was in Boston. He died, either during this voyage or
soon after his return, June 19, 1707. His brother William was
administrator, *cum testamento annexo,* and rendered an inventory,
Oct. 28, 1708. Among the items are, money received which was
due from the two-thirds of their father's estate, £47 3 9; money in
reversion expected from one-third of the father's estate, upon the
death of Mary Torrey, widow (the mother), £23 11 10; "Mem.
Logwood in the Bay of Campeachy, belonging to the deceased, not
received." [Suff. Prob., xvi. 48.]

21.

NATHANIEL SYMMES[3] (*William,*[2] *Zechariah*[1]), brother of the preceding, and youngest son of Capt. William Symmes;[2] born about 1690. His mother, in a petition to the Probate Court, March, 1692–3, prays that she may be appointed guardian to her youngest child, Nathaniel, in order that she may have legal power to improve the mill stream given to said child, by making lease of the same till said child becomes of age. The mill privilege seems, however, never to have come into his immediate possession. His brother William bought it.

He became of age about 1710 or 1711. We infer this from some receipts before us of money paid by William Symmes, in November, 1712, to Israel Walker and Oliver Noyes, who had supplied Nathaniel with goods out of their stores in Boston.

He was a cordwainer in Boston, and was living in 1720, when his mother, Mrs. Mary Torrey, in her will, made him her executor and residuary legatee. We have no further information respecting him. It is not known whether he had a family.

22. 1158968

SARAH SAVAGE[3] (*Mary Symmes,*[2] *Zechariah Symmes*[1]), eldest daughter of Maj. Thomas and Mary (Symmes) Savage; born in Boston, June 25, 1653; married Oct. 9, 1672, Hon. JOHN HIGGINSON,[3] eldest son of Rev. John Higginson, of Salem, and grandson of Rev. Francis Higginson.*

Hon. John Higginson was admitted freeman, 1677; was a selectman of Salem; representative, 1689; and member of the Executive Council of the Province from 1700 to 1719. He was also colonel of the regiment. He died March 23, 1720.

The children of JOHN and SARAH (Savage) HIGGINSON were:

+64. MARY,[4] b. Sept. 27, 1673; m. first, Thomas Gardner; m. second, Edward Weld; m. third, James Lindall.

   65. JOHN.[4]   68. SARAH.[4]
   66. THOMAS.[4]   69. ELIZABETH.[4]
   67. NATHANIEL.[4]   70. MARGARET.[4]

Of these, John, who must have been the youngest, or nearly so, was born 1698; grad. H. C. 1717; sustained the chief town offices; was a justice of the peace, and County Register. He m. first, Ruth Boardman, Dec. 1719; m. second, Esther Cabot; d. July 15, 1744, aged 46.

---

* Rev. FRANCIS HIGGINSON, son of Rev. John Higginson, was born in England in 1587. He received the degree of A.B. in 1609, at Jesus College, and the degree of A.M. in 1613, at St. John's College, both of the University at Cambridge, Eng. He was settled in the

29.

ZECHARIAH SYMMES[3] (*Zechariah,*[2] *Zechariah*[1]), eldest son of Rev. Zechariah Symmes,[2] of Bradford, and grandson of Rev. Zechariah Symmes,[1] of Charlestown; born in Bradford, March 13, 1674; married DORCAS BRACKENBURY,* Nov. 28, 1700.

He was of Charlestown, and died between 1709 and 1713. His widow Dorcas signed a deed, March 4, 1712–13.

Their children were:

+71. ZECHARIAH,[4] b. March 13, 1701–2; m. Elizabeth ———.
72. DORCAS,[4] bapt. Aug. 22, 1703; died young.
73. JOHN BRACKENBURY,[4] b. May 20, 1705; m. Elizabeth ———. [See below.]
74. WILLIAM,[4] b. Jan. 9, 1708–9; m. Mary ———. They lived in Boston, and had William,[5] b. July 30, 1730.

It is altogether probable that there are, or have been, descendants of this family. I have not found them, except they be found in the following schedule, which I make out from the Malden re-

ministry, 1615, at Claybrooke, one of the parishes in Leicester. There the Holy Spirit made him the honored instrument of saving conversion to many souls. During twelve years, he continued a strict conformist to the Established Church. But about 1627, his increased acquaintance with the Scriptures led him to embrace the principles of the Puritans. In consequence of this, he was excluded from his parish, though his people, who felt that they could not be deprived of his faithful labors, obtained permission for him to preach to them a part of the time. The next year, the intolerant measures of Bishop Laud exposed him to be brought before the High Commission Court. (For a notice of this Court, see page 1.) He then began to entertain the design of a removal to America. The Massachusetts Company, then just formed in England, having information of his purpose, invited him and another excellent minister, Rev. Samuel Skelton, to embark with a company of about one hundred new planters, whom they were intending soon to send out. Accordingly, he with his family sailed in the Talbot of 300 tons, Capt. Thomas Beecher (an excellent man who settled in Charlestown, and was one of the founders of the church there), from Gravesend, a port on the Thames, below London, April 25, 1629, and landed at Salem, June 30. He was installed as teacher of the church at Salem, the 6th of August following; Mr. Skelton being installed as pastor the same day.

There was a great mortality at Salem the ensuing winter: about one hundred, out of three hundred, the whole population, being laid low in death. Mr. Higginson lived to welcome Governor Winthrop and the large accession of new settlers who came with him in June and July, 1630; but died soon after, Aug. 6, 1630, aged 43 years. He was a man of amiable spirit, of warm piety, of exemplary life; "a man," says Edward Johnson, "endued with grace, apt to teach, mighty in the Scriptures, learned in the tongues, able to convince gainsayers."

He left, at his death, eight children; of whom the eldest was Rev. JOHN HIGGINSON, born at Claybrooke, in Leicester, Eng., Aug. 6, 1616; accompanied his father to America in 1629; served as chaplain at Saybrook, Ct., 1636–1640; in 1641, went to Guilford, Ct., and was some years colleague with Rev. Henry Whitefield, whose daughter Sarah he married; was installed pastor of the First Church in Salem, Aug. 1660; and died in that relation, highly honored, Dec. 9, 1708, at the advanced age of ninety-two, having been a minister of the gospel about seventy-two years. His children were—John, Nathaniel, Thomas, Francis, Henry; Sarah, married in 1672 Richard Wharton; Ann, m. 1682 William Dolliver, of Gloucester.

* William Brackenbury was one of the early settlers of Charlestown. He was admitted to the church in that town, Dec. 20, 1632. Anne Brackenbury, supposed to be his wife, was admitted Jan. 5, 1632–3. He was admitted freeman of the colony, March 4, 1632–3. He died in Malden, August, 1668. Alice Brackenbury, his wife, died Dec. 28, 1670, and was buried by his side in the old Cemetery in Malden.

Samuel Brackenbury, son of Samuel, and probably a grandson of William, was born in Malden, Feb. 3, 1672–3. He was a physician, died Nov. 26, 1702, and was buried in the old Cemetery in Malden. He was admitted to the church in Charlestown, Oct. 11, 1696. Dorcas Brackenbury may have been his sister.

cords, as copied in the N. E. Genealogical Register, vol. xi. pp. 129, 130, 211, 213.

Children of JOHN and ELIZABETH SIMMS, born in Malden:

75. ELIZABETH,⁵ b. May 22, 1721.
76. JOHN,⁵ b. Aug. 13, 1722.
77. MARY,⁵ b. April 16, 1724.
78. SARAH,⁵ b. March 11, 1727–8.

I am fully persuaded that John Simms, of Malden, the father of these children, is identical with John Brackenbury Symmes,⁴ the second son of Zechariah Symmes,³ husband of Dorcas Brackenbury. My reasons are — 1. The Brackenbury family lived in Malden; so did the father of these children. 2. I have before me a paper relating to the settlement of the estate of Rev. Zechariah Symmes,² or rather to some money which his children were to receive from his brother William's estate.

In this paper the heirs of Rev. Zechariah Symmes, living in 1725–6, are thus enumerated:

Mr. Scottow.
Mr. Osgood.
Mr. Stevens.
[These were husbands of three daughters of Rev. Zechariah Symmes.²]
Thos. Symmes's children.
Brackenberry Symms.
Each of these was to receive £2 0 7.

This paper appears to show that Catharine and William, children of Rev. Zechariah, had died before 1725, leaving no living issue; also Zechariah [71] and Dorcas [72], children of the third Zechariah. Some further considerations may appear in an Appendix.

31.

REV. THOMAS SYMMES³ (Zechariah,² Zechariah¹), brother of the preceding, and second son of Rev. Zechariah Symmes,² of Bradford; born there, Feb. 1, 1677–8; married, first, ELIZABETH BLOWERS, of Cambridge, a sister of the Rev. Thomas Blowers,* of Beverly. She died April 6, 1714. He married, second, HANNAH PIKE, March 28, 1715, daughter of Rev. John Pike,† of Dover, N. H. She

---

* Rev. Thomas Blowers was born in Cambridge, Aug. 1, 1677; son of Capt. Pyam Blowers of that town, by his wife Elizabeth, sister of Hon. Andrew Belcher. He graduated at H. C. 1695, and was ordained pastor at Beverly, Oct. 29, 1701, succeeding Rev. John Hale, the first minister. He died June 17, 1729, in the 52d year of his age, and 28th of his pastorate. He was a good scholar, an excellent minister, and a most useful man. He left four sons and two daughters.—Geneal. Reg., vol. viii. 179.

† Rev. John Pike was born at Salisbury, 1653; graduated H. C. 1675; ordained pastor at Dover, N. H., Aug. 31, 1681; died March 10, 1710, aged 57. His wife was Sarah, second daughter of the excellent and Rev. Joshua Moody, of Portsmouth, N. H., who was imprisoned Feb. 1684, by that worthless wretch, Edward Cranfield, Lieut. Gov. of New Hampshire, for refusing to administer to him the Lord's Supper according to the ritual of the Church of England. He was kept in prison thirteen weeks.

died in childbed, Feb. 1, 1718–19. He married, third, ELEANOR (THOMPSON) MOODY, Jan. 19, 1720–1. She was born Nov. 9, 1679, and was daughter of Benjamin Thompson, and granddaughter of Rev. William Tompson, first minister of Braintree, and widow of Eleazar Moody, of Dedham. She survived her second husband.

He was instructed in the rudiments of the Latin language by his father. His preparation for college was completed at Charlestown, under the able tuition of Mr. Emerson, a distinguished teacher. He was admitted to Harvard College in 1694, and graduated there in 1698, decidedly the first scholar in his class. He remained two years longer at Cambridge to perfect his education, through aid received from Mr. Brattle and other benefactors. He was ordained Dec. 30, 1702, the first minister of Boxford. During his pastorate there of only six years, seventy-two persons were added to that church. He met with difficulties, however, the nature of which is not known; but they greatly tried his patience, and led him, in 1706, to think of a removal. By the death of his father, March, 1707–8, the way was opened for his settlement in Bradford, a town joining Boxford, and he was installed there, December, 1708. His salary was one hundred pounds, paid in a depreciated currency. The smallness of his salary subjected him to great embarrassments, so that he could not bring up any of his sons to college as he wished, though they possessed promising talents. He was minister at Bradford nearly seventeen years, and during that time two hundred and thirty persons were added to that church. At one time, June 11, 1723, two hundred and thirty-four persons united in the communion. In the year 1720, fifty-nine persons were admitted; forty-six of them in three months, and twenty-five in one day. At the time of his death there were but one hundred and twenty families in the town.

He was a man of earnest piety. His walk was close with God, as appears from documents now in existence. He was very conscientious and punctual in the duty of secret prayer — considering this, with the daily reading of the Bible, an eminent means of security from temptations. In all his difficulties and straits he had recourse to a prayer-hearing God. He had faith in the covenant of grace. In one place he says: "I found much comfort and encouragement in pleading the covenant with God, urging the prayers laid up for me in heaven, offered by my godly ancestors. My dear children! if you ever see this, remember that you are children of many prayers. But trust not to that: pray for yourselves." May his posterity remember this! With prayer he united fasting, observing sometimes stated, and sometimes occasional seasons, for seeking the divine direction and blessing.

In sacred music he took great delight, and was himself a good singer. To this exercise he attended in his own family, on the morning and evening of every Sabbath; and in the latter part of his life, every day. He did what he could to reform the practice of

singing in public worship, which had been very low. He introduced
many new tunes, and preached on the subject. He published, in 1722,
a "Joco-Serious Dialogue concerning Regular Singing." It is full
of wit and sarcasm, and was designed to ridicule the opposers of
what he calls "regular singing," that is, singing by rule, or "singing by note," which he strongly advocated in preference to the old
method of "lining out the hymns" and singing by impulse. It is a
tract of sixty or more pages, and he informs us that he wrote it in
a single day, adding a few quotations afterward.

He also printed a sermon, entitled "The Brave Lovewell Lamented," prefixed to which is an account of the "Fight at Pig-
wacket," which is said to be the most authentic record of that
sanguinary affair.*

His other published works were: "A Legacy of Advice to the
Church of Bradford." "A Monitor for Delaying Sinners." "An
Artillery Election Sermon, 1720." "A Sermon at the Ordination
of Rev. Joseph Emerson at Malden, 1721." "A Funeral Sermon
for Rev. Thomas Barnard, 1718." "Against Prejudice."

He was a man of much intellectual ability, diligently cultivated by
close study. His library contained many of the books of his father
and grandfather, and for those days was somewhat large. He usually
reviewed his classical studies once a year. In his family he sometimes fluently rendered the Hebrew Bible into English.

In religious sentiment he was thoroughly Calvinistic. He was
diligent in visiting his people, especially the sick — always aiming
to give the conversation a religious direction. He loved to preach,
and embraced every opportunity for performing this service. In the
pulpit his manner was animated and impressive.

His constitution was naturally vigorous, and he seemed to enjoy
almost perfect health till his last sickness, which lasted only ten days.
He often expressed a desire that he might not live to be old, nor out-
live his usefulness. His wish was granted. He preached the last
Sabbath but one before he died, though in much weakness and suffering. He died of bleeding profusely at the nose, which rapidly
reduced his strength. He fell asleep in Jesus, Oct. 6, 1725, in the
48th year of his age.† "He was a public blessing, highly esteemed
in his life, much lamented at his death."‡

"The name of Mr. Symmes," says one§ who succeeded him in the

* The fight took place in the present town of Fryeburg, Maine, May 8, 1725, O. S., answering to May 19, N. S. Capt. John Lovewell, with thirty-three men, encountered a
much superior force of Indians under the noted Paugus. The Indians took them in front
and rear. The action lasted from ten, A. M., till sunset, or about ten hours. Notwithstanding the great disparity of force the Indians had the worst of it, and retired from the
field soon after sunset. Of our thirty-three men, only twelve lived to return home. Capt.
Lovewell and twelve of his men lay dead on the field.—[Symmes's Memoir; Sewall's History of Woburn.

† This account is largely derived from a memoir of Mr. Symmes, by his nearest neighbor, Rev. John Brown, of Haverhill, printed in 1726, re-printed 1816.
‡ Boston News Letter, Oct. 1725.
§ Rev. James T. McCollom, pastor in Bradford from 1854 to 1865; now pastor in Medford near Boston.

ministry, " is fragrant to this day in this vicinity. Perhaps no one in the region was more useful in the ministry." He was much beloved by his people. His children were:

By his first wife ELIZABETH. *Born in Boxford.*

+80. THOMAS,[4] b. Jan. 11, 1702–3; m. first, Martha Call; m. second, Ruth (Hall) Webber; m. third, Mary Frothingham.
+81. ANDREW,[4] b. May 20, 1704; m. Hannah ——.
+82. JOHN,[4] b. Feb. 14, 1705–6; m. first, Martha Kneeland; m. second, Philadelphia ——
  83. WILLIAM,[4] b. Oct. 23, 1707; died before the birth of Anna, the seventh child of Mr. Symmes, 1714.*

Born in Bradford.

+84. ELIZABETH,[4] b. March 3, 1709–10; m. Hon. Samuel Danforth.
+85. ZECHARIAH,[4] b. July 15, 1712; m. first, Grace Parker; m. second, Elizabeth Locke.
  86. ANNA,[4] b. April 4, 1714; admitted to the first church in Charlestown, May 31, 1741, and then unm.

By second wife HANNAH. *Born in Bradford.*

  87. ABIGAIL,[4] b. April 4, 1716.
  88. SARAH,[4] b. Sept. 30, 1717.

The foregoing is copied from the family record.

32.

WILLIAM SYMMES[3] (*Zechariah,[2] Zechariah[1]*), brother of the preceding; born in Bradford, Jan. 7, 1679–80; married ELIZABETH LANGDON, of Boston, June 13, 1706. They lived in Boston, and had:

88½. ELIZABETH,[4] b. March 20, 1706–7.

Fourth Generation.

54.

ZECHARIAH SYMMES[4] (*William,[3] William,[2] Zechariah[1]*), son of William[3] and Ruth (Convers) Symmes; born in what was then Charlestown, now the southern part of Winchester, Sept. 1, 1707; married, 1741, JUDITH EAMES, born in Woburn, March 22, 1718, eldest child of Dea. Samuel and Judith (Simonds) Eames, of Woburn. The name is of late spelled Ames, as pronounced. Dea. Eames, born in 1692, was son of Samuel born in 1664, who was a son of Robert Eames who was of Charlestown, 1651, but removed to Woburn before 1666.

---

* For this statement we have the authority of Mr. Symmes: " Advice to my dear children, Thomas, Andrew, John, Elizabeth and Zechariah," printed in connection with his memoir—William being here omitted, as not then living.

He was a farmer, and dwelt in the last house in what was then Woburn, on the road to Boston. It was opposite the Black Horse Tavern, which is still standing. The house stood on the spot where now stands the dwelling-house of Mrs. Hutchinson. It was a part of the farm of his father, Mr. William Symmes,[3] and his grandfather, Capt. William Symmes.* It is now in the town of Winchester. He died there, April 19, 1793.

His will is dated Jan. 24, 1791; proved June, 1793. He and his wife Judith, who joins in the will,† bequeath to their sons Zechariah, Samuel and William, land in Tewksbury, Woburn (the Wood-Hill lot), Medford, and elsewhere, "which we had by her father Ames."‡ They also leave a legacy to their daughter Ruth Prentice and her children. A pew in Woburn meeting-house is also bequeathed; also cattle, hogs and farming utensils.

Zechariah Symmes died April 19, 1793, aged 87. Judith, his wife, died July 24, 1795, aged 84, according to gravestone. The church record makes her but 76.

The children of ZECHARIAH and JUDITH (EAMES) SYMMES were:

89. JUDITH,[5] b. Aug. 14, 1742; died young.
+90. ZECHARIAH,[5] b. Oct. 1, 1744; m. Rebecca Tuttle.
+91. SAMUEL,[5] b. Oct. 20, 1746; m. Susanna Richardson.
92. JUDITH,[5] b. Feb. 13, 1749; m. Isaiah Dixon, of Cambridge, Nov. 16, 1773.
93. RUTH,[5] b. May 4, 1751; died young.
94. RUTH,[5] b. April 8, 1755; m. Thomas Prentice, of Cambridge, July 20, 1774.
+95. WILLIAM,[5] b. Sept. 1, 1757; m. Mary Mallet.

55.

JOSIAH SYMMES[4] (*William*,[3] *William*,[2] *Zechariah*[1]), brother of the preceding, and second son of William and Ruth (Convers) Symmes; born in the north part of Charlestown, north of Mystic Pond, April 7, 1710; never married. He was doubtless named for his maternal grandfather, Capt. Josiah Convers.

His father's large farm was divided in 1765, and about a fourth part was assigned to him. His part included the mill, the mill-pond, the house and barn. It bordered, I think, on the great road to Boston, now Main Street in Winchester. It consisted of several detached portions; one of these portions bordered on the west on the Gardiner farm (formerly Increase Nowell's) in Charlestown.

---

* The line between Woburn and Medford ran between his house and barn, his house being in Woburn, the barn in Medford.
† I have examined perhaps hundreds of wills. In no other instance have I found a wife joining her husband in a will.
‡ This expression can refer only to a part of what the testator left, for a part came from his ancestors the Symmeses.

He lived, therefore, in the extreme northerly part of Medford,* in the house standing on the bank of the Aberjona River, on the spot now occupied by John Bacon, which, since 1850, has been in Winchester. He died previous to 1780, as we learn from a quit-claim, signed by his four brothers in July of that year. He must have lived to near the age of 70.

His father, William Symmes, in 1761, conveyed to him by deed thirty acres of land near Wedge Pond, bounded N. E. on Ebenezer Convers's land in Woburn, and S. E. on the river called Symmes's River [the Aberjona].

56.

TIMOTHY SYMMES[4] (*William,[3] William,[2] Zechariah[1]*), brother of the preceding, and third son of William[3] and Ruth (Convers) Symmes; born about 1714; married ELIZABETH (or Betsey) BODGE.

He inherited a portion of his father's estate, including a portion of the mill. His land was bounded west by the mill-pond and the river; west and south by the land of his brother Josiah Symmes; south on land of his brother John Symmes and his nephew Samuel Symmes; east and west on the great road, now Main Street in Winchester. In other words, it was on both sides of the road to Boston. It was formerly in Medford; it is now in Winchester.

He died in 1784, intestate. The inventory of his estate was exhibited in court, Sept. 2, 1784, by his widow Elizabeth Symmes, administratrix. Real estate, £412; Personal estate, £72 10.

He left three children, all minors; which induces the belief that he was not married till more than 50 years of age. Of his children, Capt. Joseph Brown, of South Woburn, a near neighbor of Timothy Symmes, was appointed guardian. Elizabeth, widow of Timothy Symmes, was living in 1814.

His children were:

+96. TIMOTHY,[5] b. about 1770; m. Martha Wyman.
+97. DANIEL,[5] b. about 1778; m. Sophia Emerson.
  98. ELIZABETH,[5] b. about 1780; m. George Washington Reed, of Woburn. Published Oct. 30, 1801.
  99. WILLIAM,[5] b. about 1782.

58.

JOHN SYMMES[4] (*William,[3] William,[2] Zechariah[1]*), brother of the preceding; born about 1720; m. Nov. 7, 1754, ABIGAIL DIX, born May 21, 1733, daughter of John and Mary (Cooke) Dix, of Waltham. Mr. Dix, her father, was selectman of Waltham for several

---

* In a bond given by him Oct. 1, 1748, he is said to be of Charlestown. His house and farm were at that time in Charlestown, but annexed to Medford in 1754.

years. She was admitted to the church in West Cambridge, now Arlington, March 16, 1760.

Mr. Symmes was a farmer and lived in Charlestown until 1754, when he and his father's farm were annexed to Medford. After his marriage he continued to live in the same house with his father, on the spot where now stands the house of John Bacon, in the present town of Winchester, near where the railroad bridge spans the Aberjona River, and not far from the Mystic Station. He owned part of the mill and mill privilege; his brother Josiah the other part. Josiah's part, after his death, was divided between John and Timothy. It was more convenient for him to attend church at West Cambridge than at Woburn, and he was admitted to that church, Sept. 3, 1758, at which time his children John and Josiah were baptized. June 19, 1761, his father William Symmes conveyed to him the above John Symmes a considerable portion of his farm in Medford. His land extended to Symmes's Corner, in the south part of what is now Winchester, but was none of it on the south side of the road leading to West Medford. Forty acres, and probably more, of his land are now owned by his descendants.

His wife Abigail died March 28, 1761, aged 28. He did not marry again. He was living July 21, 1780, when he signed a quitclaim deed, together with his brothers Zechariah and William, in favor of their brother Timothy.

His children were:

+100. John,⁵ b. August, 1755; m. Elizabeth Wright.
+101. Josiah,⁵ bapt. Sept. 3, 1758; m. Elizabeth Johnson.
+102. Abigail,⁵ bapt. March 16, 1760; m. Joseph Cutter.

60.

Rev. WILLIAM SYMMES,⁴ D.D. (*William,³ William,² Zechariah¹*), brother of the preceding, and youngest son of William³ and Ruth (Convers) Symmes, born in the north part of Charlestown, afterwards included in Medford, and since 1850 in Winchester; born Nov. 1729; married, 1759, Anna Gee, daughter of Rev. Joshua Gee, pastor of the Second or Old North Church in Boston.* She died June 18, 1772, aged 38. He married, second, July 26, 1774, Susanna Powell, of Boston, b. 1729, a native of England. She died July 26, 1807, aged 79.

He graduated H. C. 1750; was tutor there, 1755 to 1758; received the degree of D.D. from that college, 1803; was ordained pastor of the North Church and Parish in Andover, now the town of North Andover, Nov. 1, 1758, and continued pastor there more than

---

* Rev. Joshua Gee [G has the hard sound], was b. in Boston, 1698; grad. at H. C. 1717; ordained pastor of Second Church Dec. 18, 1723, colleague with Rev. Increase Mather; died May 22, 1748, aged 50. He was a warm friend and promoter of the Great Revival of 1741.

forty-eight years, till his death, May 3, 1807, at the age of 77 years 6 months. Rev. Dr. Cummings, of Billerica, preached the funeral sermon, from 2 Cor. v. 1: "For we know that if our earthly house of this tabernacle," &c.

He succeeded Rev. John Barnard at North Andover, who is well remembered as a decided opposer of Whitefield and of the "Great Awakening" of 1741. Dr. Symmes is supposed to have entertained similar views, and to have been an Arminian, and very nearly if not quite a Unitarian. Rev. Bailey Loring, his successor, was an acknowledged Unitarian.

"He was," says Abbott, the historian of Andover, "distinguished for his prudence, his sound moral principle, his unshaken integrity, and his irreproachable conduct."

His children, all by first wife ANNA, were:

+103. WILLIAM,[5] b. May 26, 1760; unmarried.

104. DANIEL,[5] b. Oct. 1, 1761. He settled in Pendleton District, South Carolina; a son of his was a physician in Charleston, in that State. Perhaps Wm. Gilmore Sims, so well known a few years since as a brilliant writer of novels, was of this family, and perhaps not.

105. JOSHUA GEE,[5] b. July 11, 1763; m. Mary Elizabeth Jackson, daughter of Dr. Hall Jackson, of Portsmouth, N. H. He was a physician in New Gloucester, Me., and died at sea about 1804. His widow died at Portsmouth, Nov. 6, 1808, aged 39. [Gravestone in Portsmouth.]

106. ELIZABETH,[5] b. March 13, 1765; unm.; d. Aug. 13, 1784, aged 19.

107. THEODORE,[5] b. May 16, 1767; unm. A physician, settled in Falmouth, Me., and died in New Gloucester, Me.

108. ANNA,[5] b. April 1, 1768; m. Isaac Cazneau, probably a son of Andrew Cazneau, of Boston. After residing many years in Andover, they removed to Boston, where he exercised the trade of a book-binder. She and her husband were living there, Nov., 1811.

109. CONVERS,[5] b. July 22, 1770; died Sept. 4, 1770.

110. LYDIA,[5] ⎫ twins, born ⎰ both died the next day.
111. CHARLOTTE,[5] ⎭ Dec. 29, 1771; ⎱

62.

REV. TIMOTHY SYMMES[4] (*Timothy,[3] William,[2] Zechariah[1]*), son of Timothy[3] and Elizabeth Symmes, of Scituate, Mass.; born May 27, 1714; married, first, 1740, MARY CLEVES, daughter of Capt. John Cleves, a wealthy farmer of Aquabogue, Long Island. She died in 1746 or 1747. He married, second, 1752, EUNICE COGSWELL, daughter of Francis and Hannah Cogswell, of Ipswich, Mass.

He grad. H. C. 1733. He was ordained pastor of Millington, a parish in the town of East Haddam, Ct., Dec. 2, 1736, on which occasion Rev. Stephen Hosmer, of the First Church in that town, preached from 1 Tim. vi. 20: "O Timothy, keep that which is committed to

thy trust." He was a zealous promoter of evangelical religion, and
a warm friend of the Great Revival of 1741–2. His great activity
and fervor in this cause led to his dismission shortly after. He
then took charge of the church at Southold, Long Island. In 1744
the Presbytery of New Brunswick sent him to supply vacancies in
West New Jersey. He was pastor of the churches in Springfield
and New Providence, in that State, from 1746 to 1750, during which
time he twice sat as a member of the Synod of New York. In 1752
he removed to Ipswich, Mass., having been recommended to the people there by Rev. Nathaniel Rogers, of that place, as a man who had
been "driven from his Society in Connecticut ten years before for
being so active on the side of religion." In Ipswich he was an
assistant of Mr. Rogers; but it does not appear that he was formally
installed as colleague. He continued at Ipswich till his death,
April 6, 1756, aged 41. He had been in the ministry twenty years.

After the death of his first wife, her father, Capt. Cleves, took her
two little children and kept them till his death in 1760.

After the death of Mr. Symmes, his widow Eunice married
Richard Potter.

The children of Mr. SYMMES, by first wife MARY, were:

+112. JOHN CLEVES,⁵ b. July 10, 1742; m. first, Anna Tuthill; m. second,
     Mary Halsey; m. third, Susan Livingston.
+113. TIMOTHY,⁵ b. April 10, 1744; m. first, Abigail Tuthill; m. second,
     Mary Harker.
  114. WILLIAM,⁵ b. 1746; died in infancy.

By second wife EUNICE, born in Ipswich:

+115. EBENEZER,⁵ b. 1754.
+116. WILLIAM,⁵ b. 1756; m. Mehitable Moulton.

64.

MARY HIGGINSON (*Sarah Savage, Mary Symmes, Zechariah
Symmes*), eldest daughter of Hon. John and Sarah (Savage) Higgin-
son; born in Salem, Sept. 27, 1673; married, first, April 4, 1695,
THOMAS GARDNER, son of Thomas and Mary (Porter) Gardner, of
Salem. She married, second, April 25, 1699, Dr. EDWARD WELD,
son of Daniel and Bethiah Weld. He died Oct. 3, 1702, aged 36.
[Gravestone.] They had one son, *Daniel*, born April 13, 1700, who
died March, 1701. She married, third, May 3, 1708, JAMES LINDALL,
Esq., of Salem. She was his second wife; the former wife being
Elizabeth Curwen, daughter of Hon. Jonathan Curwen, of Salem.
This wife died May 19, 1706, aged 28.

Mr. Lindall was an eminent and prosperous merchant of Salem;
possessor of a handsome property; a deacon of the First Church in
that town; and a Justice of the Court of General Sessions. His
standing was one of the first respectability, and his connections were
with some of the influential families of the Province. He died May

10, 1753, aged 77. [Gravestone.] His wife Mary was living in 1739.

His children, by MARY HIGGINSON, were:

117. An infant son, b. April 25, 1709; died same day.
118. JAMES (Lindall), b. May 21, 1710; unm.; a merchant in Salem; died 1754.
119. VEREN (Lindall), b. May 14, 1711; died April 29, 1712.
+120. SARAH (Lindall), b. June 17, 1712; m. Lawrence Lutwyche.
+121. ABIGAIL (Lindall), b. June 16, 1713; m. Rev. William Jennison.
121½. RACHEL (Lindall), b. Aug. 9, 1714; died Sept. 9, 1714.
122. TIMOTHY (Lindall), b. April 14, 1716; merchant in Salem.

71.

ZECHARIAH[4] SYMMES (*Zechariah,[3] Zechariah,[2] Zechariah[1]*), eldest son of Zechariah[3] and Dorcas (Brackenbury) Symmes; born Charlestown, March 13, 1701–2; m. Elizabeth ——.

He lived in Boston, and appears to have died before 1725. He had by wife ELIZABETH:

123. ZECHARIAH,[5] b. Feb. 28, 1722–3.

80.

DEA. THOMAS SYMMES[4] (*Thomas,[3] Zechariah,[2] Zechariah[1]*), eldest son of Rev. Thomas[3] and Elizabeth (Blowers) Symmes; born in Boxford, Jan. 11, 1702–3; married, first, Nov. 11, 1725, MARTHA CALL, daughter of Lieut. Caleb and Ann Call, of Charlestown. She died June 19, 1733, aged 28. Caleb Call was admitted to the First Church in Charlestown, April 6, 1718, and his wife Jan. 1, 1720–1. He married, second, Dec. 11, 1735, RUTH (HALL) WEBBER, sister of Rev. Willard Hall, of Westford; born 1708, daughter of Stephen and Grace (Willis) Hall, of Medford, and widow of John Webber. She was admitted to the church Oct. 9, 1726. She died Jan. 17, 1753, aged 45.* He married, third, MARY FROTHINGHAM, July 24, 1753. She was admitted to the church in Charlestown, Feb. 10, 1740.

Mr. Symmes early submitted to the claims of the gospel, and was admitted to the First Church in Charlestown, March 27, 1720. His first wife, Martha, was admitted Oct. 9, 1726, and his second wife the same day. He was chosen deacon of said church, Feb. 5, 1752.

He passed his life, after the age of childhood, in Charlestown. He was by trade a potter, as we learn from Middlesex Deeds, vol. xxvii. fol. 57. He also kept a store. He died July 7, 1754, aged 51½ years, greatly respected.

His will is dated Dec. 10, 1753; proved July 25, 1754. He gives to his wife Mary, besides her dower, or third part of his real estate, one third part of his personal estate. The residue he gives to his four children, Thomas, Caleb, Elizabeth, Ruth, in equal portions, except that Thomas, the oldest son, " by reason of his grievous lameness," is to have two shares, or a double portion. He speaks of his late wife Ruth. Appoints as executors his wife Mary and his two sons, Thomas and Caleb. [Midd. Prob., xlvii. 150.]

Among the assets in the inventory was " Symbo, negro woman," appraised at £200; and a silver watch, £40. Whole amount of inventory, all of it personal estate, £1972 8 6.

His children by his first wife, MARTHA, were:

124. THOMAS,⁵ b. April 16, 1727; unm.; d. July 26, 1756. He was a cordwainer, and died intestate.
125. MARTHA,⁵ b. Aug. 10, 1729; d. Sept. 3, 1745.
+126. CALEB,⁵ b. Oct. 10, 1732; m. Elizabeth Hall.*

By second wife, RUTH:

127. ELIZABETH,⁵ bap. Dec. 24, 1738.
128. RUTH,⁵ bap. Dec. 6, 1741.

81.

ANDREW SYMMES⁴ (*Thomas,³ Zechariah,² Zechariah¹*), brother of the preceding, and second son of Rev. Thomas³ and Elizabeth Symmes; born in Boxford, May 20, 1704; m. HANNAH ——. He was named Andrew out of respect to Hon. Andrew Belcher, his grandmother's brother.

He lived in Boston; was a man of much respectability; was admitted a member of the Ancient and Honorable Artillery Company in 1734. He was living in 1764, when he was a witness of the will of his brother John Symmes, of Boston. He must also have

---

* The HALL FAMILY:

STEPHEN HALL, son of widow Mary Hall, of Cambridge, and probably of John Hall, was of Concord, afterwards, 1685, of Stow, which place he represented in 1689. He married, Dec. 3, 1663, Ruth Davis, daughter of Capt. Dolor Davis, of Barnstable, by his wife Margery Willard, sister of the famous Major Simon Willard, of Lancaster. Hence the name Willard among his grandson Stephen Hall's children. He had a son Stephen born 1667, who was of Charlestown, and married, first, Grace Willis, daughter of Thomas and Grace Willis. She died of small-pox, Nov. 12, 1726. He married, second, Martha Hill. He married, third, in 1739, Ann Nowell, widow of Joseph Nowell. He died Nov. 7, 1719, aged 82. He had:

> Stephen, b. Nov. 5, 1693; m. first, 1719, Anne Boylston, b. Jan. 12, 1701, second dau. of Richard Boylston, of Charlestown. She died July 3, 1734. The Boylston Family became eminent. Dr. Zabdiel Boylston, of Boston, brother of this Richard, introduced into the British dominions the practice of inoculating for small-pox, and thus saved thousands of lives. He m. second, in 1736, Elizabeth Sanders.
> Grace, b. June 17, 1697; m. Isaac Parker, of Charlestown, May 21, 1715. Their dau. Grace, b. June 21, 1716, m. Zechariah Symmes in 1734.
> Esther, b. Dec. 27, 1700; m. Peter Edes, Dec. 18, 1729.
> Willard, b. March 11, 1702-3; m. Abigail Cotton, of Portsmouth, about 1729. He was minister of Westford. Their dau. Elizabeth, b. Oct. 24, 1732, was the wife of Capt. Caleb Symmes, son of Dea. Thomas above.
> Josiah, b. May 12, 1705; d. May 20, 1706.
> Ruth, b. 1708; m. first, John Webber, of Charlestown, July 8, 1725. She m. second, Dea. Thomas Symmes. (See above.)   [Geneal. Reg., xiii. 15, 16.

been living in April, 1778, when in a legal instrument his son
Andrew has the suffix " Junior."

His children, all born in Boston, were:

129. HANNAH,[5] b. June 15, 1733; m. David Mason, Sept. 5, 1750.
+130. ANDREW,[5] b. Mar. 19, 1735; m. first, Lydia Gale; m. second, Mary
      Holmes; m. third, Mary Ann (Stevens) Symmes.
+131. EBENEZER,[5] b. Jan. 6, 1737; m. Mary Ann Stevens.
132. ELIZABETH,[5] b. March 4, 1738; m. Scarborough Hill, March 10,
      1768.
133. THOMAS,[5] b. Jan. 3, 1740.
+134. JOHN,[5] b. Feb. 5, 1741; m. Hephzibah Barrett.
135. MARY,[5] b. 174-; m. William Thompson, July 2, 1767.
135½. SARAH,[5] b. 174-; m. Samuel Martin, Sept. 22, 1779.
+136. WILLIAM,[5] b. 1753; m. first, —— ——; m. second, Elizabeth
      Russell.
136½. Another daughter, name unknown, was perhaps the wife of John
      Osborne.

82.

JOHN SYMMES,[4] Esq. (*Thomas,*[3] *Zechariah,*[2] *Zechariah*[1]), brother
of the preceding, and third son of Rev. Thomas Symmes,[3] born in
Boxford, Feb. 14, 1705–6; m. first, MARTHA KNEELAND, Dec. 19,
1728; m. second, PHILADELPHIA ——.

He resided in Boston, on the west side of the land of Col. Wendell. He was a man of high repute there, as will appear from the
following obituary notice in the *Boston Gazette and News* of March
1, 1764:

" Monday evening last, died here, after a few days illness, of a
violent fever, John Symmes, Esq., in the 58th year of his age, Lieut.
Col. of the regiment of militia in this Town. He was a gentleman
of a very courteous and affable disposition, industrious in his business, honest in his dealings with mankind, and pious towards God."

He died in Boston, Feb. 27, 1764. His will is dated on the day of
his death; it was proved March 23, 1764; and is on record in the
Suffolk Registry, vol. 63, fol. 50. He gives to his wife the use of
his real estate during her life, and to his only son Thomas Symmes,
&c. The witnesses were Richard Dana, Esq., Andrew Symmes,
Zechariah Symmes.

His wife's name—certainly uncommon for a lady—does not occur
in the will. We obtain it from the Boston town record of births,
&c.

His children, by first wife MARTHA, all born in Boston, were:

137. THOMAS,[5] b. Sept. 8, 1729; m. Rebecca Marshall, March 22, 1753.
      He was admitted a member of the Ancient and Honorable Ar-
      tillery Company in 1758. He was an only son.

By second wife, PHILADELPHIA —— :

138. ELIZABETH,⁵ b. May 5, 1745.
139. SARAH,⁵ b. Jan. 13, 1746–7.
140. GRACE,⁵ b. July 29, 1748.

84.

ELIZABETH SYMMES⁴ (*Thomas,*³ *Zechariah,*² *Zechariah*¹), sister of the preceding, and daughter of Rev. Thomas³ and Elizabeth Symmes; born in Bradford, March 3, 1709–10; m. Hon. SAMUEL DANFORTH, of Cambridge. After her father's death, 1725, she was taken into the family of Rev. Benjamin Wadsworth, president of Harvard College.

Her husband was baptized Nov. 15, 1696, in Dorchester, being son of Rev. John Danforth, of that place. Rev. John was son of Rev. Samuel Danforth, of Roxbury, who was born in England, Sept. 1626, and was son of Nicholas Danforth, who came to New England, 1634. Rev. Samuel was brother of Hon. Thomas Danforth, who was Deputy Governor of Massachusetts under Bradstreet from 1679 to 1686.

Hon. Samuel Danforth grad. H. C. 1715; was Judge of Probate, and of the Court of Common Pleas for the County of Middlesex; and was for several years President of the Executive Council. He was named Mandamus Councillor*—which means an instrument of arbitrary power under the royal government—in 1774. This last honor, although he had taken the oath for the performance of its duties, the popular clamor obliged him publicly to relinquish. Four thousand people assembled in the open air before the steps of the old Court House, in Cambridge, Sept. 1, 1774, determined to resist, at all hazards, the encroachments of the British ministry. They were aroused even to fury, and yet such order prevailed, that the low voice of Judge Danforth, now a feeble old man of seventy-eight years, was heard by the whole multitude. He addressed them at some length, and closed by giving a written promise, never "to be in any way concerned as a member of the council." His townsman, Judge Lee, confirmed his former resignation. Another townsman, Thomas Oliver, resigned the next day. Judge Danforth occupied a prominent position in his day. He sat on the bench till the Revolution, a period of thirty-four years, and died at his residence in Cambridge, Oct. 27, 1777, aged 81. Elizabeth (Symmes) Danforth, his wife, died there, Jan. 13, 1775, aged 65.

Their children were:

141. SAMUEL (Danforth), b. August, 1740; m. first, —— Watts, of Chelsea; m. second, Margaret Billings; m. third, Martha Hall

---

* The Mandamus Councillors were appointed by the king, in pursuance of the " Regulating Act," passed in May, 1774, which took away the chartered rights of Massachusetts. The people every where compelled these Mandamus Councillors to resign.—*Bancroft's Hist. U. S*, vii. 58, 95, 103, 115.

7

Gray. He grad. H. C. 1758; studied medicine; practised the healing art many years in Boston, and enjoyed a reputation as a physician seldom equalled. He continued in practice till nearly eighty years of age. "In all difficult cases his opinion was relied on as the utmost effort of human skill." He died of paralysis. Nov. 16, 1827. aged 87.

142. THOMAS (Danforth), b. Sept. 1, 1744; grad. H. C. 1762; was a tutor in Harvard College; practised law in Charlestown. Left the country with the British troops when they evacuated Boston in March, 1776, and never returned. He died in London, April, 1820. aged 76.

143. ELIZABETH (Danforth), died at Cambridge, 1816.*

85.

ZECHARIAH SYMMES[4] (*Thomas,[3] Zechariah,[2] Zechariah[1]*), brother of the preceding, and youngest son of the Rev. Thomas Symmes[3]; born in Bradford, July 15, 1712; married, first, July 10, 1735, GRACE PARKER, b. June 21, 1716, eldest dau. of Isaac and Grace (Hall) Parker,† of Charlestown, and niece of the second wife of his brother Thomas Symmes. She died March 9, 1747. He married, second, June 16, 1748, ELIZABETH LOCKE,[4] born in Medford June 17, 1716, eldest daughter of Francis[3] and Elizabeth (Winship) Locke, first of Medford, where this daughter was born, then, 1718, of Woburn, and afterwards of West Cambridge, now Arlington. Francis was son of Dea. William Locke[2], of Woburn, the part now Lexington, and grandson of Dea. William Locke,[1] of Woburn, who was born in London, Dec. 13, 1628, and came to New England in 1634, when only six years old.‡

Mr. Symmes came to Charlestown when a youth, and was admitted to the First Church in that town, Oct. 31, 1731, at the age of nineteen. His wife Grace was admitted to that church, Dec. 6, 1735.

During many years, he kept the "Cape Breton Tavern," in Charlestown, which stood near the present "Bunker Hill Tavern." It was a noted place in those days. The British troops had possession of it, after the battle of Bunker Hill, and occupied it for barracks. A granddaughter of Mr. Symmes stated that the British built a large oven near the house, the floor consisting of grave-stones found in the neighboring cemetery.

Mr. Symmes, in the latter part of his life, removed to Plymouth, and died July 12, 1772, aged 60.

A letter is on file in the Probate office, East Cambridge, written by him to his brother-in-law, Hon. Samuel Danforth, of Cambridge, and dated Plymouth, Dec. 2, 1770, asking to be excused from coming

---

* N. E. Hist. and Genealogical Register, vii. 319–321.
† See Hall family, p. 47, note. Isaac Parker was a great-grandson of John Parker, who came from Biddeford, in Devonshire, Eng. In 1629 he commenced the settlement of Parker's Island, at the mouth of Kennebec River, now the town of Georgetown, Me.
‡ Book of the Lockes, pp. 9, 24, 39.

to attend to the distribution of his father Locke's estate among the heirs, on account of his ill health, and the cold weather; his son Thomas will come in about a month.

1755, Sept. 23. Zachariah Symmes, innholder, of Charlestown, with James Osborne, miller, as surety, gives bond in the sum of £300 (equivalent to one thousand dollars) for the faithful discharge of his duties as guardian of his children by his late wife Grace, viz.: Zachary, William, John, and Isaac, all under the age of fourteen. [Midd. Prob., xlvii. 150.] This does not correspond with the record below.

The widow of Mr. Symmes married (published Nov. 15, 1776) Ebenezer Brooks, son of Jabez, of Woburn, whose first wife was her cousin, Jemima Locke, born July 4, 1718, dau. of William Locke,[2] elder brother of Francis, already mentioned. The widow Elizabeth outlived this her second husband, and died March, 1803, aged nearly 87 years.

"It is related of this family that the children of three different marriages resided under one roof in perfect harmony, viz.: the children of Ebenezer Brooks by his first wife, and the children of Zechariah Symmes by both his wives."

The children of ZECHARIAH SYMMES, by his first wife, were:

144. ZECHARIAH,[2] b. Sept. 18, 1736; m. Elizabeth ——. He was a mariner, and d. in 1765. [Midd. Prob., xlvii. 398.] He seems to have left no children.
145. WILLIAM,[2] b. Nov. 9, 1738.
146. JOHN,[2] b. Oct. 13, 1740.
+147. ISAAC,[2] b. April 10, 1743; m. Hannah Davis, March 20, 1765.

By second wife, ELIZABETH:

148. ELIZABETH,[2] b. March 26, 1749; m. Benjamin Pierce, March 28, 1771. It is said that he died in the army, and that she died of yellow fever in Boston, 1798.
149. THOMAS,[2] b. April 21, 1752; a brilliant young man, a student at Harvard Coll.; died before he graduated, about 1771.
150. ABIGAIL,[2] b. April 18, 1755; m. first, Aug. 30, 1774, Joseph Bullough (pronounced *Bullo*); lived in Newton; he was a man of large property, a native of England. She m. second, William Hayden, a native of Ireland, who also lived in Newton.
+151. SARAH,[2] b. Dec. 29, 1757; m. James Locke, b. April 7, 1752, son of Jonathan Locke, of that part of Woburn which is now the west end of Winchester. He was a soldier of the Revolution, and died at West Cambridge, July 6, 1831. She died Feb. 22, 1839, aged 81.
152. GRACE,[2] b. Oct. 11, 1760; died in infancy.

[*Book of the Lockes*, p. 71.

Fifth Generation.

90.

ZECHARIAH SYMMES[5] (*Zechariah*,[4] *William*,[3] *William*,[2] *Zechariah*[1]), eldest son of Zechariah[4] and Judith (Eames) Symmes, of Woburn; born there, in the part now Winchester, Oct. 1, 1744; m. REBECCA TUTTLE.

His father left him, in 1793, a handsome estate. He kept the "Black Horse Tavern," a noted place of resort for travellers and teamsters in those days. It was the last house in Woburn, as you approach Boston, on the east side of the Boston road, now Main Street in Winchester. It is now owned and occupied as a private dwelling by Josiah Francis Stone, Esq. He served as a soldier during a part of the Revolutionary war, previous to 1777.

His wife Rebecca died Aug. 10, 1805, aged 63.

His children were:

153. REBECCA,[6] m. Francis Wait; published April 16, 1794. They lived in Medford and had a large family.
+154. ZECHARIAH,[6] m. Hannah Richardson.
155. JOHN,[6] unm.; a blacksmith. Went to Newburyport.
156. MEHITABLE,[6] unm. She was ready to be married, but became insane and drowned herself in Mystic River.
+157. BENJAMIN,[6] b. about 1780; m. Rizpah Saunders.

91.

SAMUEL SYMMES[5] (*Zechariah*,[4] *William*,[3] *William*,[2] *Zechariah*[1]), brother of the preceding, and second son of Zechariah[4] and Judith (Eames) Symmes; born in the extreme south part of Woburn, now in the town of Winchester, Oct. 20, 1746; married, June 4, 1771, SUSANNA RICHARDSON, born in Woburn, Aug. 18, 1749, daughter of Zechariah[4] and Phebe (Wyman) Richardson, of that part of Woburn which is now Winchester.

They lived in what is now Winchester, then South Woburn, but a few rods from Medford line, on the west side of the great road to Boston, now Main Street in Winchester. Their house stood on the spot now occupied by the house of his son Horatio, and was nearly opposite the "Black Horse Tavern," already mentioned. He carried on the tailor's business, in addition to the care of a large farm, extending from the Main street across the river to the now forsaken Middlesex Canal. To the property left him by his father, he added by his own endeavors. He served as a soldier during some part of the Revolutionary war, before 1777.

He died Sept. 11, 1816, aged 70.

The children of SAMUEL and SUSANNA SYMMES were:

159. SUSANNA,⁶ b. April 1, 1772; m. Jesse Johnson, Dec. 19, 1792.
+160. SAMUEL,⁶ b. Oct. 28, 1776; m. Mary Richardson.
161. MARY,⁶ b. March 30, 1779; died at the age of 16.
161½. ZECHARIAH,⁶ b. Jan. 1, 1780; died in infancy.
+162. ZECHARIAH RICHARDSON,⁶ b. Jan. 2, 1781; m. Nancy Richardson.
+163. JOSEPH BROWN,⁶ b. Feb. 2, 1783; m. Lydia Wyman.
163½. A child ——; d. Feb. 21, 1785.
+164. JOHN,⁶ b. May 19, 1786; m. first, Abigail Green; m. second,
    Sophia Spaulding.
+165. NANCY,⁶ b. April 19, 1788; m. James Hill.
+166. STEPHEN,⁶ b. May 18, 1790; m. Priscilla Reed.
+167. HORATIO,⁶ b. Nov. 8, 1795; m. Charlotte Johnson.

95.

WILLIAM SYMMES⁵ (*Zechariah,⁴ William,³ William,² Zechariah¹*), brother of the preceding, and youngest son of Zechariah⁴ and Judith (Eames) Symmes; born in Woburn, Sept. 1, 1757; m. MARY MALLET, of Charlestown. Her father was of French descent, and her grandfather, or perhaps a remoter ancestor, fled from persecution to this country. Her mother was a Gardner, of Scotch descent, from Glasgow.

He lived in the last house in Woburn as you go south, on the west side of the road to Boston, where his father dwelt before him. It is now in the town of Winchester, a few rods from the spot where I am now writing.

He enlisted in the Continental Army, 1777, and probably served three years.

He had an only child:

+168. MARY,⁶ b. 1785; m. Rev. Jacob Coggin.

96.

TIMOTHY SYMMES⁵ (*Timothy,⁴ William,³ William,² Zechariah¹*), son of Timothy⁴ and Elizabeth (Bodge) Symmes; born about 1770; married MARTHA WYMAN, daughter of Seth Wyman, of the west side of Woburn, now in the town of Winchester.

He kept a store, first in Boston, afterwards in Medford, and for some time seemed to prosper. At length he became heavily involved in debt, and failed in business.

Dec. 1, 1797, he conveyed by deed, for three hundred dollars, to his cousin Josiah Symmes,⁵ "one half of a certain Mill right in Medford, with half the Mill Stones and Irons that belonged to said Mill, also one half of the land said mill flows, bounded on lands formerly belonging unto William Symmes, deceased, together with one half of the mill stream." [Midd. Deeds, vol. cxxvii. p. 101.]

He had many creditors, and was indebted to a large amount. The
estate was represented insolvent.   The whole amount of claims
exhibited was $10,531.40.   The estate paid only thirty-three and
one-third cents on a dollar.   He died suddenly and intestate in 1810.
Four or five years elapsed before the estate was settled.   Mrs. Martha Symmes, the widow, afterwards married Samuel Russell, and
died at the age of 93.

The children of TIMOTHY and MARTHA SYMMES were:

    169. WILLIAM,[6] b. about 1798; died in infancy.
    170. TIMOTHY,[6] b. Dec. 25, 1800; died unm. while young.
    171. WILLIAM WYMAN,[6] b. Aug. 24, 1803; d. unm. at sea, while young.
    172, 173. Two other sons died in infancy.
+174. MARTHA,[6] b. Dec. 30, 1806; m. William Wyman.

97.

DANIEL SYMMES[5] (*Timothy,[4] William,[3] William,[2] Zechariah[1]*),
brother of the preceding; born in the north part of Medford, now
a part of Winchester, about 1778; married SOPHIA EMERSON, of
South Reading.   When under seven years of age he was deprived
of his father, and Capt. Joseph Brown, a near neighbor, though living
in Woburn, was appointed his guardian.   In after life he lived
in Medford, I believe near Medford bridge, and was a blacksmith.

His children were:

    175. SOPHIA,[6] b. Oct. 10, 1801; m. ——— Eastman; she lived in
        Derry, N. H.; died 1871.
    176. SARAH WALTON,[6] b. May 8, 1803; died Oct. 9, 1804.
    177. SARAH WALTON,[6] b. Feb. 11, 1805; m. ——— Bryant; she d. Dec.
        13, 1834.
    178. HEPHZIBAH W.,[6] b. Nov. 21, 1806; died young.
    179. DANIEL,[6] b. Sept. 27, 1808; died Dec. 15, 1831.*
    180. GEORGE WASHINGTON,[6] b. Sept. 23, 1810; died June 9, 1814.
    181. HEPHZIBAH,[6] b. Dec. 27, 1812; unmarried.
+182. GEORGE WASHINGTON,[6] b. Oct. 16, 1815; m. ———.
    183. ALFRED,[6] b. April 4, 1818; lives in Westfield, Mass.
    184. EDWARD,[6] b. Feb. 2, 1821; died June 17, 1825.

100.

CAPT. JOHN SYMMES[5] (*John,[4] William,[3] William,[2] Zechariah[1]*),
eldest son of John and Abigail (Dix) Symmes; born in the north
part of Medford, now the south part of Winchester, Aug. 1755;
married Oct. 31, 1780, ELIZABETH WRIGHT, born 1757.

Her father lived on "the west side" of what is now Winchester,

---

* Daniel Symmes, formerly of Medford, Mass., died in Auburn, N. H., June 16, 1867,
aged 57.—*Boston Weekly Journal,* June 27, 1867.

among the Lockes. He had a brother Philemon and a brother John, who settled on the Ottawa River in Canada, opposite to where the city of Ottawa now is. They owned the land on which the city now stands.

Capt. Symmes was a soldier of the Revolution. He was one of the Medford company, commanded by Capt. Isaac Hall, which marched to Charlestown on the memorable 17th of June, 1775. They did not arrive on the ground till near the close of the action, when our forces were falling back from want of ammunition. It is well known that while a firm, undaunted front was presented by the men who were with Prescott in the redoubt on Breed's Hill, and with Putnam, Knowlton, Stark and Reed at the rail-fence, great numbers of the American troops refused to advance any nearer the scene of conflict than Charlestown Neck. The fire of the Glasgow frigate across the isthmus, of the Cerberus, Symmetry, and several floating batteries a little further off, the flame and smoke arising from hundreds of burning houses, and the incessant roar of the battle only a mile distant, may furnish a partial excuse. It is said that the Medford company paused at the Neck, Capt. Hall not daring to proceed.* It is also said that Sergeant Thomas Prichard, unappalled by the danger, exclaimed, "Let those who are not afraid, follow me," and with a few followers rushed to the scene of combat. This brave man was soon raised to the rank of captain, and did good service in the field near New York and elsewhere.

The enlistments in 1775 were for the term of only eight months. At the reorganization of the army, March, 1777, Mr. Symmes enlisted for three years. He was one winter in Ticonderoga. At the close of the three years he came home ragged and emaciated. He was paid in a depreciated currency, with which he bought a yoke of oxen. The oxen he sold, and took his pay in the same currency, which he kept for a short time, and then paid it all for a bag of Indian meal. Soon after he left the army, 1780, the old "continental money," of which three hundred millions had been issued, became absolutely worthless.

After leaving the army he built a wheelwright's shop at the intersection of two roads, now known as Main and Grove Streets in the present town of Winchester. It was at the locality which has since been well known as "Symmes's Corner." He also built there a blacksmith's shop. He built carts and wagons for the army in these two shops, that being the only way in which he could obtain good money. He had previously lived with his father on the river's bank, in the house where now stands the house of John Bacon. But a few years after, we suppose in 1783, he built a house for himself on what is now Grove Street, where he afterwards lived and died, as did his son Edmund after him. This house was burned, August 17, 1864.

* I have carefully examined many accounts of the battle. In none of them does Capt. Hall's name appear.

In 1793, a plan was formed by some enterprising citizens of Medford and other towns in the vicinity, for a canal to connect the waters of the Merrimack at Chelmsford with the tide water of Mystick River, near Boston. A company formed for this purpose was incorporated by the legislature, June 22, 1793, by the name of "The Proprietors of Middlesex Canal." Some years were spent in surveying and in other necessary preparations, so that it was not navigable till 1803.*

On the 17th of October, 1801, Capt. Symmes conveyed by deed a certain portion of land to the Proprietors of the Middlesex Canal, the canal passing very near it. He afterwards sold to them another portion. A bill of his now before me is for business done for the canal, in 1818–20, especially in carting materials and machines to and from Boston. Among these were steam engines to be used on the canal, as early as 1819. Mr. John L. Sullivan, of Boston, was agent for the canal, though a part of the business transacted by him was on his own private account. In 1800 or 1801, Mr. Sullivan purchased of Josiah Symmes, brother of Capt. Symmes, his share of the mill and mill-privilege, being three-fourths of the same, which had come to him from his grandfather, William Symmes.[3] Soon after this Mr. Sullivan and Capt. Symmes built a new mill-dam, which considerably increased the water fall, raising it to six feet. It flowed the land above, and interfered with the operations of the grist-mill higher up the stream, then owned by Abel Richardson. Several lawsuits with Richardson and others followed, continuing ten years or more, which were not finally settled till 1820 or later. These suits were decided against Sullivan and Symmes.

Mr. Sullivan was an enterprising man; he now owned three-fourths of the mill privilege, and at length, in 1823, Jan. 6, the other fourth part, hitherto owned by Capt. Symmes, was conveyed by him (Symmes) for one thousand dollars, to William Sullivan, of Boston, and Richard Sullivan, of Brookline, to whom their kinsman, John L. Sullivan, had, in February, 1820, conveyed his part of the premises.†

From an endorsement on the original deed, it appears that the property now conveyed consisted of two acres of land and a dwelling-house seventy feet long and two stories high, one factory dwelling-house, one workshop, one grist-mill and some other buildings.

---

* This canal was at the time regarded with much favor, and as promising to be of great public utility. But it cost a great deal of money. One hundred assessments were made between Jan. 1, 1794, and Sept. 1, 1817—the whole amount being $1,164,200, or $1,455.25 on each share. The first dividend was not declared till Feb. 1, 1819. From that time it yielded an income of less than one and a half per cent. per annum. The construction of the Boston & Lowell Railroad, in 1835, utterly ruined its business; and in 1852 its charter was surrendered and the canal sold by auction.

† Capt. Symmes, in 1801 or soon after, built a grist-mill at the eastern extremity of the milldam. The premises now conveyed by him were, "my grist-mill, and all the rights, privileges and appurtenances thereof; and all the right, title and interest which I have in the land, buildings, dam, privilege of flowing and using water on Symmes River, in Medford, my right and interest in the property being estimated as one-fourth part thereof."

The mill and mill-privilege had never passed out of the possession of the Symmes family till 1823, since the country was settled, one hundred and eighty years.

In another document of the same date, the property now conveyed is called "one fourth part of the Medford factory estate." It appears also that a trip-hammer and a turning lathe for making hubs for wheels, were reserved by Mr. Symmes, as owned by his sons John and Marshall.

Mr. Sullivan was somewhat given to scheming. The Middlesex Canal was under his superintendence, and he on his own account made steam engines at the factory on "Symmes's River," to be used for propelling boats on the canal. The manufacture of wood screws by a newly-invented machine was also prosecuted. Mr. Sullivan became involved, the whole enterprise failed, and at last he sold the whole establishment for four thousand dollars to Abel Stowell, a son-in-law of Capt. Symmes, who disposed of it to Robert Bacon, hatter, of Boston. Mr. Bacon carried it on for several years, and left it at his death to his children who now possess it. For a time it was known as " Baconville."

Capt. Symmes had a large farm and a large family. When his son John came of mature age, he gave up to him the care of the wheelwright shop, and to his son Marshall the care of the blacksmith shop. The father and sons carried on a flourishing business nearly fifty years.

He was captain of a company of Light Dragoons. He received his commission, still preserved in the family, from Gov. Sumner. He held various other offices of trust.

Twice he went to Canada to visit his youngest son Charles, who had settled on the Ottawa River, near the present city of Ottawa. Such a journey was then a formidable affair.

He died June 24, 1834, aged 79. His wife Elizabeth died July 18, 1848, aged 91.

Their children were:

+185. JOHN,[6] b. Jan. 27, 1781 ; m. Pamelia Richardson.
+186. THOMAS,[6] b. March 30, 1783 ; m. Sarah L. Wait.
+187. ABIGAIL,[6] b. Feb. 11, 1785 ; m. Elias Tufts.
+188. ELIZABETH,[6] b. April 10, 1787 ; m. Abel Stowell.
+189. MARSHALL,[6] b. July 30, 1789 ; m. Lephe Stowell.
  190. WILLIAM,[6] b. Aug. 14, 1791. When of competent age his father put him in charge of the mill. He afterwards went to Vermont, married, and died, leaving offspring of whom little is known.
+191. EBENEZER,[6] b. Aug. 17, 1793 ; m. first, Hannah Davis ; m. second, Lanissa ——.
+192. EDMUND,[6] b. Aug. 14, 1795 ; m. Elizabeth A. Smith.
+193. CHARLES,[6] b. April 4, 1798 ; m. Hannah Ricker.

101.

JOSIAH SYMMES[5] (*John,*[4] *William,*[3] *William,*[2] *Zechariah*[1]), brother of the preceding, and second son of John[4] and Abigail (Dix) Symmes, baptized Sept. 3, 1758; married ELIZABETH JOHNSON.

Who her father was we have not learned, but her brothers were Ezekiel, Levi and Reuel, and she had a sister Lucy.

He lived a bachelor till he was over fifty, then married a young girl who had been his housekeeper, and had by her six children. He never had the measles till he was about seventy, then took the disorder and died of it.

He lived in what was then the northern part of Medford, but is now in Winchester. It was near the stream known as Symmes's River. Dec. 1, 1797, he bought of his cousin Timothy Symmes one half of the mill privilege on that river. About 1800 he sold to John L. Sullivan, agent for the Proprietors of the Middlesex Canal, his interest in the mill and mill stream, it being three-fourths of the same. (See the notice of his brother Capt. John Symmes.) It would appear that he still retained some connection with the mill stream at least; for I find a document dated Boston, Nov. 3, 1821, containing an agreement between John Symmes, Josiah Symmes, and John L. Sullivan, respecting expenses incurred in defending suits against them by Abel Richardson and others.

His children were:

194. JOSIAH,[6] b. 180–; m. Sarah Butters. He was killed by the caving in of a well upon him.
195. JOHNSON,[6] married, and said to be still living in Vermont.
196. JESSE,[6] married; no issue.
197. GARDNER,[6] never married; of unsound mind; supposed to be still living in Tewksbury.
198. ELIZABETH,[6] married.
199. LUCY ANN.[6] married.

102.

ABIGAIL SYMMES[5] (John,[4] William,[3] William,[2] Zechariah[1]), sister of the preceding, and only daughter of John[4] and Abigail (Dix) Symmes; baptized March 16, 1760: m. JOSEPH CUTTER, of Woburn, afterwards of Cincinnati. She died soon after the birth of their only child:

200. ABIGAIL (Cutter), b. 1786 or 1787; m. William Woodward. This child, with her father and some of his near relatives, removed to the "Territory North-west of the Ohio River," now the State of Ohio. They went in 1789, about the time that John Cleves Symmes went, perhaps in the colony that accompanied him in that year. They settled at Hamilton, on the Great Miami River. Her father was killed by the Indians previous to 1801. William Woodward, Esq., a noted lawyer of Hamilton Co., was, in Aug., 1801, appointed guardian of the child, and afterwards married her. They had no children. He was a man of wealth, and endowed the Woodward School in Cincinnati. In 1850 he was an inmate of an insane asylum in that city. An adopted son inherited most of his property. In the decree of the Orphan's Court, August, 1801, Abigail Cutter is said to be a minor and an orphan, between the ages of fourteen and fifteen years.

103.

WILLIAM SYMMES,[5] Esq. (*William*,[4] *William*,[3] *William*,[2] *Zechariah*[1]), eldest son of Rev. Dr. William[4] and Anna (Gee) Symmes; born at North Andover, Mass., May 26, 1760; never married.

He was prepared for college at Phillips Academy, in Andover, under the tuition of that highly distinguished scholar, Rev. Eliphalet Pearson. This eminent teacher was accustomed to say, that John Lowell, John Thornton Kirkland and William Symmes were the three brightest boys ever under his instruction. He graduated at Harvard College in 1780, after which he spent some time in Virginia as a private tutor. While in this employment he kept up a correspondence with his class-mates and friends. His letters at this time are said to have been instructive and even beautiful. After pursuing a regular course of legal study in the office of that unrivalled jurist, Theophilus Parsons, in Newburyport, he was admitted to practise at the Essex bar, then including such men as Theophilus and Moses Parsons, Rufus King, Nathan Dane, Prescott, Wetmore and Bradbury. He immediately opened an office in the North Parish of Andover.

On the 3d of December, 1787, he was, while under twenty-eight years of age, chosen by the citizens of Andover as a delegate to represent the town in the Convention to be held at Boston in January following, to act on the question of the adoption of the constitution of the United States. The aspect of public affairs was dark and portentous. The people were suffering from the pressure of debt, heavy taxation and a depreciated currency. Many intelligent and upright men thought that the proposed constitution conferred on the federal government too much power; power that might and doubtless would be used for purposes of oppression. Even Samuel Adams and John Hancock had doubts whether it were best to adopt and ratify it. Patrick Henry, of Virginia, and Luther Martin, of Maryland, exerted their utmost energies against it.

Mr. Symmes at the first took a decided stand in opposition, and made far the ablest argument in the convention against it. But on hearing the arguments of Theophilus Parsons and others in its favor, he changed his views and made a speech recalling his opposition, and giving his unreserved assent to the constitution. In so doing he acted in opposition to the wishes of his constituents, expressed in a very full meeting. The course he now pursued subjected him to the popular ill will of his native parish, and even to bitter personal enmity, ultimately leading to his removal. But there is much reason to believe that it secured the adoption of the constitution not only in this State, but through the country. Had this brilliant young man persisted in his opposition, he might have led a very numerous party, even of the most ardent friends of liberty, such men as had faced the British music on Bunker Hill; and had Massachusetts, under his leading, refused to ratify the instrument, New Hampshire, New York and other States would probably have done the same. His conduct, therefore, merits the highest praise. It was an instance of the highest moral heroism.

Mr. Symmes went to Portland in 1790; entered at once upon a successful practice, and took high rank at the bar.* He was a good classical scholar, a sound lawyer, and an able advocate. His manner was formal and stately, but graceful. A letter from one of his students says: "His personal appearance was stately and dignified. He was in all respects a gentleman in his manners, and emphatically one of the old school. He was affable and polite, and commanded affection as well as respect. He may truly be said to have been one of the most imposing and influential men at that time [1805] in Portland. As a lawyer and advocate he was unsurpassed. In his efforts as a speaker there was perhaps more of the *fortiter in re* than of the *suaviter in modo*. He always touched the right string. He had great discriminating powers; no one brought out the root and truth of the case so effectually as he did, whether at the bar or at any public meeting. Great confidence was felt in his opinions on all occasions, and especially on legal questions. He was unquestionably the best and most reliable lawyer of his time in the State."

The writer of the above letter, William Freeman, of Portland and Cherryfield, then speaks of the cloud which hung over his latter days through the use of intoxicating drinks, and adds: "Often, when mellow with brandy, his favorite drink, he was brilliant, and threw more light on a subject under discussion than any other speaker."

It was probably under the influence of his favorite beverage, that a scene took place between him and Judge Thacher.† Mr. Symmes had made a motion to the court, which he was zealously arguing, notwithstanding frequent interruptions by the Judge. Thacher at last became impatient — as he was apt to be — and said: "Mr. Symmes, you need not persist in arguing the point, for I am not a Court of Errors, and cannot give a final judgment." "I know," replied Symmes, "that you can't give a final judgment, but as to your not being a *court of error* I will not say."

Mr. James Dean Hopkins, a lawyer of Portland, a cotemporary of Mr. Symmes, thus speaks of him: "Mr. Symmes was a well-read lawyer, and an able and eloquent advocate. He ranked among the first of his cotemporaries. He was also a fine classical scholar, of cultivated literary taste, and uncommonly learned as a historian. His productions in the newspapers of the time bore honorable testimony to his literary character — particularly a series of numbers, en-

---

* Mr. Symmes, as a member of the Cumberland bar, had such associates as Isaac Parker, afterwards Chief Justice of Massachusetts, Prentiss Mellen and Ezekiel Whitman, who both became Chief Justices in Maine; Stephen Longfellow, Salmon Chase, Samuel Cooper Johonnot, John Frothingham, and other eminent lawyers.

† Hon. George Thacher, of Biddeford, of the Supreme Judicial Court of Massachusetts. Maine was still a part of that State.

titled ‘Communications,’ about the year 1795, in defence of the common law. These numbers were copied into the principal newspapers throughout the Union. Mr. Symmes, with Judge Thacher and two or three others, rendered the newspapers of that period very interesting by their valuable contributions."

Mr. Symmes died Jan. 7, 1807, aged 47.

The preceding sketch has been compiled in part from Hon. William Willis's "History of the Law, the Courts, and the Lawyers of Maine," Portland, 1863, 8vo., pp. 148–151; and in part from "A Memorial Discourse of William Symmes, Esq., delivered at Andover and North Andover, in the winter of 1859–60, by Nathan W. Hazen."

112.

Hon. JOHN CLEVES SYMMES[5] (*Timothy,*[4] *Timothy,*[3] *William,*[2] *Zechariah*[1]), eldest son of Rev. Timothy[4] and Mary (Cleves) Symmes; born at Riverhead, L. I., July 10, 1742, O. S., or July 21, N. S.; married, first, about 1761, ANNA TUTHILL, daughter of Daniel Tuthill, of Southold, L. I.[*] She died in 1776. He married, second, perhaps about 1794, Mrs. MARY (HENRY) HALSEY, a sister of Col. James Henry, of Somerset Co., N. J. He married, third, at Vincennes, in 1804, SUSAN LIVINGSTON, daughter of William Livingston, Governor of New Jersey during the Revolutionary War, and sister of Brockholst Livingston.[†]

In early life Mr. Symmes was employed in teaching school and in surveying. About 1770 he removed to Flatbrook, Sussex Co., N. J. He had a farm and a house there, which continued to be his nearly or quite to the close of his life. The farm and house were called by him "Solitude," for what reason does not appear. He early took part in the great struggle of the Revolution. He was chairman of the Committee of Safety for Sussex Co. in 1774, and was a colonel, in 1775, of one of the Sussex militia regiments. In March, 1776, he was ordered with his regiment to New York, and was employed in erecting forts and batteries there and on Long Island. Early in the summer he was elected a delegate from Sussex County to the State Convention of New Jersey, which met at Burlington, June 10, 1776, and was a member of the committee which was appointed to draft a constitution for the State. Towards the close of that year he was sent by the legislature to Ticonderoga, with the delicate task

---

* JOHN TUTHILL is mentioned in Thompson's History of Long Island, as one of the principal members of the Congregational Church at Southold, at its organization by Rev. John Youngs in 1640. Southold was settled that year by a company from Norfolk, in England. Until 1674, this and two other towns at the eastern end of Long Island belonged first to the Colony of New Haven, afterwards to that of Connecticut.

John Tuthill, of Suffolk County, Long Island, probably son of the former, was a member of the General Assembly of the Colony of New York, 1695 to 1698.

† WILLIAM LIVINGSTON was the first governor of New Jersey chosen by the popular vote. This was in 1776. He was b. 1723, and d. 1790. His son Brockholst, scarcely less distinguished, was b. 1757, and d. 1823. Both were ardent friends of liberty.

of making a new arrangement of the officers of the New Jersey troops there employed. On his return he was ordered with his command to Morris County, and in December assisted in covering the retreat of Washington to the Delaware. While thus engaged, Col. Symmes attacked a detachment of eight hundred British troops under Gen. Leslie at Springfield, Dec. 14. This, it is said, was the first check to the progress of the enemy towards Philadelphia.

He was with Gen. Dickinson when he surprised the British on Staten Island. He was at Red Bank when the hostile ships came up the Delaware and attacked the fort there and Fort Mifflin. He was in the battle of Monmouth, Sunday, June 28, 1778. He conducted five expeditions to Long Island, when it was in the hands of the British. In one of the battles of the war he had three horses shot under him.

In civil life Col. Symmes rendered himself equally conspicuous. He was lieut.-governor of New Jersey one year; six years a member of the council. In 1777 he was appointed one of the associate judges of the Supreme Court of New Jersey. He served in this capacity twelve years. In 1786 he was a member of Congress from that State, and served two years.

After the war, a strong impulse was felt through the northern and eastern States, towards the settlement of the Great West. This impulse was especially strong among those who had toiled and suffered and made heavy sacrifices for the liberties of America. The "Ohio Company" was organized in Boston, March 1, 1786. It was originated by the disbanded officers of the late army. That year and the next were chiefly occupied in making surveys and other necessary preparations. The ordinance of Congress establishing the "Territory North-West of the Ohio," was passed July 13, 1787. On the 23d of the following October, Judge Symmes, together with Gen. James Mitchell Varnum and Gen. Samuel Holden Parsons, were appointed judges of the Supreme Court of the new Territory.*

The settlement of Ohio commenced at Marietta, in April, 1788, under Gen. Rufus Putnam, distinguished as an able engineer and military commander in the continental army. In the summer of that year, Judge Symmes passed down the Ohio River with a few families, but they were obliged to spend the ensuing winter in Kentucky, the settlement of which had commenced in 1770, under Daniel Boone. Judge Symmes, in 1787, contracted with Congress, in behalf of himself and his associates, for one million acres of what were called "military lands," in the south-western part of the present State of Ohio, between the Great and Little Miami Rivers. The price stipulated was sixty-six and two-third cents per acre. It is

* General Varnum was born in Dracut, Mass., 1749, but in 1787 was a resident in East Greenwich, R. I. He was a brother of Joseph Bradley Varnum. Gen. Parsons, born at Lyme, Ct., May 14, 1737, was a major-general in the continental army, and in 1787 a lawyer in Middletown, Ct.

designated on the early maps as "Symmes's Purchase." In the spring of 1789, he took possession of it with his little colony. The purchase included the land on which the cities of Cincinnati, Hamilton and Dayton now stand. By his public spirit and generous conduct, he encouraged the settlement of the whole region.

The embarrassments arising from the Indian war, which followed in 1791, hindered the settlement of the new purchase, and made it impossible for Judge Symmes to fulfil the contract, although several payments had been made on it. In 1794, after Wayne's victory, a new contract was made for 248,000 acres, which are all that are properly included in the "Symmes Purchase."

Judge Symmes selected a site for a settlement at North Bend, so called, because it is the most northerly point in the course of the Ohio, after it has passed the mouth of the Great Kanawha. It was his intention to found here a city which should become the emporium of the West. But Cincinnati and Columbia were settled about the same time; and the protection afforded to settlers against Indian hostility by the construction of Fort Washington and the presence of a military force, decided the question in favor of Cincinnati, which accordingly became the "Queen City of the West."

Judge Symmes was on the staff of Gen. St. Clair during the campaign which ended in disaster and defeat. He did not, however, neglect his judicial duties at Vincennes and other places.

During his residence at North Bend, he had frequent intercourse with the Indians, and by his kindness and uprightness was enabled to exert a great influence over them. After the treaty of Greenville, several Indians declared that during the war they had often raised their rifles to shoot him, but, recognizing him, had desisted.

He gave, either in whole or in part, a section of land to each of the eight children of his brother Timothy.

Mr. Symmes did not become rich — at least not as the word is commonly used — in consequence of his purchase. Many lawsuits arose against him,* causing no small embarrassment. Much of his land was taken from him to satisfy these demands, and sold under the sheriff's hammer as low as ten cents the acre, although some of it cost as high as twenty shillings, or $3.33 the acre. He applied to Congress for relief, but could not obtain it. In one of his letters, dated Cincinnati, Oct. 8, 1803, he speaks of being "grievously straitened and oppressed." In another, he says, "I fear I shall be ruined altogether."

I have been favored with the perusal of a series of letters from him to his brother-in-law, Col. James Henry, Lamberton, Somerset Co., N. J., bearing date from May, 1791, to May, 1813. They mostly relate to business transactions, but contain much information on family affairs. They breathe a spirit of kindness and affection for

---

* This is common in newly settled regions.

his relatives, many of whom are mentioned by name. He is careful to send his kind regards to "Mamma Henry," the mother of his second wife. It appears that he often suffered from the carelessness or injustice of others; but he maintains a cheerful, hopeful spirit through the whole.

On the 1st of March, 1811, during an absence from home of several days, his house in Cincinnati was set on fire by some malicious person who had a spite against him, and utterly consumed, with all its contents. All his papers (several barrels full), all his clothing save what he had on, "everything that could burn," were destroyed; $30,000, he says, would not repair his loss. The house alone cost him $8,000. He had nothing left but his lands, the income from which he estimated at $1,700.

The last two or three years of his life passed in much suffering from a cancer, which, commencing in the under lip, spread into his mouth and ears, and finally his throat. This dreadful malady caused his death, Feb. 26, 1814, aged 72.

The latter part of his life was spent in the family of his son-in-law, Gen. Harrison, at Cincinnati. I have before me a letter from Gen. Harrison to Col. Henry, before mentioned, dated March 4, 1814, relating to the sad event. The writer, after a visit to New Jersey, arrived at home Jan. 9, and continued with him to the last. Mr. Symmes " died with great serenity, preserving his senses till about ten minutes before his exit. On the following day I [Gen. Harrison] took his body to North Bend, where he earnestly requested to be buried. His funeral was attended by a large concourse of people, and ample justice is now done to his character, even by many who were most inveterate against him. He has appointed his grandson and myself his executors, and has given us whatever we may be able to save out of his estate. This will be nothing unless we can 'fanset' the iniquitous rules which were made under color of law, of an immense and valuable estate, which in most instances was sold for one-twentieth part of its then value."

He was buried with military honors. The procession moved from the dwelling-house of Gen. Harrison, on Front Street, in Cincinnati, and the body was interred at North Bend, in a spot selected by himself for the purpose. The following is the inscription on his tomb:

" Here rest the remains of JOHN CLEVES SYMMES, who at the foot of these hills made the first settlement between the Miami Rivers. Born on Long Island, State of New York, July 21, 1742. Died at Cincinnati, Feb. 26, 1814."

His children, all by first wife, were:

+201. MARIA,⁵ b. about 1762; m. Peyton Short.
   202, 203. Two sons, died in infancy.
+204. ANNA,⁵ b. July 25, 1775; m. William Henry Harrison.

113.

TIMOTHY SYMMES[5] (*Timothy,*[4] *Timothy,*[3] *William,*[2] *Zechariah*[1]), brother of the preceding, and second son of Rev. Timothy[4] and Mary (Cleves) Symmes; born at Aquabogue, Long Island, April 10, 1744; married, first, in 1765, ABIGAIL TUTHILL, daughter of Daniel Tuthill, of Southold, Long Island, and sister of Anna, who married the preceding John Cleves Symmes. She died in New England in 1776. He married, second, in 1778, MERCY HARKER, daughter of Rev. Samuel Harker.

He resided in Sussex County, New Jersey, during the greater part of his life, and there all his children were born. He owned a farm, but lived mainly by his trade, which was that of a silversmith. He was active in the cause of liberty in the Revolutionary War, and was a judge of the Court of Common Pleas for Sussex County.

He died Feb. 20, 1797, in his 54th year.

His children, by first wife, ABIGAIL, were:

+205. CELADON,[6] b. May 30, 1770; m. Phebe Randolph.
+206. DANIEL,[6] b. 1772; m. Elizabeth Oliver.
+207. WILLIAM,[6] b. 1774; m. Rebecca Randolph.

By second wife, MERCY:

+208. JOHN CLEVES,[6] b. Nov. 5, 1779; m. Mrs. Marianne Lockwood.
209. TIMOTHY,[6] b. 178–; d. in childhood.
+210. MARY,[6] b. 1785; m. Hugh Moore.
+211. JULIANA,[6] b. 1791; m. Jeremiah Reeder.
+212. PEYTON SHORT,[6] b. 1793; m. Hannah B. Close.
+213. TIMOTHY,[6] b. 1795; m. Ruth Spurrier.

115.

EBENEZER SYMMES[5] (*Timothy,*[4] *Timothy,*[3] *William,*[2] *Zechariah*[1]), half-brother of the preceding, and son of Rev. Timothy[4] and Eunice (Cogswell) Symmes; born in Ipswich, Mass., 1754; married, and had a family.

I have no certain information respecting this person, further than is given above. A letter from Newfield, Me., says: "During the war of the Revolution, two brothers, Ebenezer and William Symmes, came to this town, settled on farms and married." Nothing more is stated concerning Ebenezer, except that before his going to Newfield he was a sea captain.

116.

WILLIAM SYMMES[5] (*Timothy,*[4] *Timothy,*[3] *William,*[2] *Zechariah*[1]), brother of the preceding; born in Ipswich, 1756; married, Dec. 12, 1782, MEHITABLE MOULTON, of Newfield, Me. Her father removed from Hampton, N. H., to Newfield, about 1780.

9

William Symmes came to Newfield about 1780, or in the latter part of the Revolutionary War, and settled on a farm in that town. He was a deacon in the church there, and died Dec. 20, 1825, a. 70.

His children were:

214. MEHITABLE.[6]
215. ANSTICE.[6]
+216. TIMOTHY,[6] b. 1788; m. Sally Hill.
217. JAMES.[6]
218. WILLIAM.[6]

120.

SARAH LINDALL[5] (*Mary Higginson,*[4] *Sarah Savage,*[3] *Mary Symmes,*[2] *Zechariah Symmes*[1]), daughter of Dea. James and Mary (Higginson) Lindall; born in Salem, June 17, 1712; married, 1736, LAWRENCE LUTWYCHE, of Boston, a native of the county of Radnor, in South Wales.

He was a " distiller; " an occupation which, in those times, occasioned no scandal. He was a member and " vestry-man " of Trinity Church, in Boston. He died in Sept. 1740. Mrs. Lutwyche was still a widow in 1754, at the division of her father's estate. She had but one child:

219. EDWARD GOLDSTONE (Lutwyche), b. about 1737; m. 1777, Jane Rapalje. This son owned a large estate, on which he resided, in the town of Merrimack, N. H. It was on the western bank of Merrimack River, near " Lutwyche's Ferry," as it was then called. He was an influential, leading man in that vicinity; and as early as 1767, when scarcely thirty years old, commanded a regiment of militia. When the revolutionary struggle commenced, he adhered to the royal cause, as did many other men of upright lives and of the purest motives; fled to Boston during the siege; and in March, 1776, accompanied the British forces to Halifax. In 1778 he was proscribed and banished, and his valuable estate confiscated. He became a lieut.-colonel in the British army. In 1777 he married Jane, daughter of John Rapalje, or Rapalie, of Brooklyn, N. Y. She was a descendant of a Huguenot exile of that name from Rochelle, in France. Col. Lutwyche, at the close of the war, appears to have gone to England. There is no reason to doubt that he was a worthy and an estimable man. Out of respect to him, Rev. Edward Lutwyche Parker—pastor in Derry, N. H., from 1810 to 1850, a clergyman of great amiableness and worth of character—received his name.

121.

ABIGAIL LINDALL[5] (*Mary Higginson,*[4] *Sarah Savage,*[3] *Mary Symmes,*[2] *Zechariah Symmes*[1]), daughter of Dea. James and Mary (Higginson) Lindall; born in Salem, June 16, 1713; married in

Salem, May 15, 1730, Rev. WILLIAM JENNISON,[4] b. in Watertown, Feb. 6, 1706-7, second son of Samuel[3] and Mary[3] (Stearns) Jennison, of that place.*

Mr. Jennison grad. H. C. 1724; in Feb. 1728, was chosen pastor of the East Church in Salem, and ordained on the second day of May following. His prospects for a time were bright and flattering. Connected by marriage with one of the most respectable and wealthy families in Salem, and pastor of a flourishing church in that ancient town, he might promise himself a long life of comfort and usefulness. But the gay illusions of hope were changed to bitter disappointment. A general disaffection of the society towards him ere long arose, the cause of which is now unknown. Sept. 13, 1736, he asked, and soon after received, a dismission from his pastoral charge.

He preached, after this, as a temporary supply in Westborough, Holden, and other places; he also taught school in Worcester, but did not again assume a pastoral charge. He was the teacher of the public school in his native Watertown at the time of his decease, which was April 1, 1750, aged 43.

Mrs. Abigail (Lindall) Jennison died in South Danvers, now the town of Peabody, Jan. 1, 1765, aged 52. She probably resided there with her daughter, Mrs. Mary Giles. Her father, James Lindall, Esq., left her some property, which descended to her children. Her gravestone is still standing in the old cemetery in Peabody.

The children of Rev. WILLIAM and ABIGAIL (LINDALL) JENNISON, all born in Salem, were:

219½. ABIGAIL (Jennison), b. Feb. 10, 1730-1; d. in infancy.
220. WILLIAM (Jennison), b. March 19, 1731-2; m. Mary Staples. He was a physician in Mendon, the part which is now Milford. He was also engaged in trade there, and in Douglas, Sudbury, and Brookfield. He transacted a large amount of business; was a zealous and leading whig in Revolutionary times, and died in Brookfield, May 8, 1798, aged 66.

---

* The JENNISON family has been one of much respectability in England during many ages. I have before me a record of twelve generations, procured by the zeal and industry of my kinsman, Rev. Joseph Fowler Jennison, now of Canton, Mass. It begins in the time of Henry VI., who reigned from 1422 to 1461. This family possessed large estates in Lincolnshire, Norfolk, and in the vicinity of Durham and Newcastle. One of them, Rev. Robert Jennison, D.D., was "the Puritan vicar of Newcastle," his native place, from 1617 to 1632. Ralph Jennison, his nephew, was mayor of Newcastle, 1668, and received the honor of knighthood May 18, 1677.

WILLIAM JENNISON, one of this family, came from England to America in the fleet with Winthrop, in 1630. He settled in Watertown, near Boston, where he was a man of influence and distinction. He was selectman of the town, and held other important offices. He and Capt. John Underhill had charge of the military affairs of the colony of Massachusetts Bay from 1630 to 1637. He had an important command in the Pequot war. About 1645 he returned to England, as many others did, and died there.

1. His brother, ROBERT JENNISON, is the ancestor of the New England families of that name. He died in Watertown, July 4, 1690. His son,
2. SAMUEL JENNISON, b. 1645, was the father of
3. SAMUEL JENNISON, b. in Watertown, Oct. 12, 1673; d. there Dec. 2, 1730; father of
4. Rev. WILLIAM JENNISON in the text.

221. SAMUEL (Jennison), b. 1733; m. Naomi Everden.   He was a
lieutenant in the "old French war," 1756; a merchant in New
London, Ct.; afterwards dwelt in Oxford, Mass., and died there
in 1789, aged 56.

+222. MARY (Jennison), b. 1734; m. Thomas Giles.

222½. TIMOTHY (Jennison), b. 1735; d. young.

223. JAMES (Jennison), b. 1736; d. young.

126.

CAPT. CALEB SYMMES[5] (*Thomas,[4] Thomas,[3] Zechariah,[2] Zechariah[1]*), son of Dea. Thomas[4] and Martha (Call) Symmes; born in
Charlestown, Oct. 10, 1732; m. Sept. 21, 1756, ELIZABETH HALL,
born Oct. 24, 1732, daughter of Rev. Willard and Abigail (Cotton)
Hall, of Westford, Mass.*

He lived in Charlestown, in a house on or near the spot where now
stands the dry-goods store of John Skilton.   He was a master, successively, of several vessels engaged in the West-India trade. Among
the vessels in which he sailed were schooner Catharine, schooner
Greyhound, schooner Neptune, and brig Catharine.   It appears that
he was in the employ of John Hancock, of Boston, in 1764.   During the "old French war," or about 1755, he was taken prisoner by
the French, carried to France and detained there till he had acquired
a pretty good knowledge of the French language.   He was at home
in 1756.   At the time of his death he owned his house and one half
of the brig in which he sailed.

He died at St. Lucia, one of the West-India islands, Feb. 4,
1771, aged 38 years 3 mos.   He was a faithful husband, an affectionate father, a christian gentleman.

His will is dated March 3, 1757; proved May 2, 1771.   He was
then "bound on a voyage."   He gives all his estate to his wife
Elizabeth.

---

* Formerly the West Precinct of Chelmsford, incorporated as a town Sept. 23, 1729.
Rev. WILLARD HALL, b. in Medford, March 11, 1702-3, was son of Stephen and Grace
(Willis) Hall, of that town.   He grad. H. C. 1722; ordained first pastor of the church at
Westford, Nov. 15, 1727—that church being gathered and organized the same day.   He
continued pastor there more than fifty-one years, viz., till his death, March 19, 1779.   He
was probably a descendant from John and Bethiah Haule, who were dismissed from the
Boston Church, Oct. 14, 1632, and embodied into the present First Church in Charlestown,
Nov. 2, 1632.—*Am. Quar. Reg.*, xi. 377, 385.

His wife was Abigail Cotton, of Portsmouth.   His children were:

Grace, m. Benjamin Whiting.
Willard, b. June 12, 1730; married, and had seven children.
Elizabeth, b. Oct. 24, 1732; m. first, Capt. Caleb Symmes[5]; m. second, Capt. Benjamin
    Fletcher.
Abigail, b. July 19, 1734; m. —— Abbot, of Billerica.
Ann, b. April 22, 1736; m. L. Whiting, of Hollis, N. H.
Mary, b. July 30, 1738; m. Jonas Minot, of Concord, Mass.
Martha, b. June 8, 1741; died young.
Stephen, b. May 28, 1713; m. Mary Holt.   He grad. H. C. 1765; settled in Portland.
Willis, b. Nov. 14, 1747; m. Mehitable Pool.   He lived and died in Westford.   His eldest
    son Willard, b. Dec. 24, 1780, was representative in Congress from the State of Delaware, 1816-1820; afterwards judge of the District Court of the U. S.
Isaiah, b. Jan. 19, 1749.
Martha, b. July 26, 1752; m. —— Kneeland.   [*Brooks's Hist. of Medford.*

His widow Elizabeth, a woman of courage and energy, returned from Charlestown to her native Westford, in 1774, with her two little boys, Caleb and Thomas. She supported herself and them five years by shop-keeping; the Lord prospered her in so doing. She married, as her second husband, Capt. Benjamin Fletcher, Feb. 9, 1779. It is due to him to say, that he faithfully performed his duty towards her two fatherless children. He gave a deed of his farm, Dec. 6, 1788, to his step-son, Thomas Symmes, and to Levi Parker, the son of his only daughter. Capt. Fletcher died Jan. 25, 1789, in his 72d year. His widow Elizabeth died at the house of her son, Caleb Symmes, in Groton, Jan. 31, 1813, in her 82d year. She was interred at Littleton.

The children of Capt. Caleb and Elizabeth (Hall) Symmes, all born in Charlestown, were:

224. Martha,[6] b. Sept. 20, 1757; d. Sept. 30, 1767.
225. Abigail,[6] b. April 9, 1759; d. July 15, 1759.
226. Caleb,[6] b. Sept. 16, 1760; d. Oct. 11, 1761.
+227. Caleb,[6] b. March 7, 1762; m. first, Lydia Trowbridge; m. second, Mary (Chittenden) Lane.
228. Elizabeth,[6] b. Aug. 31, 1763; d. Nov. 9, 1773.
+229. Thomas,[6] b. Sept. 19, 1765; m. Rebecca Carver.
230. Willard Hall,[6] b. Jan. 21, 1770; d. Oct. 7, 1772.

129.

Hannah Symmes[5] (Andrew,[4] Thomas,[3] Zechariah,[2] Zechariah[1]), eldest daughter of Andrew[4] and Hannah Symmes; born in Boston, June 15, 1733; married Col. David Mason, of Boston, Sept. 5, 1750. He was b. 1727. She was his second wife. The first wife, married June 9, 1748, was Sarah Goldthwait.

He was a prominent man in Boston. In 1763 he founded an artillery company, known as the "Train of Artillery," the only artillery company at that time existing in Boston. This company became a celebrated military school, and furnished many excellent officers for the Revolutionary army. Gen. Knox was one of its commanders. In the year 1768, there came from London for the use of this company, two beautiful brass field pieces, three pounders, with the Province arms thereon. These two pieces constituted just one half of the field artillery with which the war of the Revolution commenced.* They were constantly in service during the war; were in many engagements; were taken and retaken many times; and finally, in 1788, the names of Hancock and Adams, "sacred to liberty,"

---

* This statement is made in the Genealogical Register, in a note on page 365, of the volume for 1852; but it cannot be true. There were at Cambridge, in April, 1775, six three-pounders and one six-pounder. At Watertown there were sixteen pieces of artillery, of different sizes, not all, however, fit for immediate use. The Americans, under Ethan Allen, took in May more than a hundred pieces of cannon at Ticonderoga.

were engraven on them by order of Congress. They are now in the Bunker Hill Monument.

Col. Mason was a distinguished officer of the Revolution, and the founder of that great national institution, the Springfield Armory. He had also a nice perception of æsthetic beauty. In his earlier years he learned painting and gilding, and studied portrait painting with that eminent artist, John Greenwood, of London, who was born in Boston, Dec. 7, 1727. He gave lectures on electricity in several towns. Franklin was a friend of his father. [*Vide* Allen's American Biography.] Col. Mason died in Boston, Sept. 17, 1794, a. 67.

The children of Col. DAVID and HANNAH (SYMMES) MASON were:

231. DAVID (Mason), b. Aug. 7, 1752.
232. ANDREW (Mason), b. Aug. 19, 1754.
233. HANNAH (Mason), b. Dec. 21, 1756.
234. ARTHUR (Mason), b. Sept. 2, 1758.
235. SAMUEL (Mason), b. April 20, 1761.
+236. SUSANNA (Mason), b. 1763; m. 1785, Rev. John Smith, D.D.

130.

COL. ANDREW SYMMES⁵ (*Andrew,⁴ Thomas,³ Zechariah,² Zechariah¹*), eldest son of Andrew⁴ and Hannah Symmes; born in Boston, March 19, 1735; married, first, Oct. 20, 1763, LYDIA GALE, daughter of Joseph and Mary (Alden) Gale.* He married, second, MARY HOLMES, of Boston. She died previous to August, 1774. He married, third, at Christ Church, Boston, Sept. 21, 1779, MARY ANN (STEVENS) SYMMES, widow of his brother, Capt. Ebenezer Symmes [131].

---

* The ALDEN FAMILY.

1. JOHN ALDEN, b. in England about 1599, is the ancestor of all who bear this widely extended name in this country. He came in the far-famed Mayflower to Plymouth, in 1620. He was not, as has been supposed, one of the Leyden church, nor did he embark in the Speedwell at Delft-Haven, July 22, 1620, O. S., with those who then and there received the parting blessing of John Robinson. That vessel stopped at Southampton to meet the Mayflower from London, and to take in provisions for the voyage. There the Pilgrims first made the acquaintance of John Alden, and thence he accompanied them to the New World.

He was distinguished for a holy life and conversation; a man of great integrity and worth, and held in great honor by the men of his time, as he has been by all succeeding generations. The compiler of this volume rejoices in calling him one of his ancestors, as do thousands of others all over the land.

He was unmarried when he came to these shores, but soon after married Priscilla Mullins, daughter of William Mullins. A romantic story of his courtship has come down to us, and may be found in Thayer's "Family Memorial." He died Sept. 12, 1687, aged 88, at Duxbury, to which place he removed about 1630. Gov. Bradford says he and Priscilla had eleven children.

2. JOHN ALDEN, his eldest son, b. 1622, went from Duxbury to Boston as early as December, 1659. He lived on what is now Alden Street, in Boston. He was captain many years of the Province Galley, and of several other armed vessels of the Colony, before it became a "Province." He m. first, Elizabeth ———; m. second, April 1, 1660, Elizabeth Everill, widow of Abiel Everill, of Boston, and daughter of Maj. William Phillips, of Saco. He died in Boston, March 14, 1702, aged 80, leaving a handsome estate.

3. WILLIAM ALDEN, his son, lived in Boston; m. 1691, Mary Drivey [Dewey?]. He was coroner in 1728, and held an inquest, July 4, in that year, over the body of Benjamin Woodbridge, slain in a duel the day before, on the Common, by Henry Phillips.

4. MARY ALDEN, daughter of William, m. Joseph Gale in the text, in 1736.

Col. Symmes resided in Boston, and was an eminent member of the community. He was distinguished by his air, manner, and entire personal appearance. He was remarkably intelligent, of great probity of character, a warm-hearted patriot and christian gentleman, and much beloved for his kindly traits of character. He was admitted in 1760 a member of the Ancient and Honorable Artillery Company, an organization of which Benjamin Lincoln, after having served in the armies of his country as major-general many years, said he deemed it an honor to be a private member.

He was one of that famous fraternity, the "Sons of Liberty,"* which originated in 1765, to oppose the execution of the Stamp Act and other arbitrary measures of the British Parliament. He was present at their memorable celebration and great dinner at the Liberty Tree Tavern, in Dorchester, Aug. 14, 1769, held in a canvas tent, " in the open field, near the barn," the rain pouring down in torrents. This was the anniversary of the hanging in effigy of Andrew Oliver, the odious distributor of stamps, on the Liberty Tree at the intersection of Washington and Essex Streets, Aug. 14, 1765. The day was held in honor somewhat as the 17th of June now is, as the time of a mighty outbreak against arbitrary power. Samuel Adams and John Adams were there. The procession, a mile and a half in length, on leaving the place, was headed by John Hancock in his splendid chariot. Gentlemen of distinction from other colonies were also there, among whom were Joseph Reed of Philadelphia, and Mr. Dickinson of New Jersey.† About three hundred and fifty persons were present; the "Liberty Song" was sung, the whole company joining in the chorus; forty-five toasts were drunk, yet no one was seen intoxicated. The company broke up between four and five o'clock in the afternoon; entered Boston before dark; marched round the State House (at the head of State Street), and then dispersed. The whole affair was conducted with perfect order, and the enthusiasm was intense.‡

In proof of the estimation in which he was held, we may mention that Col. Symmes was an intimate and confidential friend of John Hancock, before and after the Revolution. After that event, he was his aid-de-camp, and the warm friendship between them continued till death.

At the outbreak of the Revolutionary War, April, 1775, on the prospect of a siege by the American troops, Gen. Gage gave permis-

---

* This expression was first used by Col. Isaac Barré (b. 1726, d. 1802) in one of his early speeches in parliament in favor of America. It was afterwards applied to an association formed in 1765, consisting of the popular leaders and other ardent friends of liberty, and extending into all or most of the colonies. They were leagued together with the avowed determination to resist oppression to the very utmost. They held frequent meetings, kept up an active correspondence, and aided effectually in bringing on the Revolution.
† Brother of John Dickinson, of Philadelphia, author of those powerful appeals, "Letters of a Pennsylvania Farmer," written 1767.
‡ For a list of the persons present on this occasion, see " Proceedings of the Mass. Hist. Society, 1869-1870."

sion for all who desired, to leave Boston. In a few days this permission was suddenly revoked, and many respected and patriotic citizens were compelled to remain. Of this number was Col. Andrew Symmes. It so happened, therefore, that he was in Boston on the day of the battle of Bunker Hill, June 17th. On the return of the British from that sanguinary encounter, a captain of the royal army, finding himself mortally wounded, requested his bearers to take him to the house of his friend, Col. Symmes. In that house he died that evening, his young son holding his hand. Just previous to his death, Col. Symmes came in, and the dying officer said to him, " Ah! Colonel, I little thought that the bullet was cast by my American friends here to send me to my grave."

During the visit of Lafayette to this country, in 1824, while making inquiries in Boston for his old friends, he learned that Mrs. Snelling, a daughter of Col. Symmes, was alive. On her presentation to him in the evening, he said to her, in his inimitably graceful way: " Well do I remember your father, Col. Symmes. He was the first man who took me by the hand on my return to this country from France in 1780."

Col. Andrew Symmes was appointed, Aug. 5, 1774, guardian of his daughter Polly Holmes Symmes, a minor under fourteen years of age, with Ebenezer Symmes, mariner, and Benjamin M. Holmes, distiller, both of Boston, as bondsmen. [Suff. Prob., lxxiv. 17.] Benjamin M. Holmes was probably brother of the second wife.

After the death of his brother Ebenezer, Col. Symmes gave another bond, dated April 16, 1779, as guardian of the same child, with John Osborne, painter, and William Symmes, tailor, both of Boston, as sureties. [Ibid., lxxviii. 624.] John Osborne probably married his sister.

Col. Andrew Symmes died April 9, 1797, aged 61. His third wife, Mary Ann, was living as late as August, 1796.

His children, by first wife LYDIA, were:

237. MARY,[6] b. Aug. 6, 1761.
+238. LYDIA,[6] b. Dec. 18, 1768; m. Jonathan Snelling.

By second wife, MARY:
239. MARY ANN,[6] b. between 1770 and 1774.

By third wife, MARY ANN:
+240. ANDREW ELIOT,[6] m. Eliza Coffin.

131.

CAPT. EBENEZER SYMMES[3] (*Andrew,*[4] *Thomas,*[3] *Zechariah,*[2] *Zechariah*[1]), brother of the preceding; born in Boston, Jan. 6, 1737; married, first, March 21, 1763, HANNAH GREENWOOD, born 1740, daughter of Samuel and Mary (Charnock) Greenwood, of Boston.

She was a sister of the artist, John Greenwood, already mentioned. They were married by Rev. Samuel Mather.* He married, second, MARY ANN STEVENS, of Turnham Green, near London.

He lived in Boston; was a man of great courage and energy; a man of decided public spirit and patriotism. He was one of the "Sons of Liberty," and was present with his brothers on the great occasion, Aug. 14, 1769, mentioned in the notice of Col. Andrew Symmes [130]. He was a mariner, and commanded for years what was called a "king's ship" (not a man-of-war) running between Boston and London.

He died some time in 1776, in his 40th year. His widow, Mrs. Mary Ann Symmes, married his brother, Col. Andrew Symmes, Sept. 21, 1779.

He left no will. Of his estate, the widow, Mary Ann Symmes, was appointed administratrix, and as such presented an inventory, Jan. 10, 1777—the assets consisting of a dwelling-house on Middle Street, goods in the town of Littleton, &c. Her bondsmen were John Scollay, Esq., and Andrew Symmes, Jr., Gent., both of Boston.† In a subsequent account, presented Dec. 2, 1782, she charges for carting goods to and from Littleton, and from Littleton to Billerica; likewise, money "paid to his five sisters agreeably to the request of the intestate before his death;" and money "paid to his sister Mason and sister Thompson. [Suff. Prob., lxxv. 109, 194–6.]

After paying out these various charges, there was found to be a balance of personal estate amounting to £1622 6 1½. As "continental money" ceased to circulate in 1780, this balance was doubtless reckoned in a sound currency, and the amount may be stated as about $5,400. It was distributed one-third to the widow, then become a wife; two-thirds to the only daughter, Mary Ann Symmes.

---

* Samuel Greenwood, son of Samuel and Elizabeth (Bronsdon) Greenwood, of Boston, was born Aug. 15, 1694; m. Mary Charnock, his second wife, Dec. 1, 1726; was a merchant in Boston, and died Feb. 22, 1741-2. His brother Isaac Greenwood grad. H. C. 1721; was Hollis Professor of Mathematics and Natural Philosophy in that college from 1727 to 1738, and died 1745.

Rev. Samuel Mather, b. in Boston, Oct. 30, 1706, was son of Rev. Cotton Mather, by his second wife Elizabeth (Clark) Hubbard. He grad. H. C. 1723; was pastor, first, from 1732 to 1741, of the Second, or Old North Church, of which his father and grandfather had been pastors; second, of a church which separated therefrom in 1741, and built a house of worship for him at the corner of North Bennet and Hanover Streets. He died June 27, 1785. The meeting-house was purchased by the Universalists, and became the house of the First Universalist Church in Boston.

Having occasion, in the compilation of this volume, to use the records of the "Samuel Mather Church," I employed a very competent person to look them up. He made diligent inquiry of clergymen and others most likely to know, going all over Boston and spending a great portion of one day for this purpose. His search was utterly in vain. Nobody knew where they were; nobody had ever seen them. Rev. Dr. Miner, the present accomplished and able minister of the First Universalist Church, could give no clue to them. My agent was told that that society, in 1785, bought only the church edifice, nothing more.

† Dea. John Scollay was a leading man in his day. He was selectman in 1764, and held other public offices. I have heard my grandfather speak of his habitually being in the streets of a Sabbath morn, to prevent the desecration of the Lord's day. Scollay's Building was named for him. Middle Street was the northern half of what is now Hanover Street.

The only child of Capt. EBENEZER SYMMES was by his second wife:

+241. MARY ANN,[6] b. Aug. 15, 1775; m. John Greenwood.

134.

JOHN SYMMES[5] (*Andrew,[4] Thomas,[3] Zechariah,[2] Zechariah[1]*), brother of the preceding, and fourth son of Andrew[4] and Hannah Symmes; born in Boston, Feb. 5, 1741; married HEPHZIBAH BARRETT, June 1, 1766. They were married by Rev. Andrew Eliot, of the New North Church from 1742 to 1778.

He was one of the "Sons of Liberty," and was present at the great celebration in Dorchester, Aug. 14, 1769, described under the notice of Col. Andrew Symmes. He afterwards, it is said, lived in Lynn.

His children were:

242. WILLIAM,[6] had a son *William,[7]* whose daughter Susan m. a Barnes, and was living in Boston in 1867.

243. ELIZABETH.[6] m. —— Colman, and had ten daughters.

244. ABIAH.[6] m. —— Shepard, and had *Susan* (Shepard) and *John* (Shepard).

I am in doubt whether these were not the children of another John Symmes.

136.

WILLIAM SYMMES[5] (*Andrew,[4] Thomas,[3] Zechariah,[2] Zechariah[1]*), brother of the preceding; born in Boston, 1753; married, first, PRUDENCE URANN, a native of Boston, said to be a descendant of Rev. Pierre Daillé, the minister of the French Protestant Congregation in Boston, from 1696 to 1715; married, second, ELIZABETH RUSSELL, sister of the well-known Benjamin Russell, printer and publisher of the Columbian Centinel, of Boston.* She died at Ludlow, Vt., Jan. 25, 1856, in her 91st year.

He resided in Boston, and was by trade a tailor. He was also a ship-master, sailing from Boston and Philadelphia. He was one of the sureties of his brother Col. Andrew Symmes, April 16, 1779, when the latter was appointed guardian of his child Mary, by his

---

* According to Mr. Samuel G. Drake, in his "History of Boston," p. 733, there were issued in Boston, previous to Dec. 1767, only four weekly papers—the *News Letter*, commenced 1704; the *Evening Post*, 1739; the *Advertiser*, 1753; the *Gazette*, 1755. In December, 1767, two enterprising men, John Mein and John Fleming, commenced the *Boston Chronicle*. It was a high tory paper, and from the force of public opinion suspended June, 1770. All the other papers but the last continued till the Revolutionary War, 1775-6, when they were discontinued. The *Independent Chronicle* was commenced Jan. 2, 1777, and after the division of the country into parties, was the accredited and leading organ of the democratic party in New England. The *Massachusetts Centinel* was first issued in 1784, the name being changed, June 16, 1790, to *Columbian Centinel*. This paper was owned and conducted (I think from the beginning) by Benjamin Russell, a man of rare ability, and possessing in a high degree the confidence and support of the federal party. It was continued by him till about 1820, when it was merged in the *Boston Daily Advertiser.*

second wife, Mary Holmes. Also surety for him in a similar case, Aug. 28, 1787. [Suff. Prob., lxxviii. 624, and lxxxvi. 227.]

He was for a time a deputy-sheriff of the county of Suffolk, and near the close of life removed to Cambridge, where he died of consumption in 1810, aged 57. His wife's brother, Mr. Russell, was guardian to his son, then only eight years old, and took him into his family.

His children, by first wife, were:

245. MARY,[6] unmarried.
246. ELIZABETH,[6] m. John Bayley. They had a numerous family, one of whom was Dudley H. Bayley, now residing in Boston. Previous to the "Great Fire," Nov. 9 and 10, 1872, he had a "Horse Bazaar" on Federal Street, where he kept horses and carriages for sale.

By second wife:

247. An infant.
+248. WILLIAM,[6] b. 1802; m. first, Elizabeth Ridgeley; m. second, Eliza A. Mayland.

147.

ISAAC SYMMES[5] (*Zechariah,[4] Thomas,[3] Zechariah,[2] Zechariah[1]*), son of Zechariah[4] and Grace (Parker) Symmes; born in Charlestown, April 10, 1743; married, first, March 20, 1765, HANNAH DAVIS, b. Feb. 27, 1743—supposed to be a descendant of Dolor Davis, of Barnstable, 1680–1704. She died Oct. 1, 1773. He m. second, Dec. 15, 1774, HANNAH ——, b. Feb. 5, 1749, d. Dec. 13, 1783. He m. third, Oct. 24, 1784, JOANNA ——, b. Aug. 30, 1754.

He was a baker, and one of the selectmen of the town. He lived in Plymouth, Mass. He died in consequence of a fall from a horse, Saturday, Aug. 27, 1791, at 11 o'clock, A.M.

His children, by first wife, were:

249. HANNAH,[6] b. Jan. 30, 1766. She was beautiful and attractive in person; was engaged to be married, but was disappointed, and died in consequence, while yet young.
250. ISAAC,[6] b. June 5, 1767; d. Nov. 1767.
251. GRACE,[6] b. Aug. 24, 1768.
252. MARTHA,[6] b. May 6, 1770; d. Jan. 23, 1859.
+253. ISAAC,[6] b. Nov. 16, 1771; m. Mary Whitman.
254. ELIZABETH,[6] b. Sept. 16, 1773; d. May 2, 1803.

By second wife:

255. LUCY,[6] b. Sept. 14, 1775; d. Oct. 1, 1775.
+256. MARGARET,[6] b. Nov. 15, 1777; m. James Spooner.
257. SARAH,[6] b. April 24, 1779; m. Pelham Brewster, of Kingston, Mass. They had five children, names unknown.
+258. LAZARUS,[6] b. Feb. 18, 1781; m. Mary Weston.
259. LUCY,[6] b. Oct. 24, 1782; d. May 2, 1783.

By third wife:

260. JOANNA,[6] b. Oct. 14, 1785; d. Dec. 27, 1789.
261. NANCY HOLLAND,[6] b. Nov. 2, 1786.
+262. ZECHARIAH PARKER,[6] b. May 8, 1791; m. first, Elizabeth D. Berry; m. second, Elizabeth Young; m. third, Caroline F. Esty.

151.

SARAH SYMMES[5] (*Zechariah,*[4] *Thomas,*[3] *Zechariah,*[2] *Zechariah*[1]), half-sister of the preceding, and daughter of Zechariah[4] and Elizabeth (Locke) Symmes; born in Charlestown, Dec. 29, 1757; m. 1777, JAMES LOCKE, born in the west end of the present town of Winchester, then part of Woburn, April 7, 1752. He was son of Jonathan and Phebe (Pierce) Locke, of the same place.

James Locke was a soldier of the Revolution. He dwelt, successively, in Winchester, Lexington, and Arlington, the last place then known as West Cambridge. He died at the place last named, July 6, 1831, in his 80th year. His wife Sarah died Feb. 22, 1839, a. 81.

Their children, who were born at West Cambridge:

263. JAMES (Locke), b. Jan. 28, 1778; m. first, Nancy Perkins, Sept. 4, 1811; m. second, Lydia (Hills) Haskins, 1821. He resided in Maine till 1818, and then removed to Cortland, N. Y. He was a Baptist minister. He died of cholera, at Millport, Chenango Co., N. Y., Aug. 1, 1849.

264. ELIZABETH SYMMES (Locke), b. Feb. 17, 1779; m. Caleb Eames, of Wilmington, May 3, 1796. He was the sixth Caleb Eames in a direct line, who were eldest sons, and occupied the same farm. He died July 3, 1828, aged 65. She d. Oct. 1, 1844, aged 65.

Born in Lexington.

265. SARAH SYMMES (Locke), b. Nov. 16, 1782; m. Joseph Dean, of Wilmington, Jan. 1, 1807, his second wife. She died Dec. 24, 1807, aged 25.

266. WILLIAM (Locke), b. Feb. 5, 1785; d. Oct. 13, 1793.

Born in Woburn, the part now Winchester.

267. ABIGAIL BULLOUGH (Locke), b. Aug. 15, 1788; m. Aug. 9, 1812, Daniel Kingsbury, b. at Dedham, June 19, 1790. They lived in Boston. He was a housewright, and died at New Orleans in 1822.

268. THOMAS SYMMES (Locke), b. Nov. 17, 1790; m. first, Lucy Field, Sept. 26, 1814, daughter of William Field, of Windham, Me.; m. second, Experience Adams. They reside in Temple, Me.

269. JONATHAN (Locke), b. Jan. 13, 1793; d. Oct. 25, 1793.

270. MARY TUFTS (Locke), b. Oct. 24, 1794; unm. and living in 1852.

271. FRANCES STIMSON (Locke), b. Aug. 23, 1801; m. Nov. 5, 1820, Samuel Kettelle,[6] b. Nov. 29, 1791, son of Samuel[5] and Hannah (Pierce) Kettelle, of Cambridge, son of James,[4] son of James,[3] son of Jonathan,[2] son of Richard Kettelle,[1] the original emigrant, who was in Charlestown in 1635. Mrs. Kettelle is now a widow, a near neighbor of the compiler, in Winchester. The family have long resided in Charlestown.

Sixth Generation.

154.

ZECHARIAH SYMMES⁶ (*Zechariah,⁵ Zechariah,⁴ William,³ William,² Zechariah¹*), son of Zechariah⁵ and Rebecca (Tuttle) Symmes; born in the extreme south part of Woburn, now included in Winchester, 177–; married, Oct. 6, 1801, HANNAH RICHARDSON, daughter of Nathan Richardson, of Woburn.

He was by trade a cooper; lived in the south part of Woburn, now Winchester, and died there. He became, late in life, a member of the Congregational Church; his wife had long been a member.

Their children were:

272. HANNAH,⁷ b. about 1802; m. Samuel B. Tidd, March 2, 1820. They lived and died in Woburn. Had children.
273. MEHITABLE,⁷ b. 180–; m. Ira Bucknam, of Woburn; had children.
274. ZECHARIAH,⁷ b. 1807; unm.; d. April 16, 1830; said to have been an excellent young man.

157.

BENJAMIN SYMMES⁶ (*Zechariah,⁵ Zechariah,⁴ William,³ William,² Zechariah¹*), brother of the preceding, and son of Zechariah⁵ and Rebecca Symmes; born in what is now Winchester, on the border of Medford, about 1780; m. RIZPAH SAUNDERS, of Tewksbury, Mass. They were published March 25, 1809.

He lived in the south part of Woburn, and died about 1815. His widow married Charles Stackpole, of Charlestown.

The children of BENJAMIN and RIZPAH SYMMES were:

275. RISPAH,⁷ b. Jan. 26, 1810; said to have been married very young.
276. FRANCES,⁷ b. Dec. 11, 1810; m. Isaac Lathrop. He kept a hatstore in Charlestown, and died about 1850. His wife died some years previous. They left a family of six children. One of them m. Charles E. Rogers, of Charlestown, and is now living. An unmarried daughter, Mary Lathrop, is a teacher at Jamaica Plain, West Roxbury.
277. MARY,⁷ b. 1812; m. 1832, Horatio Jenkins. They resided in Boston for a time, then in Chelsea, and now in Alexandria, Douglas Co., Minnesota.
278. MARTHA SAUNDERS,⁷ b. Sept. 26, 1813; m. Henry Bursley, of Boston. They reside at No. 4 Bond Street, near Shawmut Avenue.

160.

SAMUEL SYMMES⁶ (*Samuel,⁵ Zechariah,⁴ William,³ William,² Zechariah¹*), eldest son of Samuel⁵ and Susanna (Richardson)

Symmes, of South Woburn, now Winchester; born there, Oct. 28, 1776; married, April 23, 1807, MARY RICHARDSON,[6] daughter of Joseph[5] and Abigail (Felton) Richardson, of Danvers and Woburn.

They lived in South Woburn, on what is now Washington Street, in Winchester, where their daughter Mrs. Todd now lives.

He died about 1851, aged 75.

Their children were:

279. MARY,[7] m. Andrew Todd. They are now living. Nov. 1872.
280. ABIGAIL FELTON,[7] b. Nov. 2. 1812; d. Nov. 11. 1812.
281. SAMUEL FELTON,[7] b. 1814; d. March 15, 1832, aged 18.

162.

ZECHARIAH RICHARDSON SYMMES[6] (*Samuel,*[5] *Zechariah,*[4] *William,*[3] *William,*[2] *Zechariah*[1]), brother of the preceding, and son of Samuel[5] and Susanna (Richardson) Symmes, of South Woburn, now Winchester; born there, Jan. 2, 1781; married, March 28, 1809, NANCY RICHARDSON, born Feb. 1786, daughter of Gideon Richardson, of Woburn.

They lived in what is now Winchester, on Main Street, near the mill on the Aberjona River. He died Oct. 16, 1850. His widow Nancy died at Winchester, June 21, 1871.

His children were:

282. JERUSHA RICHARDSON,[7] b. April 29, 1810; m. March 5, 1846, Joseph Wyman, of West Cambridge, now Arlington, b. Aug. 19, 1805. He died March 9, 1863. She still lives in Winchester. They had no children.
283. WILLIAM,[7] b. 1818; d. at the age of 3 years and 9 mos.
284. NANCY.[7] b. Feb. 3, 1821; m. Feb. 17, 1853, Henry Wait Howe, b. 1822, son of John Howe, who was b. in Boston, 1784. Henry W. Howe d. March 30, 1858. Their only child was *Lucy Wyman* (Howe), b. May 1, 1855; d. Sept. 16, 1855. Mrs. Howe and her sister Mrs. Wyman reside together in Winchester.

163.

JOSEPH BROWN SYMMES[6] (*Samuel,*[5] *Zechariah,*[4] *William,*[3] *William,*[2] *Zechariah*[1]), brother of the preceding; born in South Woburn, now Winchester, Feb. 2, 1783; m. LYDIA WYMAN, daughter of Daniel Wyman, of that locality, which is known as the "west side" of Winchester, formerly in Woburn. This Daniel Wyman was brother of Seth Wyman, mentioned on page 53.

He was named Joseph Brown, at the request of Capt. Joseph Brown, whose wife was Ruth Richardson, sister of Susanna Richardson, his mother. Capt. Brown was a special friend of the family. He lived in the last house but one in Woburn, on the great road to

Boston, in the midst of the Symmes family. His house stood on the lot which I now own and occupy in Winchester. He had no children, and he made Joseph B. Symmes, and a young woman who lived with him, his heirs.

Joseph B. Symmes was a farmer. He died March 22, 1850. His widow Lydia died Oct. 23, 1853.

His children were :

285. LYDIA WYMAN,[7] b. Feb. 8, 1812 ; m. Oct. 8, 1835, Jefferson Ford. He was a master of vessels trading to foreign ports. He was also a sailing-master in the U. S. Navy, in the war of the Rebellion, and died at Newbern, N. C., June 18, 1864. Children :

    286. *Caroline* (Ford), b. Dec. 16, 1837 ; m. William H. Gunnison, of Baltimore, now a clerk in the Treasury Department at Washington.

    287. *Joseph G.* (Ford), b. May 15, 1840 ; d. Oct. 23, 1850.

    288. *Sarah* (Ford), b. July 23, 1843 ; m. Charles Fitch Lunt, b. in Newburyport, July 21, 1843, now a salesman in Winslow & Myrick's store, State-Street Block, Boston.

289. JOSEPH,[7] b. Jan. 30, 1815 ; m. Hannah Wyman, sister of Joseph Wyman, of West Cambridge, now Arlington, the husband of his cousin Jerusha R. Symmes,[7] daughter of Zechariah[6] [282]. He lives in Winchester ; is engaged in the shoe business. His wife Hannah died March 23, 1871. No children.

290. GARDNER,[7] b. Oct. 18, 1816 ; m. Nov. 19, 1843, Adeline Matilda Hutchinson, of Woburn, b. in Charlestown, Dec. 17, 1821. She was dau. of Thomas and Betsey (Homer) Hutchinson. They resided in Woburn and Winchester till 1860 ; since that time mostly in Brooklyn, N. Y. While living in Winchester, he was much occupied with buying and selling real estate, building houses, and constructing public roads. He held the offices of selectman and assessor of the town several years. He built many houses in Winchester, laid out and constructed several streets, and benefited the town more than himself. He built and formerly occupied the house now occupied by the compiler. He lives in Brooklyn, but his business is with engines and machinery, in Water Street, New York. His children have been :

    291. *Gardner,*[8] b. Sept. 18, 1841 ; d. Dec. 25, 1850.

    292. *Adeline Matilda,*[8] b. Aug. 27, 1847 ; m. Edward J. Dickinson, of Brooklyn, N. Y., Oct. 12, 1869.

    293. *Lydia Gardner,*[8] b. Jan. 29, 1852 ; d. Aug. 24, 1853.

    294. *William Joseph,*[8] b. June 1, 1854.

    295. *Carrie Homer,*[8] b. April 6, 1857.

296. BETSEY CHICKERING,[7] b. April 15, 1823 ; unmarried. This name was given to her out of respect to Mrs. Betsey, wife of Rev. Joseph Chickering, pastor of the church in Woburn, then embracing most of what is now Winchester, from March, 1804, to Sept. 1821. He was afterwards settled in Phillipston, where he died Jan. 27, 1844, aged 64. Miss Betsey C. Symmes has

been a great sufferer from bodily infirmity, which she has borne with exemplary fortitude and patience. She possesses much energy of character. She resides with her sister in Winchester, the nearest neighbor of the compiler.

164.

JOHN SYMMES[6] (*Samuel,*[5] *Zechariah,*[4] *William,*[3] *William,*[2] *Zechariah*[1]), brother of the preceding; born in South Woburn, now Winchester, May 19, 1786; m. first, July 25, 1816, ABIGAIL GREEN, of Boston, b. Feb. 10, 1796. She died in Winchester, then South Woburn, Nov. 8, 1834 [Gravestone; 1835, Family Record]. He m. second, June 2, 1836, SOPHIA SPAULDING, of Lowell, b. June 22, 1792.

He was a trader in West India goods, flour, &c. He was in business one year in Fredericksburg, Va., and was during many years a merchant on the T wharf, in Boston, part of the time as partner with Daniel Cummings, part of the time with Charles Eaton, under the firm of Symmes & Eaton. He resided in South Woburn, and built a house there in 1832, or about that time. He died in Sept. 1863, aged 77. His widow Sophia died June, 1867, aged 75.

His children, all by his first wife, were:

297. ELIZA,[7] b. July 13, 1817; died at sea, on the passage homeward from Fredericksburg, Aug. 5, 1818.
+298. JOHN.[7] b. Dec. 14, 1819; m. first, Almira Stoddard; m. second, Mary Kendall Carter; m. third, Emily Carter.
+299. WILLIAM BITTLE.[7] b. June 13, 1822; m. Anna Hill.
300. DANIEL CUMMINGS,[7] b. July 3, 1827; d. in Boston, Nov. 13, 1829.

165.

NANCY SYMMES[6] (*Samuel,*[5] *Zechariah,*[4] *William,*[3] *William,*[2] *Zechariah*[1]), sister of the preceding; born in South Woburn, now Winchester, April 19, 1788; married, March 28, 1811, JAMES HILL, eldest son of James Hill, of Stoneham. He was brother of the late John Hill and the present Luther Hill, of that place.

Their children were:

301. NANCY ~~Symmes~~ (Hill). b. Feb. 22, 1812; m. Joseph Woods, from Dunstable, now a carpenter in Winchester. Children: *
302. *James (Symmes).* 303. *Andrew* (Woods).
304. CLARIMOND (Hill), a daughter, who died in infancy.
305. JAMES (Hill), lives in Lynn.
306. OTIS (Hill), m. Maria Plympton, of Medway.
307. ROWENA MARY (Hill), b. Jan. 28, 1820; unmarried; lives with her sister, Mrs. Woods.

308. PAULINA (Hill), d. in infancy.
309. WARD (Hill), d. in infancy.
310. L____ (Hill), m. Abner Hayford, of Swampscot, and is still living there. *Children : Marie, Frances [?] Hayford, Annie Rebecca J..*

166. *Abner Wendell* ..

STEPHEN SYMMES[6] (*Samuel,*[5] *Zechariah,*[4] *William,*[3] *William,*[2] *Zechariah*[1]), brother of the preceding; born in South Woburn, now Winchester, May 19, 1790; married (published Oct. 7, 1815) PRISCILLA REED, born in a part of Charlestown which is now included in the town of Arlington.

He is a farmer and lives in Arlington.

Their children were:

311. STEPHEN.[7] m. Catharine Pollard, of Bolton.
312. HARRIET PRISCILLA.[7] m. Jan. 5, 1843, Josiah Locke, son of Asa and Lucy (Wyman) Locke, of a part of Woburn which is now included in Winchester. Lucy Wyman was dau. of Daniel Wyman, mentioned under [163]. Her mother, Hannah Wright, was cousin to Pamelia Richardson, wife of Dea. John Symmes [185].
313. LOUISA,[7] died at the age of 18.
314. SARAH,[7] unmarried; lives with her father.

167.

HORATIO SYMMES[6] (*Samuel,*[5] *Zechariah,*[4] *William,*[3] *William,*[2] *Zechariah*[1]), brother of the six preceding heads of families, and youngest son of Samuel[5] and Susanna (Richardson) Symmes; born in South Woburn, now Winchester, Nov. 8, 1795; married, Nov. 11, 1819, CHARLOTTE JOHNSON, born in Lexington, July 7, 1798, daughter of Munson and Betsey (Monroe) Johnson, of Lexington, afterwards of Woburn.

He was by trade a shoemaker, and is now a *stiffener*, or maker of the stiffening part of shoes. He and his wife are still living in Winchester, in the house where he was born, and but a few rods from the spot where his grandfather Zechariah Symmes lived. He and his wife were converted in the great revival in Woburn, in 1827, when two hundred and twelve were admitted to the church by profession, and this couple among them; and they have ever since remained in covenant with God and his people.

Their children have been:

316. CHARLOTTE,[7] b. April, 1822; d. at 2 years old.
317. HORATIO,[7] b. Aug. 29, 1824; m. Rhoda Fowle, dau. of Luke Fowle, of Woburn.
318. HENRY,[7] d. at two or three years old.

11

319. HENRY WILLIAM,[7] b. Dec. 29, 1829; m. Harriet Fogg, of Harrison, Me.

320. CHARLOTTE ELIZABETH,[7] b. Jan. 30, 1833; umm.; lives with her parents.

321. SAMUEL JOHNSON,[7] b. Sept. 30, 1838; m. Eunice Fanny Forrester, of Lynnfield. They have no children.

The three sons of this family now living, reside near their father in Winchester. Stability is a marked characteristic of the Symmes family. The farm of their ancestors, William,[3] William[2] and Zechariah,[1] is but a stone's throw from their present residence.

168.

MARY SYMMES[6] (*William,[5] Zechariah,[4] William,[3] William,[2] Zechariah[1]*), only child of William[5] and Mary (Mallet) Symmes; born in South Woburn, now Winchester, Oct. 12, 1785; married, Nov. 10, 1807, Rev. JACOB COGGIN, born in Woburn, Nov. 5, 1781,* son of Jacob Coggin of that place, whose wife was a daughter of Deacon David Blanchard, of Burlington.

Jacob Coggin, the father, was a native of Woburn, descended from an early settler of that place, whose name, as given on the Town Records, is John *Craggen*. This ancestor married Sarah Dawes, Nov. 4, 1661. Mr. Jacob Coggin grad. H. C. 1763; was a school teacher by profession; taught in Woburn and elsewhere, and occasionally preached.

Rev. Jacob Coggin, the husband of Mary Symmes, grad. H. C. 1803; studied divinity with his pastor, Rev. Joseph Chickering, of Woburn; was ordained pastor of the Congregational Church in Tewksbury, Oct. 22, 1806, and continued in that relation till his death, on the afternoon of Tuesday, Dec. 12, 1854, aged 73. The colleague of his later years, Rev. Richard Tolman, in the funeral discourse, characterizes him as more earnest than brilliant, graceful rather than imposing, sensitive rather than profound; as winning the affection rather than the admiration of his hearers; as having more of the caution of Melancthon than the daring of Luther; and in his sermons dealing with the practical rather than the doctrinal. His disposition was frank, his sympathies lively, his attachments strong. During the forty-eight years of his pastorate, he retained a strong hold on the affections of his flock.

He represented the town for two successive years in the State legislature; also in the convention called to revise the State constitution in 1853. He was one of the Presidential Electors in 1852; one of the three inspectors of the State Almshouse in Tewksbury from the beginning; and chaplain of that institution till his death.

Mrs. Coggin died in Tewksbury, Sept. 18, 1856, aged 71.

---

* This date is derived from the Am. Quar. Reg., vol. xi. 379, and purports to have been furnished by Mr. Coggin himself. But Mr. Tolman, in the discourse referred to in the text, says Mr. Coggin was born Sept. 5, 1781.

The children of Rev. JACOB and MARY (SYMMES) COGGIN were:

322. ABIGAIL (Coggin), b. Sept. 28, 1808; m. C. F. Blanchard, a merchant of Charlestown. She died in 1838.

323. MARY (Coggin), b. Sept. 10, 1810; m. C. F. Blanchard, as his second wife. She is now a widow, residing in Lowell.

324. JACOB (Coggin), b. Aug. 31, 1811; m. first, Harriet P. Kittredge; m. second, Mary A. Wilkins. He is now a widower; is engaged in mercantile business in Lowell, but resides in the old paternal mansion in Tewksbury.

325. WILLIAM SYMMES (Coggin), b. Nov. 27, 1812; m. Mary Clark, Aug. 5, 1840. She was daughter of Dea. Oliver and Abigail (Richardson) Clark, of Tewksbury. Abigail, her mother, was the youngest daughter of Dea. Jeduthun and Mary (Wright) Richardson, of South Woburn, now Winchester. Mr. Coggin grad. Dart. Coll. 1834; studied divinity at Andover Theological Seminary, graduating in 1837; was ordained pastor of the Congregational Church in Boxford, Mass., May 9, 1838. He continued pastor there till May, 1868, a period of thirty years. He then, on account of ill health, asked and received a dismission. Since that time he has preached somewhere nearly every Sabbath. This year, 1872, he has been supplying the pulpit at Byfield. His ministry has been peaceful, successful and happy. In the year 1858, his parish shared in the remarkable revival of that year, and fifty-seven were added to the church. He has always borne the character of a discreet, faithful, useful minister.

326. DAVID (Coggin), b. Sept. 14, 1816; m. Ellen Kidder, dau. of Dr. Samuel Kidder, of Charlestown, Sept. 1842. He grad. Dart. Coll. 1836; was teacher and chaplain in the House of Refuge for Juvenile Offenders, at South Boston, two years, till 1838; pursued theological studies at Andover Seminary till 1841; was ordained pastor of the Congregational Church, Westhampton, Mass., May 11, 1842, and closed a pleasant and successful ministry there of ten years, by his death, April 28, 1852.

327. MARTHA (Coggin), b. Sept. 27, 1817; m. William Rogers, Esq., of Tewksbury. She is now a widow, residing in Lowell.

328. JAMES (Coggin), b. Dec. 1823; d. in 1825.

329. ELLEN (Coggin), b. May 28, 1825; m. Samuel Kidder, Jr., of Lowell. She died May 18, 1856.

174.

MARTHA SYMMES[6] (*Timothy*,[5] *Timothy*,[4] *William*,[3] *William*,[2] *Zechariah*[1]), daughter of Timothy[5] and Martha (Wyman) Symmes; born in Medford, Dec. 30, 1806; married, April 16, 1828, WILLIAM WYMAN, born in the "west side" of Woburn, now included in Winchester, May 26, 1803, son of Daniel and Hannah (Wright) Wyman, of that locality. This Daniel Wyman was a brother of Seth Wyman, grandfather to the aforesaid Martha Symmes.

William Wyman was by trade a currier. He followed this business till his health failed, then took up the business of farming. He died March 2, 1862. His widow now resides with Sylvester G.

Pierce, son of Rev. Sylvester G. Pierce, formerly pastor at Dracut, who died 1839. The younger Sylvester is son of Mr. Wyman's sister Clarimond Wyman. [See Book of the Lockes, p. 153.]

WILLIAM and MARTHA (SYMMES) WYMAN had only one child:

330. MARTHA RUTH (Wyman), b. 1833; d. July 30, 1850.

182.

GEORGE WASHINGTON SYMMES[6] (*Daniel,*[5] *Timothy,*[4] *William,*[3] *William,*[2] *Zechariah*[1]), son of Daniel and Sophia (Emerson) Symmes, of Medford; married ——.

He occupied the homestead in Medford, and was a blacksmith.

His children were:

331. LOUISA,[7] m. Charles L. Newcomb, of Boston.
332. MARY JANE.[7]
333. ABBY.[7]
334. ELLA.[7]
335. HEPHZIBAH,[7] b. about 1857.
336. CHARLES.[7]

Though I have tried, I have not been able to obtain a better record of this family.

185.

DEA. JOHN SYMMES[6] (*John,*[5] *John,*[4] *William,*[3] *William,*[2] *Zechariah*[1]), eldest son of Capt. John[5] and Elizabeth (Wright) Symmes; born in the north part of Medford, a locality now included in the town of Winchester, Jan. 27, 1781; married, June 28, 1804, PAMELIA RICHARDSON, born July 13, 1782, daughter of Dea. Jeduthun Richardson, of South Woburn, now Winchester, by his wife Mary Wright, born Jan. 29, 1741, eldest daughter of Dea. John and Mary (Locke) Wright, of Woburn.

He resided at "Symmes's Corner," in a house built by himself, in that part of Medford, which, together with South Woburn and part of West Cambridge, was incorporated as the town of Winchester. He was a good man, just and upright, and useful in his day. In addition to the cultivation of a valuable farm, part of which he inherited from his early ancestors, he carried on, during many years, the business of a wheelwright, as his father had done before him. He settled many estates of deceased persons, and held at different times most of the offices of trust in the town and parish. He attended public worship in Medford, and was a staunch supporter of civil and religious order. He was deacon of the first Congregational Church in that town from about the year 1818 till his death, which occurred Feb. 15, 1860, at the age of 79. He left a valuable estate to his children. His wife Pamelia died Dec. 1, 1845, aged 63 years and 4 months.

Their children were:

337. John Albert,[7] b. March 30, 1805; d. May 30, 1808.
338. Pamelia,[7] b. Feb. 3, 1807; m. Horatio A. Smith, May 28, 1852.
339. Mary Wright,[7] b. Oct. 26, 1809; unmarried. A lady of cultivated mind, of refined taste and extensive information; residing
in the paternal mansion. The readers of this volume are largely
indebted to her for the facts it contains relative to the Symmes
Family of Winchester. Indeed, had it not been for her, this book
probably had not been undertaken.
+340. John Albert,[7] b. Nov. 3, 1812; m. Lydia M. Smith.
+341. Charles Carey,[7] b. Nov. 15, 1814; m. Lydia F. Clark.
+342. Henry Richardson,[7] b. April 13, 1818; m. Abigail Symmes.
+343. Luther Richardson,[7] b. March 21, 1822; m. Elizabeth A. Ayer.

186.

THOMAS SYMMES[6] (*John,*[5] *John,*[4] *William,*[3] *William,*[2] *Zechariah*[1]), brother of the preceding, and second son of John and Elizabeth (Wright) Symmes; born in the north part of Medford, a locality
now belonging to Winchester, March 30, 1783; married Sarah
Lloyd Wait, daughter of Nathan Wait, of Medford.

He lived in Medford; was a farmer, and was killed in the woods
by the irregular action—what is called *slewing*—of a sled heavily
laden with fire-wood. This took place in the winter of 1811–12.

His children were:

344. Sarah Jane,[7] b. Jan. 1807; m. John Hunt, of Roxbury, as his
second wife.
345. Eliza Ann,[7] b. Aug. 1808; m. Henry Withington, of Medford.
+346. Thomas Russell,[7] b. 1812; m. Harriet Eady.

187.

ABIGAIL SYMMES[6] (*John,*[5] *John,*[4] *William,*[3] *William,*[2] *Zechariah*[1]), sister of the preceding, and daughter of Capt. John and Elizabeth (Wright) Symmes; born Feb. 11, 1785; married, May 23,
1813, Elias Tufts, born Jan. 9, 1787.

They lived in Medford. Mrs. Abigail Tufts, wife of Elias Tufts,
died in Medford, Aug. 13, 1863, aged 78 years and 6 months. Elias
Tufts died there July 18, 1868, aged 83 years and 5 months.

Their children were:

+347. Alfred (Tufts), b. July 8, 1818; m. Caroline M. Wright.
+348. Larkin Turner (Tufts), b. Oct. 28, 1821; m. Frances P. Mc-
Farland.

188.

ELIZABETH SYMMES⁶ (*John,⁵ John,⁴ William,³ William,² Zecha-riah¹*), sister of the preceding; born April 10, 1787; married ABEL STOWELL, 1814, son of Abel Stowell, of Worcester, a noted clock-maker.

His home, after marriage, was in Charlestown, where he carried on the business of a jeweller. He purchased of John L. Sullivan, for four thousand dollars, the mill privilege on the Aberjona River, in the present town of Winchester, which had, from the settlement of the country till 1823, been, partly at least, in the possession and occupancy of the Symmes Family. He had on this stream an iron-foundry. After some years, he sold it to Robert Bacon, hatter, of Boston, and it is now in the possession of Mr. Bacon's children.

Mr. and Mrs. Stowell are both deceased.

Their children were:

349. ELIZA (Stowell), b. Jan. 1815; unmarried.
350. ABEL (Stowell), b. Jan. 1819; lives in Baltimore; is a jeweller.
351. ALEXANDER (Stowell), b. Nov. 29, 1821; m. first, Esther Adams, of Billerica; m. second, Fannie Davis, of Vermont. He is a jeweller, at 16 Winter Street, Boston.
352. CAROLINE (Stowell), b. June, 1823; m. Charles Rogers, of Charles-town, Mass., and has two children.
353. EMILY (Stowell), b. Aug. 1825; unmarried; lives with her sister on Tremont Street, Boston.
354. ABBY MARIA (Stowell), b. Sept. 1829; m. John G. Hunt, of Rox-bury. They have two children. He was son of John Hunt [341], by the first wife.

189.

MARSHALL SYMMES⁶ (*John,⁵ John,⁴ William,³ William,² Zecha-riah¹*), brother of the preceding, and fifth child of Capt. John⁵ and Elizabeth Symmes; born in what was then the north part of Med-ford, now part of Winchester, July 30, 1789; married, Jan. 26, 1818, LEPHE STOWELL, born 1791, sister of Abel Stowell, the husband of her sister Elizabeth. (See preceding paragraph.) Her name, judg-ing from the name she gave to her eldest daughter, may have been RELIEF.

He pursued the business of a blacksmith at "Symmes's Corner," in what is now Winchester. He is still living in Winchester, Nov., 1872, and able to be about. His wife, Relief, died Nov. 23, 1848, aged 57.

It is a remarkable fact that he and the children of his brother Ed-mund still own fifty or sixty acres of the farm in the present town of Winchester, which was given to their ancestor, Rev. ZECHARIAH SYMMES, by the town of Charlestown, two hundred and thirty years ago. It has never gone out of the Symmes family. When transferred from one person to another, it has been by the Probate Court.

Their children were:

+355. MARSHALL,[7] b. Oct. 27, 1818; m. Abbie Stowell.
356. ELIZABETH RELIEF,[7] b. Sept. 28, 1820; d. Dec. 1, 1820.
357. HARRIET STOWELL,[7] b. Nov. 15, 1821; unmarried; resides with her father.
+358. ALEXANDER STOWELL,[7] b. Dec. 13, 1823; m. Sarah Jane Livermore.
359. PHILEMON WRIGHT,[7] b. Feb. 12, 1826; m. Eliza P. Stowell, dau. of Samuel Stowell, of Worcester. Samuel was a cousin of Abel Stowell, mentioned above. Mr. Symmes died Jan. 8, 1861. His wife Eliza died Oct. 8, 1856. No child.
+360. ELLEN LOUISA,[7] b. May 16, 1828; m. Oliver L. Wellington.
+361. CHARLES THOMAS,[7] b. March 9, 1832; m. Abby Elizabeth Hunt.

191.

EBENEZER SYMMES[6] (*John,*[5] *John,*[4] *William,*[3] *William,*[2] *Zachariah*[1]) brother of the preceding; born at "Symmes's Corner," in the present town of Winchester, Aug. 17, 1793; married, first, HANNAH DAVIS, of Wilmington, Mass., sister of the wife of Joseph Bond, of that town, the noted baker of excellent crackers. He married, second, LANISSA ———.

Mr. Symmes carried on the baking business in Hanover, N. H., as many who were students at Dartmouth College in 1825 and the following years may remember. He removed to Concord, and there had a wholesale flour store. In 1867, he removed to Medford, where he now lives on an ample income.

His children, by his first wife, were:

362. EBENEZER,[7] entered the U. S. Navy as midshipman many years ago. What has become of him we have not learned.
363. HANNAH MARIA,[7] m. Sullivan Fay, of Southboro', Mass. She is a widow, and resides with her father in Medford. She had a daughter who died.

By second wife:

364. MARY LAMSON.[7]

192.

EDMUND SYMMES[6] (*John,*[5] *John,*[4] *William,*[3] *William,*[2] *Zachariah*[1]), brother of the preceding; born at "Symmes's Corner," then in Medford, now in Winchester, Aug. 14, 1795; married, Nov. 15, 1820, ELIZABETH ANN SMITH, born Nov. 27, 1803, daughter of Elijah and Lydia Smith, of Medford.

He was a farmer: lived and died on the spot where he was born.* He died Sept. 6, 1843. The house, built by his father about 1783, was consumed by fire, Aug. 17, 1864.

His children were:

365. EDMUND AUGUSTUS,[7] b. March 2, 1822.
366. ELIZABETH ANN,[7] b. May 12, 1824; m. Hosea Dunbar, of Winchester, Jan. 3, 1847. He is a master mason. Children:
 367. *Octavia Smith* (Dunbar), b. Oct. 22, 1847; m. Thomas E. Holway, Nov. 24, 1870.
 368. *Lorenzo Atwood* (Dunbar), b. Dec. 25, 1849.
 369. *Elen Elizabeth* (Dunbar), b. Jan. 24, 1852.
 370. *Minnie Gertrude* (Dunbar), b. Jan. 20, 1856.
371. LORENZO,[7] b. Aug. 28, 1826; d. July 16, 1845.
372. LYDIA MARIA,[7] b. April 15, 1831; m. Thomas Prentiss Ayer, Dec. 12, 1854. He is a merchant in Boston, on Commercial Street, in company with Thomas Dennie Quincy, under the firm of Thomas D. Quincy & Co. He resides at "Symmes's Corner," in Winchester. One child:
 373. *Henry Prentiss* (Ayer), b. March 30, 1859.
374. THEODORE,[7] b. Aug. 11, 1835; m. Josephine G. Teel, Sept. 7, 1870. They live at "Symmes's Corner." He is engaged in business at 235 Cambridge Street, Boston.
375. SARAH SMITH,[7] b. May 11, 1840; m. Jacob Clark Stanton, Jr., a merchant in Winchester.

193.

CHARLES SYMMES[6] (*John,[5] John,[4] William,[3] William,[2] Zechariah[1]*), brother of the preceding, and youngest child of Capt. John[5] and Elizabeth (Wright) Symmes, of North Medford, now in Winchester; born April 4, 1798; married HANNAH RICKER, April 6, 1824.

In his youth, he was in the counting room of Mr. Newhall, ship chandler, in Boston. Afterwards settled in Aylmer, Canada East, on the Ottawa River, in the neighborhood of his mother's brothers.

The children of CHARLES and HANNAH (RICKER) SYMMES:

376. ABIGAIL,[7] b. Jan. 8, 1826.
377. ELIZABETH,[7] b. Nov. 17, 1829; m. Peter Aylen, July 1, 1852. Children:
 378. *Charles P.* (Aylen), b. Oct. 17, 1854.
 379. *John* (Aylen), b. May 23, 1856.
 380. *Henry* (Aylen), b. May 22, 1858.
 381. *Peter* (Aylen), b. Sept. 4, 1860.
382. SARAH JANE,[7] b. Oct. 16, 1831; m. Richard W. Cruice, Feb. 27, 1851. Children:

---

* The Symmes family are not given to change.

383. *Clara O.* (Cruice), b. Dec. 14, 1851; m. Frederick White, Dec. 5, 1871. One child:
> 384. Edith W. (White), b. Oct. 5, 1872.

384. *Jane* (Cruice), b. May 27, 1853.

+386. John Thomas,[7] } twins, born { m. Harriet Grimes.
+387. Thomas John,[7] } Jan. 26, 1856; { m. Mary Weymouth.

388. Edmund,[7] b. Feb. 6, 1858.
389. Tiberius Wright,[7] b. May 4, 1812.

201.

MARIA SYMMES[6] (*John Cleves,[5] Timothy,[4] Timothy,[3] William,[2] Zechariah[1]*), elder daughter of Hon. John Cleves Symmes,[5] by his first wife, Anna; born on Long Island about 1762; married, about 1790, Major Peyton Short, a wealthy farmer of Kentucky.

Little is known of either the husband or the wife. They lived in Lexington, Kentucky.* It is supposed that she died about 1820.

Their children were:

+390. John Cleves (Short), m. first, Betsey B. Harrison; m. second, Mrs. Mitchell, a widow, about 1850.
+391. Charles W. (Short), b. about 1795; m. ————.
+392. Anna Maria (Short), b. 1803; m. Dr. Benjamin Dudley.

204.

ANNA SYMMES[6] (*John Cleves,[5] Timothy,[4] Timothy,[3] William,[2] Zechariah[1]*), sister of the preceding, and younger daughter of Hon. John Cleves Symmes; born at Flatbrook, New Jersey, July 25, 1775; married, at her father's residence, North Bend, in what is now the State of Ohio, Nov. 22, 1795, William Henry Harrison.

Her father, in her earlier years, called her Nancy. Her mother died when she was about a year old. In her fourth year she was placed in the care of her mother's parents, Mr. and Mrs. Daniel Tuthill, at Southold, Long Island. The incidents of this journey she well remembered. The city of New York was then occupied by the British Army, and her father, though a Colonel in the American service, contrived, by assuming the British uniform, to pass the hostile lines, with his young charge, without suspicion. Her grandmother was a godly woman, whose soul had been stirred to its inmost depths by the preaching of Whitefield. From her lips Anna Symmes received her first religious instruction, which produced impressions lasting as her life. She early acquired a relish for religious reading, and committed to memory large portions of the Bible, and many

---

* Her father, in a letter to his brother-in-law, Col. James Henry, of Somerset Co., N. J., dated North Bend, May 22, 1791, says : "Poor dear Maria, she seems to be lost to us all, and buried at Lexington in a circle of strangers. She would not come here with me, nor is she willing yet to come; the fear of Indians deters her. And yet there is not the least danger. As to her health it is very poor. She is very infirm and weakly. She trembles for my safety, lest the Indians should kill me."

hymns, which she delighted to repeat after eighty years had passed away.

In early life, she enjoyed the advantages of a female school at Easthampton, L. I.,* and afterwards was a pupil of Mrs. Isabella Graham, and an inmate of her family. For that excellent woman she always cherished the highest regard.

In the autumn of 1794, her father having married again, she left her eastern home, in company with her father and step-mother; but the journey at that time was made with difficulty, and the party did not reach North Bend, her father's home, till the morning of the first of January, 1795. That region was then regarded as the *Ultima Thule* of civilization. Soon after, she paid a visit to her elder sister, the wife of Major Short, near Lexington, Kentucky; and there she first met with her future husband, Capt. Harrison, who was then in command at Fort Washington, Cincinnati. Her home was with him at that place till 1801, when, on his appointment as the first governor of Indiana Territory, then extending to the Mississippi River, she accompanied him to Vincennes, where she resided till the commencement of the war of 1812. She then returned to Cincinnati, and, after the war, removed with her family to North Bend.

She united with the First Presbyterian Church in Cincinnati, but transferred her connection to the church at Cleves, near North Bend, on its organization, and continued a member of it till her death. She could never tell the precise time of her conversion; the new life must have begun in her very early youth. She could not remember a time when she was not penitent for sin, or when she did not prefer the service of Christ to all the pleasures of the world. Her only reliance for acceptance with God, was the atoning merit of his Son, the Lord Jesus Christ.

Her influence was most happy on all who came within its reach. During the active Presidential canvass of 1840, a company of politicians from Cincinnati visited, one Sabbath day, the residence of General Harrison at North Bend. The General met them at some place near by, and extending his hand, courteously said, " Gentlemen, I should be most happy to welcome you on any other day, but if I had no regard for religion myself, I have too much respect for the religion of my wife to encourage the violation of the Christian Sabbath."†

Mrs. Harrison was not indifferent to political interests, and few were better informed on public affairs than herself. But her real life was in a higher sphere. The spirit of Christ from childhood reigned in her heart. Her chief joy was humbly to follow the Re-

---

* Both Southold and Easthampton were settled from Connecticut about 1650, and have always been pervaded by a New-England influence.

† This incident, so honorable both to Gen. Harrison and his wife, is reported by a gentleman who was present, and who furnished the biographical sketch of Mrs. Harrison which has been used.

deemer. Her love embraced all mankind. To relieve want, to succor the distressed, gave her unspeakable joy. A writer sums up her character thus:—

"She is distinguished for benevolence and piety. All who know her view her with esteem and affection. Her whole course through life, in all its relations, has been characterized by those qualifications that compose the idea of an accomplished woman."

She retained her intellectual and physical powers almost to the last, and at the age of eighty-eight was an agreeable companion both to young and old. She calmly fell asleep in Jesus, at Longuevue, the residence of her son, Hon. John S. Harrison, February 25, 1864, in her 89th year. [Cincinnati Presbyter, May 11, 1864.]

We must not omit to sketch the principal events in the life of her noble husband.

WILLIAM HENRY HARRISON was born in the County of Berkeley, in Virginia, in the year 1775. His father, Benjamin Harrison, was one of the signers of the Declaration of Independence. He graduated at Hampden Sydney College, in that State, and studied medicine; but, preferring a military life, entered the Army of the United States in 1791, with an ensign's commission, at the early age of sixteen. He soon became a lieutenant, and in 1794, as captain, had command of Fort Washington, on the ground now occupied by the city of Cincinnati. In 1797, he was appointed secretary of the Territory Northwest of the River Ohio, and, in 1799, was its first delegate to Congress. In 1801, he was appointed Governor of the newly formed Territory of Indiana, which office he held for thirteen years, during which time he resided at Vincennes.

In 1811, he defeated the Indians at the battle of Tippecanoe, receiving a bullet through his stock, without further injury. After the surrender of Gen. Hull, in 1812, he rose to the rank of Major General in the U. S. Army. In 1813, after Perry's victory on Lake Erie, he invaded Canada, and gained the battle of the Thames. A misunderstanding arising between him and Gen. Armstrong, Secretary of War, he in 1814 resigned his commission, and retired from the army, after a connection with it of nearly twenty-four years.

From this time his course was wholly in civil life. Not long after, he laid out the village of Cleves, Ohio, just back of the hills in the vicinity of North Bend, giving it that name in honor of his father-in-law, John Cleves Symmes. In 1816, he was elected to the U. S. House of Representatives from Ohio; in 1819, to the Senate of that State; and, in 1824, to the United States Senate.

In 1828, he was appointed minister of the United States to the Republic of Colombia, S. A., which position he held but one year. From 1829 to 1834, he quietly lived on his farm at North Bend. From 1834 to 1840, he served as prothonotary of the court of Hamilton county, Ohio, in which North Bend is situated.

On the 4th of March, 1841, he was inaugurated PRESIDENT OF

THE UNITED STATES, to which great office he had been elected, after a most animated canvass, by an overwhelming majority. The enthusiasm of his supporters has never been exceeded in this country. But amid the general rejoicing consequent on his election, he suddenly died just one month after his inauguration.

The children of WILLIAM HENRY and ANNA (SYMMES) HARRISON were :

393. BETSEY BASSETT (Harrison), b. 1796 ; m. her cousin, John Cleves Short. She died in 1848. He was a lawyer and farmer at North Bend.

+394. JOHN CLEVES SYMMES (Harrison), b. 1798 ; m. Clarissa Pike.

395. LUCY SYMMES (Harrison), b. 1800 ; m. D. K. Este, of Cincinnati, in 1819. He was a lawyer and judge. She d. 1826.

396. Their dau. *Lucy Ann* (Este) m. —— Reynolds, of Baltimore.

+397. WILLIAM HENRY (Harrison), b. 1802 ; m. Jane Irwin.

+398. JOHN SCOTT (Harrison), b. 1804 ; m. first, Lucretia K. Johnson ; m. second, Elizabeth Irwin.

+399. BENJAMIN (Harrison), b. 1806 ; m. first, —— Bonner ; m. second, —— Raney.

+400. MARY SYMMES (Harrison), b. 1808 ; m. J. F. H. Thornton.

+401. CARTER BASSETT (Harrison), b. 1811 ; m. Mary Sutherland.

+402. ANNA TUTHILL (Harrison), b. 1813 ; m. William H. H. Taylor.

403. JAMES FINDLEY (Harrison), b. 1818 ; d. in infancy.

205.

CELADON SYMMES[6] (*Timothy,[5] Timothy,[4] Timothy,[3] William,[2] Zechariah[1]*), eldest son of Timothy and Abigail (Tuthill) Symmes ; born in Sussex Co., N. J., May 30, 1770 ; m. Oct. 14, 1794, PHEBE RANDOLPH, said to be a cousin of the famous John Randolph of Roanoke, Va.*

He went, probably in the company led by John Cleves Symmes, in 1789, to the Territory Northwest of the River Ohio, and there took up his abode for life. Here, in Cincinnati, he bought a small lot of land for eight dollars ; built a shop eight by ten feet, and worked one year at his trade, that of a silversmith, which he had learned of his father. He then sold his lot and shop for seventeen dollars. It may well be supposed that in a new country, like that around Cincinnati in 1789, little encouragement could be found for such a business.

In 1790 he went to North Bend, and during four years took the oversight of the farm of his uncle, Hon. John Cleves Symmes. He also acted as one of the guard whose duty was to protect from the Indians the surveyors who were laying out his uncle's lands. It was then a time of war, and the Indians were troublesome.

---

* I recollect, from my early days, a pastoral, beginning,

  "Young Celadon and his Amelia were a blameless pair."

There seems to have been no price stipulated for his services; only Judge Symmes said to his nephew, "You shall never be the worse for it." The uncle afterwards gave him a section of land in Butler County, estimated to be worth eight hundred dollars, of which three hundred dollars might be considered as a present.

During his residence at North Bend he was often in danger from the savages. Once he and his brother Daniel, both being unarmed, were followed several miles by two Indians, one of whom proposed to kill them. He was prevented by the other, who maintained that they were too good to be killed.

He was a man of daring courage. At a certain time his dogs were fighting with a wounded panther, and the beast seemed to be getting the advantage. Mr. Symmes rushed into the fray, seized the animal by the fore paw and stabbed it to the heart, thus ending the conflict.

Hon. John C. Symmes, his uncle, often speaks of him with interest in his letters. In a letter to Col. Henry, of New Jersey, now before me, dated Cincinnati, Oct. 8, 1803, he says: "Celadon is very unwell. He hurt himself in the harvest field [last summer] and has never got over it. He and his brother William were both elected justices of the peace in one day by the body of the people; and the next week after, Celadon was elected captain of a company of militia; and the week following, the Governor [Dr. Tiffin, of Chilicothe] sent him a commission appointing him commissioner for leasing," &c. In a letter dated Cincinnati, Feb. 10, 1805, he calls his nephew "Major Celadon."[*]

He served several terms (seven years in all) as judge of the Court of Common Pleas of Butler County. He owned a section of land three miles south of Hamilton, Ohio, which was afterwards known as "Symmes's Corner." On the southern side of his farm he laid off two acres as a public burying-ground, which received the designation, "The Symmes Cemetery." There he was buried, dying July 11, 1837, aged 67 years, 1 mo. 11 days. [Family Record.]

Their children were:

404. WILLIAM CLEVES,[7] } twins, } d. in infancy.
405. A daughter,[7] } b. 1795; }
+406. DANIEL TUTHILL,[7] b. Nov. 5, 1798; m. Lucinda Gaston.
407. JOHN CLEVES,[7] b. 1800; a farmer in Butler Co.; d. in 1837.
+408. BENJAMIN RANDOLPH,[7] b. 1802; m. first, Eliza Gaston; m. second, Jane Pauley.
409. A son,[7] b. 1805; d. in infancy.
+410. CELADON,[7] b. 1807; m. Catharine Blackburn.
411. NANCY H.,[7] b. 1810; d. 1814.
+412. ESTHER WOODRUFF,[7] b. 1811; m. William N. Hunter.

---

* In a letter dated Cincinnati, Nov. 5, 1810, John Cleves Symmes says: "We have great crops of all kinds of grain this year. Corn at 20 cents, wheat at only 50, delivered at the Mill; Beef and Pork $2.50 per hundred weight. We begin to hope for better times."

+413. JOSEPH RANDOLPH,[7] b. 1814; m. first, Martha J. Huston; m.
      second, Mary C. Bigham.
+414. SARAH DEBORAH,[7] b. 1817; m. first, Enoch Powers; m. second,
      Joseph Danford.

206.

DANIEL SYMMES[6] (*Timothy,*[5] *Timothy,*[4] *Timothy,*[3] *William,*[2] *Zechariah*[1]), second son of Timothy[5] and Abigail (Tuthill) Symmes; born in Sussex County, N. J., 1772; married, about 1795, ELIZABETH OLIVER.

He studied at Princeton College, and went out west with his uncle. He was clerk of the court of the Territory Northwest of the River Ohio, until that Territory was discontinued. He afterwards studied law, and practised at the bar for some years. In 1802 he was elected to the senate of Ohio, and re-elected in 1803, for two years. He presided over that body as its speaker. On the resignation of Judge Meigs, in 1804, he was appointed judge of the Supreme Court of Ohio. He was captain in the militia in 1803.

He settled in Cincinnati when it was a mere village. His house, a two-story framed building, was for a time the best in the place. After the war of 1812–15, he was employed as the attorney of some persons who claimed from the United States government a large tract of land in the present State of Mississippi.* He was successful in prosecuting the claim, and received in remuneration a square league of the land included in the claim.

In 1814 he received the appointment of Register of the U. S. Land Office, in Cincinnati, which position he held until a few months before his death, which took place May 10, 1827. In that office he was succeeded by his half-brother, Peyton Short Symmes.

After his death, his widow, an excellent christian woman, married again. But this second marriage deprived her not only of her large property, but of her domestic peace; so that she obtained a divorce. There being no law in Kentucky, where she then resided, which allowed a divorced wife to resume the name she bore previous to marriage, the legislature of that State honored her by passing a special act, permitting her to bear the name of Symmes, to which she was devotedly attached. I have before me an autograph letter of hers, dated Dayton, Ohio, May 8, 1856, in which she says that in three days more she would arrive at the age of 81.

Daniel Symmes had no issue.

207.

WILLIAM SYMMES[6] (*Timothy,*[5] *Timothy,*[4] *Timothy,*[3] *William,*[2] *Zechariah*[1]), brother of the preceding, and third son of Timothy and Abigail Symmes; born in Sussex County, N. J., 1774; married, in 1796, REBECCA RANDOLPH, a sister of his brother Celadon's wife.

---

* Does this refer to the celebrated "Yazoo claims"?

He learned the trade of silversmith of his father; but after his removal to Ohio, or rather to the Territory Northwest of the River Ohio, as it was then called, he devoted himself wholly to farming. He resided in the south part of Butler County, Ohio, near what is now known as Jones's Station, on the Cincinnati, Hamilton and Dayton Railroad.

He died in 1809, leaving the children whose names follow:

415. WILLIAM F. R.,[7] b. 1798; was a grocer in Hamilton, Ohio; died in 1839.

+416. PHEBE,[7] b. 1804; m. 1826, Barnabas Hoel.

417. ESTHER,[7] b. 1806; m. James Davis, a farmer in Butler Co., Ohio.

+418. TIMOTHY,[7] b. 1809; m. Harriet Wilmuth.

208.

CAPT. JOHN CLEVES SYMMES[6] (*Timothy,[5] Timothy,[4] Timothy,[3] William,[2] Zechariah[1]*), half-brother of the preceding, and son of Timothy[5] and Mercy (Harker) Symmes; born in Sussex County, New Jersey, Nov. 5, 1779; married at Fort Adams, Louisiana, Dec. 25, 1808, Mrs. MARIANNE LOCKWOOD, widow of Capt. Benjamin Lockwood, of the U. S. Army, who had died in that year.

In early life he received a good common English education; and then, and in after life, was particularly fond of mathematics and the natural sciences.

In the year 1802 he entered the U. S. Army with an ensign's commission. In a letter, dated Cincinnati, Oct. 8, 1803, his uncle of the same name says to his correspondent and brother-in-law, Col. Henry, "Johnny Symmes is a lieutenant in the standing troops, and is beloved by his men and respected by his officers. So much for bringing up boys as they ought to be, to keep them steady to business, without discouraging them." In 1807 he was stationed at Natchez and New Orleans. "Johnny Symmes" was commissioned as a captain of infantry, Jan. 20, 1812. He was in the battle of Bridgewater, sometimes called the battle of Lundy's Lane, on the evening of July 25, 1814, and was then senior captain in his regiment. The company under his command discharged seventy rounds of cartridges, and repelled three desperate charges of the bayonet from veterans who had driven Napoleon's troops out of the Spanish Peninsula. His regiment was almost the only one which maintained its position throughout the action. In a sortie during the siege of Fort Erie, Sept. 17, 1814, he with his command captured the enemy's battery No. 3, and with his own hand spiked their heaviest cannon, a twenty-four pounder. He was universally esteemed a brave soldier, a zealous and faithful officer.*

He left the army on the general disbandment, 1816, at the close

---

* From statements made to him by Gen. Jessup. Gen. Brown, in his official report, makes honorable mention of the bravery of Capt. Symmes in this battle.

of the war, and took up his residence at St. Louis, where he was engaged, for about three years, in furnishing supplies to the troops stationed on the Upper Mississippi. Contrary to the usual experience, he did not make this business profitable, and he left it in 1819.

Capt. Symmes has become extensively known as the author of a "Theory of Concentric Spheres and Polar Voids," which he promulgated at St. Louis in 1818, and which attracted considerable attention about the year 1824. We will here present, in as few words as possible, the substance of this theory, and the arguments by which the author attempted to sustain it. For this we are indebted to a book written by James McBride, Esq., of Hamilton, Ohio, entitled "Symmes's Theory of Concentric Spheres, demonstrating that the earth is hollow, habitable within, and widely open about the poles." On page 28 of this book we read: "According to Capt. Symmes, the earth is composed of at least five hollow concentric spheres, with spaces between each, and habitable, as well upon the concave as the convex surface. Each of these spheres is widely open about the poles.

"The north polar opening is believed to be about four thousand miles in diameter, the south six thousand; and that they incline to the plane of the equator at an angle of about twelve degrees. The highest point of the northern polar opening is near the coast of Lapland, on a meridian passing through Spitzbergen; the lowest point will be found in the Pacific Ocean, about N. latitude fifty degrees, on or near a meridian passing through the mouth of Cook's River.

"The lowest point of the southern opening will be found in the South Pacific, about latitude forty-two degrees south, and longitude one hundred and thirty degrees west. The highest point will be found in about latitude thirty-four degrees south, and longitude fifty-four degrees west."

The main arguments used in the book already referred to, in support of the position assumed in the title, are these:

First. An argument is drawn from the laws of GRAVITATION. If, as philosophers have supposed, the matter of which the earth is composed was first created in a fluid or semi-fluid state, and set rapidly revolving on its axis and in its orbit around the sun, the power of gravitation and the centrifugal force, united, would, it is argued, cause the matter to arrange itself in a series of concentric spheres. This point is discussed at length on philosophical principles, which cannot here be mentioned. Illustrations are drawn from well-established facts; e. g., if water be poured on a rapidly-revolving grindstone, instead of settling around the axis, it will form itself into a series of concentric spheres around the sides. Again, if a magnet be placed under a paper on which iron or steel filings have been poured, they will be drawn, not into a solid mass, but into concentric curves. Again, meteoric stones are not solid, but hollow.

Secondly. In all his works God never seems to use more material than is needful to accomplish the object in view. Straws, bones, some plants, even the hairs of our heads, are hollow. Why then suppose our earth to be a solid sphere, when a hollow globe would answer every purpose just as well, with a great saving of stuff?

Thirdly. Celestial appearances favor the theory suggested. The author maintains that the rings of Saturn, the belts of Jupiter, and the circles around the poles of Mars, prove these planets to be concentric spheres with polar openings; and that similar appearances are not observed on the other planets, is because their poles are never presented to our view. The spots on the sun and the cavities on the surface of the moon are holes, formed by portions of their outer crusts falling inwards. All the planets seem to be hollow spheres.

Fourthly. Terrestrial facts favor this theory; such, for example, as the following. Arctic navigators have discovered that great multitudes of rein-deer, white bears and foxes, musk oxen, ducks and geese, and vast shoals of whales, herrings and other fish, migrate southward from the regions of the north pole in the spring, and in very fine condition. In autumn they return to the northerly regions, where they propagate their species. Is it not evident, therefore, that beyond the most northern discoveries yet made, there must be a vast region, embracing both land and water, and very fertile and salubrious? Such a region as is indicated by these facts can exist only on the supposition that the earth is hollow, habitable within, and widely open about the poles; and through these polar openings these animals find entrance to and egress from the interior.

The objections and difficulties which lie in the way of this theory are met with answers and solutions which are highly ingenious, and sometimes apparently conclusive. The author of the theory was intensely desirous to have it subjected to the test of actual experiment. On the 10th of April, 1818, he issued a circular from St. Louis, asking to be furnished with an outfit of one hundred brave companions, well equipped, to set out from Siberia in autumn, with rein-deer and sleighs, to pass over the ice of the Frozen Ocean. Thus furnished, he engaged to explore the concave regions, and to discover a warm, or at least a temperate country, of fertile soil, well stocked with animals and vegetables, if not with men, on reaching about sixty-nine miles beyond north latitude eighty-two degrees. Having made the discovery, he would return the next spring.

Capt. Symmes long contemplated such an expedition in order to verify his theory. Twice—in March, 1822, and December, 1823—he asked Congress for an appropriation for this purpose. But Congress did not see fit to grant his request, and he had not sufficient funds to carry into effect his long-cherished object. He lectured on the subject in Cincinnati and other towns in Ohio, 1820–25; in Philadelphia, New York, Boston, and other eastern cities in 1826.

Wearied and worn out by his constant labor and excitement, he

13

died May 29, 1829, aged 49 years and 6 months. He was buried
the next day with military honors, in the old cemetery at Hamilton,
Ohio. His monument, erected by his son Americus Symmes, is sur-
mounted with a *hollow sphere* of carved stone, about one foot in
diameter. The pedestal bears on its sides inscriptions; on the
south side commemorative of his daring bravery in battle, and on
the north side announcing him as a philosopher and the originator
of Symmes's "Theory of Concentric Spheres and Polar Voids."
"He contended that the earth is hollow and habitable within."

His namesake and uncle gave him a valuable section of land near
Hamilton, Ohio. He removed to it in 1824, but, as may well be
supposed, his estate was insolvent at his death, and his affairs greatly
embarrassed, demanding the most vigorous exertions of his eldest
son Americus to provide for the widow and the family. Mrs. Marianne Symmes, the widow, made her home most of the time with her
eldest son Americus, and died at Mattoon, Illinois, on a visit to her
son, Dr. William H. H. Symmes. Aug. 5, 1864.

Capt. Symmes was a man of great simplicity and earnestness of
character, high-minded, honorable, honest, exemplary, in every walk
in life; beloved, trusted and respected by all who knew him. The
lady whom he married came to him with a family of five daughters
and one son by her former husband. These children were brought
up and educated by him as his own.

So entirely convinced was he of the soundness of his theory, that
for ten years, though laboring under great pecuniary embarrassment,
and buffeted by the ridicule and sarcasm of an opposing world, he
persevered in his endeavors to convince others and interest them in
it. The theory finally cost him his life.

The children of Capt. JOHN CLEVES SYMMES were:

+419. LOUISIANA,[7] b. Feb. 5, 1810; m. first, James W. Taylor; m. sec-
       ond, Joel Baker.

+420. AMERICUS,[7] b. Nov. 2, 1811; m. first, Ann Milliken; m. second,
       Frances Scott.

+421. WILLIAM HENRY HARRISON,[7] b. May, 1813; m. first, Phebe A.
       Waven; m. second, H. Bargen.

  422. ELIZABETH,[7] b. 1814; d. at Newport, Ky., in 1821.

+423. JOHN CLEVES,[7] b. 1824; m. Marie Lepowitz.

210.

MARY SYMMES[6] (*Timothy,[5] Timothy,[4] Timothy,[3] William,[2] Zechariah[1]*), sister of the preceding, and daughter of Timothy[5] and Mercy
(Harker) Symmes, born in Sussex County, New Jersey, 1785; married HUGH MOORE, 1805.

He was a merchant in Cincinnati. She died in 1834.

Their children were:

424. MARGARET (Moore), b. 1806; d. in infancy, 1806.
+425. MARY ANN (Moore), b. 1809; m. James B. Marshall.
426. JULIA SYMMES (Moore), b. 1811; d. in infancy, 1812.
427. DANIEL SYMMES (Moore), b. 1817; d. in infancy, 1819.
+428. HUGH MONTGOMERY (Moore), b. 1819; m. first, Margaret Crane; m. second, Clara Harris.
+429. JOHN CLEVES SYMMES (Moore), b. 1822; m. Emily Wright.
430. LUCY (Moore), b. 1824; m. 1855, Rev. William W. Wright, of Dunnon Springs, Ky. They had:
    431. *Lucy* (Wright), b. 1856.
    432. *Alice* (Wright), b. 1858; d. 1860.
433. JANE (Moore), b. 1826; m. 1856, Charles E. Matthews, a mathematician, of Walnut Hills, Ohio. They had:
    434. *Fanny* (Matthews), b. 1857.
    435. *Charles Edward* (Matthews), b. 1859.

211.

JULIANA SYMMES[6] (*Timothy*,[5] *Timothy*,[4] *Timothy*,[3] *William*,[2] *Zechariah*[1]), sister of the preceding, and daughter of Timothy[5] and Mercy Symmes; born in Sussex County, New Jersey, 1791; married, 1811, JEREMIAH REEDER.

She came from her eastern home to Ohio in 1800. Mr. Reeder, whom she married, was a native of Pennsylvania, and in 1811 was a merchant in Cincinnati. In 1818 they removed to a farm below Cincinnati, which had been bequeathed to her by her uncle, Hon. John Cleves Symmes. Mr. Reeder there engaged largely in the nursery business. A few years after, they returned to the city, and he resumed his former occupation, continuing it until his death. He acquired considerable property, but lost most of it by indorsing for some of his friends. After his death Mrs. Reeder removed to her farm, where she died in 1844.

Their children were:

436. ANNA HARRISON (Reeder), b. 1813; unm.; d. in 1836.
437. JOHN CLEVES (Reeder), b. 1815; d. 1818.
+438. ALLEN LAKE (Reeder), b. 1817; m. Lydia A. Elliot.
439. HARRIET HENRIETTA (Reeder), b. 1819; d. 1824.
440. DANIEL OLIVER (Reeder), b. 1824; a nursery-man near Cincinnati.
+441. MARY SYMMES (Reeder), b. 1824; m. William R. McAllister.

212.

PEYTON SHORT SYMMES[6] (*Timothy*,[5] *Timothy*,[4] *Timothy*,[3] *William*,[2] *Zechariah*[1]), brother of the preceding, and son of Timothy[5] and Mercy Symmes; born in Sussex County, New Jersey, in 1793; married HANNAH B. CLOSE, in 1819.

He went to Ohio in his childhood, and was one of the pioneers of the West. He passed his life in Cincinnati, and was one of its most respected and valued citizens. His name stands intimately connected with every important social improvement made in the Queen City. He took a deep interest in the cause of education, and did much to promote the efficiency and success of the public schools. He had refined literary tastes, and was a man of much culture. He wrote often in prose and verse, for papers and magazines. He was distinguished for purity of character, and was courteous and pleasant in social life. He was fond of humor and excelled in wit, but not at the expense of others. He was apt with the pencil, and could draw the human countenance with remarkable success. He gave much time to the affairs of the city, in the City Council and in the Board of Health, of which he was a member from 1830 to 1850, as well as in the Board of School Trustees from 1833 to 1849. He was one of the Trustees of Cincinnati College, an active member of the Horticultural Society, and prominent as a member and corresponding secretary of the Pioneer Association. He succeeded his brother Daniel, in 1827, as Register of the U. S. Land Office in Cincinnati. He was the last male survivor of the family of the elder John Cleves Symmes, the purchaser and pioneer settler of the wilderness of the northwest, between the Great and Little Miami, where those flourishing cities, Cincinnati, Hamilton and Dayton now stand.

He died of a paralytic stroke, on the afternoon of Saturday, July 27, 1861, aged 69, at the house of his son-in-law, Charles L. Colburn, at Mount Auburn, near Cincinnati, where he had been resting for a few weeks, during the heat of the weather. On the morning of that day he had attended the weekly meeting of the Cincinnati Horticultural Society at its rooms in the city. His funeral was attended on Friday, Aug. 2, by many of the old pioneer families, and the body deposited in the Spring Grove Cemetery. [Cincinnati Daily Gazette.]

The children of PEYTON S. SYMMES were:

442. WILLIAM,[7] b. 1820; d. same year.
+443. MARY SUSAN,[7] b. 1822; m. Charles L. Colburn.
444. ELIZABETH,[7] b. 1825; m. Langdon H. Haven, 1845, a merchant of the city of New York. Children:
    445. *Henry Langdon* (Haven), b. 1846.
    446. *Ethan Allen* (Haven).
447. RACHEL ANNA,[7] m. Henry B. Skinner, merchant, of Boston. Child:
    448. *Henry C.* (Skinner).
+449. HENRY EDWARD,[7] b. 1835; unm.
450. HARRIET LOUISA,[7] d. 1852.
451. DANIEL CLEVES.[7]
452. ETHAN ALLEN.[7]
453. ALLEN CLEVES.[7]

213.

TIMOTHY SYMMES⁶ (*Timothy,*⁵ *Timothy,*⁴ *Timothy,*³ *William,*² *Zechariah*¹), brother of the preceding, and youngest son of Timothy⁵ and Mercy (Harker) Symmes; born in Sussex County, New Jersey, 1795; married RUTH SPURRIER, 1817.

He was a farmer at North Bend, Ohio, and died on his farm in 1822.

His children were:

454. CAROLINE,⁷ b. 1819; m. first, 1832(?), Joseph Tincher, a cabinet-maker and farmer in Kentucky; m. second, Charles L. Palmer, of St. Louis. She died in 1855. Children:

  455. *Timothy Symmes* (Tincher), b. 1834; engineer on steamboat navigation.

  456. *Julia Ann* (Tincher), b. 1836; m. 1855, John G. Keady, tailor, of St. Louis.

  457. *Caroline* (Tincher), b. 1839; d. 1841.

  458. *Henry J.* (Tincher), b. 1841.

  459. *Caroline* (Palmer), b. 1851.

  460. *Edward A.* (Palmer), b. 1853.

+461. HENRY HARKER,⁷ b. 1821; m. Belinda Sedam.

462. JULIA,⁷ b. 1823; d. 1834.

216.

TIMOTHY SYMMES⁶ (*William,*⁵ *Timothy,*⁴ *Timothy,*³ *William,*² *Zechariah*¹), son of William⁵ and Mehitable (Moulton) Symmes; born in Newfield, Me., about 1788; m. SALLY HILL, of Newfield. He was a deacon in the church in that town forty years; a member fifty years. He died Aug. 27, 1866. [See Christian Mirror, Sept. 7, 1866.]

They had:

463. EBENEZER,⁷ b. May 9, 1822; m. May 31, 1854, Olive Frances Moulton, b. May 3, 1829, daughter of Samuel Moulton, of Newfield. She died June 3, 1858, aged 29 years 1 mo. Their daughter:

  464. *Mary Ella,*⁸ b. Oct. 29, 1855; was living Dec. 13, 1868.

222.

MARY JENNISON (*Abigail Lindall, Mary Higginson, Sarah Savage, Mary Symmes, Zechariah Symmes*), daughter of Rev. William and Abigail (Lindall) Jennison; born in Salem, 1734; married in Salem, Nov. 4, 1753, THOMAS GILES,⁴ born Feb. 1730–1, youngest son of Samuel³ and Susanna (Palfrey) Giles, of that place.*

---

* The GILES FAMILY.

Sir EDWARD GILES, of Bowden, in Devonshire, England, 1620, was sheriff of that county, a member of the third parliament of James the First, 1620–1, and one of the Patentees in the Great Charter granted by that monarch, Nov. 3, 1620, usually called the Plymouth

He was a substantial mechanic, a cabinet-maker, which trade he learned of his father. He resided in South Danvers, now Peabody, which till June 16, 1757, was the Middle Parish in Salem. Tradition reports that they commenced married life in a style above what they were able to support, induced, no doubt, by their connection with the wealthy family of the Lindalls; and thus became reduced in their worldly circumstances.

He was a soldier in the "Old French War," 1755–1762, the war which resulted in the expulsion of the French from Canada. He suffered much on the Canada frontier. When the encroachments of the British ministry, long patiently endured, at length aroused all the colonies to an armed resistance in 1775, Thomas Giles was among the first who repaired to the Revolutionary standard. He was in the battle of Bunker Hill, and fought with undoubted courage. Just as he was about to fire away his last cartridge, he was heard to exclaim, "Heaven direct the charge!" The fatigue and exhaustion of that very warm day proved too much for him; and on the next day, or day after, in a tailor's shop in Medford, he suddenly fell and instantly expired, June 18, 1775, in his 45th year.

His wife, a minister's daughter, was, for those times, a well educated woman, and possessed great worth of character. She died at Salem, Nov. 1784, aged 50.

Their children were:

+471. THOMAS (Giles), b. Oct. 6, 1754; m. Mary Soper Marshall.
  472. MARY (Giles), b. Feb. 1, 1756; m. Solomon Stevens.
  473. SAMUEL (Giles), b. April 6, 1757; m. Laurana Holmes, 1783.
  474. ABIGAIL (Giles), bapt. Jan. 24, 1759; d. young.
  475. ELIZABETH (Giles), bapt. Nov. 2, 1760; d. young.

Charter, which Prince, in his N. E. Chronology, styles "the great civil basis of all the subsequent patents which divided New England." Sir Edward Giles was a leading Puritan, and took an interest in the colonization of the New World. His coat of arms is still used by our family. He had no children.

1. EDWARD GILES, supposed to be a relation of his, came to this country probably in 1631, when the tide of emigration was perceptibly quickened. He was admitted a freeman of the Massachusetts Colony, May 14, 1634. Soon after his arrival, he married the widow BRIDGET VERY, who was from Salisbury, in Wiltshire. A grant was made to him, in 1636, of one hundred and twenty acres of land near Cedar Pond, in the south-westerly part of what is now Peabody. He died previous to 1650, but Bridget, his widow, lived till 1680.

Their children were Mehitabel,[2] Remember,[2] Eleazar,[2] and John.[3]

2. ELEAZAR GILES, son of Edward and Bridget Giles, b. Nov. 1640; m. first, SARAH MORY, of Lynn, Jan. 25, 1664–5, who died May 9, 1676. He m. second, ELIZABETH BISHOP, of New Haven, Sept. 25, 1677. She was born July 3, 1657, and was the daughter of James Bishop, Esq., of New Haven, who was Secretary of the New Haven Colony, 1661, before its union with Connecticut; representative of New Haven, 1665; and Deputy Governor of Connecticut from 1683 to 1695, except when the government was suspended by the usurpation of Andros in 1687 and 1688.

Eleazar Giles lived in Salem, the part which is now Peabody, all his days. He was a husbandman of respectable standing, and died in 1726, aged 86. His widow Elizabeth died 1733, aged 76. He had six children by his first wife, and nine by the second.

3. SAMUEL GILES, the fifth son of Eleazar and Elizabeth, b. Dec. 17, 1694; m. Sept. 10, 1719, SUSANNA PALFREY, youngest daughter of Walter Palfrey,[2] sail-maker, of Salem, who was a grandson of Peter Palfrey,[1] of that place. Peter Palfrey, John Balch, and John Woodbury, were the three "honest and prudent men" who remained with Roger Conant at Salem, in 1627, when all the other persons of the colony, discouraged with ill success, abandoned the plantation. Samuel Giles was father of Thomas Giles in the text.

176. WILLIAM (Giles), bapt. Feb. 28, 1762; m. ——.

177. JAMES LINDALL (Giles), bapt. March 30, 1766; m. first, Anna Page; m. second, Martha Bellamy.

178. ABIGAIL (Giles), bapt. May 7, 1769; m. first, Robert Watson; m. second, Adna Bates.

Three of the above-named sons, Thomas, Samuel and William, as well as their father, were in the military service of their country during at least a part of the Revolutionary struggle. For a full account of the Giles Family, from the beginning, see the GILES MEMORIAL, by the compiler of this work.

227.

CALEB SYMMES[6] (*Caleb,[5] Thomas,[4] Thomas,[3] Zechariah,[2] Zechariah[1]*), son of Capt. Caleb[5] and Elizabeth (Hall) Symmes; born in Charlestown, Mass., March 7, 1762; married, first, LYDIA TROW-BRIDGE, in Westford, Nov. 23, 1784. She was born in Shirley, Mass., Dec. 25, 1762, dau. of Thomas and Lucy Trowbridge. She died in Groton, Mass., Dec. 5, 1812, and was buried in Littleton on the 7th. Thomas was son of Rev. Caleb Trowbridge, of Groton. Mr. Symmes married, second, MARY (CHITTENDEN) LANE, a widow, dau. of Calvin and Sally Chittenden, in Charlestown, the marriage ceremony by Rev. James Walker, July 20, 1820. She was born in Malden, March 19, 1781; died in Charlestown, Sept. 13, 1826, and was interred in Malden, Sept. 14.

In his childhood Mr. Symmes was fond of study, and obtained some knowledge of Latin and Greek. He afterwards learned the trade of a blacksmith. He resided, after marriage, in West-ford, till about 1792; in Hollis, N. H., one year; in Peterborough, N. H., about the same length of time. In 1796 his mother bought a farm of one hundred and twenty acres in the south part of Gro-ton, Mass., of her brother-in-law, Capt. Jonas Minot, father of Judge Minot, of Haverhill, Mass., to which place they removed the same year. After his first wife's death he lived in Charlestown.

He died, trusting in Christ, at Malden, near Boston, Dec. 15, 1843, aged 81 years 9 months, and was interred in the family tomb in the old cemetery in Charlestown, Dec. 23.

His children, by first wife LYDIA, were:

Born in Westford.

+479. CALEB,[7] b. Sept. 1, 1786; m. Mary Bowers.

+480. BETSEY,[7] b. Sept. 5, 1788; m. Joshua Mixter.

481. LYDIA,[7] b. Jan. 11, 1791; unm.; she was a member of a Baptist church nearly fifty years, and an eminently useful person; d. in Boston, Jan. 4, 1857. Her end was perfect peace.

Born in Hollis, N. H.

+482. LUCY,[7] b. June 29, 1793; m. John Clement.

Born in Groton, Mass.

+483. WILLARD HALL,[7] b. March 26, 1796; m. Sally Parker.

+484. CALVIN,[7] b. March 8, 1798; unmarried.

485. HARRIET,[7] b. May 19, 1802; never married. This estimable lady has been a worthy member of the Episcopal church for the last thirty-one years. She has taken a warm interest in this Family History, and has contributed much to its completeness, especially in the record of her father's and grandfather's descendants. She resides with her brother Caleb's widow, No. 8 Joiner Street, Charlestown.

+486. MARY,[7] b. Nov. 16, 1805; m. William C. Paterson.

By second wife, MARY, and born in Charlestown :

+487. THOMAS,[7] b. Dec. 13, 1823; m. first, Mary Mitchell; m. second, Sarah Ellen Bowers.

229.

THOMAS SYMMES[6] (*Caleb,[5] Thomas,[4] Thomas,[3] Zechariah,[2] Zechariah[1]*), brother of the preceding, and son of Capt. Caleb and Elizabeth (Hall) Symmes; born in Charlestown, Sept. 19, 1765; married REBECCA CARVER, born July 3, 1766, youngest child of Ensign Benjamin and Edea Carver, of Westford.* Her mother, Edea Fletcher, was sister to Capt. Benjamin Fletcher, his step-father.

He went with his mother, in 1774, to Westford, where she married Capt. Fletcher in 1779. He was brought up, under Capt. Fletcher, to the business of husbandry, to which he added that of a cooper. He was unsuccessful in business, as many were in the pinching times that followed the war of the Revolution. He found it necessary, in 1796, to dispose of his interest in the farm at Westford, which had belonged to Capt. Fletcher, and removed to Ashby, where Dr. Thomas Carver, his wife's brother, was the practising physician. He bought a farm there, and engaged in trade, but soon sold out, and in 1799 returned to Westford. He bought a small place in the south part of Westford, which, with some additions since made, remains in the hands of his descendants.

He was a man honest, industrious, and of exemplary life; a church-going man, and very careful in observing the sabbath. He was fond of church music, and took part in the devotions of the sanctuary.

* The CARVER FAMILY.

1. ROBERT CARVER, said to be a brother of John Carver, the first governor of Plymouth Colony, was born in England, 1594; came to Marshfield, in Plymouth Colony, 1638; died 1689, aged 86.

2. JOHN CARVER, his son, b. 1637; m. Melicent Ford, of Marshfield. He died 1679, aged 42. Children: *William, John, Robert, Eleazar,* DAVID, *Elizabeth, Mercy,* and *Anna.* Robert and David seem to have settled in Canterbury, Ct.

3. DAVID CARVER, son of the preceding John, first appears on the town records of Canterbury, Ct., in 1719. He died Sept. 17, 1727. By a second wife, SARAH BUTTERFIELD, of Chelmsford, Mass., he had a son—

4. BENJAMIN CARVER, born in Canterbury, Ct., Dec. 10, 1722. His mother, after the father's death, returned to her native Chelmsford, of which Westford (incorporated 1729) was then a part. He passed his life in Westford; owned a valuable farm near the centre of that town, part of which is still owned by his descendants; m. EDEA FLETCHER, about 1745, and had nine children : *Sarah, Benjamin, Jonathan* (representative, 1783), *Thomas,* M.D., of Ashby, *Edea,* m. Dr. Charles Proctor, of Westford, *Martha, Benjamin, Mary,* and *Rebecca,* the wife of Thomas Symmes in the text. He d. July 18, 1804, in his 82d year. Edea, his widow, d. Aug. 1813, aged 89.

He died Sept. 1, 1817, aged 52, nearly. His widow Rebecca remained at the homestead till 1832, when she removed to the house of her son Edward, where she died, Nov. 17, 1836, in her 71st year.

The children of THOMAS and REBECCA (CARVER) SYMMES were:

Born in Westford.

+188. THOMAS,⁷ b. March 27, 1790; unm.; d. Nov. 27, 1816.
489. PATTY CARVER,⁷ b. Aug. 14, 1791; d. June 28, 1795.
490. SUSANNA BANCROFT,⁷ b. July 5, 1793; d. April 13, 1813.
+491. EDEA FLETCHER,⁷ b. Aug. 2, 1795; m. Cephas Drew.

Born in Ashby.

492. MARTHA,⁷ b. May 4, 1797; d. April 24, 1820.

Born in Westford.

493. CALEB,⁷ b. Nov. 15, 1800; d. March 29, 1821.
494. ELIZABETH HALL,⁷ b. April 16, 1803; d. 1805.
+495. EDWARD,⁷ ⎫ twins, born ⎰ m. Rebecca P. Fletcher.
+496. EDMUND,⁷ ⎭ April 1, 1806; ⎱ unmarried.

236.

SUSANNA MASON⁶ (*Hannah Symmes,*⁵ *Andrew,*⁴ *Thomas,*³ *Zechariah,*² *Zechariah*¹), daughter of Col. David and Hannah (Symmes) Mason; born in Boston, 1763; married, 1785, Rev. John Smith, D.D., Professor of the Latin, Greek, Hebrew and Oriental Languages in Dartmouth College, Hanover, N. H. She was his second wife.

Her husband was son of Joseph and Elizabeth (Palmer) Smith; was born at Rowley, Mass., Dec. 21, 1752, and died at Hanover, N. H., April 30, 1809, in his 57th year. He studied divinity with the Rev. Eleazar Wheelock, D.D., first president of Dartmouth College; graduated at that institution, 1773; was tutor there from 1774 to 1778; and was Professor of the Latin, Greek, Hebrew, and the Oriental Languages from 1778 till his death. He was also pastor of the church at Hanover; associate pastor with president Wheelock from 1773 till 1779, when Dr. Wheelock died; associate pastor with Rev. Sylvanus Ripley from 1776 till Mr. Ripley's death, Feb. 5, 1787; after which he was sole pastor till his own decease. He had a great reputation as a linguist. He published a Latin Grammar, a Greek Grammar, a Hebrew Grammar, Cicero de Oratore, with notes and a memoir; besides several ordination sermons. His first wife was Mary Cleveland, daughter of Rev. Ebenezer Cleveland, of Gloucester, Mass., Y. C. 1748.

When I was a student and a resident at Hanover, I heard frequent and honorable mention made of Professor Smith. I was personally acquainted with Madam Smith, his widow—a lady of very respectable abilities. She told me of revolutionary scenes, and in particular of her making up, with the help of her sister, cartridges, and casting musket balls for the American army; melting domestic

14

utensils, such as pewter plates, for the purpose. She died at Hanover, Dec. 20, 1845, aged 82.

The children of Prof. JOHN and SUSANNA SMITH,* so far as they have come to my knowledge, were:

497. JOHN WHEELOCK (Smith), b. April 25, 1786; never married. He grad. Dart. Coll. 1804; studied law; began practice in Boston, 1808; was forced by ill health to go abroad; travelled in various parts of Europe, and died in London, Feb. 19, 1814, in his 28th year.

498. SAMUEL MASON (Smith), b. 1792; d. at Hanover, April 15, 1813. He was then on his last year in college.

238.

LYDIA SYMMES[6] (*Andrew,[5] Andrew,[4] Thomas,[3] Zechariah,[2] Zechariah[1]*), daughter of Col. Andrew Symmes[5] by his first wife, Lydia Gale; born in Boston, Dec. 18, 1768; m. July 2, 1795, JONATHAN SNELLING, son of Joseph[4] and Rachel (Mayer) Snelling, of Boston.†

Mr. Jonathan Snelling was, for the greater part of his life, master of the Centre School in Boston, universally respected and beloved for his excellent qualities of mind and heart. In his school he was efficient, discriminating and successful.

Mrs. Lydia Snelling died in 1844. They had seven children, the eldest of whom was

501. ANDREW SYMMES (Snelling), b. in Boston, July 19, 1797; m. April 9, 1829, ELIZA TEMPLETON STRONG, b. Dec. 7, 1804, d. April 24, 1869, the dau. of Benjamin Strong, merchant, of New York, who d. Jan. 27, 1851, aged 80, by his wife Sarah (dau. of Jotham Weeks), who d. May 1, 1843, aged 78. Mr. Andrew S. Snelling was educated in his father's school, in the Boston Latin School, and in the Medford Academy under the teaching of that

---

* A daughter of Prof. Smith by his first wife Mary Cleveland, Abigail (Smith), in 1800 became the wife of Cyrus Perkins, M.D., b. in Middleboro', Mass., Sept. 4, 1778, d. 1849, an eminent physician in New York city, and also professor of Anatomy and Surgery in Dartmouth College from 1810 to 1819.

† The SNELLING FAMILY.
  1. JOHN SNELLING, son of Thomas Snelling, of Chaddlewood in Plympton St. Mary, Co. of Devon, Eng., came to New England about 1657, and died in Boston, 1672.
  2. JOSEPH SNELLING, son of John, b. 1667; d. Aug. 15, 1726; father of eleven children, according to Savage, of whom was—
  3. JONATHAN SNELLING (Capt.), b. Dec. 29, 1697; commanded the corvette Cæsar, of 20 guns, fitted out by the Province as a part of the expedition to Louisburgh in 1745, and was a prominent actor in that affair, reflecting so much honor on the provincial arms.
  4. JOSEPH SNELLING, b. Dec. 5, 1741; m. Oct. 13, 1762, Rachel Mayer, b. April 19, 1743, and d. June 9, 1837, aged 95, having borne eleven children. He was one of the active and energetic men who brought on and carried out the Revolution. His course made him obnoxious to Gen. Gage, and having left Boston with a friend on a visit to Cambridge, his return to Boston was prevented. He forthwith went back to Cambridge, joined the army there under Gen. Ward as a commissary, and returned to Boston when the siege was ended. He died Feb. 6, 1816, aged 75.
  5. JONATHAN SNELLING, husband of Lydia Symmes in the text.

eminent master, Dr. Luther Stearns.* He chose and has successfully pursued a mercantile life. In 1827 he removed to New York, and was for a long time an importing and shipping merchant. He is still living, in New York, 1873, though not in active business. His children have been :

507. *Georgiana* (Snelling), b. Jan. 28, 1830; m. Dr. John C. Peters.

503. *Frederick Greenwood* (Snelling), b. July 26, 1831; grad. New York Univ., M.D.; living in New York in 1873.

504. *Edward Templeton* (Snelling), b. March 2, 1835; living in New York, 1873.

505. *Eliza Strong* (Snelling). b. Feb. 14, 1838; m. Dr. M. Clymer.

506. *Grenville Temple* (Snelling), b. Nov. 5, 1841; d. Jan. 3, 1856, aged 14, while on a visit to Chicago with his parents.

240.

ANDREW ELIOT SYMMES[6] (*Andrew*,[5] *Andrew*,[4] *Thomas*,[3] *Zechariah*,[2] *Zechariah*[1]), half-brother of the preceding, and only son of Col. Andrew Symmes[5] by his third wife Mary Ann (Stevens) Symmes; born in Boston; married ELIZA COFFIN, daughter of Hon. Peleg Coffin, a native of Nantucket and a member of Congress from the district in which Nantucket was situated. He was an intimate and confidential friend of Caleb Strong, the excellent governor of this commonwealth. He resided in Boston, and was one of the firm of [Samuel] Torrey, Symmes & Co., from 1806 to 1810.

He had two daughters :

507. ELIZA,[7] m. first, John Thorne, of Brooklyn, L. I.; m. second, William Raymond Lee Ward, formerly of Salem, Mass., now, 1873, a broker in New York city. She and her husband are both living. By her first marriage she had one child, a son, George Winthrop (Thorne), who m. a Miss Beckwith, but is now a young widower.

508. MARY ANNE,[7] m. Frederick A. Heath, of Brookline. She died about a year after marriage.

241.

MARY ANN SYMMES[6] (*Ebenezer*,[5] *Andrew*,[4] *Thomas*,[3] *Zechariah*,[2] *Zechariah*[1]), only daughter of Capt. Ebenezer[5] and Mary Ann (Stevens) Symmes; born in Boston, Aug. 15, 1775; married her cousin, JOHN GREENWOOD, April 22, 1802. The marriage took place at St. George's [Hotel?], Hanover Square, London.

Her father dying when she was less than two years old, she was

---

* Luther Stearns, born Feb. 17, 1770; died April 30, 1820; was eldest son of Hon. Josiah Stearns, of Lunenburg, and brother of Hon. Asahel Stearns, Professor of Law in Harvard College, 1817 till his death in 1839. Luther Stearns had been tutor at Cambridge; afterwards studied medicine; settled in Medford, and became eminent as a physician.

His nephew, Luther Stearns Cushing, has been a judge of the Inferior Court, and is the author of Cushing's Manual of Parliamentary Rules.

left in the care of her mother. Some time afterwards, Dr. Samuel Danforth, her father's uncle by marriage, became her guardian, and so continued till she was twenty-one years of age. The final settlement is indicated by a receipt signed by her, dated London, Jan. 12, 1797, on record in the Probate Office, Boston.

Her mother being of English birth, it appears that she passed several years in and near London, with her mother's friends, previous to 1800; and there she found her husband.

Her husband, John Greenwood, born Oct. 5, 1772, was a son of John Greenwood, born in Boston, Mass., Dec. 7, 1727, who went to England; was an artist; passed many years in London; m. Dec. 17, 1769, Frances Stevens, b. Jan. 18, 1744, sister of Mary Ann Stevens, wife successively of Capt. Ebenezer Symmes and his brother Col. Andrew Symmes, of Boston. John Greenwood, Sen., died at Margate, Sept. 15, 1792.

John Greenwood, Jr., the husband of Mary Ann Symmes, above, was at one time an auctioneer in London. He is said to have been, 1808 to 1814, chief scene painter of Drury-Lane Theatre. Byron pays him a compliment in his "English Bards and Scotch Reviewers," in the lines where, satirizing the drama of his day, he exclaims:

> " Lo ! with what pomp the daily prints proclaim
> The rival candidates for Attic fame !
> In grim array though Lewis' spectres rise,
> Still Skeffington and Goose divide the prize.
> And sure *great* Skeffington must claim our praise,
> For skirtless coats and skeletons of plays,
> Renowned alike ; whose genius ne'er confines
> Her flight to garnish Greenwood's gay designs."•

The children of John and Mary Ann Greenwood were:

509. John Danforth (Greenwood), b. in London, Jan. 4, 1803; m. a Miss Field, near London; emigrated to New Zealand, after 1825.
510. Frederic (Greenwood), b. Oct. 5, 1804; came to Boston in 1820, after the death of his parents, to his uncle Jonathan Snelling; was adopted by Mr. Samuel Torrey, but died July, 1821.

248.

WILLIAM SYMMES[6] (*William*,[5] *Andrew*,[4] *Thomas*,[3] *Zechariah*,[2] *Zechariah*[1]), only son of William[5] and Elizabeth (Russell) Symmes; born in Boston, 1802; married, first, 1826, Elizabeth Ridgeley, a native of England. She died in Dorchester, in 1833, aged 26. He married, second, Eliza A. Mayland, May 2, 1836.

His father dying when he was but eight years old, his mother's

---

• In a note the poet informs his readers that Mr. Skeffington is the " illustrious author " of several comedies, of which he says " baculo magis quam lauro digne ;" for whose success the writer was much indebted to the scene painter, Mr. Greenwood. Matthew Gregory Lewis, a celebrated writer of plays, is intended in the lines in the text. He is known as Monk Lewis, from being the author of a novel entitled " The Monk."

brother, Hon. Benjamin Russell, was his guardian. He spent much of his early life in his family. He was a harness-maker in Boston, and has lived in Boston, Dorchester and Framingham. He and his wife are living in Framingham, March, 1873.

His children, by first wife, were:

511. CHARLES,[7] b. Feb. 11, 1827 ; m. Cleora Dunbar, daughter of Hon Frederick Dunbar, of Ludlow, Vt. He now, 1872, is a farmer in Waupaca, Wisconsin.
512. WILLIAM HENRY,[7] b. March 29, 1829 ; m. Rhoda Bray, of Rockport. She is not now living. He was a sailor nine years ; was in the War of the Rebellion. He now lives in Boston, and has some office in the Suffolk Jail in Charles Street; house, Bradford Street.
513. SARAH ELIZABETH,[7] b. March 13, 1831 ; m. Amasa D. Cunningham, of Cambridge, a horticulturist. They live in Boston Highlands, formerly the town of Roxbury.

By second wife :

514. CHARLOTTE RUSSELL,[7] b. May, 1837 ; m. Nelson H. Hull, of Durham, Ct. He was in the "lamp business" at Meriden, Ct. He is not now living. She resides with her parents, in Framingham. Has one child.
515. HENRIETTA RUSSELL,[7] b. July 5, 1838 ; unm. She is at present, Jan. 1873, in Southington, Ct.
515a. HUBBARD WINSLOW,[7] died.
515b. HUBBARD WINSLOW,[7] died.
516. THEODORE WHITE,[7] b. Feb. 17, 1844 ; m. Amanda Colburn, of Groton, Mass. They live in Plantsville, Ct. He is a clerk.

253.

ISAAC SYMMES[6] (*Isaac,*[5] *Zechariah,*[4] *Thomas,*[3] *Zechariah,*[2] *Zechariah*[1]), son of Isaac and Hannah[5] (Davis) Symmes ; born in Plymouth, Mass., Nov. 16, 1771 ; married, Jan. 1, 1798, MARY WHITMAN, who was born Aug. 19, 1778.

We suppose he lived in Plymouth, Mass.; possibly in Kingston, an adjoining town.

Their children were:

517. ISAAC,[7] b. Sept. 27, 1798.
518. HANNAH,[7] b. May 6, 1801.
+519. WILLIAM,[7] b. Aug. 19, 1802 ; m. first, Mary D. Washburn; m. second, Caroline H. Jameson.
+520. MARY WHITMAN,[7] b. Oct. 29, 1805 ; m. Alden Sampson.
521. MARTHA,[7] b. Jan. 12, 1809.
522. DANIEL,[7] b. Nov. 1820 ; m. Selina A. Weston.

256.

MARGARET SYMMES[6] (*Isaac,*[5] *Zechariah,*[4] *Thomas,*[3] *Zechariah,*[2] *Zechariah*[1]), half-sister of the preceding; b. Nov. 15, 1777 ; married JAMES SPOONER.

He was a trader in Plymouth, Mass.

Their children were:

523. JAMES (Spooner), unmarried; is said to be a clergyman; lives in Plymouth, Jan. 1873.
521. EPHRAIM (Spooner), m. ———; is living, 1873, in Plymouth, and has children.
525. MARGARET (Spooner), unmarried; lives in Plymouth, 1873.
526. GEORGE (Spooner), ... "went south and died there."

258.

LAZARUS SYMMES[6] (*Isaac,[5] Zechariah,[4] Thomas,[3] Zechariah,[2] Zechariah[1]*), brother of the preceding; b. Feb. 18, 1781; married, Nov. 7, 1802, MARY WESTON, b. 1784, daughter of William Weston, of Plymouth, Mass.

"Their home was in Plymouth; but the last part of their lives they spent mostly with their children." Mr. Symmes died Jan. 25, 1851, aged 70. Mrs. Symmes died Dec. 4, 1863, aged 79.

Their children were:

527. ELIZA,[7] b. 1803; d. 1804.
528. WILLIAM,[7] b. June 1, 1805; m. in Boston, April, 1834, Jane G. Pratt, a widow; was a sea-captain; d. at sea, 1836.
529. ELIZA ANN,[7] b. Jan. 17, 1808; m. in Plymouth, Sept. 29, 1828, John W. Newman, of Lancaster, Mass. She now resides in Wakefield. Their son (530), Dr. J. Frank Newman, is a dentist in Boston.
531. COLUMBUS,[7] b. Sept. 28, 1813; d. May 19, 1827.
532. WASHINGTON,[7] b. Aug. 29, 1816; m. Juliette Jones, in Philadelphia, where they reside. Children:
    533. *William.[8]*
    534. *Mary.[8]* m. James Patterson. They live in Washington, D. C.
535. HARRIET,[7] b. Jan. 27, 1819; m. in Plymouth, 1838, to Rensselaer Barker, of East Boston.
536. MARY,[7] b. March 16, 1823; m. at Hartford, Ct., Oct. 15, 1850, to James B. Richards, of New York. She d. Feb. 5, 1872.

262.

ZECHARIAH PARKER SYMMES[6] (*Isaac,[5] Zechariah,[4] Thomas,[3] Zechariah,[2] Zechariah[1]*), brother of the preceding; born in Plymouth, Mass., May 8, 1791; m. first, ELIZABETH DUKES BERRY, b. Aug. 16, 1791, died Nov. 23, 1834; m. second, ELIZABETH YOUNG, who died Dec. 17, 1840; m. third, CAROLINE FOX ESTY, b. April 21, 1808, now deceased.

Mr. Symmes died Sept. 6, 1865.

His children, by first wife, were:

537. DAVID MASON,[7] b. Sept. 23, 1815; unmarried; a "jobber."
538. PARKER,[7] b. March 19, 1817; died at sea, Sept. 1838.

+539. LEWIS,[7] b. April 17, 1819; m. Sarah P. Hood.

540. HENRY,[7] b. Jan. 25, 1822; m. Almira W. Wiley. He was a shoe-maker; lived in Beverly and Lowell, Mass., and d. Oct. 27, 1869. His wife is living in Lowell. One child:

    541. *Lucy*,[8] b. June 6, 1852.

542. STEPHEN,[7] b. March 20, 1824; a shoemaker in Beverly; m. Jan. 8, 1846, Sarah D. Hildreth, b. Sept. 21, 1827, daugh. of James Hildreth, a blacksmith, of Hopkinton, N. H. Only child:

    Freddie H.,[8] b. July 28, 1869; d. Aug. 3, 1869.

+543. CHARLES,[7] b. April 10, 1827; m. Nancy Duffee.

543½. ANN,[7] b. Nov. 23, 1828; d. young.

544. RICHARD,[7] b. Sept. 25, 1830; unmarried; a shoemaker.

By second wife :

545. RUFUS WILLIAM,[7] b. Dec. 2, 1836; m. 1867, Mary E. Page, dau. of William Page, of Newburyport, Mass. Resides in Beverly; a trader. Only child:

Walter,[8] b. March 14, 1870.

By third wife :

546. PARKER FOX,[7] b. Sept. 5, 1842.

546½. JOANNA A.[7]

Seventh Generation.

298.

JOHN SYMMES[7] (*John*,[6] *Samuel*,[5] *Zechariah*,[4] *William*,[3] *William*,[2] *Zechariah*[1]), eldest son of John[6] and Abigail (Green) Symmes, of South Woburn, now Winchester; b. Dec. 14, 1819; married, first, ALMIRA STODDARD, of Woburn. She died previous to 1845. He married, second, June 9, 1845, MARY KENDALL CARTER, of Albany, N. Y. She was born June 14, 1827, daughter of Levi and Cynthia (Kendall) Carter, residents in Albany, but not natives of that place. She died at Burlington, Mass., June 11, 1860, aged 33. He married, third, at Lexington, Mass., June 30, 1861, EMILY CARTER, born in North Bridgton, Me., Sept. 13, 1832, daughter of Henry and Hannah (Cochran) Carter. She was cousin to the second wife—Henry, her father, being brother of Levi Carter, already mentioned. Hannah Cochran, wife of Henry Carter, was an Andover woman.

Mr. Symmes was by trade, originally, a carpenter, and worked in the sash and blind business. He has resided in Naples, Me., Burlington, Mass., Lawrence, Mass., and now lives on Elm Street, in Winchester. He goes to Boston daily, where he is superintendent of the large piano-forte manufactory of Hallett, Cumston & Co.

There were no children by the first wife, at least none that lived.

Children by second wife:

547. EMMA SOPHIA,⁸ b. in Winchester, Feb. 11, 1846; unmarried, and
     lives with her father.
548. WILLIAM FRANKLIN,⁸ b. in Naples, Me., July 31, 1849.
549. CHARLES AUGUSTUS,⁸ b. in Naples, May 31, 1851; d. July 31,
     1851.
550. MARY ELLA,⁸ b. in Naples, Sept. 2, 1853.
551. ARTHUR CARTER,⁸ b. in Burlington, Sept. 15, 1855; d. Nov. 9,
     1856.
552. CHARLES KENDALL,⁸ b. in Burlington, Jan. 24, 1858.
553. ABIGAIL GREEN,⁸ b. in Burlington, June 4, 1860; d. Aug. 26,
     1860.

Child by third wife:

554. EDWIN ALBERT,⁸ b. in Lawrence, Mass., May 22, 1865.

299.

WILLIAM BITTLE SYMMES⁷ (*John*,⁶ *Samuel*,⁵ *Zechariah*,⁴ *William*,³ *William*,² *Zechariah*¹), brother of the preceding; b. June 13,
1822; married ANNA HILL, of Portsmouth, N. H., Feb. 11, 1847.

He lives in New York city, or very near there, and is connected
with a clothing store in that city.

Only one child:

555. WILLIAM,⁸ b. July 31, 1851.

340.

JOHN ALBERT SYMMES⁷ (*John*,⁶ *John*,⁵ *John*,⁴ *William*,³ *William*,² *Zechariah*¹), son of Dea. John⁶ and Pamelia (Richardson)
Symmes; born at "Symmes's Corner," in what was Medford, but is
now included in Winchester, Nov. 3, 1812; married LYDIA MARIA
SMITH, June 1, 1839.

He kept a store in South Woburn, now the centre of Winchester.
He was to have taken the wheelwright's business from his father's
hands, with his brother Luther, and moved to the homestead for this
purpose, but died from a cut on the knee, Feb. 19, 1849, aged 36
years and three months.

He had but one child:

556. AMELIA MARIA,⁸ b. March 24, 1841.

341.

CHARLES CAREY SYMMES⁷ (*John*,⁶ *John*,⁵ *John*,⁴ *William*,³ *William*,² *Zechariah*¹), brother of the preceding; born Nov. 15, 1814;
married, Nov. 10, 1840, LYDIA FLETCHER CLARK, daughter of Dea.
Oliver Clark, of Tewksbury, Mass., by his first wife, and half-sister
to Hon. Oliver Richardson Clark, of Winchester, and Rev. Edward

Warren Clark, of Claremont, N. H., they being children of the second wife.

He went to Aylmer, Ottawa Co., Canada East, when sixteen years of age, as clerk to his uncle Charles Symmes [193], a lumber merchant there. After his marriage, 1840, he and his brother Henry succeeded to the uncle's business. He died of cholera at Three Rivers, Canada East, Aug. 4, 1854. His widow Lydia died at Aylmer, C. E., March 26, 1859.

Their children, all born at Aylmer, were:

557. CHARLES HENRY,[8] b. Oct. 31, 1841; d. Oct. 3, 1858.
558. EDWARD CAREY,[8] b. Oct. 1844; d. Feb. 1846.
559. CATHARINE NOEL,[8] b. Dec. 25, 1846; d. Dec. 1846.
560. FRANCIS EDWARD,[8] b. Sept. 12, 1851. After his mother's death, as above, her brother, Rev. Edward W. Clark, above mentioned, adopted this her only living child, and had his name changed to Francis Edward Clark. He is now a member of Dartmouth College, and it is expected that he will graduate in the summer of 1873.

342.

HENRY RICHARDSON SYMMES[7] (*John*,[6] *John*,[5] *John*,[4] *William*,[3] *William*,[2] *Zechariah*[1]), brother of the preceding; born April 13, 1818; married, March 25, 1842, his cousin ABIGAIL SYMMES,[7] [376], b. Jan. 8, 1826, daughter of his father's youngest brother Charles, of Aylmer, Canada East.

He resided some years at Aylmer, where he was editor of a paper. In 1858, he removed to Three Rivers, in the same province, and has since been superintendent of Public Works on the River Saint Maurice.

His children have been:

561. HENRY CHARLES,[8] b. April 18, 1843; m. Jennie Brown Thompson, Aug. 22, 1867. They live at Hamilton, Canada West. Child:
    562. *Herbert Ormsby*,[9] b. Sept. 20, 1872.
563. JOHN ALBERT,[8] b. May 28, 1845.
564. MARY ELIZABETH,[8] b. Jan. 4, 1848.
565. EDWARD,[8] b. Feb. 3, 1850; d. Dec. 10, 1850.
566. WILLIAM,[8] b. Oct. 25, 1851.
567. HANNAH PAMELIA,[8] b. March 25, 1854.
568. LUTHER RICHARDSON,[8] b. Aug. 22, 1856.
569. MARGARET McDOUGAL,[8] b. Aug. 5, 1858.
570. FREDERIC,[8] b. Nov. 11, 1859; d. March 28, 1867.
571. FANNY,[8] b. Sept. 5, 1861; d. 1861.
572. KATE FRANCES,[8] b. Jan. 12, 1863.
573. CHARLES,[8] b. July 18, 1864; d. 1864.
574. AGNES ADELAIDE,[8] b. Jan. 25, 1866.

15

343.

LUTHER RICHARDSON SYMMES[7] (*John,[6] John,[5] John,[4] William,[3] William,[2] Zechariah[1]*), brother of the preceding, and youngest son of Dea. John[6] and Pamelia (Richardson) Symmes; born March 21, 1822; married, Nov. 1, 1848, ELIZABETH ABBY AYER, daughter of Nathaniel Ayer, formerly of Charlestown, and more recently of Winchester, and sister of Thomas Prentiss Ayer [372].

He resides at the old homestead at "Symmes's Corner," in what is now the south part of Winchester, formerly the north part of Medford, on the spot where he was born. He was for some time a wheel-wright, following the business of his father and grandfather. He is now the efficient superintendent of the upper portion of the Charles-town Water Works, which derive an unfailing supply from Mystic Pond, near to which is "Symmes's Corner," and Mr. Symmes's house. North of this beautiful sheet of water, and immediately contiguous to it, was the farm granted to his ancestor, Rev. Zechariah Symmes, two centuries and a quarter ago.

Only one child:

575. ALICE FRANCES,[8] b. Sept. 13, 1851.

346.

THOMAS RUSSELL SYMMES[7] (*Thomas,[6] John,[5] John,[4] William,[3] William,[2] Zechariah[1]*), son of Thomas[6] and Sarah Lloyd (Wait) Symmes; born 1812; married HARRIET EADY, of Canada.

He lived at Aylmer, Canada East, and died a few years ago.

Their children were:

576. ELIZABETH.[8]
577. SARAH.[8]
578. THOMAS RUSSELL,[8] lives in Medford, near Boston.
579. ALBERT.[8]
580. JANE,[8] d. 1870.

347.

ALFRED TUFTS[7] (*Abigail Symmes,[6] John,[5] John,[4] William,[3] William,[2] Zechariah[1]*), son of Elias and Abigail[6] (Symmes) Tufts; born in Medford, July 8, 1818; married CAROLINE M. WRIGHT, of North-field, March 5, 1843. She was born March 16, 1820.

Their children were:

581. ARTHUR THOMPSON (Tufts), b. Feb. 9, 1844; m. Lizzie P. Herrick, of Brattleboro', Vt., Oct. 5, 1869.
582. EDWARD ALBRO (Tufts), b. July 19, 1845; d. Aug. 3, 1848.
583. ABBY THERESA (Tufts), b. Nov. 1, 1846; d. Sept. 25, 1861.
584. CHARLES ALFRED (Tufts), b. May 9, 1848; d. Sept. 8, 1849.

585. LIZZIE ELLEN (Tufts), b. Aug. 6, 1850 ; m. George D. Moore, of Somerville, May 30, 1871.
586. EMMA SHEPARD (Tufts), b. May 30, 1852 ; m. Allston M. Redman, of Medford, May 30, 1871.
587. FLORA LYMAN (Tufts), b. Oct. 9, 1855 ; d. July 23, 1865.
588. ANNA CAROLINE (Tufts), b. May 6, 1857.
589. FANNIE GERTRUDE (Tufts), b. Jan. 6, 1859.

348.

LARKIN TURNER TUFTS⁷ (*Abigail Symmes,*⁶ *John,*⁵ *John,*⁴ *William,*³ *William,*² *Zechariah*¹), brother of the preceding; born in Medford, Oct. 28, 1821 ; married FRANCES PARTHENIA McFARLAND, of Skowhegan, Me. She was born in Anson, Somerset Co., Me., Dec. 15, 1829. They were married at East Boston, Dec. 2, 1856, by Rev. William H. Cudworth.

At present, they live in Chelsea.

Their children :

590. FREDERIC SUMNER (Tufts), b. in Leavenworth, Kanzas, Nov. 6, 1860.
591. VIRGINIA PEARSON (Tufts), b. in Medford, Mass., March 29, 1865.

355.

MARSHALL SYMMES⁷ (*Marshall,*⁶ *John,*⁵ *John,*⁴ *William,*³ *William,*² *Zechariah*¹), eldest son of Marshall⁶ and Lephe (Stowell) Symmes ; born in what is now the south part of Winchester, Oct. 27, 1818; married, June 17, 1846, ABBIE STOWELL, born Aug. 16, 1824, dau. of Samuel Stowell, of Worcester, who was cousin of Abel Stowell, already mentioned as the husband of his aunt Elizabeth Symmes. [See p. 86.]

They live at "Symmes's Corner," in the south part of Winchester, in the house formerly owned and occupied by Gov. John Brooks.

Their children :

592. FRANCES LOUISA,⁸ b. April 26, 1847 ; d. Aug. 25, 1849.
593. FREDERIC MARSHALL,⁸ b. Aug. 13, 1850.
594. ELLA LEPHE,⁸ b. May 28, 1852.
595. WALTER FAY,⁸ b. Aug. 1. 1854.
596. ANNA ELIZA,⁸ b. Feb. 16, 1857.
597. SAMUEL STOWELL,⁸ b. Oct. 22, 1858.
598. ALBERT HENRY,⁸ b. Aug. 11, 1860 ; d. April 28, 1861.
599. ABBIE ELIZABETH,⁸ b. Aug. 2, 1862.

358.

ALEXANDER STOWELL SYMMES⁷ (*Marshall,*⁶ *John,*⁵ *John,*⁴ *William,*³ *William,*² *Zechariah*¹), brother of the preceding; born

Dec. 13, 1823; married, Jan. 27, 1852, SARAH JANE LIVERMORE, of Watertown, born Dec. 7, 1830.

They reside in Medford.

Their children, all born in Medford, are:

600. ADDIE MARIA,[9] b. March 23, 1853.
601. ARTHUR COTTING,[9] b. Feb. 9, 1856.
602. MARY ELLEN,[9] b. May 9, 1858.
603. JENNIE.[9] } twins; b. }
604. NETTIE.[9] } April 1, 1861. } d. Nov. 12, 1861.
605. SARAH ELIZABETH,[9] b. July 3, 1863.
606. LILLIAN FRANCES,[9] b. Oct. 17, 1865.
607. IDA LIVERMORE,[9] b. June 9, 1871.

360.

ELLEN LOUISA SYMMES[7] (*Marshall*,[6] *John*,[5] *John*,[4] *William*,[3] *William*,[2] *Zechariah*[1]), sister of the preceding; born May 16, 1828; married, Oct. 30, 1851, OLIVER LOCKE WELLINGTON, of Medford, son of Isaac, who may have been son of Abraham[6] and Elizabeth (Lawrence) Wellington, and grandson of William Wellington,[5] of Waltham. For his pedigree, see Dr. Henry Bond's Watertown Genealogies, pp. 627–635.

They live in Medford, and their children were born there, as follows:

608. ELLEN SYMMES (Wellington), b. Dec. 9, 1853.
609. HARRIET STOWELL (Wellington), b. Sept. 19, 1855.
610. FRANK OLIVER (Wellington), b. Aug. 2, 1857.
611. HERBERT MARSHALL (Wellington), b. June 24, 1859; deceased.
612. HARRY EUGENE (Wellington), b. Nov. 29, 1861.

361.

CHARLES THOMAS SYMMES[7] (*Marshall*,[6] *John*,[5] *John*,[4] *William*,[3] *William*,[2] *Zechariah*[1]), brother of the preceding, and youngest child of Marshall[6] and Lephe (Stowell) Symmes; born March 9, 1832; married, March 30, 1863, ABBY ELIZABETH HUNT, born Feb. 28, 1843, dau. of John Hunt, of Roxbury, and sister of John G. Hunt, who was the husband of Abby Maria Stowell [354].

Children:

613. IRVING LIVINGSTON,[9] b. July 13, 1866.
614. CHARLES HERBERT,[9] b. Nov. 15, 1869.

386.

JOHN THOMAS SYMMES[7] (*Charles*,[6] *John*,[5] *John*,[4] *William*,[3] *William*,[2] *Zechariah*[1]), son of Charles[6] and Hannah (Ricker) Symmes; born at Aylmer, Canada East, Jan. 26, 1836; married HARRIET GRIMES, April 5, 1860.

Children :

615. SARAH D.,⁸ b. Jan. 24, 1861.
616. CHARLES W.,⁸ b. Sept. 9, 1863.
617. HANNAH E.,⁸ b. Feb. 26, 1867.

387.

THOMAS JOHN SYMMES⁷ (*Charles,⁶ John,⁵ John,⁴ William,³ William,² Zechariah¹*), twin brother of the preceding ; born at Aylmer, Canada East, Jan. 26, 1836; married MARY WEYMOUTH, April 17, 1865.

Children :

618. CHARLES THOMAS,⁸ b. Jan. 17, 1866.
619. EDMUND,⁸ b. Jan. 3, 1868.
620. DANIEL WEYMOUTH,⁸ b. Jan. 30, 1870.
621. THOMAS JOHN,⁸ b. Dec. 13, 1871.

390.

HON. JOHN CLEVES SHORT⁷ (*Maria Symmes,⁶ John Cleves Symmes,⁵ Timothy,⁴ Timothy,³ William,² Zechariah¹*), son of Major Peyton and Maria (Symmes) Short, of Kentucky; b. about Oct. 1790; married, first, his cousin, BETSEY BASSETT HARRISON, born at North Bend, on the Ohio River, 1796, eldest child of William Henry and Anna (Symmes) Harrison. She died in 1848, and he married, second, a widow MITCHELL, about 1850.

He lived at North Bend, Ohio; was engaged in agricultural pursuits; had some acquaintance with law; was for a time judge of the Court of Common Pleas for Hamilton County, in which North Bend is situated; and was a member of the legislature of Ohio. While the rebel John Morgan was pursuing his devastating march in Kentucky, in July, 1862, and had even crossed the Ohio into Indiana, and Cincinnati was threatened, Mr. Short gave one thousand dollars to the authorities there towards putting that city in a proper state of defence.

He had several children, whose names are unknown to the compiler.

391.

DR. CHARLES W. SHORT⁷ (*Maria Symmes,⁶ John Cleves Symmes,⁵ Timothy,⁴ Timothy,³ William,² Zechariah¹*), brother of the preceding; born about 1795; married ――――.

He was a physician in Louisville, Ky.

His children were :

625. MARY (Short), m. ―― Richardson, a merchant, of Louisville.
626. WILLIAM (Short), m. Matilda Strader. He was a farmer in Ky.
627. JANE (Short), m. Dr. Butler, a physician, of Louisville.

628. SARAH (Short), m. Dr. Tobias Richardson, a physician, of Louisville.
629. LUCY (Short), m. ——Kincaid, a lawyer. (?)
630. ALICE (Short).

392.

ANNA MARIA SHORT[7] (*Maria Symmes,*[6] *John Cleves Symmes,*[5] *Timothy,*[4] *Timothy,*[3] *William,*[2] *Zechariah*[1]), sister of the preceding; born 1803; married, 1821, Dr. BENJAMIN DUDLEY, a physician, of Lexington, Ky.

Their children were:

631. CHARLES W. (Dudley), b. 1822; m. Margaret A. Johnson. He was a planter, near Lake Washington, in Mississippi. Child:
632. *Charles W.* (Dudley), b. 1856.
633. WILLIAM A. (Dudley), b. 1824; m. Mary J. Hawkins. He is a lawyer, in Lexington, Ky. Children:
634. *B. Winslow* (Dudley), b. 1846.
635. *Charles* (Dudley), b. 1849; d. 1859.
636. *William* (Dudley), b. 1851.
637. *Mary W.* (Dudley), b. 1852.
638. ANNA M. (Dudley), b. 1827; m. Edward A. Tilford, of Lexington, Ky., a lawyer.

394.

JOHN CLEVES SYMMES HARRISON[7] (*Anna Symmes,*[6] *John Cleves Symmes,*[5] *Timothy,*[4] *Timothy,*[3] *William,*[2] *Zechariah*[1]), eldest son of Gen. William Henry Harrison, President of the United States, by his wife Anna Symmes;[6] born at North Bend, Ohio, 1798; married, 1819, CLARISSA PIKE, dau. of Gen. Zebulon Pike.

He resided at Vincennes, Ind., and was for some time Receiver of the Public Moneys at that place. He died in 1830.

Children:

639. A daughter, m. John Hunt. Had children as follows:
640. *Symmes Harrison* (Hunt).
641. *Clara Pike* (Hunt).
642. *Mary* (Hunt).
643. A daughter, m. —— Roberts. Had *James Montgomery* (Roberts).
644. CLARA (Harrison), m. first, Dr. T. M. Banks; m. second, —— Morgan, of Fort Wayne, Ind., a merchant. Three children by Mr. Morgan:
645. *Symmes Harrison* (Banks), b. 1846.
646. *Mary* (Banks).
647. —— (Banks).
648. WILLIAM HENRY (Harrison), m. ——. Had two children.
649. MONTGOMERY PIKE (Harrison). He was educated at West Point, where he graduated, June 30, 1847; commissioned as 2d lieutenant in the 5th Reg't U. S. Infantry, Sept. 11, 1847. He served in the Mexican war. After its close, he was with his regiment

in Texas, and as he was returning from Santa Fe, with a detachment of soldiers under Capt. Randolph B. Marcy, he got separated from them and was cruelly murdered by Indians, near the Colorado River, Texas, Oct. 7, 1849.

650. JOHN CLEVES SYMMES (Harrison). He was a soldier in the Mexican war.

397.

WILLIAM HENRY HARRISON⁷ (*Anna Symmes,⁶ John Cleves Symmes,⁵ Timothy,⁴ Timothy,³ William,² Zechariah¹*), brother of the preceding; born 1802; married JANE IRWIN.

He was a graduate of Transylvania University, Ky., but spent his life as a farmer at North Bend, Ohio, and died about 1838.

Their children were:

651. WILLIAM HENRY (Harrison).
652. JAMES FINDLEY (Harrison), m. Caroline Allston. He was educated at Cincinnati College and at West Point, and studied law at Cincinnati. He served as Adjutant in the Cincinnati Regiment in the war with Mexico. After the war, he settled on a farm near Dayton, Ohio, where he still resides. Children:
 653. *William Henry* (Harrison).
 654. *James Findley* (Harrison).

398.

JOHN SCOTT HARRISON⁷ (*Anna Symmes,⁶ John Cleves Symmes,⁵ Timothy,⁴ Timothy,³ William,² Zechariah¹*), brother of the preceding; born 1804; married, first, LUCRETIA K. JOHNSON; m. second, ELIZABETH IRWIN.

He is a graduate of Cincinnati College; resides at North Bend; and is a lawyer by profession. He was a member of Congress from Ohio, in 1855.*

His children are:

655. BETSEY H. (Harrison), b. about 1825; m. Dr. George C. Eaton, a physician at North Bend, Ohio. Four children.
656. WILLIAM HENRY (Harrison), b. 1827; d. 1829.
657. SARAH (Harrison), b. about 1830; m. —— Devine, of Iowa.
658. IRWIN (Harrison), b. 183–; m. Bettie Shute. Resides at Indianapolis. He is a graduate of Miami University, at Oxford, Ohio. He raised a company for the three months' service in 1861, of which he was captain. He was in the battle of Rich Mountain, in West Virginia, July 11, 1861. At the expiration of the three months' service, he was commissioned lieut.-colonel of the 27th Reg't Ind. Vols.; but the ill health of his family compelled him

---

* It seems there were two Johns in Gen. Harrison's family who came to mature years and had families of their own.

to leave the army in the summer of 1862. He has several children.

659. BENJAMIN (Harrison), b. 183–; m. Carrie Scott. Resides at Indianapolis. He also is a graduate of Miami University, at Oxford, Ohio, and is a lawyer. In 1860 he was chosen Reporter of the Supreme Court of Indiana. On the breaking out of the war in 1861, he entered the military service as colonel of the 10th Reg't Indiana Vols. He rose to the rank of brigadier-general, and distinguished himself as a good officer. Since the war, he has been engaged in the profession of the law, at Indianapolis. In the celebrated Clem case, a difficult affair, which had four different trials, Gen. Harrison was the leading prosecutor. In the fourth and last, at Lebanon, Ind., 1872, he was opposed, on the defence, by Hon. D. W. Voorhees, of Terre Haute. Gen. Harrison is at the head of his profession in Indiana, and indeed in the West.

660. JENNY (Harrison), b. 183–; m. Samuel Morris.
661. CARTER (Harrison).
662. ANNA (Harrison).
663. JOHN (Harrison).
664. JAMES FINDLEY (Harrison), b. 1847.
665. JAMES IRWIN (Harrison), b. 1849.

399.

DR. BENJAMIN HARRISON[7] (*Anna Symmes,*[6] *John Cleves Symmes,*[5] *Timothy,*[4] *Timothy,*[3] *William,*[2] *Zechariah*[1]), brother of the preceding; born 1806; married, first, —— BONNER; m. second, —— RANEY.

He graduated at Cincinnati College, and studied medicine in Baltimore. He closed his life at New Orleans in 1840.

Children:

666. JOHN C. (Harrison), b. 183–; m. Mary Harrison. A banker in Indianapolis.
667. WILLIAM HENRY (Harrison), b. 1839; d. 1850.
668. BENJAMIN (Harrison).

400.

MARY SYMMES HARRISON[7] (*Anna Symmes,*[6] *John Cleves Symmes,*[5] *Timothy,*[4] *Timothy,*[3] *William,*[2] *Zechariah*[1]), sister of the preceding; born 1808; married, 1829, Dr. J. F. H. THORNTON, a physician of North Bend, Ohio.

Children:

669. WILLIAM HENRY HARRISON (Thornton), b. 1831; a farmer of Monroe Co., Ill.
670. CHARLES (Thornton), b. 1832; a physician, in Cincinnati.
671. ANNA HARRISON (Thornton), b. 1835; lives at Newstead, Ohio.
672. LUCY H. (Thornton), b. 1837; d. 1839.

673. ALICE E. (Thornton), b. 1838.
674. FITZHUGH (Thornton), b. 1842.

401.

CARTER BASSETT HARRISON⁷ (*Anna Symmes,⁶ John Cleves Symmes,⁵ Timothy,⁴ Timothy,³ William,² Zechariah¹*), brother of the preceding; born 1811; married, 1836, MARY SUTHERLAND.

He graduated at Miami University, Oxford, Ohio, in 1833; attended law lectures in Cincinnati, and completed his legal studies with the eminent lawyers, Schenck and Crane, at Dayton, Ohio.

He accompanied his father, Gen. William Henry Harrison, afterwards President, to Colombia, as private secretary. He had commenced a brilliant career as a lawyer, in Hamilton, Ohio, but it was cut short by his untimely death in 1839.

He had one child:

675. ANNA C. (Harrison), b. 1837.

402.

ANNA TUTHILL HARRISON⁷ (*Anna Symmes,⁶ John Cleves Symmes,⁵ Timothy,⁴ Timothy,³ William,² Zechariah¹*), sister of the preceding, and dau. of Gen. William Henry Harrison by his wife Anna Symmes; b. 1813; married Col. WILLIAM HENRY HARRISON TAYLOR, a grand nephew of her father.

He has served as clerk of the court and deputy sheriff of Hamilton Co., Ohio; and also as post-master of Cincinnati. He has also been colonel of the Fifth Cavalry Regiment of Ohio.

To his worthy lady the reader is indebted for most of the information touching the descendants of her father, Gen. Harrison. She died July 5, 1865.

They resided some time at Cleves, near North Bend, Ohio; more recently at Minneapolis, Minn.

Children:

676. WILLIAM HENRY HARRISON (Taylor), b. 1837.
677. LUCY S. (Taylor), b. 1838.
678. ANNA HARRISON (Taylor), b. 1840; d. 1840.
679. JOHN THOMAS (Taylor), b. 1841.
680. MARY F. (Taylor), b. 1843.
681. ANNA C. (Taylor), b. 1844.
682. BESSIE S. (Taylor), b. 1846.
683. FANNIE E. (Taylor), b. 1848.
684. VIRGINIA B. (Taylor), b. 1849.
685. JANE H. (Taylor), b. 1852.
686. NELLIE B. (Taylor), b. 1853.
687. EDWARD EVERETT (Taylor), b. 1856.

16

406.

DANIEL TUTHILL SYMMES[7] (*Celadon,[6] Timothy,[5] Timothy,[4] Timothy,[3] William,[2] Zechariah[1]*), son of Celadon[6] and Phebe (Randolph) Symmes; b. in Butler Co., Ohio, Nov. 5, 1798; m. May 8, 1823, LUCINDA GASTON, dau. of Joseph and Martha (Hutton) Gaston.*

He passed his life in agricultural pursuits in his native place, was a leading man in that vicinity, and died somewhat prematurely, Aug. 14, 1830, in his 32d year.

Children:

688. PHEBE,[8] b. 1825; d. same year.

+689. JOSEPH GASTON,[8] b. Jan. 24, 1826; m. Mary Rosebrook Henry.

+690. FRANCIS MARION,[8] b. Nov. 18, 1827; m. Mary Jane Dunn.

691. SAMUEL,[8] b. 1832; d. 1842.

408.

CAPT. BENJAMIN RANDOLPH SYMMES[7] (*Celadon,[6] Timothy,[5] Timothy,[4] Timothy,[3] William,[2] Zechariah[1]*), brother of the preceding; born 1802; married, first, ELIZA GASTON, 1826. She was sister of Lucinda Gaston, wife of Daniel Tuthill Symmes. He married, second, JANE PAULEY, 1835.

He has always resided in the vicinity where he was born, and has devoted himself to the pursuits of agriculture. He was for a long time captain of a company in the militia, and also justice of the peace. In 1840, he built a hotel on the southwestern corner of the section of the land which had been the property of his father, three miles south of Hamilton, Ohio. To this locality he gave the name "Symmes's Corner;" whence the name of the village which has since

* JOSEPH GASTON was of Huguenot origin. Early in life he removed from Washington County, in Western Pennsylvania, to Abbeville District, South Carolina. Encouraged by the success of the British troops, in 1780, the tories infested that whole region, and the friends of liberty, for self-protection, formed themselves into armed bands, under Cols. Thomas Sumter, Francis Marion, Andrew Pickens, George Rogers Clarke, Campbell, Cleveland, Shelby, and others. The tories were for the most part worthless, unprincipled and cruel men. Gaston joined one of the patriot bands, we believe that of Marion. Once he was captured by the tories, who also killed one of his brothers. The tories ordered him to give up all he had. He delivered to them all but a guinea he had secreted in his watch-pocket. They then said they would search him, and if they should find anything they would kill him. On this he suddenly exclaimed, "Oh yes! I have a guinea in my watch-fob." This saved his life.

He married Martha Hutton, April, 1783, who was born April 25, 1763, and died Nov. 21, 1821. She was a woman of earnest patriotism and indomitable resolution. The fire kindled in her bosom by the terrible outrages of the tories never died out. A brother of hers was killed in the American army during the Revolution. She, her sisters, and their mother, suffered much from the tories, who would wantonly destroy what they could not use. Her grandson, who supplies these facts, has often slept on a feather bed, which they saved from the tories by forcing it up with a pole in a large hollow tree, out of sight, leaving the pole standing to hold it up. They buried their dishes, hid away their clothing, and secreted their food. In later days, she would spend hours in relating to her children the trying scenes of that period.

In 1809, Mr. Gaston with his family removed from Abbeville District, S. C., to the northern part of Hamilton Co., Ohio, and thus came into the vicinity of the Symmes family. They moved in a wagon, accompanied by four other families. Five weeks were spent on the way. They camped out at night, cooking their food by fires in the woods, having family worship night and morning, and resting on the Sabbath day.

sprung up in that vicinity. In 1844, he removed to the "Corner," and kept the hotel himself for many years. He also served as postmaster of that village from that date to 1861. He still resides at "Symmes's Corner."

His children have been, by first wife, ELIZA:

692. CELADON CLEVES,⁸ b. 1828 ; d. 1829.
+693. MARTHA JANE,⁸ b. 1829 ; m. John Watson.
694. ISAAC WATTS,⁸ b. 1831 ; d. 1835.
+695. PEYTON RANDOLPH,⁸ b. 1833 ; m. Elizabeth Kingery.

By second wife, JANE:

696. CELADON HUTTON,⁸ b. 1836 ; m. Sarah Tuley, 1862.
697. SAMUEL WILEY,⁸ b. 1839 ; d. 1839.
+698. JAMES RIGDON,⁸ b. 1840 ; m. Maria Hagerman.
699. ELIZA GASTON,⁸ b. 1843 ; d. 1844.
700. JOSEPH ERSKINE,⁸ b. 1845.
701. CATHARINE JANE,⁸ b. 1847.

410.

CELADON SYMMES⁷ (Celadon,⁶ Timothy,⁵ Timothy,⁴ Timothy, William,² Zechariah¹), brother of the preceding; born 1807; married, 1828, CATHARINE BLACKBURN.

He is a well-to-do farmer in Butler Co., Ohio; a member of the Presbyterian church. After his brother Daniel died, he was guardian of his three fatherless, helpless children, and acted towards them the part of a father.

Children:

702. BENJAMIN,⁸ b. 1830. He is a farmer at Symmes's Corner, near Hamilton, Ohio.
703. Infant son,⁸ b. 1832; d. 1832.
704. JOHN MILTON,⁸ b. 1833; a farmer and carpenter at Symmes's Corner.
705. DANIEL TUTHILL,⁸ b. 1836 ; m. 1860, Mary H. Vinnedge. He is a farmer at Symmes's Corner. Had :
    706. *Georgetta,*⁹ b. 1861.
707. JOSEPH CLEVES,⁸ b. 1840 ; m. 1863, Martha Smith.
708. AARON BLACKBURN,⁸ b. 1843.
709. CELADON JASPER,⁸ b. 1845; d. 1848.
710. HANNAH CATHARINE,⁸ b. 1848.

In this family the reader will observe seven sons in succession.

412.

ESTHER WOODRUFF SYMMES⁷ (Celadon,⁶ Timothy,⁵ Timothy,⁴ Timothy,³ William,² Zechariah¹), sister of the preceding; born 1811; married, 1827, WILLIAM NOBLE HUNTER.

He was a farmer in Butler Co., Ohio; an elder in the Presbyterian church many years, and a very worthy man.

Children:

711. ANDREW (Hunter), b. 1829. He devoted himself to the gospel ministry, and entered Hanover College with this purpose, but was called away by death in 1848, at the commencement of his course.
712. SARAH JANE (Hunter), b. 1835; m. 1857, William Hall Huston, a farmer, living at Symmes's Corner, already mentioned.
    Children:
    713. *Edward C.* (Huston), b. 1858.
    714. *William Clay* (Huston), b. 1859.
    715. *Sarah Elizabeth* (Huston), b. 1860.
716. CALVIN SYMMES (Hunter), b. 1839; a farmer at Symmes's Corner.
717. LUCINDA SYMMES (Hunter), b. 1841; m. 1864, John A. Compton.
718. JOHN CLEVES (Hunter), b. 1843; a college student, and a soldier in the late war.
719. PHEBE CATHARINE (Hunter), b. 1845.
720. WILLIAM NOBLE (Hunter), b. 1847.
721. ALEXANDER (Hunter), b. 1849.
722. ESTHER (Hunter), b. 1851.
723. MARY CLARA (Hunter), b. 1853.
724. CELADON JASPER (Hunter), b. 1856.

413.

JOSEPH RANDOLPH SYMMES[7] (*Celadon,[6] Timothy,[5] Timothy,[4] Timothy,[3] William,[2] Zechariah[1]*), brother of the preceding; born 1814; married, first, 1840, MARTHA J. HUSTON; married, second, 1847, MARY C. BIGHAM.

He is a farmer, near Hamilton, Butler Co., Ohio; a man of strict integrity and unusual strength of character. He is now, Dec. 1872, an elder in the First Presbyterian Church in Hamilton, Ohio.

Children by first wife, MARTHA:

725. JOHN HUSTON,[8] b. 1840; d. 1840.

By second wife, MARY:

726. JAMES BIGHAM,[8] b. 1848; d. 1849.
727. WILLIAM,[8] b. 1851.
728. MARTHA,[8] b. 1853; d. 1856.
729. JOHN CLEVES,[8] b. 1855; d. 1858.
730. CELADON,[8] b. 1857; d. 1858.
731. MARY CATHARINE,[8] b. 1859; d. 1861.
732. JOSEPH CLEVES,[8] b. 1861; d. 1863.
733. PHEBE RANDOLPH,[8] b. 1864.

414.

SARAH DEBORAH SYMMES[7] (*Celadon,[6] Timothy,[5] Timothy,[4] Timothy,[3] William,[2] Zechariah[1]*), sister of the preceding, and youngest child of Celadon[6] and Phebe (Randolph) Symmes; born 1817; married, 1834, ENOCH POWERS, a farmer, of Symmes's Corner, near Hamilton, Ohio; married, second, 1860, JOSEPH DANFORD.

Children :

734. ESTHER ANN (Powers), b. 1834; m. first, 1853, Charles Hunt, of Symmes's Corner, a wagon-maker; m. second, 1859, Joseph Miller, a farmer. Children :
    735. *Scott Powers* (Miller), b. 1859.
    736. *William Elliot* (Miller), b. 1862.
737. NANCY CAROLINE (Powers), b. 1836; d. 1842.
738. MARTHA JANE (Powers), b. 1841.
739. SARAH ELLEN (Powers), b. 1843; m. 1859, Amos Danford, of Symmes's Corner. Two children, both deceased.
740. JOHN WELLER (Powers), b. 1846; d. 1847.

416.

PHEBE SYMMES[7] (*William,[6] Timothy,[5] Timothy,[4] Timothy,[3] William,[2] Zechariah[1]*), dau. of William[6] and Rebecca (Randolph) Symmes; born 1804; married, in 1826, BARNABAS HOEL, a farmer, of Hamilton Co., Ohio. She died in 1855.

Her children were :

741. LUCINDA (Hoel), b. 1827.
742. JANE (Hoel), b. 1828.
743. WILLIAM (Hoel), b. 1831.
744. REBECCA S. (Hoel), b. 1834; m. 1851, Edwin T. Jordan, of Mount Pleasant, Ohio. Children :
    745. *Frances A.* (Jordan), b. 1857.
    746. *Florence M.* (Jordan), b. 1859.
747. CATHARINE (Hoel), b. 1856.
748. MARTHA A. (Hoel), b. 1838; m. 1857, Oscar Smith, a machinist, of Hamilton, O. They have :
    749. *Ida* (Smith), b. 1858.
750. SARAH J. (Hoel), b. 1840.
751. JACOB (Hoel), b. 1843.
752. JOSEPH (Hoel), b. 1846.

418.

TIMOTHY SYMMES[7] (*William,[6] Timothy,[5] Timothy,[4] Timothy,[3] William,[2] Zechariah[1]*), brother of the preceding; born in Butler Co., Ohio, 1809; married, 1830, HARRIET WILMUTH.

He was a farmer in Butler Co., Ohio, and died 1838.

Children :

753. HESTER A.,[8] b. 1831 ; m. 1850, James Hargan, of Cincinnati, O.,
   a locksmith. She d. 1854. Children :
   754. *Mary V.* (Hargan), b. 1851 ; d. 1852.
   755. *George* (Hargan), b. 1853 ; resides at Madison, Ind.
756. WASHINGTON,[8] b. 1832 ; d. 1848.
757. JEFFERSON,[8] b. 1834; m. 1857, Ellen H. Dixon. Resides at Chicago ; is a broom-maker. Has two children.
758. TIMOTHY,[8] b. 1837 ; at Chicago, a broom-maker.

419.

LOUISIANA SYMMES[7] (*John Cleves,[6] Timothy,[5] Timothy,[4] Timothy,[3] William,[2] Zechariah[1]*), dau. of Capt. John Cleves Symmes ;[6]
born at Bellefontaine, Missouri,* Feb. 5, 1810 : married, first, at
Hamilton, Ohio, 1832. JAMES W. TAYLOR, merchant, of Frankfort, Ky.
He died in 1838. She married, second, 1844, JOEL BAKER, a grocer,
in Cincinnati.

Her two oldest sons died within a week of each other, in 1853.
The shock to the mother was so severe, that she followed them
just a week afterwards.

Children :

759. RICHARD CLEVES (Taylor), b. 1833 ; a military student, at Drennon Springs, Kentucky ; d. 1853.
760. JAMES W. (Taylor), b. 1835 ; a military student ; died 1853, just
   as he was about to graduate at the Military Academy, Drennon
   Springs, Ky. Both he and his brother Richard died of typhoid
   fever.
761. AMERICUS STANLEY (Baker), b. 1845.
762. MARY SYMMES (Baker), b. 1848.

420.

AMERICUS SYMMES[7] (*John Cleves,[6] Timothy,[5] Timothy,[4] Timothy,[3]
William,[2] Zechariah[1]*), brother of the preceding, and eldest son of
Capt. John Cleves Symmes ;[6] born at Bellefontaine, Nov. 2, 1811 ;
married, first, 1832. ANNA MILLIKEN, of Hamilton, Ohio, dau. of Dr.
Daniel Milliken. She died there, Jan. 5, 1839. He married, second,
at Louisville, Ky., 1840, FRANCES SCOTT, dau. of Maj. Chasteen Scott,
of Boone Co., Ky.

His father died when he was but little more than seventeen years
of age, leaving on his hands an estate encumbered with debt, and a
widowed mother and three children besides himself to provide for.
The responsible task was well performed.

He resided at Hamilton, Ohio, till 1850, then removed to Covington, Ky. In 1852, he removed to a fine farm, three miles south-east
of Louisville, Ky.

---

* A garrison post, sixteen miles above St. Louis. It was afterwards destroyed by the
caving in of the bank of the river.

Children by first wife:

763. ANTHONY LOCKWOOD,[8] b. 1835; m. 1857, Mary E. Culver. He
is a coal-dealer in Louisville, Ky. Children:
    764. *Ella,*[9] b. 1858.   } Twins.
    765. *Charles,*[9] b. 1858; d. 1859. }
766. JAMES TUTHILL,[8] b. 1857; was a military student; d. 1854.
767. DANIEL CLEVES,[8] b. 1859; of Louisville, Ky.; was a captain in
the rebel army, and fought bravely on the side of the "Confederacy." He was taken prisoner by a kinsman in the U. S.
Army. [See 695.]

By second wife:

768. FLORENCE,[8] b. 1841.
769. SCOTT,[8] b. 1843.
770. AMERICUS,[8] b. 1846.
771. WILLIAM,[8] b. 1848.
772. HENRY,[8] b. 1852.
773. LILLY,[8] b. 1855; d. 1856.
774. IDA,[8] b. 1858.
775. A daughter,[8] b. 1861.

421.

DR. WILLIAM HENRY HARRISON SYMMES[7] (*John Cleves,*[6]
Timothy,[5] *Timothy,*[4] *Timothy,*[3] *William,*[2] *Zechariah*[1]), brother of the
preceding, and son of Capt. John Cleves Symmes;[6] born at Bellefontaine, May, 1813; married, first, PHEBE A. WAYNE, at Greyville,
Ill., 1840. She died there, 1851. He married, second, Mrs. H.
BARGEN, 1853, at Shawneetown, Illinois, a niece of the noted Benjamin Hardin, of Kentucky.

He studied medicine in Frankfort, Ky.; graduated at the Medical
College, Cincinnati, O., in 1837. He practised medicine some years
in Ohio; in 1857, removed to Mattoon, Illinois; and is now a physician in Kansas City, Missouri.

Children by first wife:

776. WILLIAM SCOTT,[8] b. 1841.
777. LITTLETON FOWLER,[8] b. 1843.
778. ALICE,[8] b. 1845.

By second wife:

779. OLIVER REEDER,[8] b. 1854.
780. IDA CARR,[8] b. 1855.

423.

CAPT. JOHN CLEVES SYMMES[7] (*John Cleves,*[6] *Timothy,*[5] *Timothy,*[4] *Timothy,*[3] *William,*[2] *Zechariah*[1]), brother of the preceding, and
youngest son of Capt. John Cleves Symmes;[6] born at Newport,
Ky., Oct. 25, 1824; married, in 1862, at Berlin, Prussia, while
sojourning in Germany, MARIE LEPOWITZ, of Posen, in Prussian
Poland.

He graduated at the U. S. Military Academy, West Point, in 1847, at the head of his class, and with a higher "general merit" in studies than any other student of that institution had ever exhibited. He was second lieutenant of Artillery immediately on his graduation, July 1, 1847; and two months afterwards, Aug. 30, became Acting Assistant Professor of Ethics, &c., in that institution. He was transferred to the Ordnance Department, Aug. 24, 1849; and was, unsolicited, made a captain of infantry by the Secretary of War, on the formation of new regiments, in 1855, but declined the appointment, preferring the artillery service.

After this he was stationed at Fort Leavenworth, in Kansas, and was promoted to be captain of Ordnance, but was compelled to retire from active service on account of sickness and weak eyes contracted at that station. He made, from time to time, fifteen breech-loading guns and a cannon, all different. He has invented a new species of arms, which he proposes to call the "Simz Rifle," and the "Simz Cannon;" also an air-engine, which he calls "The Simz Power."

He is now on the invalid list, and since Sept. 1862, has resided in Berlin, Prussia, where he had a son:

781. JOHN HAVEN CLEVES,⁸ b. 1866.

425.

MARY ANN MOORE (*Mary Symmes,⁶ Timothy,⁵ Timothy,⁴ Timothy,³ William,² Zechariah¹*), daughter of Hugh and Mary (Symmes) Moore; born in Cincinnati, 1809; m. 1829, JAMES B. MARSHALL.

They dwelt in Covington, Ky. He was an editor.

Children:

782. JOHN (Marshall), b. 1831; a commission merchant in Covington, Kentucky.
783. MARY SYMMES (Marshall), b. 1833; d. 1833.
784. HUGH HUMPHREY (Marshall), b. 1834; d. 1835.
785. LOUIS ISHAM (Marshall), b. 1836; a commission merchant.
786. WILLIAM HENRY HARRISON (Marshall), b. 1838; d. 1853.
787. KATE BURNEY (Marshall), b. 1840.
788. JULIA SYMMES (Marshall), b. 1843.
789. LUCY JANE (Marshall), b. 1848; d. 1849.
790. JOHN CLEVES SYMMES (Marshall), b. 1851; died 1860.

428.

HUGH MONTGOMERY MOORE (*Mary Symmes,⁶ Timothy,⁵ Timothy,⁴ Timothy,³ William,² Zechariah¹*), brother of the preceding; born in Cincinnati, 1819; married, first, MARGARET CRANE, of Hamilton, Ohio, 1842; married, second, CLARA HARRIS, of South Carolina, about 1853.

He lived in Hamilton, Ohio, and died 1854.

Children:

791. MARY SYMMES (Moore), b. 1843 ; d. 1843.
792. CHARLES (Moore), b. in South Carolina, about 1853.

429.

DR. JOHN CLEVES SYMMES MOORE (*Mary Symmes,* *Timothy,* *Timothy,* *Timothy,* *William,* *Zechariah*), brother of the preceding; married, 1851, EMILY WRIGHT.

He was a physician in Cincinnati, and died in 1860.

Children:

793. CHARLOTTE EMILY (Moore), b. 1853.
794. CLEVES MONTGOMERY (Moore), b. 1855.

438.

ALLEN LAKE REEDER (*Juliana Symmes,* *Timothy,* *Timothy,* *Timothy,* *William,* *Zechariah*), son of Jeremiah and Juliana (Symmes) Reeder; born in Cincinnati, 1817; married, 1841, LYDIA A. ELLIOT.

He was a nurseryman in Cincinnati.

Children:

795. JULIA ANN (Reeder), b. 1842.
796. LAURA GRAHAM (Reeder), b. 1844.
797. WILLIAM ELLIOT (Reeder), b. 1846.
798. EDWARD OLIVER (Reeder), b. 1851.
799. CHARLES STANLEY (Reeder), b. 1853.
800. ALLEN HARRISON (Reeder), b. 1861.

441.

MARY SYMMES REEDER (*Juliana Symmes,* *Timothy,* *Timothy,* *Timothy,* *William,* *Zechariah*), sister of the preceding; born 1824; married, 1845, Dr. WILLIAM R. McALLISTER.

He was a physician in Troy, Tennessee.

Children:

801. FRANCES ELIZABETH (McAllister), b. 1845.
802. JULIA SYMMES (McAllister), b. 1851.
803. WILLIAM CLEVES (McAllister), b. 1857.
804. HUMPHREY MARSHALL (McAllister), b. 1860.

443.

MARY SUSAN SYMMES[7] (*Peyton S.,* *Timothy,* *Timothy,* *Timothy,* *William,* *Zechariah*), daughter of Peyton Short Symmes,[6] of

17

Cincinnati; born there, 1822; married, 1847, CHARLES L. COLBURN, hard-ware merchant.

They live at Mount Auburn, near Cincinnati. He is of the firm of Latimer, Colburn & Lupton, hardware merchants, 55 West Pearl Street, Cincinnati.

Children:

805. CHARLES (Colburn), b. 1850.
806. JAMES LUPTON (Colburn), b. 1852.
807. MARY GLIDDON (Colburn), b. 1857.

449.

MAJ. HENRY EDWARD SYMMES[7] (*Peyton S.,*[6] *Timothy,*[5] *Timothy,*[4] *Timothy,*[3] *William,*[2] *Zechariah*[1]), brother of the preceding, and son of Peyton S. Symmes,[6] of Cincinnati; born in Cincinnati, 1835; never married.

When the war of the rebellion broke out, in April, 1861, he entered with ardor and energy into the great struggle against the enemies of the Union. In a very few days he left his native city at the head of a company of nearly one hundred men. This was afterwards known as Co. C, in the 5th Reg't Ohio Vols. This regiment was chiefly made up of Cincinnati young men, the flower of that city. At the end of the three months term, for which it originally enlisted, it was mustered for three years. Its first campaign was in West Virginia. They were first under fire in the affair of Blue's Gap, near Romney, so called because it is a narrow ravine between two high hills, the ravine in one place only twenty feet wide. It was on the 8th of January, 1862, and the snow was six inches deep. In this affair, Capt. Symmes led the advanced guard, of one hundred and fifty men, in most gallant style, and was in the thickest of the fight, till the enemy, though strongly posted, made a hasty retreat.

The regiment bore a conspicuous part in the battle of Winchester, March 23, 1862; joined Gen. McDowell, at Fredericksburg, May, 1862; were actively engaged in the battles of Port Republic, June 9, Cedar Mountain, Aug. 9, in the second battle of Bull Run, Aug. 29, in the battle of Antietam, Sept. 17, in the defence of Dumfries against the attack of the rebel Stuart, Dec. 27, all in 1862; in the battle of Chancellorsville, May 1, 2, and 3, of Gettysburg, July 2, 3, and 4, and of Lookout Mountain, Nov. 23, 24, and 25, 1863. In these severe engagements the regiment lost the greater part of its men.

In Jan. 1864, Capt. Symmes was promoted to be major. Col. John H. Patrick, who commanded the regiment, was killed by a concealed rebel, and Maj. Symmes succeeded to the command, but received a mortal wound from a rebel in a rifle-pit, of which he died at Chattanooga, in May or June, 1864, being only 29 years of age.

461.

CAPT. HENRY HARKER SYMMES[7] (*Timothy,[6] Timothy,[5] Timothy,[4] Timothy,[3] William,[2] Zechariah[1]*), only son of Timothy[6] and Ruth Symmes; born 1821; married BELINDA SEDAM, 1846.

His home is St. Louis, Mo.; but he has passed the greater part of his life on the Ohio, Mississippi, and Missouri rivers, as pilot, mate, and captain of steamboats. Thirteen steamers are recollected of which he has been captain and owner-in-trust. He is noted for great bodily strength. Frequently, when two men have been fighting, he has gone up to them, and taking one in each hand, has held them apart until their rage subsided.

Children:

808. CREED F.,[8] b. 1851; d. 1853.
809. MARY,[8] b. 1854.
810. SCOTT HARRISON,[8] b. 1856; d. 1857.
811. RUT. A.,[8] b. 1859.

471.

THOMAS GILES (*Mary Jennison, Abigail Lindall, Mary Higginson, Sarah Savage, Mary Symmes, Zechariah Symmes*), eldest son of Thomas Giles by his wife Mary Jennison; born in South Danvers, now Peabody, Oct. 6, 1754; married, June 22, 1780, MARY SOPER MARSHALL,* born in Boston, Aug. 9, 1756, dau. of Zerubbabel and Elizabeth (Soper) Marshall, of that city.

He learned the trade of sail-maker, of Nicholas Lane, at his loft on Union Wharf, in Salem. He was reputed an excellent workman.

At the breaking out of the Revolutionary War, he, with all the ardor of youth, took arms in behalf of his country, and continued in the military or naval service until the very close of the war. Of this

---

* In the first generation of New-England people were many families of the name of MARSHALL. I find more than twenty men of mature age bearing that name in New England, previous to 1650. Their posterity are now widely scattered.

1. JOHN MARSHALL, a progenitor of Mary Soper Marshall, in the text, was a native of Scotland. He came to this country about 1650, but was *not* one of the Scottish prisoners sent over by Cromwell after the battle of Dunbar. He lived in Boston, near the intersection of Hawkins and Sudbury Streets, and died there in the autumn of 1672.

2. JOHN MARSHALL, his second son, was born in Boston, Oct. 2, 1664, and married in Braintree, May 12, 1690, Mary (Sheffield) Mills, dau. of Edmund Sheffield, and widow of Jonathan Mills, all of Braintree. Edmund Sheffield, born in England about 1615, may have been a distant relative of Edmund, lord Sheffield, one of the patentees of the Great Charter for New England, granted Nov. 3, 1620. He lived in that part of Braintree which is now Quincy, as did also his son-in-law Marshall. Both were highly respectable men, men of deep and fervent piety.

3. Rev. JOSIAH MARSHALL, born Nov. 28, 1700, was the only son of John Marshall, who lived to mature years. He grad. H. C. 1720, and was pastor of a church in Falmouth, in Barnstable Co., Mass. I am not quite *sure* that Zerubbabel Marshall, in the text, was his son: but there is ample evidence that Zerubbabel Marshall married Elizabeth Soper, who was a daughter of Mary Marshall, sister of Rev. Josiah, and daughter of John Marshall, of Braintree. The parties to this marriage were probably cousins. It is not strange that town records sometimes fail us. They were then imperfectly kept. Mrs. Mary (Marshall) Giles, in the text, assured the compiler that she was great granddaughter of John and Mary (Sheffield) Marshall, of Braintree, above named.

the proof is abundant and satisfactory; and it was a case which had few parallels in the history of that great struggle. The records show that he enlisted May 15, 1775, in Col. Moses Little's regiment of eight months' men. This service ended with the year; but he re-enlisted at its close; and again enlisted May 3, 1777, in the 13th Mass. Reg't of continental troops, commanded by Lieut.-Col. Calvin Smith, for three years, and obtained an honorable discharge at the end of that period. His discharge, dated May 2, 1780, is still in existence.

He then returned to his friends, and was married. But the very day before his "intention of marriage" was recorded by the town clerk of Boston, he shipped as sail-maker of the armed ship Mars, in the service of the State of Massachusetts, under the command of that brave and efficient officer, Capt. Simeon Sampson, of Kingston, Mass.

He was sail-maker of the Mars from June 8, 1780, to March 12, 1781. He was then transferred to the continental frigate ALLIANCE, the "crack ship" of the American Revolution, then lying in the port of L'Orient, in France, under the command of that meritorious officer, Capt. John Barry. He was sail-maker of the Alliance, as he had been of the Mars.

He was in the Alliance, May 28, 1781, when she had that severe encounter with two English armed ships, the Atalanta, of 16 guns and 130 men, and the Trepassy, of 14 guns and 80 men, and took them both. There was no wind, and the sea was perfectly smooth. The Alliance was becalmed, and lay like a log in the water. The other vessels got out their sweeps [oars] and selected their positions at will. The cannon was well served on both sides. At length the ensign of the Alliance was shot away, and the crews of the hostile ships quitted their guns and gave three cheers for victory. The ensign was replaced; a light breeze sprung up, the men fought with new courage, and pouring a heavy broadside into the antagonist ships, compelled them both to haul down their colors.

The Alliance was in several engagements. Once she was chased by a squadron of English frigates, one of which, the Sibyl, venturing too near, was repulsed with heavy loss on the part of the enemy.

The Alliance brought the Treaty of Peace to Boston, in April, 1783. At the close of the war there remained only two frigates in the U. S. Navy, the Alliance and the Hague. The Alliance filled a place in the public mind like that which, after the war of 1812, was occupied by the Constitution. She was afterwards sold and converted into an Indiaman. [Cooper's Naval History; Lossing's Field-Book of the Revolution.]

Thomas Giles had his full share of peril and hardship, during the eight years of his patriotic service. It is painful to reflect that for all this hardship and peril, he received nothing by way of recompense beyond the supplies furnished to him in camp and on shipboard. Nor have his family ever received a dime by way of pension or otherwise. Even the bounty for enlisting, which was to be thirty pounds, or one hundred dollars, was *never paid*. Nothing was paid him at the close of the war; not even in continental money, which was then utterly worthless. He was credited on the books of the government with services rendered, at forty shillings, or $6.66, a month; but the amount was never paid. The credit remains on those books uncancelled to this day; and the government still owe his family for those eight years' hard service. THE DEBT HAS NEVER BEEN PAID. Let the reader take his pen and calculate what it may amount to, at this time, with ninety years' interest! The matter was brought to the notice of Congress, twenty years ago, and relief asked for his family. The justice of the claim was fully acknowledged, and a bill was reported for their relief; but through the opposition of the southern members, ever ready to manifest their hatred of the North, the bill failed.

After the war, Thomas Giles took up his residence in Boston, his wife's native place. In April, 1786, he removed to Sandy Bay, then a precinct of Gloucester, but since Feb. 1840, a distinct town by the name of Rockport. He continued to work at his trade, that of a sailmaker—being an approved workman—till his decease, Nov. 18, 1795. The man who had braved death in every form, on the battlefield and the man-of-war's deck, came to his end in an unthought-of way, by slipping into an open well while attempting to draw water.

He left little or no property; his best years having been given, without recompense, to his country. His widow was left in embarrassed circumstances. A descendant of the princely family of the Lindalls, she had no earthly resources but her own energy and resolution. But her courage did not fail. She opened a little shop, and by the blessing of God was enabled to keep her children together, to provide for them decently, and to train them for respectability and usefulness. She lived to see them all, except one, who died young, comfortably settled around her. She died at Rockport, Sept. 27, 1822, aged 66. The compiler has a full remembrance of her. She was his grandmother; and her husband, the sailmaker of the frigate Alliance, was his grandfather.

The children of THOMAS and MARY (MARSHALL) GILES were:

Born in Boston.

╂812. BETSEY SNOW (Giles), b. March 29, 1781; m. Josiah Vinton, of Boston.

813. MATTHEW SMITH (Giles). b. Aug. 16, 1784; m. first, Sally Webster; m. second, Lydia (Lee) Clifford.

814. THOMAS (Giles), b. Nov. 16, 1785; m. first, Olive Tarr; m. second, Mary Cotton Holmes. He was a most excellent man. His son Walter Harris Giles was a missionary of great worth in Western Asia.

Born in Rockport.

815. MARY (Giles), b. Sept. 3, 1787; m. Daniel Smith Tarr.
816. SAMUEL (Giles), b. Aug. 22, 1789; m. Margaret (Davis) Norwood.
817. ABIGAIL (Giles), b. July 11, 1791; d. Jan. 31, 1799.
818. WILLIAM (Giles), b. Sept. 16, 1793; m. Hannah Gott.
      For a full account of this family, see the "Giles Memorial," by the
compiler.

479.

CALEB SYMMES[7] (*Caleb,[6] Caleb,[5] Thomas,[4] Thomas,[3] Zechariah,[2]
Zechariah[1]*), eldest son of Caleb[6] and Lydia (Trowbridge) Symmes;
born in Westford, Mass., Sept. 1, 1786; married, in Charlestown,
Jan. 27, 1814, by Rev. Jedidiah Morse, D.D., MARY BOWERS, born
in Littleton, Mass., Dec. 26, 1793, dau. of Samuel and Lucy (Allen)
Bowers.

He had no trade; for some years was employed in farm-work.
He came to Charlestown at twenty years of age.   The embargo and
war followed; the times were hard, and money difficult to obtain.
He was happy, therefore, to get anything to do.   At length he became funeral undertaker, and did the most of that sort of business
in Charlestown for several years.   He was a man of good common
sense and sound judgment. His company was sought by the young
for the information he could impart of "the olden time." He gave
his children a good school education, fitting them for usefulness in
future life.   He enjoyed a competency through life, and left a competency to his family.

He died in Charlestown, Dec. 8, 1856, and was interred in the
old cemetery there.   His wife, who has long been a member of the
First Congregational Church there, still survives, Feb. 1873.

Their children, all born in Charlestown, were:

+819. MARY BOWERS,[8] b. Dec. 1, 1814; m. Joseph Parsons Moulton,
         of Woburn Centre.
+820. CALEB TROWBRIDGE,[8] b. Feb. 23, 1817; m. Nancy Richardson.
+821. LYDIA MARIA,[8] b. Aug. 11, 1819; m. Josiah Thomas Reed.
 822. SAMUEL BOWERS,[8] b. Oct. 25, 1821; d. June 17, 1828.
+823. MARTHA ELIZA,[8] b. April 26, 1824; m. Thomas D. Demond.
 824. LEONORA WARNER,[8] b. Oct. 5, 1826; m. Bradford Erastus Gline,
         June 15, 1848.   He was born in Westmoreland, N. H., Sept.
         10, 1824, son of Phinehas and Betsey (Hodges) Gline. Is a
         grocer in Charlestown.   No children.
      All the above children of mature age, except Martha Eliza, were mar-
ried by Rev. William Ives Budington, then pastor of the First Church
in Charlestown, Mass., now of Brooklyn, N. Y.

480.

BETSEY SYMMES[7] (*Caleb,[6] Caleb,[5] Thomas,[4] Thomas,[3] Zechariah,[2]
Zechariah[1]*), sister of the preceding; b. in Westford, Mass., Sept. 5,

1788; married in Charlestown, by Rev. William Collier, May 27, 1819, JOSHUA MIXTER, born in Palmer, Mass., June 23, 1779, son of Phinehas and Sarah (Shaw) Mixter.

For some time he was employed in the Armory at Springfield, Mass. He was afterwards a dealer in provisions in the Faneuil-Hall Market, Boston, and a member of the Baptist Church.

He died in Charlestown, Nov. 30, 1842. His wife died in Charlestown, Dec. 19, 1854. They lie side by side, with their son Phinehas, in the Bunker-Hill Burial Ground.

Their children, born in Charlestown, were:

825. PHINEHAS (Mixter), b. Sept. 4, 1822; d. in Charlestown, April 30, 1846.

826. CALVIN SYMMES (Mixter), b. Aug. 27, 1832; m. Rebecca (Stevens) Golbert, Aug. 17, 1856. He served in the armies of his country, during the late civil war, from April, 1861, to Dec. 1864. At the outset of the war he enlisted in the 5th Reg't. Co. B, Mass. Vols., Col. Samuel C. Lawrence. These were "three months' men." He was in the first battle of Bull Run, July 20, 1861; got separated from his company, lay down in the woods and slept all night. In the morning he walked to Washington, twenty-five miles. He came home soon after, and in October enlisted in the 22d Mass. Reg't, Co. B, under Col. Jesse A. Gove, and continued to serve till Dec. 1864. In April, 1865, he was a clerk in the Sanitary Commission, Washington. He is now in Boston.

482.

LUCY SYMMES[7] (Caleb,[6] Caleb,[5] Thomas,[4] Thomas,[3] Zechariah,[2] Zechariah[1]), sister of the preceding; born in Hollis, N. H., June 29, 1793; married in Charlestown, by Rev. Bartholomew Otheman, Nov. 20, 1823, to JOHN CLEMENT, born in Centre Harbor, N. H., April 12, 1799, son of John and Ann (Adams) Clement.

He was a maker of soap and candles. They dwelt in Charlestown, Mass., Dover, N. H., and Exeter, N. H., and were members of the Methodist church.

He died in Exeter, Feb. 20, 1870. His wife survives, Jan. 1873. Has been a consistent and worthy professor of religion nearly sixty years.

Their children, born in Charlestown, were:

827. ELMIRA (Clement), b. Sept. 30, 1824; d. Nov. 26, 1825.

828. JOHN WESLEY (Clement), b. July 1, 1826. He spent five years in California, from Oct. 1849, to Sept. 1854. In Aug. 1861, he enlisted in the 3d N. H. Reg't, Co. B; was in the attack on James Island, Charleston harbor, June 18, 1862, when the regiment lost 103 in killed, wounded and missing. They were exposed to three cross fires for two hours. He was also at the capture of Fort Wagner. During his whole service, though often exposed, he received no injury. Born in Dover, N. H.

829. LUCY ANN (Clement), b. Sept. 24, 1828.

Born in Exeter.

830. FRANCES ASBURY (Clement), b. Sept. 22, 1830 ; d. in Exeter, Aug. 27, 1832.
831. MARTIN VAN BUREN (Clement), b. April 11, 1836 ; d. in Exeter, Jan. 13, 1863.

483.

WILLARD HALL SYMMES' (*Caleb,* *Caleb,* *Thomas,* *Thomas,* *Zechariah,* *Zechariah'*), brother of the preceding; named for his ancestor, Rev. Willard Hall, of Westford; born in Groton, Mass., March 26, 1796; married, Feb. 5, 1819, SALLY PARKER, born in Littleton, Mass., Nov. 2, 1802, dau. of Ebenezer and Sally (Bowers) Parker.

They lived in Charlestown, and their children were born there. He left Charlestown for New York, on business, Dec. 25, 1824, and it is supposed died soon after.

Children :

832. CALVIN, b. Dec. 25, 1819 ; m. in Charlestown, Feb. 22, 1849, Martha Ann Rice, b. in Charlestown, March 7, 1824, dau. of Samuel Rand and Ann (Caldwell) Rice. He is a carpenter ; resides in Charlestown ; no children.
833. CHARLES, b. Oct. 12, 1821 ; d. Jan. 29, 1823.
834. SARAH ANN, b. July 26, 1823 ; m. first, in Charlestown, June, 1844, James Lawrence Murphy, a brass-founder and coppersmith, b. in Catskill, N. Y., 1815, d. in Charlestown, Dec. 11, 1845 ; m. second, Sept. 26, 1855, Isaac McCausland, b. in Fredericton, N. B., Feb. 4, 1827, son of Alexander and Margery McCausland, and a harness-maker by trade. Now resides at Fredericton, N. B. ; keeps a jewelry store. Her child :
   835. *Lawrence Leopold* (Murphy), b. Nov. 15, 1845 ; d. Jan. 23, 1848.

484.

CALVIN SYMMES' (*Caleb,* *Caleb,* *Thomas,* *Thomas,* *Zechariah,* *Zechariah'*), brother of the preceding, and son of Caleb⁶ and Lydia Symmes; born in Groton, Mass., March 8, 1798; never married.

It may be said of him that he was a born mechanic. When he was a little boy, he was always using a jack-knife; and wherever there was a little water-fall he would place a water-wheel made by himself. When eighteen years of age, his adventurous spirit moved him to go to sea. He was absent five years, and made two voyages, visiting Antwerp, the Hawaiian and Marquesas Islands, Sumatra and China. At one island the ship was in want of charcoal, and he made some, to the great delight of the natives.

After his return, he was employed as a machinist at Great Falls, Somersworth, and Dover, N. H., and at Manayunk, seven miles from

Philadelphia; but when or where he learned the business, his friends never knew. He was subsequently employed by a company to go to Mexico and set up a factory there. He succeeded well, and gained golden opinions.

After this, he hired a small factory in Troy, N. Y., employing sixteen or twenty people in spinning cotton warp. He resided in Troy about two years, his sisters Lydia and Harriet being with him.

In politics he was a decided whig, and a great admirer of Henry Clay. He died suddenly in Troy, Nov. 4, 1848, aged 50, greatly lamented by his friends; and his remains were deposited in the family tomb in Charlestown.

486.

MARY SYMMES[7] (*Caleb,[6] Caleb,[5] Thomas,[4] Thomas,[3] Zechariah,[2] Zechariah[1]*), sister of the preceding; born in Groton, Mass., Nov. 16, 1805; married in Charlestown, March 22, 1832, WILLIAM CAMPBELL PATERSON, born in Galston, Ayrshire, Scotland, May 28, 1810, son of George and Martha (Armor) Paterson.

When her husband was eight years old, his father removed to Glasgow, Scotland. At the age of twelve, William was apprenticed to his mother's brother, John Armor, tailor, of Glasgow. At nineteen, he crossed the Atlantic to visit his brother James, who then resided at Ramsay, Canada West. In that place, and in Derby, Vt., he stayed two years, working at his trade. In April, 1831, he came to Boston, and became acquainted with his future wife.

In June, 1834, he and his wife sailed from New York to Liverpool, and thence went to Glasgow. They resided in different places in Scotland, and returned to New England in January, 1841.

He had been a member of the Salem Church, in Boston, but in 1842 he and his wife joined the First Baptist Church in Charlestown. About 1847, by the advice of friends, and his own previous inclination, he engaged in theological studies, and not long after was ordained to the work of the ministry. He was pastor of the Baptist Church in East Dedham, Mass., from June, 1848, until January, 1862. At the date last mentioned, he was appointed by Governor Andrew chaplain of the 1st Mass. Reg't of Cavalry, stationed at Beaufort, S. C. He was present at the attack on James Island, near Charleston, in June, 1862. He obtained a discharge from the army, Aug. 29, 1862. In 1865, he was chaplain of the Prison at Dedham, Mass. During the last eight or nine years, he has been engaged in various secular pursuits, preaching occasionally. He now resides at South Boston.

Children:

836. MARTHA TROWBRIDGE (Paterson), b. in Boston, July 29, 1833; d. in Greenock, Scotland, Dec. 25, 1837.

18

837. HARRIET SYMMES (Paterson). b. in Glasgow, Scotland, Nov. 23,
          1855; died there, Oct. 11, 1856.
838. MARY (Paterson), b. in Greenock, Jan. 8, 1838; d. there, Oct. 17,
          1839.
839. MARTHA JANE (Paterson), b. in Charlestown, Sept. 7, 1844; m. at
          South Boston, Feb. 27, 1873, Caleb Swann French. b. at South
          Woburn, now Winchester, Jan. 14, 1842, son of Caleb and Caro-
          line Colson French. They reside at West Rindge, N. H.

487.

THOMAS SYMMES[7] (*Caleb*,[6] *Caleb*,[5] *Thomas*,[4] *Thomas*,[3] *Zecha-*
riah,[2] *Zechariah*[1]), half-brother of the preceding, and son of Caleb[6]
and Mary (Chittenden) Symmes; born in Charlestown, Dec. 13, 1823;
married, first, in Charlestown, by Rev. Benjamin Tappan, Sept. 23,
1849, to MARY MITCHELL, b. in Charlestown, Oct. 17, 1822, dau. of
John and Sarah (Phipps) Mitchell. She died April 12, 1850. He
married, second, at Milford, Mass., June 25, 1854, SARAH ELLEN
BOWERS, born in Littleton, Mass., May 18, 1827, dau. of Samuel and
Mary (Downing) Bowers, and half-sister of his brother Caleb
Symmes's wife.

In his fifteenth year he enlisted in the U. S. Navy, and served in
the Sloop-of-War Cyane, Capt. Percival. He left the service when
twenty-one, and went to California, upon the acquisition of that
country by the United States. He was not successful there; he returned to his native place, and some time after became an officer in
the State Prison, in Charlestown.

He was Acting Master of the U. S. ship Pocahontas from Sept.
1861, till Sept. 1862, in the South Atlantic Squadron, under Commodore Dupont. He was at the capture of Port Royal, S. C., Nov. 7,
1861. From Oct. 1862, to Aug. 1863, the ship belonged to the West
Gulf Squadron, under Admiral Farragut; from Nov. 1863, till the
close of the war, to the North Atlantic Squadron, under Admirals
Phillips and Porter. During a part of this time he served on
board the U. S. ship Agawam. He was highly approved as an
officer, and might have remained in the navy, but the charms of
domestic life prevailed, and March 4, 1865, he obtained his discharge.

He now resides with his family in Waltham, Mass., and is connected with the well-known Waltham Watch Manufactory.

Children, all by second wife:

840. MARY ELIZABETH,[8] b. in Charlestown, May 30, 1857.
841. CALEB CHITTENDEN,[8] b. in Charlestown, Sept. 13, 1859; a fine
          Latin scholar.
842. THOMAS FORESTUS,[8] b. in South Reading, now Wakefield, June 8,
          1863.

488.

THOMAS SYMMES[7] (*Thomas,[6] Caleb,[5] Thomas,[4] Thomas,[3] Zechariah,[2] Zechariah[1]*), eldest son of Thomas[6] and Rebecca (Carver) Symmes; born in Westford, Mass., March 27, 1790; never married.

He was for a short time a lieutenant on board of a privateer in the war of 1812. He was taken prisoner, carried to Halifax, and confined in the prison on Melville Island, where he remained till the war was over, his health good, though otherwise suffering greatly.

Writing from Philadelphia, April 29, 1815, he says: "I arrived in the brig Herald, eight days from Halifax." From Philadelphia he proceeded to Charleston, S. C., and engaged as a clerk in a dry-goods store. Subsequently he engaged in that business for himself, acquired a competency, and returned to Massachusetts in 1839.

After the death of his father, in 1817, he supplied the place of a father to the other children. His purse was always open to the needs of the family. He lost his life in that fearful storm, Nov. 27, 1846, by the stranding of the Steamer Atlantic, on Fisher's Island, at the entrance of Long Island Sound. Many others perished at the same time. He was on his way to Washington to spend the winter. Three weeks afterwards, his body was recovered and brought to Westford for interment.

491.

EDEA FLETCHER SYMMES[7] (*Thomas,[6] Caleb,[5] Thomas,[4] Thomas,[3] Zechariah,[2] Zechariah[1]*), sister of the preceding ; b. in Westford, Mass., Aug. 2, 1795; married, in Westford, April 2, 1822, CEPHAS DREW, born in Halifax, Mass., April 21, 1797.

He was a farmer, and settled in Westford.

Children:

843. THOMAS (Drew), b. April 20, 1826 ; m. April 25, 1858, Sarah Elizabeth Wilson, b. in New Orleans, March 21, 1831, dau. of Seth Wilson, of Billerica. He is a farmer in Westford. Children :
   844. *Ernest,* b. March 12, 1859.
   845. *Ellen P.,* b. June 27, 1861.
   846. *Mary E.,* b. March 11, 1864.

847. GEORGE (Drew). b. Dec. 14, 1828 ; m. Sarah J. Ober, b. Oct. 12, 1835, dau. of Benjamin I. Ober. He is a carpenter in Westford. Children :
   848. *Edea J.,* b. Dec. 4, 1864.
   849. *Emma F.,* b. Nov. 22, 1867 ; d. June 20, 1870.
   850. *Annie Mabel,* b. March 5, 1872.

495.

EDWARD SYMMES[7] (*Thomas,[6] Caleb,[5] Thomas,[4] Thomas,[3] Zechariah,[2] Zechariah[1]*), brother of the preceding, and son of Thomas[6] and Rebecca (Carver) Symmes; born in Westford, Mass., April 1, 1806; married, Nov. 19, 1840, REBECCA PIERCE FLETCHER, born March 30, 1814, dau. of Capt. Aaron and Sally (Keep) Fletcher, of Carlisle, Mass.*

In 1826 he was employed in the machine-shop of the Hamilton Manufacturing Company, Lowell. In 1827, was in the service of the Merrimack Manufacturing Company, in the same city. He passed a little more than a year in a manufacturing establishment in Saco, Me., 1828 and 1829. Returning to his mother's house in Westford, 1829, he studied surveying; taught school the following winter, and again in the winter of 1830–31. He was assistant in a retail store in Westford, in the summer of 1831; and in trade on his own account there from May 1, 1832, till Sept. 17, 1838. At the last date he removed to Lunenburg, in Worcester Co., and engaged in trade there till the spring of 1840, when he returned to Westford and resumed store-keeping in that place. In the spring of 1843, he removed to the old homestead of his grandmother, widow of Caleb Symmes, which he had purchased in 1832, where he has since pursued the business of farming; occasionally serving as a surveyor of land.

He has a special taste for genealogy, and has rendered important aid to the compiler of this volume.

His children, all born in Westford:

851. WILLIAM EDWARD,[9] b. Sept. 5, 1841.
852. THOMAS EDMUND,[9] b. Oct. 28, 1843; grad. H. C. 1865; is now a school teacher in Boone Co., Ind.
853. JOHN KEELER,[9] b. Nov. 5, 1845; d. Oct. 6, 1848.
854. SARAH REBECCA,[9] b. Oct. 20, 1847; d. Oct. 5, 1848.
855. CALEB,[9] b. Sept. 11, 1849; d. same day.
856. CARVER,[9] b. Feb. 9, 1851.
857. FLETCHER,[9] b. Sept. 10, 1852.
858. HARRIET ELIZABETH,[9] b. Aug. 19, 1854.

496.

EDMUND SYMMES[7] (*Thomas,[6] Caleb,[5] Thomas,[4] Thomas,[3] Zechariah,[2] Zechariah[1]*), twin brother of the preceding; born in Westford, Mass., April 1, 1806; never married.

His childhood and youth were spent in his native town, Westford. In 1829, he joined his brother Thomas, who was doing well in the dry-goods business in Charleston, S. C. In 1832, he returned to Massachusetts, and during some years was a clerk in stores in Boston. He went into business there on his own account, in 1836. Three

---

* Capt. Aaron Fletcher, born Nov. 18, 1777, was son of Henry Fletcher, of Westford. The father, Henry, was born Aug. 17, 1751. He married, Nov. 30, 1773, Deborah Parker, who was born June 6, 1751, and was a sister of David Parker, who married Martha, dau. of Benjamin Carver. The wife of Capt. Aaron Fletcher was Sally Keep, born Nov. 10, 1781.

years later, he removed to Charlestown. Having long been desirous
of going West, his wish was gratified in 1842, when he made ar-
rangements with a merchant then in Boston from Wisconsin, to go
out with him. His brother Thomas accompanied him on the journey
thither. He spent several years in Wisconsin, mostly in the city of
Madison. Late in 1846, the distressing news reached him of the
death of his excellent brother Thomas, in the steamer Atlantic, as
already mentioned. This sad and melancholy event caused his return to New England, and he spent a year or more in Westford.
After another stay in Wisconsin of two or three years, he came back
in 1850, and not long after commenced business in Lexington, Mass.,
where he continued twelve years. Having acquired a competency,
and his health failing, he gave up active business in 1863. He now
resides in Framingham.

519.

Capt. WILLIAM SYMMES[7] (*Isaac,[6] Isaac,[5] Zechariah,[4] Thomas,[3]
Zechariah,[2] Zechariah[1]*), son of Isaac[6] and Mary (Whitman) Symmes;
born Aug. 19, 1802; married, first, March 4, 1832. MARY D. WASH-
BURN, who was born Aug. 17, 1805, and died Feb. 7, 1837; married,
second, Nov. 27, 1841, CAROLINE H. JAMESON, born July 16, 1816.

He lives at Kingston, Mass.; is a ship-master, and is said to be a
skilful navigator.

Children, by first wife:

859. WILLIAM WHITMAN,[8] b. Feb. 7, 1834; d. July 1, 1857.

By second wife:

860. CARRIE FRANCIS,[8] b. Aug. 22, 1842.
861. JOHN JAMESON,[8] b. May 9, 1844; deceased.
862. FRANK JAMESON,[8] b. June 7, 1847; a graduate of the Scientific
School at Cambridge. In 1866, he was Acting Assistant Engineer in the U. S. Navy.
863. ALEXANDER BEAL,[8] b. June 27, 1849; d. Sept. 26, 1849.
864. MARY WHITMAN,[8] b. Oct. 17, 1859; d. April 5, 1860.

520.

MARY WHITMAN SYMMES[7] (*Isaac,[6] Isaac,[5] Zechariah,[4] Thomas,[3] Zechariah,[2] Zechariah[1]*), sister of the preceding; born, I suppose, in Kingston, Mass., Oct. 29, 1805; married, Dec. 2, 1827,
ALDEN SAMPSON,[6] born in Duxbury, an adjoining town, April 23,
1804, son of Constant[5] and Rebecca Partridge (Alden) Sampson.
Rebecca, his mother, b. Aug. 1777, was dau. of Col. Ichabod Alden,
of Duxbury, who was slain, 1778, in the hideous massacre at Cherry
Valley, N. Y.[*]

---

[*] The massacre was perpetrated Nov. 11 and 12, 1778, by a party of tories under Walter
N. Butler, accompanied by Mohawk Indians under Brant. [See Simms's History of Schoharie County; Stone's Life of Brant, &c.]

Alden Sampson, in 1863, resided in Charlestown; had resided there eighteen or twenty years, and was a master caulker in the U. S. Navy Yard.

Their children were:

865. WILLIAM ALDEN (Sampson), b. Dec. 29, 1829. He went to California when twenty or twenty-one years of age, and was brutally murdered, with another American, in their tent, by a party of Mexicans, July 18, 1851, for the gold they had collected. He was found alive two hours after the attack, and was able to give an account of the affair. The Mexicans were armed; the Americans unarmed, but made what resistance they could.

866. MARIANNA (Sampson), b. Nov. 2, 1832; unm.; living in 1863.
867. GUSTAVUS (Sampson), b. March 26, 1834; d. May 15, 1834.
868. GUSTAVUS (Sampson), b. Sept. 12, 1836; d. Nov. 9, 1836.
869. ISAAC DAVIS (Sampson), b. Feb. 5, 1838; d. March 29, 1838.
870. FRANCES MARIA (Sampson), b. Sept. 26, 1840; d. Jan. 18, 1841.
871. WINSLOW (Sampson), b. Dec. 26, 1843; living in 1863.
872. ASAPH HOLMES (Sampson), b. Oct. 4, 1845; d. Aug. 26, 1846.
873. MARTHA ALICE (Sampson), b. May 31, 1849; d. Aug. 4, 1849.

Of this numerous family, only two were living in 1863.

539.

LEWIS SYMMES' (*Zechariah P.,*[6] *Isaac,*[5] *Zechariah,*[4] *Thomas,*[3] *Zechariah,*[2] *Zechariah*[1]), son of Zechariah Parker Symmes;[6] born April 17, 1819; married, Nov. 24, 1842, SARAH P. HOOD, dau. of Samuel and Abigail Hood. Samuel Hood, a mariner, died at the age of 74. His wife Abigail died, aged 76. The dates were not given to me, nor was the place of their residence stated.

Lewis Symmes is a shoemaker; I suppose, of Beverly.

Children:

874. LEWIS HENRY,[8] b. Sept. 10, 1843; d. Feb. 24, 1858.
875. WILLIAM ALBERT,[8] b. March 15, 1846; a teacher in N. Carolina.
876. SARAH ELLEN,[8] b. Jan. 12, 1860.

543.

CHARLES SYMMES' (*Zechariah P.,*[6] *Isaac,*[5] *Zechariah,*[4] *Thomas,*[3] *Zechariah,*[2] *Zechariah*[1]), brother of the preceding, son of Zechariah Parker Symmes;[6] b. April 10, 1827; married, April 11, 1850, NANCY DUFFEE, dau. of James Duffee, blacksmith, from Nova Scotia.

His place of residence is unknown to the compiler; perhaps Beverly.

Children:

877. MARY A.,[8] b. May 30, 1851.
878. CHARLES A.,[8] b. Oct. 20, 1852; a shoemaker.
879. JAMES A.,[8] b. July 14, 1855.
880. SAMUEL A.,[8] b. Dec. 27, 1858.
881. GEORGIANA,[8] b. Dec. 25, 1860.
882. HENRIETTA,[8] b. June 14, 1862.

Eighth Generation.

*Many names belonging to the Eighth Generation have already found a place under
the Seventh.*

689.

REV. JOSEPH GASTON SYMMES⁸ (*Daniel T.,*⁷ *Celadon,*⁶ *Timothy,*⁵ *Timothy,*⁴ *Timothy,*³ *William,*² *Zechariah*¹), son of Daniel Tut-
hill⁷ and Lucinda (Gaston) Symmes; born in Fairfield township,
Butler Co., Ohio, Jan. 24, 1826; married, May, 1854, MARY ROSE-
BROOK HENRY, dau. of Rev. Symmes Cleves Henry, D.D., of Cranbury, New Jersey. Dr. Henry's father's sister, Mary Henry, was
the second wife of Hon. John Cleves Symmes. [See p. 61.]

He graduated at Hanover College, Ind., 1851, and at the Theological Seminary at Princeton, New Jersey, 1854. In the Seminary
just named, he was chosen Spring Orator for 1853, which is there
esteemed a great honor. He was licensed to preach by the Presbytery of New Brunswick, N. J., in 1854, and was ordained pastor of
the First Presbyterian Church in Madison, Indiana, by the Presbytery
of Madison, in the same year. In 1857, he became pastor of the
First Presbyterian Church in Cranbury, N. J., the place having
become vacant by the death of his father-in-law.

At Madison, the church published one of his sermons, entitled
"Predestination and Prayer." I have before me a printed sermon
of his, preached at Cranbury, Nov. 21, 1863, on occasion of the
National Thanksgiving, it being the first thanksgiving appointed by
a President of the United States, unless on some special occasion. I
also have before me a printed Address delivered by him before the
Loyal Leagues of South Brunswick and Monroe, N. J., June 1, 1865.
Both of these discourses are clear and decided utterances in con-
demnation of the great sin of slavery, and both do honor to the
author's mind and heart. He was very earnest and decided in the
cause of union and humanity during the great war against the southern rebellion, and took a leading part at the dedication of the Soldiers' Monument at Cranbury, Aug. 1, 1866. He still remains at
Cranbury, 1873.

His children are:

883. HENRY CLEVES,⁹ b. at Madison, Ind., May 9, 1855.
884. FRANK ROSEBROOK,⁹ b. at Madison, Oct. 24, 1856.
885. ADDISON HENRY,⁹ b. at Cranbury, N. J., Nov. 1858.
886. JOSEPH GASTON,⁹ b. at Cranbury, May 3, 1870.

All now living, Dec. 1872.

690.

REV. FRANCIS MARION SYMMES[8] (*Daniel T.,*[7] *Celadon,*[6] *Timothy,*[5] *Timothy,*[4] *Timothy,*[3] *William,*[2] *Zechariah*[1]), brother of the preceding; born in Fairfield township, Butler Co., Ohio, Nov. 18, 1827; married, March 15, 1855, MARY JANE DUNN.

He graduated at Hanover College, Ind., 1852, and at the Theological Seminary, Princeton, 1855. He was licensed to preach by the Presbytery of Oxford, Ohio, in 1856, and was ordained pastor of the Presbyterian Church at Pleasant, Ind., by the Presbytery of Madison, in 1856. He had previously preached there as a supply for one year. In Aug. 1861, he became pastor of the Presbyterian Church at Vernon, Ind., where he continued till April, 1864. The summer of that year he spent at Crawfordsville, Ind. After preaching four months to a feeble church in Brazil, Indiana, he took charge of the Independent Presbyterian Church at Bedford, Ind., a church which had been formed by the union of an Old School church with one of the New, and not connected with any Presbytery. This charge he resigned in April, 1867, and passed the ensuing summer in mission work. In the autumn, he took charge of the Presbyterian Church in Lebanon, Ind., which he retained till October, 1872. He then removed to Crawfordsville, and is now prosecuting mission work in Alamo Church, ten miles from that city, and in one other, half the time in each. Besides which, he superintends and teaches five classes in the Crawfordsville graded schools, thus performing more than the work of two men.

At Lebanon, a member of his church, who had been subjected to discipline, brought an action before the Circuit Court for an alleged libel, but lost the case.

Mr. Symmes sometimes pays his *devoirs* to the Muses, as will appear by what follows.

DIALOGUE SONG BETWEEN A CITIZEN AND A RETURNING SOLDIER.

BY REV. FRANCIS MARION SYMMES,

Formerly of Bedford, Indiana, now of Crawfordsville, Indiana.

Citizen.   Say, soldier brave, whence do you come,
      So lightsome and so cheery,
   With joyful heart, returning home,
      All war-worn and so weary?

Soldier.   From war's red field in "Dixie Land,"
      Where camp-fires long were burning,
   From dangers thick on every hand,
      Right glad am I returning.

Chorus.   Long live our land, our native land,
      And those who dared defend her,
   And victory, by land and sea,
      May Heaven always send her.

Citizen.   Where are the ones who went with you,
    When war began its drumming,
  But numbered with the missing now ;
    Say, soldier, are they coming ?

Soldier.   Some foremost in the fighting fell ;
    Died many sick and wounded,
  While thousands starved, Oh ! sad to tell !
    By rebel guards surrounded.

Citizen.   How long you fought, tell, soldier, tell,
    And when you that have ended,
  How the " Confederacy " fell,
    And how its hosts were rended.

Soldier.   For four long years we fought, and then,
    Pray listen to my sonnet,
  What rebels were not caught or slain
    Were taken in a bonnet.

Citizen.   My soldier brave, what shall be done
    With rebels small and great ones,
  Who all this course of ruin run,
    The first one and the late ones ?

Soldier.   Let Jeff. and all his leaders hang,
    As Haman, high and handy,
  And let the rest, not to be long,
    Go settle up with " Andy."

Citizen.   The " Butternut," my soldier man,
    It will not do to slight him,
  Who did all things 'gainst " Uncle Sam,"
    But take up arms and fight him.

Soldier.   The mark of Cain be on his head,
    Reproaches on him banging,
  And let him live in fear and dread,
    Not good enough for hanging.

A CHRISTMAS RHYME.

BY UNCLE FRANC M. SYMMES.

Christmas Eve.

Oh, Christmas dear,
  You are so near,
I'll off to bed and not be cross,
  For on this night,
  If folks say right,
I'll get a call from Santa Claus.

But will he come
  Into my room,
And fill my stocking full of things?
  I'll feign to sleep,
  And lie and peep,
And see if he has any wings.

'Tis only Pa,
  Or else my Ma,
That does it all in Santa's name.
  But if they will
  Just only fill
My stocking up, 'tis all the same.

19

I tell you all
You need not call
A dozen times to make me hear.
You need but say
" 'Tis Christmas day,"
And I'll be up, my mother dear.

Oh, I can't sleep,
My eyes will peep
To see what all is going on.
I wonder too
What they will do
When-down-to-sleep-ing-t-ha-ve-g-o-n-e.

Christmas Morning.

My Christmas gift!
My Christmas gift!!
My father, mother, Joe and Jake!!!
My stocking! He-e,
Now let me see—
I've candy, toys, and nuts, and cake.

His children are:

887. SAMUEL DUNN,[9] b. Oct. 20, 1856.
888. LUCINDA SOPHIA,[9] b. April 26, 1859.
889. JOSEPH GASTON,[9] b. Nov. 7, 1862.

693.

MARTHA JANE SYMMES[8] (*Benjamin R.,*[7] *Celadon,*[6] *Timothy,* *Timothy,*[4] *Timothy,*[3] *William,*[2] *Zechariah*[1]), daughter of Benjamin Randolph Symmes, of Symmes's Corner, near Hamilton, Ohio; born 1829; married, 1846, JOHN WATSON, a farmer, formerly of Springdale, Ohio. A man of integrity, an elder in the United Presbyterian Church. They now live in Illinois.

Their children were:

890. ROBERT (Watson), b. 1847; d. 1849.
891. ELIZA JANE (Watson), b. 1849.
892. CATHARINE BELL (Watson), b. 1853.
893. PHEBE LUCINDA (Watson), b. 1858.

695.

PEYTON RANDOLPH SYMMES[8] (*Benjamin R.,*[7] *Celadon,*[6] *Timothy,*[5] *Timothy,*[4] *Timothy,*[3] *William,*[2] *Zechariah*[1]), brother of the preceding; born 1833; married, 1856, ELIZABETH KINGERY.

He has been engaged in the pursuits of agriculture; but has also borne arms in the service of his country. He was a soldier in the 69th Reg't Ohio Vol. Inf., Co. B, under command of Capt. Gibbs. He was stationed the greater part of the time at Camp Chase, Columbus, Ohio, guarding prisoners. One day he discovered that he had under his charge a cousin, Capt. Daniel Cleves Symmes, of Louisville, Ky. [767], son of Americus Symmes.

He resides at College Corner, Ohio.

Children :

894. ELIZA JANE,[9] b. 1857 ; d. 1861.
895. EDWIN CLARENCE,[9] b. 1859 ; d. 1863.

698.

JAMES RIGDON SYMMES[8] (*Benjamin R.,[7] Celadon,[6] Timothy,[5] Timothy,[4] Timothy,[3] William,[2] Zechariah[1]*), brother of the preceding; born 1840 ; married, 1860, MARIA HAGERMAN.

He is a farmer, at Symmes's Corner, Butler Co., Ohio.

Children :

896. ELLA BELL,[9] b. 1861.
897. MARTHA JANE,[9] b. 1862 ; d. 1863.

812.

BETSEY SNOW GILES (*Thomas Giles, Mary Jennison, Abigail Lindall, Mary Higginson, Sarah Savage, Mary Symmes, Zechariah Symmes*), eldest child of Thomas and Mary (Marshall) Giles; b. in Boston, March 29, 1781 ; married, April 7, 1800, JOSIAH VINTON, born in Braintree, July 27, 1777, eldest son of Josiah and Anne (Adams) Vinton, of that town.*

Josiah Vinton was a dry-goods merchant in Boston, from 1797 to 1824. He commenced with nothing but an upright heart and a good name ; and though his gains were moderate and his success not uninterrupted, he ultimately acquired a handsome property. He united with the Old South Church, Boston, in 1803. In 1822, he joined the new church in Essex Street, of which in Feb. 1823, he was elected

---

* The VINTON FAMILY.

1. JOHN VINTON, the ancestor of this Family in America, is supposed to have been of French extraction; the son or grandson of some pious Huguenot, exiled from France for religion's sake. He was probably born in England, not far from 1620, since he was a young man in 1648, when we first hear of him. He came to New England about 1640, and settled in Lynn, probably in that part which is now the town of Saugus. He died in New Haven, Ct., 1663. By his wife ANN he had seven children, between 1648 and 1662, of whom the eldest son was

2. JOHN VINTON, born March 2, 1650; married, Aug. 26, 1677, HANNAH GREEN, born 1660, dau. of Thomas Green, of Malden. He was a worker in iron, a "forgeman;" was successful in business; lived in Malden till 1695, when he removed to Woburn, and devoted himself to agriculture. He died Nov. 13, 1727, aged 77.

3. THOMAS VINTON, second son of the preceding, born in Malden, Jan. 31, 1686-7; married, Aug. 10, 1708, HANNAH THAYER, of the very respectable Thayer Family of Braintree. He came to Braintree under twenty years of age; was a "bloomer," which means that he was employed in the Braintree Iron-Works. By his activity, enterprise and thrift, he was enabled to purchase the Braintree Iron-Works in 1720; and died, possessed of a handsome property, Jan. 18, 1757, aged 70.

4. THOMAS VINTON, his eldest son, born in Braintree, Aug. 22, 1711; married MEHITABLE ALLEN, born 1717, dau. of Joseph Allen, of Braintree. He was a blacksmith, like his father and grandfather; had a good property; had ten children, and died Feb. 28, 1776, aged 62. His youngest son,

5. JOSIAH VINTON, born April 25, 1755; married, 1776, ANNE ADAMS, b. 1757, of the celebrated ADAMS Family of Quincy, which has furnished two Presidents of the United States. He was a silversmith by trade, which he pursued for about twenty years, and then gave it up for commerce and agriculture. He died Dec. 27, 1843, aged 88. His wife Anne died Dec. 18, 1851, aged 95. They were the parents of Josiah Vinton in the text.

deacon. In March, 1836, after a residence of eleven years in East Braintree, he removed to South Boston; was chosen deacon of Phillips Church, in that place, and continued to reside there till his death. He died of apoplexy, without a struggle or any apparent pain, Oct. 17, 1857, a. 80. His wife Betsey d. Aug. 9, 1849, a. 68.

Their children were:

898. JOHN ADAMS (Vinton), b. Feb. 5, 1801; m. first, June 6, 1832, Orinda Haskell, of Hanover, N. H.; m. second, Feb. 24, 1840, Laurinda Richardson, of Stoneham. Mass.

899. GEORGE (Vinton), b. Aug. 13, 1803; m. first, Charlotte W. Callender, Sept. 14, 1826; m. second, Mary Callender, Nov. 28, 1841, sisters, daughters of Joseph Callender, of Boston.

900. ELIZA ANN (Vinton), b. Jan. 31, 1806; never married; resides in South Boston.

901. NANCY ADAMS (Vinton), b. Oct. 26, 1807; m. William V. Alden, of Boston, Nov. 28, 1833.

902. MARY MARSHALL (Vinton), b. March 30, 1809; d. Oct. 31, 1821.

903. ALFRED (Vinton), b. Dec. 28, 1815; m. Sarah Martin, of Lancaster, Pa., Feb. 20, 1839.

904. FREDERIC (Vinton), b. Oct. 9, 1817; m. first, Phebe Worth Clisby, of Nantucket, Sept. 13, 1843; m. second, Mary Blanchard Curry, of Eastport, Me., at Boston, June 1, 1857.

905. HARRIET NEWELL (Vinton), b. March 8, 1819; never married; resides at South Boston.

Rev. John A. Vinton, the eldest of these children, prepared for college at Phillips Academy, Exeter, N. H.; graduated at Dartmouth College, 1828; and completed a full course of theological study at Andover, 1831. He received ordination as a minister of the gospel, May 16, 1832; and has labored in the ministry, for a longer or shorter period, in Bloomfield (now Skowhegan), New Sharon, Exeter and Bristol, all in Maine; in Chatham, Kingston and Stoneham, in Massachusetts; in West Randolph and Williamstown, in Vermont. He was also chaplain of the State Almshouse, Monson, Mass., 1859–60. During the last twenty years he has been chiefly retired from the ministry by reason of ill health, and has devoted himself to literary pursuits. From 1852 to 1870, he dwelt in South Boston; since 1870, in Winchester, Mass.

819.

MARY BOWERS SYMMES[8] (*Caleb,*[7] *Caleb,*[6] *Caleb,*[5] *Thomas,*[4] *Thomas,*[3] *Zechariah,*[2] *Zechariah*[1]), eldest child of Caleb[7] and Mary (Bowers) Symmes; born in Charlestown, Dec. 1, 1814; married, Sept. 15, 1840, JOSEPH PARSONS MOULTON,[*] born in Newfield, Me.,

---

[*] The town of Moultonborough, N. H., was named in honor of Gen. Jonathan Moulton, of Hampton, in that State, and a kinsman of him in the text. That officer, as Captain Moulton, led a body of eighty resolute men to Norridgewock, Maine, took it by surprise, and utterly destroyed that nest of savage Indians, with Sebastian Rasle, their spiritual adviser and guide, Aug. 23, 1724. Rasle was as much of a savage as any of them. The Indian chieftains, Mogg, Bomazeen and others, were slain on that day, and New England thus freed from evils it long had suffered.

Aug. 29, 1814, youngest son of Simeon and Sally Moulton, of that place. The father of Simeon removed from Hampton, N. H., to Newfield, and Simeon himself was born there.

Mrs. Moulton, previous to marriage, was a successful teacher in Boston, Charlestown, and other places.

He is a carpenter by trade; lived in Charlestown several years; afterwards in Woburn Centre. He and his wife are members of the Congregational church.

Children, born in Charlestown:

906. ISABEL (Moulton), b. Nov. 17, 1812.
907. MARY PARSONS (Moulton), b. May 7, 1845; d. April 2, 1848.
908. CALEB SYMMES (Moulton), b. Jan. 13, 1847; m. May 7, 1871, Mary Jane (Lunt) Hoyt, dau. of Silas Lunt, of Lynn.

Born in Woburn.

909. FANNY (Moulton), b. April 18, 1849; d. Aug. 11, 1849.
910. ROGER HUTCHINSON (Moulton), b. Sept. 17, 1851; d. Sept. 3, 1865.
911. SAMUEL BOWERS (Moulton), b. Nov. 3, 1856; d. Sept. 12, 1857.
912. JOSEPH HERBERT (Moulton), b. Jan. 12, 1858.

820.

CALEB TROWBRIDGE SYMMES[8] (*Caleb,[7] Caleb,[6] Caleb,[5] Thomas,[4] Thomas,[3] Zechariah,[2] Zechariah[1]*), brother of the preceding; born in Charlestown, Feb. 23, 1817; married, by Rev. William Ives Budington, Oct. 28, 1841, to NANCY RICHARDSON, born at Woburn, July 9, 1819, dau. of Job and Nancy Richardson, of that place. Job Richardson was son of Edward and Sarah (Tidd) Richardson, of "Button End," Woburn.

For nearly thirty years, or since 1843, he has been the faithful cashier of the Lancaster Bank, in the town of Lancaster, Mass., where he resides. He and his wife are members of the Congregational Church, and are represented as being worthy and conscientious persons, " serving God, it is said, with his prayers, his strength, and his money."

913, 914. They have had two children, who both died in infancy.

821.

LYDIA MARIA SYMMES[8] (*Caleb,[7] Caleb,[6] Caleb,[5] Thomas,[4] Thomas,[3] Zechariah,[2] Zechariah[1]*), sister of the preceding; b. in Charlestown, Aug. 11, 1819; married, April 20, 1848, JOSIAH THOMAS REED, born in Burlington, Mass., Nov. 11, 1821, son of Isaiah and Sally (Ellsworth) Reed.

They live in Charlestown. He was a grocer on Main Street, in that city; now a dyer of kid gloves. They are members of the Winthrop Church. He is an active and liberal man.

Children :

915. GEORGE HYDE (Reed), b. April 17, 1849 ; d. Oct. 25, 1849.
916. 917. Twin sons, b. Oct. 3, 1850 ; both died the next day.
918. MARY ELIZA (Reed), b. Feb. 17, 1852.

823.

MARTHA ELIZA SYMMES[8] (*Caleb,[7] Caleb,[6] Caleb,[5] Thomas,[4] Thomas,[3] Zechariah,[2] Zechariah[1]*), sister of the preceding; born in Charlestown, April 26, 1824; married in Charlestown, by Rev. Benjamin Tappan, Oct. 28, 1852, to THOMAS DENNY DEMOND, b. in Rutland, Mass., Nov. 16, 1814, son of Daniel and Hannah Demond.

Previous to marriage, she was an approved teacher in Charlestown and other places.

He was a merchant in State Street, Boston.　They resided at 124 Webster Street, East Boston.

Children :

919. GEORGE ALBERT (Demond), b. Feb. 26, 1854.
920. JOSEPH MILES (Demond), b. Feb. 15, 1856 ; d. Sept. 27, 1860.
921. MARY SUSAN (Demond), b. Jan. 10, 1858 ; d. Sept. 26, 1860.
922. EDWARD GRIFFIN (Demond), b. July 24, 1859 ; d. Sept. 26, 1860.
923. WARNER (Demond), b. Oct. 5, 1861.
924. MARTHA SYMMES (Demond), b. Jan. 25, 1864 ; d. Dec. 8, 1867.
925. LINCOLN GRANT (Demond), b. March 9, 1867.
926. CHARLES DENNY (Demond), b. Dec. 12, 1869.

Three children of this family were buried at the Forest Hills Cemetery, Dorchester, the same afternoon, Friday, Sept. 28, 1860.

SUPPLEMENT.

[Pages 6–8.]

THE subject of the Antinomian Controversy of 1637 is treated in full, in a monograph by the compiler of this volume, and published in the "Congregational Quarterly" for April, July, and October, 1873. It is there shown, that notwithstanding what is often supposed, and the harsh aspect of the case, as it meets the eye of a careless observer, the treatment of Mrs. Hutchinson and her followers was not only an absolute necessity, if the colony was to survive the vigorous assault made upon it by these persons, but that they were in fact treated with much lenity and forbearance; and that the affair was not at all a religious persecution, as has often been represented, but a proceeding based on political grounds and no other.

[Pages 16, 17.]

Mrs. Ruth Willis and Mrs. Deborah Prout, daughters of Rev. Z. Symmes, were living and testified in Probate Court, Dec. 28, 1676.

[Page 27.]

The second wife of Timothy Symmes [14], Elizabeth Norton, was daughter of Capt. Francis Norton. She married Capt. Ephraim Savage, as his third wife, and died April 13, 1710.

[Page 28.]

Timothy [31] died on the day of his birth. The mother died twelve days after.

[Pages 31, 32.]

According to Lewis's History of Lynn, the Squaw Sachem, in 1639, sold to Charlestown "all that parcel of land which lies against the ponds of Mystic, together with the said ponds, all which we reserved from Charlestown and Cambridge, this deed to take effect after the death of me, the said Squaw Sachem." The consideration was, "the many kindnesses and benefits we have received from the hands of Capt. Edward Gibbons, of Boston." This deed must have included the Symmes farm.

[Page 36.]

William Simmes was, in 1725, "a youth," on board of some vessel, whose name is not given, sailing from Boston to a foreign port. [Geneal. Register, xxi. 367.] This must have been William, born in Charlestown, Jan. 9, 1708–9, son of Zechariah³ and Dorcas (Brackenbury) Symmes [74]. Perhaps he was ancestor of the Simes or Symes Family of Portsmouth, who say their ancestor was a sea-captain.

[Page 37.]

On further consideration, I am inclined to doubt as to John Simms, of Malden, being a descendant of Rev. Zechariah Symmes. It is more likely that he was brother of Stephen Sims, who was of Boston, 1720–1730.

[Page 48.]

The list here given of the children of Andrew Symmes is not altogether correct. In the settlement of his son Ebenezer's estate, 1782, it is stated that Ebenezer had five sisters then living, one of whom, the settlement states, was Mrs. Mason, and another Mrs. Thompson. Of the other three, we now learn one was Mrs. Susanna Drew, and one was Mrs. Experience Perkins, whose husband was father of Dr. Cyrus Perkins, of Dartmouth College. [See page 106, *note*.] There is a mistake about the fifth sister, but the compiler knows not how to correct it.

[Page 62.]

OUR WESTERN EMPIRE.

On the 7th of April, 1788, the first permanent settlement was made in the Northwestern Territory, now containing the populous, flourishing and mighty Western States of the American Union. Previously that whole region was a howling wilderness, into which no white man had ventured, except a few daring explorers. But the era of emigration had come, and it dawned in Massachusetts. On the 25th of January, 1786, the newspapers of that Commonwealth contained a notice requesting " all good citizens who wished to become adventurers in the delightful region known as the Ohio country," to hold meetings and choose delegates to a convention in Boston on the 1st of March. The movement resulted in the purchase of a million and a half acres of land of Congress by "The Ohio Company," and the sending out of a colony to begin its occupation. When these venturesome pioneers got to Pittsburg, then the extreme western limit of civilization, they had to spend three months in building boats to convey themselves and their effects down the river. About noon of the 7th of April, 1788, they reached Fort Harmer, where the town of Marietta now stands.

There began the settlement of the Northwest. Providentially, by the famous ordinance of '87, that whole region had been devoted to freedom, and the soil proved most congenial for the growth of free institutions. Only the historian's pen can record the ever-increasing miracle of subsequent progress, variegated as it was, though hardly checked, by the terrors and occasional reverses of Indian warfare. In 1798, the settlers were enabled to avail themselves of the permission contained in their organic law, to form a territorial legislature when they comprised "five thousand free male inhabitants of full age." In 1799 Congress divided the territory by establishing the new Territory of Indiana; and in 1802, Ohio, then containing a population of 45,365, according to the previous census, was admitted as a State into the Union. Indiana followed fourteen years afterward, Illinois in sixteen, and thenceforward the procession swelled, till the grand constellation of commonwealths became as we now see it—the present pride and the future strength and hope of the nation.

The first organized movement for the settlement of the Great West dates from June, 1783, in the camp of the American army, then soon to be disbanded. In that month, under the lead of Gen. Rufus Putnam, the chief engineer of the army, a native of Sutton, Mass., and a son of Elisha Putnam, of Danvers, a plan was formed, which, while provision would be made for the disbanded officers and soldiers, would also contribute greatly to the future security and strength of the nation. A petition was drawn up and presented to Congress by the officers, with this end in view. A letter, addressed by Gen. Putnam to Gen. Washington, contained *the first suggestion of dividing the western lands into townships of six miles square*, a plan soon after adopted and continued to this day. On the first of March, 1786, the "Ohio Company" was formed at Boston, in pursuance of a circular addressed by Gen. Putnam and Gen. Benjamin Tupper to the officers and soldiers of the army, as well as other good citizens, disposed to remove to the West. During the year 1787, an arrangement was effected with Congress. On the 7th of April, 1788, Gen. Putnam, with a party of forty emigrants, arrived at the mouth of the Muskingum and commenced the first permanent settlement of the territory northwest of the Ohio. They called their village Marietta, in honor of Marie Antoinette, the friend of their country, the queen of France.

[Page 69.]

A CHAPTER OF REVOLUTIONARY HISTORY.

[Furnished by Isaac J. Greenwood, of New York.]

Lt.-Col. David Mason.

David Mason, born in 1727, learned, during his earlier life, the art of painting and gilding, and then portrait-painting of John Greenwood, in Boston. He also delivered lectures on electricity in various towns. From Allen's American Biography, we learn, further, that "Dr. Franklin was a friend in his father's house. In the French war he was a lieutenant, and understood well the art of gunnery, commanding a battery of six cannon at Fort William Henry. He was there taken prisoner, but was released in the woods by the kindness of a French officer. In 1763, he organized the first artillery company in Boston. In 1774, he was appointed engineer. Two brass cannon, which the British seized in Boston, he secretly carried off, concealed in loads of manure. His wife Hannah (eldest daughter of Andrew Symmes, of Boston, and whom he had married in 1750) cut out five thousand flannel cartridges. From Salem, April 19, 1775, he marched to Medford with four or five hundred men." Three days thereafter, being on a furlough at Salem, the Massachusetts Committee of Safety despatched a courier to request his attendance, and he was ordered to provide one field piece ready for action, and to put the remainder, consisting of eight 3-pounders and three 6-pounders, in thorough order. At the same time another courier was sent to the residence of Col. Richard Gridley, at Stoughton, requiring the immediate attendance of himself and son Scarborough Gridley. Col. Gridley, who had already served during the French war as chief engineer, was again appointed to that position, April 26, by

20

the Massachusetts Provincial Congress, in the forces being raised by that colony, and William Burbeck was appointed an engineer. Soon after this, a Train or Regiment of Artillery was projected, and, on June 21st, the Provincial Congress issued commissions to Burbeck as lieut.-colonel, David Mason as 1st-major, and Scarborough Gridley as 2d-major. The command had been secured to Col. Gridley as major-general, a rank not subsequently recognized by the Continental Congress. This regiment, with one company of the Rhode-Island Train, commanded by Maj. John Crane, comprised all the artillery actively employed in 1775, at the siege of Boston.

Nov. 17, 1775, Col. Gridley, on account of his advanced age, was superseded, through appointment of the Continental Congress, by Henry Knox. His son Scarborough had been discharged, soon after the battle of Bunker Hill, for some lack of judgment or indiscretion there exhibited. Upon the reorganization of the army in January, the officers of the Artillery Regiment were Henry Knox, colonel; William Burbeck, 1st lieutenant-colonel; David Mason, 2d lieutenant-colonel; and John Crane, 1st major. In April, Capt. John Lamb (then a prisoner at Quebec) was appointed 2d major. On the nights of Saturday, Sunday and Monday, March 2, 3 and 4, previous to taking possession of Dorchester Heights, a vigorous bombardment and cannonade was kept up from Cobble Hill, Lechmere's Point, and Lamb's Dam, with a view of diverting the enemy's attention. Unfortunately, on the first night, one 13-inch and two 10-inch iron mortars were burst. On Sunday night, while Washington himself was present, it is said, a brass 13-inch mortar was likewise burst, and Lt.-Col. Mason slightly wounded. This was the only brass mortar in the camp, and had been taken on the ordnance-brig Nancy, by Commodore Manly.

April 3d, Washington issued his orders to Col. Knox, that the artillery and ammunition should be forwarded to New York, whither Lt.-Col. Burbeck should proceed by the most direct road without any delay; Lt.-Col. Mason to follow as soon as he was able to travel. The former, fearful of forfeiting the four shillings sterling per diem, which had been settled on him for life by the Province of Massachusetts, refused, in a letter to Col. Knox, of April 12, to quit his native State, and was in consequence dismissed the service by the Continental Congress during the following month.

Mason, who succeeded him in rank, came on to Norwich with the ordnance, and in consequence of his ill health, was permitted to travel thence to New York by land. After the battle of Long Island, and the retreat from New York to Westchester, it becoming evident that the enemy would make a vigorous movement westward through the Jerseys, Washington wrote to Knox from White Plains, Nov. 10, desiring him to take into consideration a proper partition of the field artillery, and not to delay in despatching "those destined for the western side of Hudson's river. With respect to yourself," he continues, "I shall leave it to your own choice to go over or stay; if you do not go, Col. Mason must." Four days after, he urged on Congress the necessity of largely increasing the field artillery, and on December 20 communicated, in a letter, which was read on the 26th, a plan of Col. Knox for the establishment of a Continental Artillery, with magazines, laboratories, &c. The question had already been under discussion, however, and on Dec. 21st and 24th Congress had resolved to establish three magazines, with laboratories attached—one in Virginia, another at Carlisle, Pa., and a third at Brookfield, Mass.; and on the 28th, the President of Congress wrote to the Council of Massachusetts Bay, desiring them to contract with proper persons for erecting the magazine in that State, sufficient to contain 10,000 stand of arms, and 200 tons of gunpowder, and also for erecting an adjacent laboratory, and to take such measures as they judged necessary for the immediate execution of the same.

Some steps were taken towards establishing the works at Brookfield, but the location did not meet the approval of Knox, who had been appointed brigadier-general of Artillery, Dec. 23, 1776, and on Feb. 1, following, he addressed a letter to Gen. Washington, pointing out the superior advantages of the town of Springfield as a place for the contemplated cartridge laboratory and cannon foundry. Washington, on the 14th, advised Congress, in a letter from Morristown, that in consequence of Gen. Knox's opinion, he had ordered the works to be begun at Springfield.

The care of the ammunition and the manufacture of cannon and musket-cartridges, had, previous to this, been entrusted to Ezekiel Cheever, Esq., appointed Aug. 17, 1775, by Gen. Washington, as commissary of artillery stores, with brevet rank of colonel, and to this gentleman, and to Lt.-Col. David Mason, was given the charge and superintendence of the new works. These latter were at first located on the Main street, but during the year 1778 they were removed to the Hill, where a square of ten acres, the old town training-field, had been secured.

Col. Mason continued to reside at Springfield. Allen mentions that he sold his State securities "at a great loss, for two or three shillings on the pound." In 1786, he became lame, and remained so until his death, which occurred at Boston, Sept. 17, 1794, at the age of 67. "He was a christian eminent for love to God and man. His daughter Hannah married Capt. John Bryant, of Boston, and died at Springfield. Susannah married Prof. John Smith, of Hanover, N. H. Mary married Daniel Tuttle, of Boston. His grandson, John Bryant, merchant of Boston, married Mary, a daughter of Prof. Smith by his first wife Mary Cleveland."

[Pages 11, 23, 31, 41.]

WINCHESTER, MASS.

The territory now embraced in the town of Winchester may be considered as in some sort the cradle of the Symmes Family in America. Rev. Zechariah Symmes, the progenitor of those who write their names in the manner now indicated, was, it is true, the minister of Charlestown, and dwelt there from 1634 till his death in 1671. But in those early days Charlestown included much of what is now Winchester, and for some years the whole of it; and the Symmes farm given to him by Charlestown, was nearly all of it in Winchester, and part of it remains in the hands of his descendants to this day. The town last named was the residence of his son William, and it is supposed has since contained more of his descendants than any other town, at least in New England.

It is a very pleasant town. The natural features are attractive, and greatly embellished by cultivation. Its rounded hills afford many fine prospects; a beautiful stream of water, called the Aberjona River, passes through the midst of it. Only eight miles from Boston, with railroad trains running through its centre thirty times a day, it is a desirable place of residence. The inhabitants are mostly of a highly respectable character, many of them doing business in Boston. From Boston, therefore, they derive largely their manners and customs, and are inclined to be formal, stately, distant and reserved, like the city folks. It is hard for a stranger to get acquainted. They do not readily admit strangers into their society. The members, for instance, of the Orthodox Church have their social gatherings at their vestry four or five times during the winter season, which are not always well attended; and the Winchester folks think this must suffice. Those who cannot be present on such occasions, have little or no opportunity of mingling in society.

As a large proportion of the men of business, if not nearly all, are, during all the hours of every day in the week, the Sabbath excepted, occupied with engrossing affairs in Boston and elsewhere, the consequence is the affairs of the town are sometimes committed to men not the most competent; to men governed more by the letter of the law than by its spirit, and therefore liable to pursue a course of conduct which may find its excuse, but never its justification, in the statute book. Consequently there is sometimes loss and suffering.

There is no species of injustice more afflictive or more glaring than is often perpetrated under color of law. Human law is imperfect at best, and may sometimes operate to the disadvantage of the innocent and the helpless. The law, which is intended for the protection of the community, often becomes an engine of severe oppression. Long-continued observation has taught me that persons may often be found to lay hold of plausible but wrong interpretations of law for purposes of oppression: Cruel wrongs are thus committed for which no redress can be obtained. If the sufferer complain, he is gravely told that the law allows it.

It is to be feared that this has sometimes been the case in this pleasant town of Winchester, more especially in the assessment and collection of taxes. Were this the place to publish the particulars, a case might be related, on what is supposed to be good authority, which would fully justify, it is believed, all that is here said of this liability to injustice in the matter of taxation. In the case alluded to, great suffering was caused to one who was ill able to bear it.

Since Winchester became a town, the population has greatly increased from various sources.

APPENDIX I.

THE SIMS OR SYMMES FAMILY IN ENGLAND.*

WE are able to trace back the Family bearing the name of Sims, Symmes, or something equivalent, about five hundred years. It is without doubt an old Saxon Family, and the name may have been borrowed from the second son of the patriarch Jacob; *Sims*, meaning simply, *Son of Simeon*.†

John Symmes, priest, was appointed Rector of Stotesbury, by the Prior and Convent of St. Andrew, Oct. 13, 1390.

John Symme was chosen Bailiff‡ of the city of Canterbury in Kent, Sept. 14, 1392.

The principal seat of the Family, however, at least of that part of it with which this volume is chiefly concerned, appears to have been, in the early time, in Northamptonshire, in England. Some branches of it still exist in the neighborhood of Daventry in that county. It has been connected with some of the most honored English families.

In Baker's History of Northamptonshire, Part II., p. 330, there is a reference to Bridge's work, Part I., p. 48, where it is mentioned that the church of Daventry,§ in that county, contained, " at the east end of the south aisle upon a blue stone, the effigies of a man and his wife, with the following inscription on a brass plate: " for the solle of William Symnes, sometyme . . . . . es his wife, which William departed . . . . . June, A.D. 1547." Underneath were figures of five sons and five daughters.

1547. William Symes, or Symmes, just mentioned, at his death, in 1547, was seized of estates in Daventry, held of the duchy of Lancaster. [Baker's Northamptonshire, Part II., p. 306.]

1576. John Symes, or Symmes, was bailiff of Daventry, in 1576, and was named as one of the principal burgesses or citizens, fourteen in number, in the earliest extant charter of the corporation of Daventry, 18 Elizabeth, 26 March. The list of bailiffs begins in 1574, with the name of John Symes.

---

* For much that immediately follows, the compiler is indebted to the researches of George C. Mahon, Esq., of Framingham, Mass., and of Mr. Isaac J. Greenwood, of New York City.

† Parallel to which is *Adams*, meaning *son of Adam*; *Abrams*, for *Abraham's son*; *Davis*, for *David's son*; *Peters*, for *Peter's son*; *Roberts*, for *Robert's son*; and so on without end.

‡ A bailiff, the dictionaries say, was a sheriff's deputy and assistant. Some writers make it equivalent to mayor.

§ The borough of Daventry is ten miles west of Northampton, and seventy-two northwest of London.

1591. May 1.   Richard Symes, of Stareton (Staverton), a short distance west of Daventry, was recommended to Lord Treasurer Burghley as a retainer. [Vide Calendar State Papers.]

1592.   To Edward Symes, apparently a younger son of the before mentioned William of Daventry, was granted a coat of arms; or rather some addition was then made to the ancient arms of the Symmes Family.

1593.   Richard Symes, or Simmes, gentleman, son of Edward and grandson of the above mentioned William Symes, in April, 1593, purchased the manor of Drayton, near Daventry, from Anthony Chester, Esq., afterwards Sir Anthony Chester, bart., and died 6 Sept. following, seized of the manor and lands of Drayton, Staverton and Kislingbury; leaving Richard Symes or Simmes his son and heir, aged 21 years. [Baker, ii. 348.]

1602.   Richard Symes, the son and heir just mentioned, alienated his manor of Drayton to Richard Raynsford, Esq. [Ibid.]

In the Records of the Herald's College, Bennett's Hill, London, Mr. Mahon, my informant, found the name spelled variously, thus: Symes, Symmes, Syms, and Simmes.   The autograph of William Symes occurs in C. 14, 1619, p. 56.   In the private sketch-book of the Herald who made out the grant of 1592, he spells the name Syms.   The Heralds of the present day corrected Mr. Mahon for pronouncing the name *Sims*, with a short vowel, instead of *Symes*, with a long vowel.   But the diversities in the ancient spelling indicate that the short sound gives the true pronunciation.   Mr. Mahon says that the Irish branch, from which he is descended, has never pronounced the name otherwise than *Sims*, though written formerly Symes, or Symmes, indifferently, and for the last one hundred years invariably Symes.

When in Northamptonshire, Mr. Mahon made inquiries as to the present state of the Family.   He learned that though ancient, it is not now very opulent.   From personal inquiry, it appeared that there are many members of the Family still existing in the neighborhood of Daventry, principally small landed proprietors, whereas their ancestors in that vicinity owned large estates.   They still retain an aristocratic, haughty, proud spirit— what might be called *touchy*—so that he did not like to approach them, lest they should manifest some contempt for the Irish branch even of their own blood.

We find in Burke's General Armory, the arms of Symmes of Daventry, in the county of Northampton, granted to Edward Symes in 1592, viz.: Ermine, three crescents, gules.   Crest, a head in helmet, or, plumed azure, the beaver up, the face proper.   Motto, *Droit et loyal*.

The same coat of arms is borne by the Symes Family of Ballybeg, county of Wicklow, Ireland, which is an offshoot of the Symmes Family of Daventry.   It is also borne by the Symmes Family in America.

Pedigrees of the Symmes Family of Welton, one mile north of Daventry, are in the British Museum.   Harleian MSS. 1094, fol. 1885 b.   1184, fol. 180 b.   1553, fol. 118 b.   See Index of Pedigrees in the British Museum, by Richard Sims of the MS. Department in that institution.

From the Symes Family of Northamptonshire is descended a branch which took root in the county of Wexford in Ireland, some time previous to 1688.   The arms are, with a slight exception, the same.   A member of this branch, a merchant there, supplied some ships to bring over the army of the Prince of Orange, afterwards king William III., in the year just mentioned.

The Irish branch throve rapidly and multiplied.   From them sprung the Symeses of the neighboring county of Wicklow. At least, it is known that they all are descendants of the Family in Northamptonshire.

In 1795, the British authorities in India, alarmed at the rapid and extensive conquests of the new Burman dynasty in the vast regions beyond the Ganges, sent an embassy to promote a good understanding between themselves and the Burman monarch. At the head of this embassy was Col. Michael Symes, who spent some time in that country, and after his return published an interesting work, in two volumes, affording much light in regard to a portion of the earth previously almost unknown. It was entitled, "An Account of the Embassy to Ava." Col. Symmes was descended from the Irish branch, from that portion of it known as the Symeses of Ballyarther, or more briefly, of Bayley. He died in 1809, leaving behind him a very full history of the Symes Family from their first settlement in Ireland, and showing their alliances with many of the best Anglo-Irish and Irish families.

My informant, Mr. George C. Mahon, now a resident of Framingham, but having business in Boston, is descended from the Symes Family in England; the line being as follows:

1. JEREMIAH SYMES, a younger son of a Northamptonshire family, came to Ireland in the reign of Charles II. For faithful services, he received from king William III. a grant of lands in Middleton, in the county of Wexford. His wife was BARBARA PAYNE, an English woman, sister of the private secretary of James II., the last man who suffered the torture of the boot in Scotland. Jeremiah Symes had several sons, of whom the fourth was:

2. JOHN SYMES, married —— Sandham, and lived at Coolboy. His wife's mother was a Mitchelbourne, whose father assisted conspicuously in the defence of Londonderry in 1689. John Symes was the father of:

3. Rev. ABRAHAM SYMES, D.D., of Hillbrook, in the county of Wicklow. His wife was Anne, daughter of Thomas Le Hunte, an eminent Dublin advocate, whose mother was a Miss Legge, a niece to the Earl of Dartmouth, whose family name is Legge. The mother of Anne Le Hunte was Alice Ryves, daughter of a dean of St. Patrick's. The mother of Alice Ryves was a Miss Maude, sister to Sir Cornwallis Maude. The Maude Family is connected with the Lowther, De Clifford, Percy and Mortimer Families in England, and through them with the royal line of Plantagenet. The first Le Hunte came to Ireland in Cromwell's time, as Col. Le Hunte. He was commander of Cromwell's body guard, and received large grants of land in the county of Wexford. [See Pendergast's Cromwellian Settlement of Ireland.] Rev. Dr. Symes was father of:

4. MARY ANNE SYMES, of Glencraig-Hollywood, in the county of Down in Ireland, who died unmarried, and at an advanced age, about 1865. She had a sister, who also lived and died in Ireland, the mother of George C. Mahon, Esq., of Framingham, Mass., my informant.

SIMES OR SYMES OF SOMERSETSHIRE.

1581. William Simes, of this county, was living in this year.

1623. John Symes was member of parliament for this county. He was living, 1637, a justice of the peace for the county. He was a staunch adherent to the party of the king; was fined by the parliament for his loyalty £945, and paid the same, March 8, 1647. Pardon was granted, however, Dec. 31, 1647, and the sequestration of his estate taken off. He appears to have been living in 1664.

He was of Pounsford, a tything, in the parish of Petminster, four miles south by west of Taunton.

Pedigrees of the Symes or Sims Family of Pounsford, county of Somers, may be seen in the British Museum, Harleian MSS., 1141, fol. 57 b, and fol. 67. Also, 1145, ff. 85 b and 97. Also, 1559, ff. 120, 187.

SIMS OF DEVONSHIRE.

Pedigree of the Devonshire Sims of Pounsford, in British Museum, Harl. MSS. 1091, fol. 133.

The coats of arms of this and the Somersetshire Syms Families differ materially from those of Northamptonshire.

SIMS OF YORKSHIRE.

George Symme, of Mark, county of York, was fined by parliament £22. for his loyalty in the civil war.

Pedigrees of Symmes or Symes, of Yorkshire, are in the British Museum, Harl. MSS. 1394, fol. 249. Also, 1145, fol. 29 b. Also 1420, fol. 176.

SYMMES OF LONDON.

[From Cal. of State Papers.]

1589, July 21. Randall Symmes will furnish, on twelve days' warning, a certain quantity of provision, arms and munition.

1603, Aug. 6. To John Syme was granted a gunner's place in the Tower; a warden's place in the Tower, Feb. 27, 1604. Reported as lately deceased, March, 1625. He was probably the John Syme, a Scotsman, to whom was granted denization, July 28, 1609.

1636. John Symms had been a citizen of London. This year his widow married Richard Phillips, of Limehouse, in Middlesex, east of London; the latter being a widower at that time. Susan Symms, a daughter, had married Thomas Stebranck, late coachman to Sir Edward Barkham.

1654. Thomas Symes, vintner, had a lease of the White Cross Tavern, London.

OTHERS OF THE NAME OF SYMMES.

John Sym, or Syms, a Scotsman, born 1580, was living 1636, minister of Leigh, in Essex. A volume in 4to. by him, entitled "Life's Preservative against Self-killing," was printed 1637, with his portrait prefixed.

John Sims was a Baptist minister, who preached at Hampton in England, about 1646. An act of parliament had been passed against unordained ministers, in virtue of which he was apprehended while on a journey to Taunton, some letters which he was to deliver to pious friends taken from him, and he was examined before some court for preaching without being ordained, and for denying infant baptism.*

Walter Symmes, of West Wittering, co. Sussex, for adhering to the royal party and assisting forces raised against parliament, was fined £86, and his estate sequestered. He rendered [surrendered] before March 1, 1643, and his fine of £34 was accepted, March 23, 1647–48.

---

* Neal's History of the Puritans, vol. iii. p. 553.

1647, Oct. 2. Edward Symmes, confined in the county jail of North-amptonshire, under sentence of death, was pardoned by the [Long] Parliament. His offence was probably of a political nature.

1650, March. Major John Symes, an officer of Lord Inchiquin's Horse in Ireland, was taken prisoner by Cromwell's forces, brought to Cashel, tried and shot. His widow Margery was living 1663, with four children.

1651, Nov. 20. The House of Commons considered the petition of Ann Symms, widow of Jonas Symms, who had died in the service of parliament.

1654. In the church at South Lynn, county of Norfolk, is a stone in memory of Lidia, daughter of Mr. Jenkinson, merchant, and wife of Mr. John Sims, merchant and alderman. She died 1654.

1656. William Sims was public lecturer of the borough of Leicester, and confestor of Wigston's Hospital.

1662–3, March. Robert Symmes, chief salt-petre man of the late king at Oxford, having spent £1207, "his whole estate," in providing material for the said services, his widow Margaret petitions for relief and a pension.

1681–2. William Symes received the degree of B.A. at Queen's College, Cambridge; and of M.A. at Baliol College, Oxford. He became Master of St. Saviour's School at Southwark, on the Surrey side of the river Thames, but reckoned a part of London.

1691. Rev. William Syms, M.A., was Rector of the church of Chisle-hurst in Kent, near Bromley, eleven miles from London, from May 17, 1686, until deprived in 1691. [Possibly the same person.]

1713, May 2. A Bill was read in the House of Lords, for enabling Symes Perry to change his name of Perry to Symes, according to the will of John Symes, Esq., deceased. Request granted.

1739. Rev. Joseph Simms, M.A., was curate of the church of Bromley in Kent, ten miles from London.

1739. Rev. Robert Simms was inducted into office this year as Rector of the church of Woolwich in Kent, ten miles from London.

Richard Simms, Esq., was of Mount Pleasant, in the Parish of Bexley in Kent. His wife, a sister of Sir Robert Austen, died 1743.

John Symes, Esq., lived in the manor-house of Newbury, in the Parish of Crayford in Kent. 1797.

John Sim of Penhill, in the Parish of Bexley, in Kent, was a subscriber to Greenwood's Epitome of Kent, published 1838.

Richard Sims, of London, was in 1856, and perhaps is now, an officer of the British Museum, in charge of the MS. Department, and is extensively and favorably known in both hemispheres for his labors in that department, and as the author of a "Manual for the Genealogist, Topographer, Antiquary and Legal Professor." [See N. E. Hist. and Geneal. Reg., xi. 83.]

There was a Prof. Syme, of Edinburgh, in 1869.

The "Wars of the Roses," which commenced in 1459, and ceased at the accession of Henry VII. in 1485, constituted a period of great disquiet and suffering in England. Seven or eight bloody battles were fought; suffering and distress abounded on every side; and a cotemporary writer observes, that "their own country was desolated by the English as cruelly as the preceding generation had wasted France." At that time it is supposed that many families left the kingdom; and it is quite probable that this included some of the Symmes Family. In this manner we may account for a branch of that family in the northern kingdom. The tradition is, that at a subsequent period numbers of them returned to England, as we know some did on the accession of the Stuart dynasty to the English throne.

21

APPENDIX II.

PERSONS BEARING THE NAME OF SYMMES IN AMERICA,
WHO WERE NOT DESCENDANTS OF REV. ZECHARIAH SYMMES.

There were other emigrants from Great Britain to America of the name of Symmes and names equivalent, besides Rev. Zechariah Symmes and his family. The name, though differently spelled, has the same sound throughout.

Simon Sims was a passenger for Virginia, July 6, 1635. [Hist. and Gen. Reg., iv. 61.] The king in council, jealous of the growing prosperity of New England, and having got Virginia into his hands, had issued an order, Feb. 21, 1633–4, detaining the ships then in the Thames bound for this country, and restraining all further emigration to these parts. As no restraint was placed upon emigration to Virginia, it is supposed that many persons and families took that colony on their way to New England.

SIMS FAMILY IN MAINE.

John Symes, of Scarborough in Maine, took the oath of allegiance to Massachusetts, and was admitted freeman of that colony, July 13, 1658. [Geneal. Reg., iii. 194.]

As all the people below Wells were driven away by the Indians about 1692, his family may have shared the same fate, and it may be that some persons of the name whom we find living in Massachusetts fifteen or twenty years later, were his descendants.

SIMS OR SIMES FAMILY IN NEW HAMPSHIRE.

JOHN SIMES, it is said, came from England about 1736, and settled in Portsmouth, N. H. He was a ship-master, and had one son Joseph and five daughters, from whom are descended all of the name in that vicinity, and some living elsewhere.

Dorothy Simes, supposed to be a daughter of this Capt. John Simes, married Humphrey Fernald, Dec. 3, 1741. Both parties were of Portsmouth. Anna Simes, supposed to be another daughter, married, Nov. 17, 1747, John Nutter, born Feb. 24, 1721, son of Hatevil Nutter, of Newington, N. H. She was born Oct. 20, 1727, and died Aug. 11, 1793. Hannah Simes, another daughter, married Moses Noble, of Portsmouth, N. H., Dec. 7, 1756. He died May, 1796, aged 65. His wife Hannah survived him two years. They had eleven children. [Geneal. Reg., xiii. 341.]

Joseph Simes, the only son of Capt. John Simes, was by trade a painter. He was a highly esteemed citizen of Portsmouth, and chairman of the board of selectmen in 1776. He had six sons and four daughters. The sons were—John, Thomas, Mark, William, George and Joseph. My informant is not quite sure that the last of these names is correct, as the person died quite young.

It appears very probable that of these sons, John and William went to Lynn and Boston, and had families there at the period of the Revolution.

The children of John Simes, son of Joseph, who lived in Lynn, and whose wife was Hannah Dart, were as follows. They have been, in the body of this work (page 71), wrongly credited to another John Symmes.

William, his son, had a son *William*, whose daughter Susan married —— Barnes. She was living in Boston in 1867.

Elizabeth, daughter of John, married —— Colman ; had ten daughters.

Abiah, another daughter, married —— Shepard ; had a daughter Susan Simes (Shepard) who married, first, —— Gardner ; second, —— Nelson, of Boston. Abiah had also a son John (Shepard).

William, fourth son of Joseph Simes, of Portsmouth, appears to have lived in Boston and had issue, as follows :

William Simes.

Elizabeth Simes, married Josiah Stoddard, and had William (Symmes) Stoddard, Susan, Isaiah, Edward, Elizabeth, Albert, Ephraim, Almira, Mary Augustus (Stoddard).

Luther Simes, who had by first wife : John, unm.; Elizabeth (m. James Arkurson, ropemaker in Brighton) ; Luther, 3. By second wife, whose name was Reney, or Irene ——, five children, viz., Sarah, William, Thomas, Anne, b. 1839, Joseph P. B.

John Simes.

Thomas Simes.

George Simes, fifth son of Joseph, and grandson of Capt. John Simes, of Portsmouth, was the father of William Simes, a merchant of that city, who was mayor there in 1861 ; and 1862 had a son William Simes, Jr., and another son, Joseph S. Simes, who are of the firm of Simes & Farley, doing business at No. 10 Central Street, Boston, and boarding at the Pavilion, on Tremont Street.

Ex-Mayor Simes, in a letter, speaks of a cousin, Stephen H. Simes, who must therefore be a son of his uncle Thomas or his uncle Mark. Ira H. Simes, of Lowell, stands in the same position ; and so, I suppose, does Capt. Jonathan C. Simes.

Mrs. Mary H. Simes (formerly Miss Noble, of Portsmouth) married, Jan. 21, 1804, Capt. Hiram Rollins, born July 6, 1767, son of John Rollins. She was his second wife, and he was her second husband.

SIMS OR SIMES FAMILY IN MASSACHUSETTS.

In the body of this work, page 18, *note*, mention was made of "Sarah Simes, of Cambridge, Mass. Bay in New England," whose will, dated April 4, 1653, we found in the Probate Office in East Cambridge. We ventured the conjecture in that note, and on page 21, that the testatrix was the first wife of Capt. William Symmes.² It now appears conclusively that this conjecture is not justified. Miss Sarah Simes had a grant of land in 1639 ; and therefore could not be the wife of Capt. William Symmes, or of any other man. She was undoubtedly a maiden, a lady of wealth and respectability, and a member of the church. She died at Cambridge, June 10, 1653. This is all we know about her, beyond what the will itself contains.

We find in Boston, in 1720, Stephen and Elizabeth Sims, who had the following children, all born in Boston:

John, born June 22, 1720.
Stephen, born July 14, 1721 ; died young.
Elizabeth, born Dec. 1, 1722.
Mary, born May 4, 1724.
Stephen, born May 23, 1728 ; died young.
Stephen, born Jan. 23, 1729–30 ; married, first, Sarah Norris, May 30, 1750 ; married, second, Judith Stoneman, March 27, 1768.

Stephen, the father of the above children, must have been bereft of his wife Elizabeth by death, for he married Lydia Nowell, Sept. 27, 1750.

He seems to have had a brother John Symes, who married, first, Mercy Youngman, March 13, 1734 ; married, second, Elizabeth Dickman, Feb. 3, 1737.

John, the brother of the above Stephen Sims, was a "mariner." His will, dated May 3, 1764, to which he made his "mark," was witnessed by William Sinclair and William Dickman, the latter of whom was probably his wife's brother. The will was proved June 14, 1765, when Elizabeth his wife, the executrix, presented it in court. In it he speaks of wife Elizabeth, and of his children Mercy, wife of Thomas Barns of Boston, rope-maker, Isaac and Elizabeth. Recorded Suff. Prob., lxiv. 182.

Elizabeth Simmes, of Boston, widow (doubtless of the above John), made her will Aug. 2, 1793 ; proved May 26, 1795 ; and gave all her estate to Sarah Clemens, of Boston, "single woman, spinster," but says nothing about any one being of kin to herself. [Suff. Prob., xciv. 47.]

When documents are wanting, there is no end to conjecture. We now conjecture that John Simms, of Malden, whose four children, born from 1721 to 1728, are mentioned on page 57 of this volume, was brother of the above-named Stephen Sims, of Boston.

James Syme and Sarah Vassall were married at King's Chapel, Boston, Dec. 29, 1763.

Abigail Symmes and Col. Nathaniel Barber were married at Christ Church, Boston, July 14, 1782.

John Simmes and Sally Thompson were married by Rev. Samuel Stillman, July 21, 1796.

Samuel Symmes and Polly Bumstead [Burchsted?] married by Rev. John Eliot, Aug. 16, 1796.

Samuel B. Symmes, of Boston, sail-maker, died intestate, and James Burchsted, of Boston, shipwright, appointed administrator, Sept. 20, 1802. [Suff. Prob., c. 404.]

Joseph Sims, a rich tea merchant, of Boston, married the daughter of a Plymouth man, whose name is not given, and "built a fine house in South Plymouth," six miles from the principal village." This was about 1850 or 1860.

There was a family of the name of Sims, or its equivalent, in Salem, Mass., soon after 1700. Hannah, daughter of Mr. Richard Sims, was baptized at the First Church in Salem, July 31, 1707. As the prefix *Mr.* was at that time not applied indiscriminately, we infer that "*Mr.*" Richard Sims was a man of some note. This daughter Hannah became the wife of Jeffrey Lang, of Salem, and had by him : *Richard*, b. Dec. 23, 1733 ; *Han-*

nah, b. May 1, 1735, and *Nathaniel*, b. Oct. 17, 1736. Mr. Richard Sims probably died in 1716, for we find that Richard, son of Hannah, the widow of Richard Sims, was bapt. at Salem, June 17, 1716. [Records of the First Church, Salem.]

From the Records of the First Church, Salem, we obtain the following list of the children of Edmund and Sarah Sims:

Edmund, bapt. June 26, 1726.
Benjamin, bapt. Sept. 29, 1728.
Sarah, bapt. May 9, 1731.
Ann, bapt. March 1, 1733.
Mary, bapt. June 15, 1735.
Angel, bapt. Feb. 25, 1738-9.
George, bapt. Nov. 8, 1741.

Widow Sarah Sims died at Salem, May, 1789, aged 88 years.
The above family belonged to the First Church in Salem.

The Salem Directory for 1872 contains the names of Mrs. John D. Sims, who lives at 301 Essex Street, and her son, Henry Osgood Sims, who boards with her. She was the daughter of Henry Osgood, of Salem, and the widow of a Sims, a sea-captain, or in some way connected with the sea, and who was a resident in Portsmouth, or Greenland, N. H., connected therefore with the Simes Family there already mentioned.

SYMS FAMILY IN WESTERN MASSACHUSETTS.

A settlement had been commenced at Squakeag, or Northfield, on the Connecticut River, in Massachusetts, before "Philip's War." The inhabitants were driven away by the Indians in September, 1675. The progress of the settlement was slow, and it was not incorporated as a town till Feb. 22, 1713. On the records of the town we find notice of a grant, April 4, 1721, to William Syms, of a house-lot of seven and one-half acres, of ten acres on Moose Plain, and ten acres on South Plain, on condition that he continue an inhabitant of Northfield four years from that date, and fence and improve his home-lot within two years from that date. This of course indicates that he was a new comer, comparatively a stranger there. We have no means of ascertaining the place of his former abode, or from what branch of the Syms family he sprung. The Northfield settlers were largely from New Haven, Wallingford, and the vicinity of Hartford, Ct. The Northfield records contain no births, marriages or deaths of his family.

Since the foregoing notice was written, Rev. J. Howard Temple, of Framingham, a diligent antiquary, from whom it was received, has furnished the following additional from the Northfield records:

"Married, Jan. 24, 1732-3, Israel Woodward, of Lebanon, Ct., to Mary Sims." He says, furthermore, "Israel Woodward's grandfather, and some of his relatives, were residents in Northfield in 1685, and a number of other emigrants to Northfield about 1720, removed from Lebanon and that vicinity in Connecticut."

In 1731, William Syms received a grant of a lot in the First Division of Commons, of 8¾ acres, and another lot of 19 acres.

Danger from Indian hostility being apprehended, a military force was raised in 1722, and Fort Dummer built on the Connecticut River in 1724. William Syms served as a corporal in 1722, and at Fort Dummer in 1724. Fort Dummer was then within the jurisdiction of Massachusetts, receiving its name in honor of William Dummer, Lieut.-Governor and Acting Governor of that Province.

In June, 1755, *Captain* Sims was in command of a fort at Keene, N. H.

About the year 1741, about twenty towns, by a decree of the Privy Council of England, were separated from Massachusetts and annexed to New Hampshire. At this time, it is probable, the northern part of Northfield was made into a town, and called Winchester, N. H. This seems to explain how it happened that Capt. William Syms, in 1743, was taxed in the town last named.

SYMMES FAMILY IN VERMONT.

Alexander Symmes, with his wife and their two children, Campbell and Agnes, emigrated from Renfrew, in Scotland, and settled in Ryegate, Caledonia Co., Vermont. They were part of a colony from Scotland who had purchased lands on the Connecticut River, in Vermont, now constituting the towns of Ryegate and Barnet. In those towns the Scottish element has ever since been predominant. Part of the colony had arrived before the Revolutionary war commenced, and part were on their way when the vessels in which they were embarked were detained by the British authorities, and all the men capable of bearing arms were impressed for the military service. The remainder, disheartened, returned home, though some came to this country after the peace.

Alexander Symmes and his family safely reached America before the war. His son Campbell, who was thirteen at the time of the emigration, and who followed farming, married Abigail Doying, of Pembroke, N. H. Their children were:

Abigail, born Oct. 16, 1787; married Jonas Tucker, of Newbury, Vt. She is a widow, and is still living in Ryegate. No children.

Agnes, born July 20, 1791. She is deceased; left no children.

Alexander, born Nov. 13, 1792; deceased; left three sons and four daughters.

James, born July 2, 1794; died in his eighteenth year.

Robert, born April 7, 1796; still living in Ryegate; had four sons and seven daughters.

Campbell, b. Nov. 9, 1797; deceased; left two sons and three daughters. His widow and children are living in Ryegate.

William, born July 14, 1799; now residing in Lunenburgh, Vt.; had five sons and five daughters.

John Henderson, born Oct. 4, 1801. [See below.]

David, born July 24, 1803; died recently in Brooklyn, California, where he and his family had lived about fifteen years. He had five sons and two daughters.

Daniel, born Jan. 17, 1806; died in Kentucky, young and unmarried.

Timothy, born July 31, 1807; deceased; left two sons and one daughter. His widow and children reside in Baltimore, Md.

Margaret Jane; have no record; m. George Donaldson. Both are deceased; left four daughters, one of whom lives with her aunt Abigail.

Rev. John Henderson Symmes, the eighth in the above list, graduated at Dartmouth College in 1830. He pursued theological studies in the Seminary of the Reformed Presbyterian Church in Philadelphia; united with the General Assembly of the Presbyterian Church, and became pastor of the Presbyterian Church in Columbia, Lancaster Co., Pa., in the autumn of 1833. In 1840, he became pastor of the First Presbyterian Church in Lansingburg, N. Y., and in 1844 became pastor of the First Presbyterian Church in Cumberland City, Md. In 1862, the War of the Rebellion having broken out, and nearly all the families of wealth and social influence taking part with the rebels, and Mr. Symmes not being able to sympathize with them, the church in Cumberland was nearly broken up, and he resigned his pastoral charge. Being strongly urged to become chaplain of the Second Regiment of Maryland Volunteer Infantry, composed principally of men from Cumberland and the vicinity, he yielded, and served in that capacity three years.

He has now, Oct. 1872, been pastor of the First Presbyterian Church in Conshohocken, Pa., nearly five and a half years. Conshohocken is on the river Schuylkill, about twelve miles from Philadelphia, connected with that city by the Philadelphia & Norristown Railroad.

He married, March 7, 1833, Catharine McAdam, daughter of Thomas McAdam, of Philadelphia. They have no children.

SIMMS FAMILY OF NEW YORK, PHILADELPHIA, ETC.

William Simmes was married to Mary Barrick, in the Dutch Church of New York, May 11, 1701. He was a joiner, lived in his own house on Pearl Street, and died 1735, leaving a widow and three daughters—Mary, Ruth and Charity; also an undutiful son James, whom he cuts off with a shilling.

Thomas Simmes was a petitioner among the Protestants of New York, in December, 1701.

W. J. Symes was a merchant in New York about 1860. His father came from Devonshire, Eng.

Hugh Sim graduated at the College of New Jersey, Princeton, in 1768.

William D. Simms, at same College in 1801; and John D. Simms at same in 1806.

John G. Sims, at same College 1809.

Alexander D. Sims, at Union College in 1823.

Simms's History of Schoharie County, N. Y., was written by Jeptha Root Simms, born in Canterbury, Ct., in 1807. He lived in New York city in 1851. [See Allibone's Dict. of Authors, and Drake's Biog. Dict.] In that history the fearful devastations committed by the tories and Indians from 1775 to 1778, are related. Mr. Simms is the author of several other works.

Clifford Stanley Sims, of Philadelphia, says that his branch of the family was driven out of Scotland into England by political troubles some time between 1450 and 1550. Part of them returned to Scotland, some remained in England. He is from the Scottish branch.

Sarah Symmes, of Philadelphia, married Robert Hewes Hinckley,[7] son of Capt. Robert Hinckley,[6] by his wife Esther Messinger, daughter of Daniel Messinger, of Wrentham, Mass. The date of the marriage is not given; but as the father was born in 1774, and died on his farm at Milton, near Boston, Jan. 26, 1833, a reasonable conjecture may be made. Mr. Hinckley was the sixth in descent from Gov. Thomas Hinckley, born in England about 1618, governor of Plymouth Colony. [See N. E. Geneal. Reg., vol. xiii. pp. 208–212.]

William Gilmore Simms, LL.D., was born in Charleston, S. C., April 17, 1806; and died there June 11, 1870. He was of Irish descent, and a well-known author of novels. [See Drake's Amer. Dict. of Biography.]

His father, of the same name, married Harriet Ann Augusta Singleton, of a Virginia family. He, the father, was once a merchant in Charleston. He removed to Tennessee, and served in the war against the Creeks and Seminoles. The son came to New York in 1852. [See Duyckinck's Cyclopedia of American Literature, and Drake's Dict. American Biography.]

LANCASTER SYMES, OF NEW YORK.

We are indebted in great part to Mr. Isaac J. Greenwood, of New York, for the following sketch of a man somewhat noted in his day.

Immediately after the news arrived in New York of the deposition of James II. from the throne of England, much confusion prevailed in that city. There were two parties, each striving for the ascendancy; the tory party, or the friends of aristocratic and arbitrary power, and the party of the common people. It was necessary that something should be done immediately for the preservation of order. A Committee of Safety assumed the task, and gave a commission to Jacob Leisler, the head of the popular party, to take possession of the fort at New York and to assume the government. This he did without opposition, June 8, 1689.

The government of Leisler was regarded as only temporary, and to be superseded on the arrival of a governor bringing a commission from the new king. On one of the last days of January, 1690–1, some transports arrived, having on board two companies of foot under the command of Major Richard Ingoldsby, a kinsman of Sir Henry Ingoldsby. With the major came his brother-in-law LANCASTER SYMES, at that time a lieutenant of infantry. This lieutenant, in company with Lieut. Matthew Shank, went to demand the surrender of the fort from Leisler.

It appears that Ingoldsby had no right to make such a demand, for he produced no order from the king, nor from the new governor, who, it was known, had been appointed, but did not arrive till near two months afterwards.

It seems clear, therefore, that Leisler acted rightly in refusing to deliver up the fort to Ingoldsby. He promised obedience to Col. Henry Sloughter, the new governor, when he should arrive, and on the evening of his arrival, March 19, 1690–1, Leisler sent to receive his orders. The next morning he asked, by letter, to whom he should surrender the fort. The letter was unheeded; and Sloughter, giving no notice to Leisler, commanded Ingoldsby to arrest Leisler, his son-in-law Milborne, and the Council of the Province. To gratify the tory party, Leisler and Milborne were brought before a tory tribunal instituted by Sloughter, condemned as guilty of high treason, and in a drenching rain executed on the gallows, May 16, 1691. Impartial history brands the transaction as a foul judicial murder.

It is painful to find a man bearing the name of SYMES implicated in such an affair. It is painful, moreover, to find him in high favor with such a profligate, unscrupulous wretch as Sloughter. The latter, writing to Charles, duke of Bolton, asks that nobleman's "favor that Lancaster Symes may be confirmed as lieutenant, for," he says, "he is a good soldier and qualified in every respect." The next year, the young lieutenant, so recommended, obtained the rank of captain, and a few years later that of major. Sloughter dying suddenly, July 23, 1691, was superseded by Ingoldsby as commander-in-chief, and he by Col. Benjamin Fletcher, who arrived as governor, Aug. 28, 1692. Capt. Symes was despatched by him to England, to recruit the two companies of grenadiers stationed at New York and Albany. On his return he entered into trade in the city of New York, still retaining his military position.

In the Dutch Church in New York, Nov. 4, 1694, he married CATHA-RINE, widow of James Larkin, and daughter of Matthias De Hart, who, when a widower, married the widow Johanna De Wit. Catharine De Hart was baptized in the Dutch Church, Jan. 21, 1673.

Nov. 11, 1695, Capt. Lancaster Symes and wife petitioned for a confirmation of a tract of land on the boundary line of New York and New Jersey, between the Hudson River and Ovepeck's Creek, formerly granted by the governor of New Jersey to Balthazar De Hart, uncle to Mrs. Catharine Symes. In the course of a few years, Capt. Symes received a grant of all the lands on Staten Island, not already covered by a patent; also of an extensive tract of land on the west side of Hudson River, in Orange County. Besides the possessions already mentioned, Capt. Symes appears to have held an extensive and valuable leasehold estate in the city of New York. It had formerly belonged to Gov. Dongan; but he, owing £200 to James Larkin, the former husband of Mrs. Symes, and not able to pay, executed a mortgage to Symes. April 12, 1694, upon his property in New York; part of it lying near the water just east of the Battery, and part eastward of the Meadows (or Park) between the present Nassau Street and Park Row. The sum for which the mortgage was given was not paid, and March 25, 1698, the mortgage was superseded by a lease of the premises for fourteen years, " at the rent of one pepper-corn a year."

Meanwhile, Capt. Lancaster Symes, intent on the acquisition of wealth, and enjoying his fine mansion at Whitehall in New York, formerly the residence of Gov. Dongan, had wholly neglected his military duties, while continually receiving the stipulated pay. Gov. Bellamont, arriving in New York, April, 1698, and finding how matters, under the connivance of Ingoldsby and Gov. Fletcher, had for two years stood, suspended Lancaster Symes from his military rank, declaring that he ought to be broken.

Capt. Symes was present in July, 1701, at a conference with the Five Nations, held at Albany. One year after, he again visited that town in the suite of the newly arrived governor, Edward Hyde, lord Cornbury. The latter personage, though a cousin of Queen Anne,* reached this country, as is well known, in straitened circumstances, and on his removal from the gubernatorial chair in 1708, was still detained in the city by his creditors. On his succeeding to the title of Earl of Clarendon, at the death of his father in October, 1709, Capt. Symes came to his relief with sundry loans, and he departed for England at the close of July, 1710.

Capt. Symes continued to reside in the city of New York quite a number of years; became one of the vestry of Trinity Church, and in 1704 was admitted to the freedom of the city.

On giving up a mercantile life, he seems to have removed to Albany. In the summer of 1726, he was one of the two representatives chosen for Orange County, and held his seat in the General Assembly from the 29th of September following until his death, which took place in the earlier part of 1729. During his membership, his name as Major Symes is of frequent occurrence in the journals of the Assembly.

We find no will of Major Symes; but a will of Major Richard Ingolds-

---

* Both were grandchildren of Edward Hyde, first Earl of Clarendon.

22

by, his brother-in-law, dated Stillwater, Albany Co., Aug. 31, 1711, proved at New York, Oct. 8, 1719, mentions his two nephews Lancaster and Richard Symes. The elder of these, Lancaster, became a freeman of New York in 1737. That one of these sons married and had issue, we learn from the will of Mrs. Catharine Symes, of New York, widow of Major Lancaster Symes, which mentions her granddaughter Susanna Catharine Symes living with her, and also Elizabeth Symes, quite young, sister of said Susanna, and their brother Lancaster Symes. This will is dated June 24, 1749; proved Jan. 23, 1750. This third Lancaster Symes died 1759, without issue.

The elder of these sisters, Susanna Catharine, was, in 1754, wife of Rev. John Ogilvie, the Episcopal minister at Albany, and afterwards assistant minister of Trinity Church, New York. At the time last mentioned, she had received, under the wills of her grandfather, grandmother, father and brother, large estates in the Provinces of New York and New Jersey, in Holland and elsewhere. She died previous to April 17, 1769, when Mr. Ogilvie married a second wife, Margaret, widow of Philip Philips, and daughter of Nathaniel Marston, merchant, of New York. Mr. Ogilvie died Nov. 26, 1774, aged 51.

The BOSTON DIRECTORY for 1872, contains the following names:

Symmes, Alfred, boards 1618 Washington Street.
  Miss Anna, house 6 Greenville Place.
  Jacob P., 1 Bath Street, house 265 Bowen Street.
  Rufus K., watchman Faneuil Hall Market, boards 11 Lyman St.
  Sarah W., teacher in Mather School, boards Winter St., Wd. 16.
  Selwin, printer, house 122 Leverett Street.
Simms, George, salesman, cellar 17 Commercial Street.
  Thomas, carpenter, 111 Northampton Street.
Simes, Joseph S. (Simes & Farley), 10 Central Street, boards Pavilion, 57
  Tremont Street.
  William, Jr., 10 Central Street.
Symes, Albert, teamster, boards 13 Preble Street.
  Charles, tin-smith, house 13 Preble, Washington Village.
  Charles, Jr., brass-worker, house Preble, Washington Village.
  Joseph H., brass-moulder, boards 13 Preble, Washington Village.
  James R. (Park, Symes & Co.), 120 Milk, house 181 Bowen St.
  William H., porter, 13 Custom House Street, house 180 Seventh
  Street, South Boston.
  William H., Jr., carpenter, boards 12 Crescent Place.
Sims, Benjamin William, sail-maker, house 7 Orange Lane.
  William A., laborer, house 7 Orange Lane.
  Charles, clerk, boards 9 Florence Street.
  Mrs. Isabella, house 2 Vincent Court.
  Oliver, 6 Faneuil Hall Square, house Cambridge Street.

SIMS AND ITS EQUIVALENTS IN NEW YORK CITY.

The NEW YORK DIRECTORY contains the following. The name is spelled in no fewer than seven different ways: *Sim, Simes, Sims, Simms, Syms, Symes*, and lastly, *Symmes*.

In the Directory for 1789, the first of the series, the name does not occur.

The Directory for 1800 has Sim, William, a clerk in the Loan Office; Simes, Elizabeth; Sims, Tobias, butcher.

1811. Sims, John, teacher; Sims, Michael, coachman.

1818. Sims, Francis, carpenter; Symes, John, cooper; Sims, Palin, carpenter. This name is found in the Directory every year till 1840. There were subsequently in New York several carpenters of the name of Sims, probably relatives of this man.

1820. Simms, Robert B., gunsmith. This man is found every year till 1841. In 1840, and afterwards, we find several gunsmiths of the name, or something like it.

Simms, Thomas S., carpenter, and every year till 1831.

Simms, William, hair-dresser, and so on till 1828.

Syms, John, cordwainer, also 1821, 1822.

1821. Sims, Charles; Sims, John, coachman; Sims, Peter, carpenter, also 1822, 1823.

Simms, John C., hair-dresser, and till 1828.

Syms, Mary, widow, seamstress, and till 1829.

1823. Simms, Thomas A., merchant.

Syms, John, shoe-store, and every year till 1842.

1824. Simms, James H., turner; Simms, Robert, merchant.

1825. Simms, William, carpenter, and so on till 1840.

Simms, Julia, widow; Simms, Mary, widow of Thomas, till 1831.

1826. Simms, Thomas S., grocer; also 1827.

1828. Simms, Edward.

Simms, Thomas, hatter, and till 1840.

Sims, Orrin H., mason, and till 1839. He seems to have died in 1842.

Syms, Samuel, shoe-maker, shoe-store, 1829; boot-maker, 1837, and till 1845.

1829. Simms, Thomas S., drug-broker till 1835, afterwards auctioneer till 1843.

Simms, William P., wheelwright; also 1839 to 1844.

1830. Sims, John M., coach-maker; also 1837.

1831. Simms, Jeptha R., author of the History of Schoharie County, N. Y.

Symmes, D. & T., grocers.

1832. Sims, Samuel, butcher, till 1840.

Simms, John, hair-dresser, till 1839.

1834. Sims, Martin, carpenter; also 1838, 1839.

Simms, Ebenezer W., mason, till 1854.

Symes, Mary; Symes, Mary, widow of William [hair-dresser?].

1836. Simms, John, hatter; also 1845.

Syme, James, M.D., till 1845, then chemist till 1860 or after.

1838. Simms, Robert W., gunsmith.

Simms, Robert L., teas, till 1844.

Simms, Samuel D., butcher.

Simms, William, mason; also 1839, '40, '41; carpenter from 1841 to 1850.

Symes, Mary, widow of John L., and till 1855.

1839. Sims, Orrin H., Jr., mason, till 1850. The "Junior" omitted after 1842.

Sims, Samuel M., butcher, and till 1865.

Sims, William S., mason, till 1844.

Sims, Frances H., widow of Peter, till 1844.

Sims, Thomas, porter, till 1860 ; tavern-keeper, 1840–41.
Sims, William E., painter, till 1841.
Simms, Matthew, porter-house, till 1841.
Simms, William, hatter.
Syme, Rev. Daniel, teacher : also 1840.
Syms, William, gunsmith, till 1842.
Symes, Samuel J., gunsmith, till 1845.
Symes, William, milkman, till 1855.

1840. Sims, David, contractor.
1841. Sims, Robert, grocer ; carpenter, 1842 ; clerk, 1842.
1842. Simes, Sarah, boarding-house, till 1865, or after.
Sims, Martin, fruit ; carpenter, till 1855.
Sims, Hannah, widow of Palm, carpenter, till 1845.
1843. Sims, David, carman, till 1860.
Sims, Linsley D., accountant, afterwards of Montreal.
Sims, William, laborer, till 1860.
Syme, John, druggist ; also 1841.
Symes, William J., importer.
1844. Simes, William, furniture, till 1850.
Symes, William T., blacksmith, till 1855.
1850. Sim, Robert, shipwright.
Sims, John D., merchant, till 1860, or after.
Simms, Charles & David T., carpenters.
Simms, George, pattern-maker ; 1860, carriage-trimmer ; 1870, machinist.
Simms, Henry A., brewer.
Simms, Philip, merchant, till 1865.
Simms, Robert, coachmaker.
Simms, Robert B., cooper.
Simms, Thomas Scott, agent ; broker, 1854.
Sims, Jane, widow, seamstress, till 1870.
Sims, Robert, hatter.
Sims, William H., brewer.
Syms, John G., Samuel R., and William J. (partners), gunsmiths, till 1870.
Symes, John L., wheelwright, till 1865.
1855. Sims, Eliza, widow of John, till 1870.
Sims, Margaret, widow of Orrin H. See 1839.
Sims, James Marion, doctor, till 1870.
Sims, Patrick, carpenter, till 1870.
Sims, William P., carriage-maker, till 1865.
Simms, Charles E., butcher, till 1870.
Simms, Horatio, lawyer, till 1870.
Simms, Mary, widow of David T., till 1860. See 1850.
Simms, Robert B., gas-metres till 1860 ; cooper, 1870.
Simms, William, carpenter, till 1870.
Simms, William, police, till 1870.
1860. Sims, Cicero H., safe-maker, till 1865 ; machinist, 1870.
Sims, Daniel, clerk.
Sims, John H., clerk.
Sims, James, carpenter.
Simms, Augustus L., painter.
Simms, John G., U. S. H.

Simms, Isabella, widow of Charles, boarding-house, till 1870.
Simms, Maria, widow of Ebenezer W., till 1870. See 1834.
Simms, John E., milkman ; 1870, butcher.
1865. Sims, Jasper H., printer, till 1870.
Sims, John, coals ; engineer, till 1870.
Syme, Charles, U. S. Army.
Syme, David, tailor.
1870. Sims, Alfred, plumber.
Sims, Henry, mason.
Simms, Jacob H., agent.
Simms, Samuel S., hatter.
Syme, William, lawyer.

Many of the above, perhaps the greater number, are of foreign birth.
There are several other names in the Directory for 1860 and 1870, for
whom room could not be found.   In the volume for 1870 are several Ger-
mans bearing the names of Siems, Semm, and Semmes.

The MONTREAL DIRECTORY for 1865, and later, has :

Sims, John, laborer.
Sims & Pigeon, lumber.
Symm, Hugh, machinist.
Simms, Robert, Charles and Francis H. (partners), commission merchants.
Simmes, Charles H. and Linsley D., in New York 1843.
Simmes, James, laborer.
Simmes, James Campbell, P. O. clerk.
Symmes, Albert, produce merchant.

There are none of the name in the Quebec Directory for 1871.

INDEX I.

DESCENDANTS OF REV. ZECHARIAH SYMMES, BEARING HIS NAME.

The figures before each name denote the year of birth; the figures after the name denote the consecutive number under which the birth is recorded. The interrogation mark (?) intimates uncertainty as to the year.

☞ Those who are known to have died young are omitted.

ERRATA.—EDWARD SYMMES,⁷ No. 495, on page 140. Line 3 from top, for "Keep" read *Neck.* In the next paragraph, the closing sentence should read—" In the spring of 1831, he removed to the old homestead of his mother, the widow of Thomas Symmes, which descended to her children in 1836," &c.

23

DESCENDANTS OF REV. ZECHARIAH SYMMES, BEARING OTHER NAMES.

[For Explanations, see Index I.]

INDEX III.

NAMES OF PERSONS WHO HAVE MARRIED DESCENDANTS OF REV. ZECHARIAH SYMMES.

The year of MARRIAGE, when known to the compiler, precedes the name. The figures after the name denote the consecutive number belonging to the DESCENDANT with whom the marriage was contracted.

The interrogation point [?] implies doubt as to the year.

INDEX IV.

PERSONS INCIDENTALLY MENTIONED.

The figures preceding the name indicate the year when the transaction occurred, in connection with which the individual is mentioned.
The figures following the name denote the PAGE where the name appears.

INDEX V.

MISCELLANEOUS.

☞ The figures denote the PAGE.